W9-BOO-443

57.
3-00

She couldn't marry Zach.

For a second Beth was stunned by her own thoughts. Not marry Zach? Impossible. Zach was a part of her already. Without him, she wouldn't be whole. She couldn't leave him. She would never survive.

But to stay, to become his wife, would be equally devastating, if not more so. She simply couldn't chance it. If she failed to tell him the truth, how could she handle the pain in his eyes when he wanted to make love and she refused him?

Pain as sharp and biting as a hot knife sliced through her, bending her double. Zach deserved better than half a woman; he deserved a whole woman who could meet his needs both physically and mentally. She could do neither.

Only because she loved him could she let him go.

Coming in September 1997 from
MIRA Books and
MARY LYNN BAXTER

LONE STAR HEAT

MARY LYNN BAXTER

A Day in April

MIRA BOOKS

ISBN 1-55166-165-9

A DAY IN APRIL

Copyright © 1992 by Mary Lynn Baxter.

MIRA and the star colophon are trademarks of MIRA Books.

Printed in U.S.A.

Heartfelt gratitude to Susie Cox and
DeReigh Meyer at The Clothes Rack
for their help and expertise.
Also to Glenda Duke and Leigh Duke
at The Look.

Thanks, ladies. *A Day in April* couldn't
have been written without you.

Prologue

Fall, 1989

Beth Melbourne had been certain she had no more tears to shed, that past heartaches had robbed her of that cleansing luxury. She was wrong. Tears had filled her eyes the instant she'd received the call that her best friend lay in the hospital, dying.

Now, a day later, as she walked through the doors of the small hospital in her hometown of Shawnee, Louisiana, tears once again threatened. She felt lost for a moment, powerless and afraid.

Blinking furiously, she angled down a long hall, cognizant of the stares from the hospital personnel. Some she recognized; some she did not. But now was not the time to stop and make small talk. She was on a mission, a mission of mercy. She had to see Rachel before it was too late.

When she reached room 121, Beth paused outside the door and breathed a silent prayer, asking for strength to face the task that lay before her.

She had just placed her hand on the knob when she heard a sound behind her. For a moment she froze, fearing it would be Zach. He was the last person she wanted to see.

Forcing herself to show none of the raw emotions churning inside, Beth turned, then watched in relief as a somber woman in a white uniform approached.

"Hello. I'm Jill Renfro, Rachel's day nurse."

Beth cleared her throat. "I'm Beth Melbourne."

"Ah, yes, you're the friend Zach . . . Mr. Winslow spoke about. He said you were expected."

"Where . . . is Mr. Winslow?"

"He went to check on Amanda, but I expect him back shortly."

Another surge of relief stampeded through Beth. For the time being, at least, she was spared an encounter with Zach. Suddenly sensing that the nurse expected her to say something in response, she stammered, "How . . . how is Rachel?"

The nurse's eyes held sympathy, though it seemed only professional. "Not good, I'm afraid. She's very sick."

"Is it all right if I go in now?"

"Of course. If you need me, I'll be at the nurses' station."

The door was ajar. Once the nurse walked away, Beth hovered just inside, unsure of her next move. Even though the room was cloaked in dimness, she could see that it contained very little: a sink, a clumsy wing-back chair and the bed. Bouquets of flowers splattered the windowsill with vibrant color, but they did nothing to dispel the shadows that clung to the walls and furniture.

Rachel, a pale replica of her former self, lay unmoving on the big bed. Taking an intense, piercing breath, Beth stepped closer. One of Rachel's arms lay on the sheet. The other rested on a splint that was attached to a tube and bottle hanging from a nearby stand. Her fingers were curved into her palms like a baby's; the blue veins and small bones of her hands were visible beneath the transparent skin.

Her face, always tanned before, was now drained of color. The harsh treatments had depleted her thick, dark hair. Death itself seemed a tangible part of the sterile room.

Oh, Rachel, Beth cried silently, how can that be? How could she be dying, when she had so much to live for? She was only thirty-four years old, Beth's own age, for God's sake. It wasn't fair; it simply wasn't fair.

"Is everything all right?" the nurse whispered from the door. Her face was grave.

Rachel opened her eyes and looked as if she were trying to focus them. "Beth . . ." she breathed.

Behind her, Beth heard the door close softly.

"I'm . . . here, honey." Beth tiptoed to Rachel's bedside, then eased down into the chair beside the bed and took hold of the limp, outstretched hand. She was dry-eyed and controlled, but it wasn't easy. Her body throbbed with the effort of that composure.

Rachel's mouth trembled. "I'm . . . so glad you came." Her sunken eyes pooled with tears as she peered up at Beth.

Beth answered with a smile that twisted into a grimace. She savagely fought the wetness that stabbed her eyes. "You knew I'd come."

"When did you get here?"

"I just this minute drove into town."

"You . . . must be tired."

"Shh, don't worry about me. I'm fine."

"I prayed that you'd . . . get here in time."

"Oh, God, Rach—" Beth's voice broke; she couldn't go on. Then, swallowing the lump in her throat, she added, "I would have been here long before now, only I didn't know. Why wasn't I told you were sick?" Beth's delicate features bore the ravages of anguish. "Why did you keep it from me?"

"I . . . thought I could beat it, that's why." Rachel's words were faint but audible, her gaze intent.

"Maybe you still can."

"No." A single tear slipped from the corner of Rachel's right eye and disappeared onto the sterile white pillowcase. "It's too late. The doctors say the cancer's all through me now." She paused and took a quivering breath. "That's why I had . . . Zach call you."

"No," Beth said desperately. "There has to be more they can do. I won't let you give up."

"I'm so tired...so tired of fighting." Rachel's hand came up to touch Beth's face. "We've shared so much, haven't we? So much pain, so much heartache, more than two friends ought to have to share."

Beth could only nod, shutting her eyes tightly. She couldn't cry. Not now. She had to be brave. At last she opened her eyes to find Rachel's closed. She lay still, too still. Then she spoke. "Beth . . . ?"

"I'm here."

"I dreamed . . . dreamed you . . . never forgave me about Zach."

Beth's heart almost stopped beating. "Of course I did," she said softly. "I forgave you a long time ago. Don't you remember?"

Rachel's wide-open blue eyes had a sudden clearness in them. "Zach . . . never stopped loving you, you know."

Beth held herself tightly. "No!"

"It's okay." It was just a whisper.

"No, you're wrong, Rach, you're wrong." Without warning, Beth's entire body began to shake, and her breath came in jerky little spurts. "He . . . he loves you."

As if Beth's words hadn't registered, Rachel went on, "And I want you to know that when I'm gone, you and Zach have my blessing . . ."

"Oh, please, Rachel, don't do this to me," Beth pleaded. "What you're thinking is impossible, and no matter how much you might want me to, I can't promise . . ."

"But there's one thing you *can* promise me. . . ."

Beth leaned closer as Rachel's voice grew fainter. Alarmed, she whispered, "You're wearing yourself out."

"No. Please, you have to hear me out."

"All right," Beth whispered, a catch in her voice. "Tell me."

With what strength she had left, Rachel squeezed Beth's hand. "It's Amanda."

"What—what about Amanda?" Beth croaked. Fear of what was coming rose like hot bile in the back of her throat.

The line around Rachel's colorless lips eased, and she smiled whimsically. "You know...what a joy she's been to me."

"Yes...I know."

"Promise me you'll continue to see her. I want you to always be a part of her life."

Suddenly the senseless horror of what was happening to Rachel, what she was asking of her, came crashing down on Beth's shoulders, and she almost broke under the immense strain. Struggling to hold up, she looked past Rachel toward the window, as if seeking a reprieve. Only a dreary sky met her gaze. No sun today, just gray and dismal, like a reflection of her heart.

"Beth..."

"Oh, Rachel, do you know what you're asking?"

"Yes." An unlikely flush of color rose in Rachel's cheeks and clung there.

"What about...Zach?"

Rachel smiled through her tears. "Don't you worry about him. He'll come around." She paused and drew a deep, shuddering breath, as if digging for the strength to continue. "It's...just that he's had so much pain so close together. He's...not thinking straight right now."

"You rest, okay?" Beth pleaded. "You're talking too much."

"Will you help him with Amanda, no matter what he says?" Rachel's breathing was ragged, her eyes frantic. "Promise me!"

Unchecked tears streamed rapidly down Beth's face. "Yes...I promise."

"Thank you," Rachel wheezed, the pallor in her face making her appear yellow.

"Rachel!" Beth's voice was hoarse.

Rachel's lids fluttered. "I'm . . . tired, so tired."

"I should go and let you rest," Beth said, wiping at her eyes, her nose.

It was only after Beth stood, leaned over and kissed Rachel on the forehead, that Rachel whispered close to her ear, "When . . . when I die, the pact we made dies, too. Remember that."

"Rachel, Rachel," Beth sobbed, staring down at her longtime friend, as if to memorize everything about her.

"Shh...don't cry.... I'm not afraid.... Don't forget, you promised. . . ." Suddenly her voice faded into nothingness.

Beth watched Rachel's eyelids flutter again, then close. For an instant Beth was too panic-stricken to move. Finally forcing her legs to move, she crossed to the door and jerked it open. Nurse Renfro was coming toward her.

The instant she saw Beth's face, she rushed past her into the room.

"Nurse . . . is she . . ." Beth couldn't go on, fear sucking the breath from her lungs.

"No," the nurse responded. "She's asleep."

Somehow Beth dragged herself away from the door, slumped heavily against the nearest wall and took several deep, gulping breaths. They didn't help. Closing her eyes, she finally gave in to the wave of nausea churning inside her.

"Oh, Rachel, Rachel," she whimpered again, repeating the words over and over with a gasping horror in her voice, "what have I done?"

But she knew what she had done. She had made a promise she wasn't sure she could keep.

Part I

One

Summer, 1973

Sunbeams filtered through the trees and sparkled off the water in the kidney-shaped pool. Beth smiled to herself, wiggling into a more comfortable position in the chaise longue.

The air carried the intoxicating scent of periwinkles and roses. Somewhere close by, a dog barked in a serene and relaxing way.

She lifted her head toward the sun, and a tiny breeze touched her face like a caress. How great life was, she thought, flicking absently at a mosquito humming around her head. If she had anything to complain about, it was the unseasonably warm summer that all of southern Louisiana was experiencing. The heat was frightful. Coupled with that was the humid breeze from the west to contend with, a breeze that coated the entire town with the stench from Southland Paper Mill.

Although Beth inhaled a whiff and frowned, the smell didn't chase her away or dent her sense of well-being and contentment. She had grown up hearing her daddy say, "That's money you smell, and don't you ever forget it."

She hadn't, since it was money from that mill that was paying for her wedding. In thirty-five days, seven hours and twenty minutes, she would be repeating her vows. What more could a girl ask?

"Mrs. Zachery Winslow," Beth whispered aloud. The name rolled off her tongue sounding so good, so exactly right, that she hugged herself and giggled.

Zach. Just thinking about him and that upcoming day filled her with excitement, though mixed with that excitement there was a tad of fear, as well. Would she make Zach a good wife? Would she be able to satisfy him?

He had always been a part of her life. In fact, she couldn't remember a time when Zach hadn't been the *most important* part of her life. But then, she had never questioned his presence. Their fathers were partners in the mill, Shawnee's largest employer. Not only were they business partners, but they were neighbors, as well.

Still, that togetherness hadn't been what bonded her and Zach. While their families moved in the same social circles, they rarely socialized individually. It had seemed at times that each family went out of its way to avoid doing just that.

Always looking for an excuse to be around Zach, Beth had approached her daddy one day and asked why they never had the Winslows over for dinner or vice versa.

"It's simple, my dear," Foster had replied. "Taylor and I are under each other's feet all day. When we leave the mill, we both need a reprieve."

She'd had to be satisfied with that explanation and had eventually come to accept it. Nonetheless, the adults' cockamamy reasoning hadn't kept her away from Zach.

She had adored him, and spent her early years tagging after him. He had always been her hero. Four years her senior, he had taught her how to swim, how to ride, and helped her with her homework.

Together they had tramped through the woods picking blackberries and fished in the nearby creek using worms that he had made her put on the hook herself, laughing all the while.

There had been escapades just to get his attention. Beth had climbed one of the huge oak trees on his lawn and pretended she couldn't get down. He had shinnied up the tree and made a big deal out of helping her down. It was only after his arms were around her that she had admitted she'd been teasing. Although he'd swatted her playfully on the butt, he hadn't turned her loose.

Another memorable incident was the time Zach had swung the hammock too high and tossed her out. She had pretended to be hurt. He'd bent over her and pleaded with her to open her eyes. She had, of course, only to wink at him and grin. He hadn't thought it funny and had been furious at her for scaring him out of ten years' growth, or so he'd said.

She had idolized him. But that was understandable, because Zach was unique. Zach was unpredictable. Yet they shared a rapport.

He had spoiled her; she realized that now, but at the time she hadn't thought of herself as greedy in demanding his undivided attention. Though he'd been extremely popular and was usually in the company of a crowd of peers, especially girls, he was never too busy to talk to her.

It was only after Rachel Carrington moved to Shawnee and the two of them became firm friends that she gave Zach any breathing room.

By then, however, Zach had been unwilling to let Beth out of his sight, so he'd taken both girls under his wing. They had become a threesome. On the weekends they would pile into his Mustang and cruise the local Dairy Queen to see who was dating whom.

On one occasion, when Rachel hadn't been asked to an important dance and both girls were bemoaning the fact, Zach had placed his arms around their shoulders.

"How 'bout if I escort the two of you?" he'd drawled, grinning broadly. "I'll enjoy watching the other guys turn green with envy."

Beth had seen the cow-eyed look Rachel had bestowed on Zach when she thanked him profusely. Zach, in turn, had ruffled Rachel's hair. Beth had realized then that Rachel was as smitten with Zach as she was. Although she loved Rachel dearly, she had felt a twinge of jealousy. Zach belonged to her. She didn't want to share him with anyone, not even a dear friend.

Before, though she hadn't altogether understood why, she had experienced a funny feeling in her stomach whenever he looked at her. Nor had she understood why she'd felt ill and agitated when he looked at other girls or took them out.

Afterward, Beth had become aware of herself as a female and had begun to see the mature Zach in a different light. She fantasized that one day he would kiss her and tell her she was special.

That time came the summer she turned sixteen. She and Zach had been playing tennis, and she had accidentally twisted her ankle. Zach had come to her rescue, sweeping her into his arms. With her fingers locked behind his neck, their eyes had met. Something had flashed between them, something deep and sweet and tender.

"Oh, Beth," he whispered, "what am I going to do about you? I'm crazy in love with you."

He'd kissed her deeply then, and while her senses were spinning, her mind was denying what her instincts were telling her. This was her surrogate older brother, her best friend. But wasn't this what she'd wanted? What she'd ached for? The kiss had left her head hammering and her heart beating out of control. In the end, instead of feeling embarrassed or ashamed, she had felt exhilarated and honored. She had wanted more.

From then on they were inseparable. And though Beth suspected that Rachel was also in love with Zach, nothing was ever said. It was an established fact that it was Beth Zach loved and was going to marry.

The majority of her friends, Rachel included, couldn't wait to graduate and leave Shawnee. Not so with Beth. Why, she couldn't imagine living anywhere else. She loved this small town with its oak-lined streets, its mix of the old and the new: office buildings springing up close to old ground-hugging landmarks depicting the glory days of the South as well as its downfall.

Withered old-timers sat on sidewalk benches around the square, chewing tobacco, talking of horse racing or the old days on the cotton and pecan plantations.

Shawnee was a good place to live, a good place to work, and a good place to rear children. That was exactly what Beth wanted to do. Marry Zach, settle in Shawnee and have his children.

Newcomers often said Shawnee was cliquish and that people were a tad snobbish, that instead of saying welcome, they often said, "Now, who is your family?"

Well, maybe there was some truth in that, but even so, the good far outweighed the bad, and that was what Beth dwelled on.

Recognizing the song that suddenly blared from the radio beside her as one of Zach's and her favorites, Beth reached over and switched the volume louder. The lyrics to "Behind Closed Doors" throbbed in the air. She hummed to the lyrics.

"Lord a mercy, child, you're going to be deaf as sure as the world."

Beth turned her head and leisurely smiled at the robust black woman who stood in the French doors shaking her head.

"Oh, come on, Jess, don't tell me you don't like Charlie Rich. Anyway, it's better than Tricky Dick and that Watergate stuff." She frowned. "That's all you hear these days."

Jessie Hollister wiped her hands on the white apron tied around her waist. "Huh. It doesn't matter what I like, child. It's your daddy I'm thinking about. You know how he's always popping in unexpected. And you also know he hasn't been in the best of moods lately."

Beth's smile slipped as she leaned over and turned down the radio. "You're right," she said, looking at Jessie once again. "I just wish he and Trent could get along better."

"I know you do, honey." Jessie's smile was indulgent. "But time will take care of a lot of your daddy's problems with your brother."

Beth's face brightened. "I hope you're right."

"How 'bout if I bring you some fresh-baked tea cakes and a glass of lemonade?" Jessie asked.

"Mmm, sounds great. And, Jess, please don't forget to pack a basket for Zach and me. When he gets off work this afternoon, we're going on a picnic."

Jessie's round face crinkled in a grin. "Why, I've already made a batch of fried peach pies, Zach's favorite."

"Thanks, Jess," Beth said sweetly. "I owe you one."

Jessie snorted good-naturedly. "Seems to me you owe me more than that."

Beth was still smiling long after Jessie had gone back inside the house. The competent black woman was a fixture at Cottonwood, and Beth couldn't imagine life without her. She was all things to her: substitute mother, friend and housekeeper, all rolled into one. She would miss her terribly.

But then, leaving home was all part of growing up, Beth knew. Still, it wouldn't be easy. Her eyes wandered toward the house, standing tall, bathed in the bright sunlight. The glorious structure with its Tara-style columns, glittering chandeliers and curving staircase was a place of magic, ethereal in its tranquil beauty.

So what if it was in dire need of a paint job both inside and out, that the plaster was cracked inside in various rooms, and that the rugs and drapes needed replacing? For the longest time Beth had hounded her daddy to make repairs, but he always brushed her aside with the promise, "Soon, honey, soon."

Still, those imperfections failed to detract from its beauty. But then, Cottonwood was more than just a house; it was an institution. It had history. The Melbournes had owned it for generations, and according to her daddy, his ancestors had thought there was nothing this side of heaven that could compare with it.

Beth agreed, especially now that the trees were in full bloom, as were the lawns and sweeping meadows beyond. Past the meadows, a driveway curved through the huge oaks where blackbirds gathered, and the pebbles became variegated with light and shadow.

In the far distance stood a barn, a racetrack and stables where her daddy's prized quarter horses munched on the abundant clover blanketing the meadows.

No matter where she lived, Cottonwood would always be close to her heart, always be her home. Her roots were something no one could ever take from her.

But then, she wasn't going far. Simply next door.

Beth removed her sunglasses and squinted. Though she couldn't see Wimberly, Zach's home, from where she sat, it was there, as pretentious and elegant as Cottonwood, if not more so.

Suddenly her lips tightened, and a nameless fear flooded through her. If only they didn't have to live there. She gave her head a hard shake to clear it of all unwanted thoughts. But the thoughts persisted. It wasn't that she didn't like Wimberly or think it was lovely. The problem was Zach's daddy, Taylor. There was something about him that gave her the willies. And that concerned her, for Zach's sake as well as her own.

But she wouldn't think about that now. She refused to let anything dampen her day.

"Hey, friend, you aren't getting too much of this July sun, are you?"

At the sound of the loud, unexpected voice, Beth bolted upright. "Lordy, Rachel, you nearly scared me half to death."

Rachel shrugged, then grinned. "Sorry. Just thought I'd stop by a minute. I'm on the way to the bank for Mamma."

Beth watched Rachel Carrington with admiration as she sauntered closer, then plopped down into the chair next to her. Rachel was eighteen years old, Beth's own age, and pretty. Dark hair framed an oval face with wide-spaced blue eyes and high cheekbones. Beth, envious of her olive complexion, swore it was to die for.

"You know, ever since graduation Mamma thinks I don't have anything better to do than run her errands," Rachel was saying.

"Well, now that all our graduation parties are over, you don't."

Rachel rolled her eyes. "Thanks. A fine friend you are."

"I thought I heard you, Rachel, honey, so I added a few extra cookies and lemonade."

Both girls turned their attention to Jessie, whose hands were occupied with a tray loaded with goodies.

Rachel smiled. "If you ever get tired of working for these people, you know where you'll be welcome."

"Hush your mouth, Rachel Carrington," Beth responded, grabbing a magazine off the nearby table and fanning herself. "Jessie'll never leave Cottonwood."

"That's right, Beth. The Lord willin', I'll die right here."

Rachel sighed audibly. "Oh, well, I can tell Mamma I tried."

The silence continued long after Jessie had scuttled off, as both girls were busy nibbling the appetizing sweets.

After chasing a bite of tea cake down with the last of her lemonade, Beth finally said, "After you go to the bank, why don't you put on your swimsuit and come sun with me, not that *you* need any more sun. You're brown as a berry."

Rachel scoffed, "By that time you'll already be burned to a crisp."

"I'll have you know," Beth said airily, "I mixed iodine with baby oil, which guarantees a tan without burning." Pausing, Beth perused her own body. "But yuk, I know I look ghastly."

"No way, friend. You couldn't look ghastly if you tried." Rachel smiled without envy. "Even all greased up, you look good."

And she did. Beth's face was a sculptor's dream. Flawless features and creamy skin were enhanced by enormous brown eyes, which reflected both innocence and amusement. Her hair, parted in the middle and hanging straight to her shoulders, was the color of butterscotch.

In spite of her delicate bone structure, Beth was not the least bit angular. She had full breasts and softly rounded hips. Her legs were long and thin. Clothes, for which she had an instinctive flair, always draped her slender frame with exquisite perfection.

"Flattery will get you everywhere," Beth teased, "but we both know that's all it is." She paused and rubbed more oil on her bare stomach. Then, changing the subject, she said, "When you come back, I want us to try lemon juice on our hair." She grinned. "*Glamour* says it's supposed to make it shine."

Rachel lifted a dark eyebrow. "Sounds interesting, only I can't come back this morning. Mamma has some other things for me to do today—work on my wardrobe, for one."

Beth scooted to the edge of the chair. "Oh, Rach," she began on a wail, "just think, soon everything's going to be so different. You'll be going off to the university, and I'll be getting married."

"Yeah, I know." Rachel made a face. "I'm going to miss you, too. But we both know nothing ever stays the same."

Beth adjusted her sunglasses closer to the bridge of her nose. "I bet you'll be so busy you won't even write." Her tone held a petulant ring.

"Me?" Rachel grinned a Cheshire-cat grin. "You'll be the one who'll be too busy to write. Why, I bet Zach won't let you out of the sack long enough—"

Beth's face and neck flushed red. "Rachel Carrington! I'm shocked."

"No, you're not, because you know it's the truth."

Beth giggled. "You're right, I do. And I can't wait."

"Reckon there's another specimen walking around on this earth that looks as good as Zach?"

Beth smiled while her eyes took on a dreamy glaze. "No, never. And it's downright disgusting whenever he walks into a room, how the other girls' eyes stick to him like decals."

"Tut, tut, your claws are showing."

"I know, I'm awful," Beth admitted, "but I can't help it. Lord knows, I'm too jealous for my own good."

Rachel laughed, only to turn suddenly serious. "All I can do is keep hoping that one of these days maybe I'll stumble across someone as wonderful as Zach."

"Of course you will." Beth's tone had chilled somewhat, slightly miffed at the thought that Rachel might still harbor feelings for Zach. "Your knight in shining armor is out there. I know he is. And when you find him, you'll be as happy as I am."

Rachel stood abruptly. "Well, speaking of happy, if I don't get to the bank and back home, Mamma's going to have my hide." She pushed a hand through her short curls. "If you're not doing anything this afternoon, maybe I could come back."

"Sorry, but Zach's taking me on a picnic."

Rachel grinned another knowing grin. "Well, y'all have fun."

Beth answered her grin with a flushed face, then said, "I'll see you later, hear?"

When she was alone again Beth grabbed the brush on the table beside her and ran it through her long hair, wincing each time she hit a tangle. Then, looking down at her arms, she decided that Rachel was right. She'd gotten enough sun for one day. After slipping into her thongs, she reached for her paraphernalia and headed toward the cool comfort of the glassed-in sun porch.

Beth had just stepped inside when she heard voices coming from the library to the left of where she stood. Holding her breath, she paused and listened. Despite the television blaring in the kitchen, she could hear the heated exchange.

In fact, the whole world could hear it, Beth thought with a sinking heart. Her daddy and brother were shouting, or rather, her daddy was shouting at her brother again.

Knowing that it was probably unwise to interfere, she stayed where she was. But when it looked as if there was no end to the quarrel in sight, Beth made her way to the open door and stopped on the threshold.

Her daddy was standing in the middle of the large room that housed a prized Seignoret cabinet and mahogany bookcases jammed with books. An assortment of Clementine Hunter paintings covered the wall by her brother. Both seemed oblivious to her presence.

Foster Melbourne, a tall, robust man with a thatch of prematurely gray hair and a big Teddy Roosevelt mustache, towered over his son.

"Damn it, boy, can't you do anything right? This is the third time I've been called to the principal's office, and the summer-school term has just started."

Trent, though only twelve years old, was not cowed. He stood up to his father with a belligerent look on his face, which Beth knew only angered Foster that much more.

"I told you," Trent was saying, his lower lip trembling ever so slightly, "it wasn't my fault. Johnny Grimes started the fight."

Beth stared at her brother, taking in the pale, pinched features, the swollen right eye, the lock of dark curly hair that was matted with blood from the small cut on his forehead. She had to quell the urge to go to him, fling her arms around his thin shoulders and tell him that everything was going to be all right. She couldn't, because instinct told her that everything was *not* going to be all right.

"The hell with Johnny Grimes!" Foster bellowed. "To hear you tell it, it's always somebody else's fault, never yours. When are you going to stop behaving like poor white trash and act like a Melbourne?"

He paused and rubbed the back of his neck with his left hand. "I wish you were more like your sister. Why, she's never given me a minute's trouble."

"Yeah, well, everybody can't be perfect like her!" Trent cried suddenly, bitterly. "She thinks her sh—"

Red faced, Foster raised his hand as if to strike his son. "Now, listen here, boy! I won't have you talking about your sister like that!"

"Daddy, don't!"

Beth wasn't even aware that she'd cried out until both pairs of eyes swung in her direction. For a moment no one moved; no one said a word.

Foster cleared his throat at the same time that he lowered his hand, though he never took his eyes off Beth. "How long have you been standing there?"

"Long enough," Beth said in a weak voice.

"I guess you know your brother's in trouble, then? Actually, they expelled him from summer school."

Beth switched her gaze to her brother. "Trent, what happened?"

Trent didn't answer. Instead, he glared at her, then whirled and ran toward the door. When he would have skirted past her, Beth reached out and caught him by the arm.

"Trent, please, I want to talk to you."

"But I don't want to talk to you," he spat, his eyes narrowed slits. "It's all your fault."

A sob caught in Beth's throat. "Trent, please," she begged, "you're not being fair."

Trent jerked his arm out of her grasp. "Leave me alone. Don't you understand? I hate you! I *hate* you!"

Two

Oak trees loaded down with Spanish moss towered over the grassy embankment; birds making melodious music rivaled the nearby creek as it gurgled over the rocks. The succulent smell of wildflowers flavored the air and sweetened the earth.

Though Beth, lying on a hand-pieced quilt and cradling her head in the palm of one hand, appreciated the beauty surrounding her, that was not what was on her mind at the moment. Zach was the target of her concentration. She watched as he ambled toward the shiny blue Pontiac GTO his parents had given him for graduation and opened the trunk. Sporting the easy grace of an athlete, he tossed the empty picnic hamper inside and slammed the lid shut.

Twisting halfway around, Zach smiled his cocksure smile, his eyebrows rising and lowering Elvis-Presley-style, as he sauntered toward her once again. No doubt about it, Zach Winslow was beautiful. And he was hers. Though his tall, rock-hard body, clad in cutoffs and a muscle shirt, was impressive, it was his eyes that set him apart. They were a watery green color, like celery, and contrasted perfectly with his dark hair and long, thick lashes.

Though not perfect, his features were close enough to perfection that he could be labeled handsome. Yet a rugged edge gave him a somewhat dangerous look, a look that never failed to draw a throaty groan from her.

Earlier, when she'd heard him drive up, Beth had dashed down the stairs, confident she looked her best in a pair of yellow shorts and a white halter top. Laughing, she had thrown her arms around Zach's neck. After swinging her around and kissing her hotly on the lips, Zach had bounded out the door with her and they had climbed into his GTO. While the radio blared "Raindrops Keep Falling On My Head," they had sped down a country lane that led to their favorite picnic spot.

Even after they had gotten settled, they hadn't said much, especially Beth, until the majority of the food Jessie had prepared for them had disappeared and they had drunk a half bottle of Boone's Farm apple wine.

Now, as Zach eased his lanky frame down onto the quilt in front of her, Beth continued to devour him with her eyes.

"I'm waiting for you to tell me," he said into the silence.

A frown creased Beth's smooth forehead. "Tell you what?"

"What's been bothering you ever since I picked you up."

Beth smiled and shook her head. "I can't fool you for a minute, can I?"

"Nope. So, let's hear it. I can't have my bride-to-be worrying about anything." He grinned. "Anyway, who wants a wife with worry wrinkles on her face?" With his index finger, Zach traced a line down the center of her forehead.

Smiling sweetly, Beth innocently placed a hand on his thigh and then, without warning, grasped several hairs and yanked. Hard.

"Ouch!" Zach scowled. "Why'd you do that?"

"Because you insinuated I had wrinkles, that's why."

He gently yanked a handful of her hair. "Payback time."

They both laughed. Then Zach's face sobered again. "Are you gonna tell me?"

Beth sighed. "It's nothing new, actually. Daddy and Trent had a fight."

His eyebrows met in a frown. "Another one?"

"Uh-huh."

"What happened this time?"

"Trent got expelled from summer school, and Daddy had to leave work and go to the principal's office. Wow, was he mad." Beth paused and drew a ragged breath. "He shouldn't have been. It's his fault, you know. He spends more of his time at the racetracks than he does with Trent." Beth's face clouded. "I feel so sorry for my brother, even though at times I could wring his neck."

"Sounds like normal brother-and-sister love to me." Zach exhaled slowly. "But it's obvious that where Trent is concerned, your old man has never played by the rules. I'm concerned about him, too." He was quiet for a moment, as if lost in thought.

"A penny," Beth said, angling her head.

"What?"

"A penny for your thoughts, silly. You know."

The dent in Zach's brow became more pronounced. "They aren't worth even that."

"They are to me."

"Actually, I was thinking about how much Trent reminds me of myself at that age." Zach grew pensive. "I was never allowed to make mistakes. My parents expected me to be perfect, to behave like an adult."

"Ah, so that's why you sometimes act like a thorny old man?" Beth asked, a gleam in her eye, determined to remove that sad look from Zach's face. Too, the thought of him being mistreated as a child was unbearable.

"Sure you don't mean horny?"

Beth gave a start, only to then smile in response to the answering gleam in his eyes. "You're . . . you're impossible," she sputtered.

"I know. That's why you're crazy about me."

The slap on his leg seemed to have the desired effect. He sobered and asked, "What about Gran? Can't she do anything with Foster?"

Grace Childress, affectionately known as Gran, was Beth's maternal grandmother. Just thinking about her and her soothing self-confidence brought a smile to Beth's face. Unfortunately, though she was a major player in their lives, she had very little influence over her stubborn son-in-law.

Beth voiced her thought. "Gran's wonderful, all right. She more than does her part, but it's impossible for her to always be there to pick up the pieces following one of Trent's and Daddy's arguments. You...you know what the problem is, don't you? What it boils down to?" Tears sprang into Beth's eyes. "Daddy's never forgiven Trent for living while Mamma died. It just kills me that he blames his son for something Trent can't help."

Zach pinched the bridge of his nose. "Well, as I said before, it's no secret that Foster resents that boy."

"And it's Daddy's fault that Trent resents me. If only he'd stop throwing me up to Trent." Beth sighed. "He's always comparing us. It's crazy. Daddy never reprimands me, while Trent can't do anything to please him."

"I'm sure he doesn't mean half the things he says," Zach pointed out quietly.

"I'm sure he doesn't, either." Beth's teeth touched her lower lip. "Daddy's wonderful. I adore the ground he walks on, but when it comes to my brother, he's a hopeless case."

"Well, I would imagine it hasn't been easy rearing the two of you alone. On second thought, I'm sure it hasn't been easy for any of y'all."

Zach's uncanny insight into her problems both comforted and reassured her. He was only twenty-two, but he had a wisdom far beyond his years, which she knew stemmed from the way he'd been reared.

"You're right, it hasn't. But Trent, especially, has suffered. Daddy—well, he doesn't show his feelings. He's not a toucher...." Beth's voice faltered. "What Trent needs is a mother. I...I tried to talk to him, only, only..." She paused again and screwed up her face. "Oh, Zach, he...he told me he hated me, that his problems are all my fault."

A furrow appeared between Zach's eyes. "He didn't mean that, baby. He's just a mixed-up twelve-year-old."

"He *did* mean it. I truly believe he hates me. And I feel so helpless, so useless." A plaintive note entered Beth's voice. "I...I've tried to be a mother to him, but I've failed."

Zach drew her close against him. "You're being too hard on yourself. You haven't failed. If anyone's a failure, it's Foster."

Beth pulled back so she could look into his face. "I've told him over and over that Trent is special in his own right, that he should be proud of him, too."

"Only he won't let himself."

"Right. I don't know why, and neither does Gran. But what I do know is that Trent is really upset, and he won't let me help him."

"He'll get over his anger. Just give him time. And I promise we won't desert him. He can spend as much time with us as he wants."

"Maybe if you talked to him it would help." Beth pinched her fingers together. "You know, he thinks the sun rises and sets on you."

"I'll give it my best shot. Don't you worry about it. Trent'll come around. You'll see."

"He has to," Beth said fiercely. "He just has to."

'How 'bout a little more wine? It'll make you feel better." He reached over and grabbed the bottle, and once he'd filled their glasses, Zach raised his and gave her a slow smile. "To us."

Beth's gaze came up level with his. "To us."

They sipped in silence for a moment; then, without taking his eyes off her, Zach reached for her glass and set it alongside his on the edge of the quilt.

"You're beautiful, Beth Melbourne," he said softly. "Especially today."

Even after all this time, the husky tone of his voice could still cause that funny feeling in the pit of her stomach. Beth swallowed hard.

"Your hair." Though he angled his head, his husky-toned voice didn't change. "It looks different."

Grinning, Beth pulled a segment of the silky mass away from her neck and let it slip through her fingers. "I used lemon juice on it."

"Lemon juice." Zach looked astonished. "God, that sounds awful."

Beth lifted her chin. "Only because you don't understand. It's supposed to make it shine."

"Well, it damn sure looks good, all right," he said, reaching out and using a handful of it to slowly draw her closer. His eyes were on her, soft and warm like spring sunshine.

At that moment Beth felt a tightness in the back of her throat, an overwhelming tenderness for him. His lips, when they met hers, tasted more intoxicating than the wine they had consumed.

Having been lovers for nearly a year, they were familiar with each other's bodies. But it had been only through loving patience that Zach had taught her how to please, how to satisfy him.

"Do you know what you do to me?" His voice was a nervous shiver as he pushed himself against her.

"I hope so," she whispered and caught her breath, feeling his strength.

Suddenly her need for him betrayed her, and she moved even closer; at the same time she slipped a hand underneath the damp material of his shirt, touching his body. As she explored, ridge upon ridge of strong, solid muscle rolled and flexed beneath her greedy hand.

"Oh, Beth," Zach said, grinding his lips against hers and rolling her onto her back. Once she was on the ground, he tore his mouth from hers and moved it to her breast.

She felt herself convulse when his lips made damp, sucking noises through the cotton cloth, capturing a nipple between his teeth.

Their panting, at first low and soft, suddenly turned harsh and urgent. As if from afar, Beth was certain she heard someone whispering, "Please, please," but she couldn't tell who spoke the words.

With a muttered curse, Zach suddenly broke the embrace to rise over her, balancing himself on one knee.

"Damn clothes!" His words were muffled as he ripped off his shirt in one frenzied motion, letting it fly. Rocking back on his feet, he grabbed the edge of her shorts as she pushed them down. They, too, drifted high in the air.

Tangled arms and hands slowed the rush they made to remove the remaining clothes from each other's bodies. The heat of desire, threatening to consume them, made the task too urgent for laughter and teasing.

When they were finally naked, compelling need drew them back together.

Zach immediately moved atop her, his sex grazing her thigh and stomach. Dizzily she clung to him as he rubbed himself against her, softly, evenly.

"Oh, Zach, please, stop teasing." Yet her hands teased him, too, increasing the tension and the pleasure until it became unbearable for both.

"Like that, huh?"

"Yes, oh, yes," Beth cried as his lips found her breast at the same time that he thrust into her. She could not slow her breathing, feeling him inside her like the heavy pulse of a second heart.

The sun shone and the wind whistled through the trees, lifting the edges of the quilt. They were aware of nothing except each other.

When their bodies moved as one and he spilled into her, their cries of passion filled the heated summer air with the sound and scent of primitive life. And the earth beneath them seemed to move.

The empty wine bottle lay warming in a stray stream of sunlight that had slipped between the barricading leaves of the old oak above them.

The young lovers lay on their sides, face-to-face, stomach to stomach, their eyes shut. The hot air moistened their bodies, while their intertwined legs grew slicker and wetter. Still, neither moved to fully embrace the other as they played a lover's game of chicken.

"You awake?"

"Mmm, just barely," Zach murmured.

Beth rubbed her foot up and down his leg in a slow motion. He had been quiet for so long, she had thought he had dropped off to sleep.

"You remember when we first met?"

His eyes flickered open. "You mean we actually met? I thought we were born knowing each other."

"Hey, I'm serious."

"So am I."

Beth stuck her tongue out at him. "No, you're not. You're teasing me, even though what you said was romantic."

He rolled his eyes. "Okay, it was a day in April. Right?"

"The fifth, to be exact."

He looked skeptical. "You're puttin' me on. You don't remember the exact date."

Beth turned her Technicolor smile on him. "Well, it sounded good, anyway."

"You're bad," he whispered before kissing her soundly.

"Oh, Zach, I can't wait till we're married."

"Me either."

She fingered her engagement ring, a three-carat, oval-shaped diamond in a gold mounting, then held it up so that the sun hit it just right. She watched it glow like the early-morning dew. "Do you think there will be a lot of people at our wedding?" she asked, lowering her hand.

"Suppose so," he drawled. "Especially since everybody in town seems to have been invited."

"Not everybody, silly."

"Who'd you leave off the invitation list, the town drunk?"

She slapped him playfully. "That's not funny."

"Didn't mean it to be." He kissed her again. "Do you love me?"

When she could speak coherently, she whispered, "You know I do."

"I wish to hell these weeks would hurry up and pass. I can't wait to get you all to myself."

"I feel the same way, only..." Beth's voice faltered, and her eyes darkened.

"Only what?" He sounded tense.

"Nothing," she said hurriedly.

"You don't want to live at Wimberly, do you?"

She struggled to her knees and peered down at him.

"I know you're not wild about my parents, especially Daddy."

"Oh, Zach, that's not true," Beth said lamely. "It's just that..." Again she faltered, wishing she could say what was on her mind.

No matter how hard she tried, she couldn't conquer her uneasiness about Taylor Winslow. She knew where that uneasiness stemmed from, though she hated to admit it even to herself. It was the way he looked at her, as if an evil hunger lurked beneath his civilized veneer. And his reputation with women merely intensified her feelings.

She had kept those feelings well hidden from Zach. She didn't intend to let them surface now.

"Like yours, my dear ole Daddy has his faults, too."

"But you still love him." Beth said the words quietly.

Zach's eyes narrowed and turned hard. "Yeah. But I could kill him sometimes for the way he treats Mamma, the way he flaunts his affairs in front of her."

"Why does she put up with it?" Beth asked softly, plucking at the hairs on his chest. She saw his distress and knew there was something he wasn't telling her, something painful. She wouldn't press him, though.

"Beats me."

They were silent for a minute; then Beth sidled up to him once again. "Well, just as long as you don't let any of your daddy's bad habits rub off on you."

He grinned. "Like father, like son, huh?"

"You just try it and see where it gets you."

"Oh, so now you're threatening?"

"No," she said with innocent calmness, "I'm just saying that I'll..." She mouthed the last part, as if the air had ears.

Zach laughed, a big, room-rocking laugh that seemed to reach the sky. "Why, Beth Melbourne, such nasty talk!"

"But you love it," she whispered against his lips.

"I love you," he said seriously.

"That's why I don't care where we live, as long as we're together."

"Are you sure? Because we can get a place of our own. It's just that when Mamma offered us my grandmother's old apartment, I snapped it up."

"Because it's rent free. I know."

"What's wrong with that?" Zach pulled back slightly. "After all, it'll give us a chance to save for our dream house. And it's not like we'll see them all the time, because we won't."

Beth rubbed her hand up and down his arm. "I promise you, it'll be all right."

They were silent for another long moment; then, changing the subject, Beth said brightly, "It's going to be so much fun decorating the apartment with all our gifts. There's so much more I want to do."

"Whoa! Slow down. Don't plan too far in advance. Come September, remember, you've got to start school."

Beth's mouth turned downward. Zach had insisted she go to school, and while a degree was important to her, it wasn't top priority at the moment.

Zach looked at her strangely. "What's the matter? Did I say something wrong?"

"No, only..."

He tweaked her nose. "Only what?"

"It's just that I'd like to concentrate on being your wife before I tackle anything else."

He seemed surprised by her comment. "You'd really like to postpone going to the university?"

Beth didn't hesitate. "Yes. I've given it a lot of thought, too. By the time the second term rolls around, I'm sure I'll be ready. If not, then the summer term." Beth paused and fingered a string of Spanish moss that had fallen onto the quilt. "After all, you're going to need my undivided attention now that you're working full-time at the mill."

Zach's face sobered. "True, especially since I plan to implement some of those new ideas I learned at the university."

"You mean you plan to try."

Zach smiled ruefully. "Yeah, you're right. I should rephrase that. To paraphrase the old saying, 'It's hard to teach an old dog new tricks.' While Foster and Taylor aren't old, they're sure as hell set in their ways. Why, just the other day I heard Daddy say, 'There's no reason to change that, son. After all, we've been doing it that way for forty years.'"

Beth giggled, then apologized. "Sorry, but you mimicked Taylor perfectly. Still, I know how frustrated you must be."

"You're right. I *am* frustrated. I didn't spend four years busting my behind in engineering school for nothing. And it's not as if I'm suggesting changes where they aren't needed. The mill needs modernizing. I have the answer to the sludge problem that's causing tons of trouble. And air pollution—God knows, we need to make improvements there, or the government's going to step in and do it for us.

"And last, but not least, is the number two boiler. If something's not done, it's liable to blow sky-high." His eyes gleamed fiercely. "I have the solutions to all those problems, and if they'll let me, I can increase production twofold."

He could, too. Beth had all the confidence in the world in him. When it came to the mill, to making paper, he seemed to have been blessed with added insight. He'd always had a knack for spotting trouble and automatically smelling out the way to fix it.

"In light of all that, you're definitely going to need my undivided attention." She nibbled on his earlobe. "I need to be studying you rather than freshman English 101."

Zach's arms tightened around her. "Mmm, that sounds good to me."

"Oh, Zach, we're going to have such a wonderful life together."

"Perfect, you mean, don't you?"

"Of course it'll be perfect, especially when we have a baby."

His eyes darkened. "It will be kinda nice watching my son feast on your breast."

Beth blushed, and her breath caught in her throat.

Zach chuckled. "It amazes me that I can still make you turn red."

"Speaking of babies, how long am I going to have to take birth control pills?"

Zach widened his eyes. "Don't tell me you're already thinking about getting pregnant?"

Beth's face softened. "You know I am."

He bent over and traced her lips with the tip of his tongue. "Just hearing you talk about having my baby is making me hard again." He reached for her hand and placed it on him. "See," he said thickly.

Pinpoints of ecstasy swept through Beth. "Make love to me again," she pleaded. "Now."

He needed no second invitation.

Three

The sky was gray and blustery with clouds. Even though more rain was likely, the sun occasionally broke through and silhouetted the twin stacks of the number one and two boilers.

Squinting against the glare, Zach ran his hands through his already-mussed hair. Where the hell was his daddy? And Foster Melbourne? Both men were to have been in his office half an hour ago. No wonder the mill was in such a shambles, he thought, aggravation forming a tight ball in his stomach. When the bosses elected to put pleasure before business, the results could be both costly and deadly, which fit the current scenario here to a tee.

How could his daddy and Foster justify playing with their employees' lives? That was the question he'd been asking himself since he'd gone on the payroll full-time.

Granted, six months was not a long time, but it was long enough to know the mill was in trouble—both financially and managerially, that it was losing money by the fistful. And he hadn't even seen the books.

He shouldn't have been surprised, he told himself with a grimace. His daddy was too busy chasing skirts to tend to the mill, and Foster was too busy chasing horses. It didn't take a rocket scientist to figure out that all they cared about was reaping the benefits from the business. Well, enough was enough. Someone had to be responsible.

That someone was himself, but he wanted to do it his way. He wanted control. He'd told himself from the moment he'd walked into this dingy cubbyhole that was his office, he was going to make a difference. He didn't intend to let anything stop him. He liked taking the inside track. In a race. In business. Anytime. Anywhere. He liked getting there first.

Therein lay the trouble. All his life his parents had tried to control him. They had tried to mold him into being what they wanted him to be, continually stressing who he was. To them, the Winslow name was synonymous with royalty.

"You're a Winslow," his mother would say to him in her perfectly modulated voice. "You must remember never to do anything that would undermine that."

Zach had taken delight in doing just that, having learned early on that being born with a silver spoon in his mouth was more of a curse than a blessing. He guessed what irked him the most was the hypocrisy of the rich and famous. You could sin, but only if your sin remained behind closed doors. No one must ever know.

He would never forget the day after he turned nine. He had overheard his mother and daddy arguing. It was late, and he'd been unable to sleep, so he'd decided to wander downstairs and get some cookies. The door to his parents' room was cracked slightly. When he'd heard his mother's furious but tear-filled voice lashing out at his daddy, he'd paused and peered inside.

"How dare you flaunt your affairs in my face?" Marian Winslow was saying. "Haven't you any shame?"

Taylor stepped closer until he was looming over her. "I'll dare anything I damn well please, and you'll keep your mouth shut," he sneered. "If you weren't so frigid in bed, I might not have to go elsewhere."

"If I'm frigid, it's because you've made me that way." Marian was openly weeping now.

Taylor's hand pawed the air. "Oh, for god's sake, spare me. Just shut up your sniveling and go to bed."

"I'm warning you, Taylor—"

Marian got no further. Taylor's hand shot out and smacked her across the face. "And I'm warning you—"

Acting on instinct alone, Zach pushed the door the rest of the way open. "Don't!" he cried, his eyes blazing in his pinched, pale face. "Don't you hit my mamma again, you hear? Don't you dare!"

Taylor's booze-reddened face drained of color. Marian's hand went to her mouth, but she was unable to smother the whimper that escaped.

"Dammit, boy, I'll have your hide for eavesdropping!"

Marian turned on her husband, shaking uncontrollably. "You'll do no such thing. Leave the boy alone." Then, turning toward Zach, she walked closer to him, her arms outstretched, a pleading look on her face. "Zachery, honey, I can explain. . . ."

With huge tears running down his cheeks, Zach shook his head violently and stumbled backward. When he reached the door, he spun and ran.

His mother followed him to his room to try to explain. Even then, she hadn't been able to find the right words.

"Oh, Zach, you're too young to understand." She paused and sniffed back the tears. "Please, I want...want you to forget what you saw tonight. Pretend it never happened."

"But, Mamma, why did he hit you?" Zach cried, gazing up at her, his chin wobbling.

"Oh, son, there are just some things a woman has to put up with. All you have to remember is that we love you and always will."

Regardless of how hard he tried, he was unable to forget the incident. It wasn't until later that he realized it was at that moment he'd ceased to be a child. He had witnessed a dark side of life that had stolen his innocence, made him face life's harsh reality. That incident also spawned two other truths that Zach was forced to face. One was that his mother would do anything to remain Mrs. Taylor Winslow. The other was that he could not change his parents or the code by which they lived; he could only change himself and make sure he didn't repeat their mistakes.

From then on, throughout his school years, he'd gone to great lengths to distance himself from the snobbery he lived with at home. But it hadn't been easy. He deliberately set out to prove that he was a regular guy. He became known as the class daredevil, the leading prankster.

As a result, he never once lived up to his academic potential. He was an underachiever because he was too busy having a good time and excelling in sports, especially football. He'd been addicted to it as surely as some of his classmates had been addicted to alcohol. The teachers had adored him, and he'd gotten away with it. He could smile that smile of his and they would turn to putty.

His parents had not wanted him to play ball and had fought vehemently against it. His mother had been certain he would break every bone in his body and be maimed for life. She hadn't been far from wrong. During his senior year in high school he had severely injured his knee. His dreams of playing college ball had vanished like leaves in a windstorm.

With his dreams of gridiron fame and glory nothing but a fading memory, he had turned his grit and determination toward learning everything he could about the paper industry, because by then he was head over heels in love with Beth and was dreaming of a future at home in Shawnee.

Ah, Beth. Thoughts of her came as a welcome reprieve to the trek down memory lane that had ripped open an old wound. Zach found that his tightly wound nerves had untangled. She had that effect on him. But then, Beth was his life. Beth was the air he breathed. He couldn't imagine life without her.

No matter how discouraged or down-and-out he became, thinking about her never failed to buoy his spirits and put things in their proper perspective. Or cause his pulse to hammer, he thought, a grin inching its way across his mouth.

In his mind's eye, he saw Beth standing nude in the shower, beckoning him to join her under the streaming water. He saw her sitting in the lounge chair on the deck, the breeze teasing her hair. He could hear her throaty voice as she laughed....

For some crazy reason, the first time they had made love jumped to the forefront of his mind. His grin widened.

It hadn't been planned. Maybe that was what had made it so unforgettably special.

They had been on a picnic much like the one they'd been on three days ago. It had been a sultry Saturday afternoon, and rain had threatened all day. But they hadn't minded, knowing that, if they had to, they could find shelter in an old deserted cabin on the Melbourne estate, which they had often played in as youngsters.

Their horses had been tied to a nearby tree, and they were sprawled on a blanket that Zach had removed from his saddlebags. They had finished eating an hour earlier and had returned from a trek through the woods. They were kissing hot and heavy.

"Sweet, sweet Beth," Zach breathed against her lips, "you do such wonderful things to my body."

"Like what?" she demanded innocently.

He nipped at her lips. "Like make me hard. But you know that, don't you?"

"Which means you want me."

"Oh, baby, I want you all the time."

Every time he was near her, he thought he would die from wanting her so much. But he hadn't taken her. Even though their petting had advanced, he hadn't seen her completely naked. For one thing, he hadn't thought she was ready. They had only been dating seriously for a short time, and he hadn't wanted to rush her. Still, he ached to make love to her.

"Oh, Beth, you're driving me nuts," he whispered, lifting her T-shirt and greedily suckling one breast and then the other.

Moaning, she held his mouth in place while lifting his shirt and massaging his back. It was only after he slipped his hands inside her panties that he paused and looked at her.

"Please," she panted, her eyes slightly glazed, "don't stop."

He eased one finger, then two, inside her warmth. She found even breathing was difficult while he gently moved his fingers.

"You're so tiny, so wet."

"Oh, Zach," she moaned again.

"It's your turn to touch me," he said thickly, moving her hand to cover the thickness in his jeans.

Her breath caught.

"Unzip my jeans."

Boldly, she did just that. When his hardness was visible, she again caught her breath and hesitated.

"Go ahead, touch me like I'm touching you."

She stared at him wide-eyed. "Are you sure?"

"Please . . . Beth . . ." he ground out. "I'm sure."

Her eyes were dark with passion as she circled him with tentative fingers. To Zach they felt like satin. It was all he could do not to come in her hand.

"Oh, Zach," she said breathlessly. "It's . . . it's perfect."

"You think so, huh?" he asked with an agonized chuckle.

"What . . . what do we do now?"

"What do you want to do?"

"Go . . . go all the way," she said in raspy spurts.

"Oh, baby..."

He got no further. Not only did a clap of thunder invade their paradise, but lightning danced across the sky, as well.

"Come on, let's head for the cabin."

They didn't make it. Halfway there the sky opened, and by the time they raced inside, they were drenched. Without hesitation they stripped off their soggy clothes and stood facing each other in the dim light.

"You're something," he whispered, awestruck by her full, bare breasts, nipples that shone like petals, softly rounded hips and thin, endless legs.

"So are you," she whispered in turn.

He felt his control slipping. "Come here."

With lips pressed together hotly, they lowered themselves to the cot, the only piece of furniture in the room, and intertwined their legs.

"Oh, God, Beth," he gasped, finally letting go of her mouth. "I don't know how much more of this I can stand. I want you so much. But—"

"And I want you," she whispered urgently. "Now. This minute. I don't want to wait."

Following those words, she boldly took his steely hardness in her hand and placed it between her thighs.

"Beth, Beth," Zach wheezed. "We...we shouldn't...."

"Please, Zach," she all but begged. "I want to feel you inside me."

"Oh, baby, I want that, too, only it's too dangerous. You could get pregnant."

"I know," she wailed. "Only..."

"How 'bout if we compromise?" He could hear his hoarse voice reverberate within his chest. "I'll just put it part of the way inside, then I'll stop, okay?"

"Oh, Zach, I'll settle for anything as long as you love me."

But he'd been unable to hold to his promise. When he'd penetrated her wetness, they had both lost control, and he'd ended up filling her completely. It was only after their passionate moans had subsided that he realized what he'd done.

Panicking, he pulled his sweat-slicked body off hers and stared at her, his eyes dark with remorse and pain. "Did I . . . hurt you?"

Dots of color stained Beth's cheeks. "A little, but I don't regret it," she murmured softly, almost shyly.

"Oh, baby, baby, I'm sorry," Zach whispered, his eyes wandering over her. It was then that he saw the drying blood on her legs. He raised horror-filled eyes. He tried to say something, but nothing could get past the lump in his throat.

Beth smiled at him with infinite sweetness. "Shh, don't say anything. It's all right. Trust me."

And it had been. Luckily she hadn't gotten pregnant, but he had never loved her again without taking precautions.

Feeling his body respond to his thoughts, Zach shifted his feet uncomfortably and forced his thoughts off Beth.

Then, sighing deeply, he turned his back on the gray day and stared instead at the gray interior in front of him. A large, scarred desk, two dingy-looking filing cabinets, a table with an automatic coffee maker, and two chairs comprised the only objects in the room. He could live with the charming decor, as it was only temporary. Since he'd come to work full-time he'd drawn up plans for a separate office building.

That project was just one among many he wanted to discuss with Taylor and Foster.

Shifting his gaze to the detailed list in front of him, Zach sat down at his desk and picked up his pen. He was writing furiously, adding to the list, when Taylor strode through the door, impeccably dressed, as usual, in a navy suit and red paisley tie.

Zach deliberately glanced at his watch. "'Bout time," he drawled.

Ignoring his son's sarcasm, Taylor went to the make-shift coffee bar in the corner and helped himself to a generous cup.

Zach watched as his daddy's hand shook, and grimaced inwardly. The features of Taylor's face seemed flat, and his complexion was sallow, as if he hadn't seen the sun all summer. Besides his roving eye, Taylor had another problem. The bottle. Everyone knew it; too bad he didn't. Though it galled him, Zach had to admit that his daddy, despite his superficial scars, had yet to show the deep physical signs of most substance abusers.

At fifty-six, he still posed quite a commanding figure. Like Zach, he was tall. Beyond that, there was little resemblance. Taylor had a swarthy complexion, a nose that was a shade too long and a forehead that was too high. In his favor were a set of evenly matched teeth and a headful of brown hair devoid of gray. When it suited him he could turn on his Southern charm, which was any time a beautiful woman was around.

That laid-back charm could turn deadly without warning, Zach knew. Taylor Winslow did not like to be crossed. When thwarted, the line of his chin made you think of a granite cliff. Zach's mother had told him that he had inherited that trait.

"Where's Foster?" Taylor demanded, as if it had just dawned on him that his partner was missing.

Disgusted, Zach shook his head. "Probably forgot, which is just as well. I'd like to talk to you alone, anyway."

"You got a burr up your butt this morning?" Taylor asked, easing onto the nearest chair and pulling a cigarette out of his pocket.

Zach leaned forward and rested his elbows on the desk. "The burr I've got up my butt is the mill." His tone matched the coldness in his eyes. "It's suffering from neglect, Daddy, and you and Foster can't keep ignoring that."

Taylor lit his cigarette and drew on it. "I'll admit we've hit on some hard times, but it's not losing money."

"Well, it sure isn't making any, either."

"It's doing all right," Taylor said stubbornly. "We're paying our workers."

The cigarette hung from his lower lip like a scab. Zach turned away, disgusted. "There's no way you can ignore the fact that we laid off twenty-five hands last week."

"Well, we'll be calling them back before long." Taylor spoke in a low tone, as if to defuse his son's anger.

"Daddy, please, listen to me. Let's spend some money. We need to modernize the number one paper machine and put in a new boiler—"

Taylor lunged to his feet. "You can't come in here and start making changes and demanding things! Things just don't work that way."

A slow red flush mounted Zach's face, but his cool, even voice didn't change. "Why not? After all, this is the seventies, not the forties, which is the way you two are running things around here."

The heavy muscles of Taylor's jaw tightened into ugly knots. "You're entitled to your opinion."

"Beth warned me it wouldn't be easy," Zach mumbled, more to himself than to Taylor.

But Taylor heard him, and his features twisted. "Beth. What the hell does she know about all this? She couldn't care less about the mill. All she cares about is getting all dolled up for you."

Zach hung on to his temper by a thread. "When are you and Mother going to get over being jealous of Beth?"

Taylor scowled down into his coffee. "Jealous? Who's jealous?"

"All right, we'll play it your way for now." Zach's face hardened. "Let it be known here and now that if our living at Wimberly doesn't work out, we'll move in a heartbeat."

"See here, boy, you're way out of line."

A smirk flirted with the corners of Zach's lips. "Yeah?"

An uneasy silence fell over the room.

Zach was the first to break it. "Back to the mill. I want to be involved. I want to get production back on track."

"I don't see anything wrong with that," Taylor said, eyeing a long ash on his cigarette.

"But first, I want to see the books." Zach spoke deliberately and watched as his words sank in. "And there's more. I want to be a partner. Now."

Taylor looked as if he might explode. His face turned redder than his tie. "I'll take it up with Foster, but I'm making no promises."

Zach stood. "Either I become a partner soon, or I'll walk out, leaving you and Foster to drown in your own incompetence."

With that he made his way out the door, leaving Taylor behind, his mouth gaping.

Four

"Do you have to go?" the young woman whispered in a husky voice, at the same time languorously stretching like a cat who'd just finished a bowl of rich cream. "It's only six o'clock," she added on a peevish note.

Taylor Winslow, sitting on the edge of the bed, cut Carolyn an exasperated glance before zipping his pants. "For crying out loud, you've screwed my brains out already. As it is, I won't be worth a damn today."

She giggled and began to trail a blood-red fingernail down his back, leaving a thin white mark. "Good."

Taylor faced her, swallowing hard. "You're not playing fair, honey. You know I have to go." Still, he couldn't stop himself from touching her. Twisting his lips, he leaned over and took a nipple between his teeth, while his hand found the shadow between her legs.

She whimpered and began to move.

Not only was she beautiful, but was she ever a good lay, Taylor thought, basking in the sensations shooting through him. He couldn't remember when he'd felt so drained, both mentally and physically. Yet he was hard again and knew he could take her without regrets or second thoughts. When it came to sex lately, he seemed to be insatiable. Maybe it was his way of escaping from the pressures at work and at home.

He had met Carolyn in a bar several weeks ago, and since then he'd spent as many nights as he could in her bed. He didn't know much about her, except that she was about his son's age and she worked at the local grocery. That was all he wanted to know. The less he knew about his lovers, the better.

"Take off your pants," she ordered urgently, taking her hand and placing it over his hardness.

Taylor sucked in a harsh breath, but at the same time he did her bidding.

Thirty minutes later, Wimberly was quiet when he let himself in the side door off the newly modernized utility room. Zach, it appeared, had already left for the mill, as his GTO wasn't in the garage. Carmen, the housekeeper, hadn't arrived yet. Marian, he knew, would still be asleep.

He needed a drink, badly. On the way from Carolyn's small apartment on the other side of town, he'd emptied the flask of whiskey he kept in the glove compartment of his Cadillac. That hadn't been nearly enough. He was nervous, too, noticing how his hands shook as he helped himself to a generous cup of coffee, already brewed thanks to the automatic timer. Then he grabbed a bottle from the cabinet and laced the coffee with a generous portion of whiskey.

After sitting down at the table in the glassed-in breakfast room, Taylor sipped continually from his cup until he felt his insides unwind. Outside the French doors that opened onto a long gallery, birds chirped and squirrels scampered from one oak tree to the other. He failed to notice; his thoughts were centered on himself and his problems. He needed all his faculties about him this morning, because he planned to approach Foster about making Zach a partner.

Nearly a week had passed since his son had confronted him with his ultimatum. He couldn't put off making a decision much longer. He knew Zach well enough to know that he'd meant what he said.

Zach was like himself: headstrong, impulsive and self-centered enough to bulldoze aside anyone who got in his way. Still, he didn't like being pushed into a corner. Marian had tried that more than once, only to find that it wouldn't work.

Zachery, however, was a different matter. There were few things in life that Taylor cared about. His son was one of them; the Winslow name was another. He enjoyed clout, the reverence associated with the name. It meant something, meant that *he* was something. He was proud of his standing in the town, too. He was on the board of the local bank and chairman of various organizations around town.

He also cared about Wimberly. He would die before he would leave this elegant old home, with its graceful white pillars and beautifully landscaped gardens. Both his father and his grandfather had been born here. While not steeped in quite the same amount of history as the neighboring Cottonwood, it nonetheless could hold its own.

At one time he had cared about Southland with the same passion. No more. The problems associated with the mill had stymied that passion.

He couldn't pinpoint the exact time his interest had begun to erode. Early on, he couldn't wait to get to work, to embrace the challenges he knew were waiting for him. That same enthusiasm had once driven Foster, as well. It seemed like only yesterday that he and Foster had been strapping young bucks eager to prove they were capable of carrying on the tradition of their fathers, who had founded Southland together.

For years they had taken great pride in doing just that. But then something had happened. Foster became more interested in horses than in the mill. At first he hadn't let that outside pleasure interfere with business. But then Taylor began to notice that projects that were Foster's sole responsibility were left undone or botched.

One such debacle had forced him to confront Foster, no longer willing to cover for him.

"That new generator just isn't cutting it," he'd said, seething. "It's already cost us a bundle."

Foster's shoulders had bowed. "It's being worked on even as we speak."

"That's the problem!" Taylor had exploded. "If you hadn't taken the first bid just so you wouldn't have to fool with it, we wouldn't be in this shape."

Foster had pulled on one end of his mustache while his face turned redder. "Just what are you getting at?"

"You spend too much time at the racetracks and not enough on business." Taylor had pounded a fist on his desk. "That's what I'm getting at."

Foster had looked as if the veins in his face were about to pop. "What I do here or anyplace else is none of your business. You'd best keep that in mind."

With that, Foster had stormed out the door and slammed it behind him.

Since that day their relationship had never been the same. Taylor knew Foster had never forgiven him for bringing his mistakes to light and confronting him. Not that Taylor cared. He hadn't cared then, and he damn sure didn't care now. About Foster or the mill.

So why didn't he just inform Foster that he was making Zach a partner, thus giving him carte blanche to implement his new ideas? A sudden smirk rearranged Taylor's lips. In light of his partner's own problems, he knew Foster wouldn't say a damn word.

Was he dragging his heels because he still considered his son a young whippersnapper with a lot to learn? Simply because Zach had graduated from the university with those newfangled ideas didn't mean he knew how to run a company.

Taylor knew the mill was in trouble. But he had his pride, and it galled him to think that Zach had to sweep up his and Foster's messes.

On the other side of that coin, though, he'd been grooming Zach all his life to take over the mill. Maybe that time had simply come sooner than he'd anticipated. What harm could it do? The more he thought about it, the better it sounded. After all, it would leave him free to pursue his other interests.

A harsh chuckle altered Taylor's features as his latest conquest, Carolyn, came to mind. There was something about her that bewitched him. She reminded him of someone. He frowned, trying to think who it was. After taking another healthy drink from his cup, it hit him.

Beth. She reminded him of an older, more mature Beth Melbourne. Taylor's frown erupted into a full-blown scowl. Zach was wrong. He wasn't jealous of his future daughter-in-law. He wanted a grandson to carry on the Winslow name. If Beth was the chosen one, then so be it. Too bad, though, that she didn't like him. She would never admit that, probably didn't even realize it herself. But Taylor knew. He had caught her looking at him as if he was some varmint that had crawled out from under a rock, which neither surprised nor upset him.

Beth thought she was something special, with hair that shone as brightly as trapped sunlight and high, firm tits. He had to agree, she was. Even as a youngster, she was a looker. But, amazingly, she had made an even more beautiful woman.

He could recall the moment he had first noticed that she had become that woman. It was still imprinted on his brain. He'd gone to his partner's house to discuss a pressing business matter. When he'd stepped into the backyard, Beth had been poised to dive into the water.

The silhouette of her trim sixteen-year-old body, highlighted by pert, budding breasts and long, shapely legs, had caused an unwitting tightening in his crotch. He had just licked his lips when she turned and saw him. In that instant something strange had flickered across her face. Later, after mulling it over, he'd been certain it was fear he'd seen there.

But instead of feeling shame for lusting after his partner's daughter and his son's girlfriend, he'd felt randy as hell, despite the fact that both men would have killed him if they'd known his thoughts.

Yet he hadn't been able to stop himself from looking, from wishing....

For sure, she was one little filly that needed a heavy hand. He just hoped Zach was up to the challenge.

"Well, well, I see you finally made it home."

At the sound of his wife's cutting voice, Taylor swung around, and when he did, cold coffee sloshed over him. "See what you made me do!" He jumped up, then reached for a towel on the Empire sideboard behind him and attacked the dark stain on the front of his shirt.

Marian stepped farther into the room, and without saying anything further, helped herself to some coffee. Equally silent, Taylor watched her every move, his eyes hooded.

Damned shame, he thought, that someone as lovely as his wife of twenty-five years could be such a big disappointment. At fifty-two she was still a fine-looking woman, especially when she had her frosted blond hair parted in the middle and pulled away from her stunning profile in a chignon at the nape of her neck. Her figure wasn't too shabby, either. Under the free-flowing robe, her still-high breasts were silhouetted. Tall and statuesque, she carried herself as though she were a queen. An ice queen, he had learned shortly after they were married.

She hadn't liked his method of lovemaking, she'd told him when they had returned from their honeymoon. Still, she had tolerated him, because she had liked being Mrs. Taylor Winslow and she'd wanted a child.

Having come from a family with bloodlines but no cash, she had convinced him one evening when he was half drunk that with her beauty and his brains they would make a good match. If he hadn't been half lit, he would have realized after he'd taken her virginity in the car that same night that she hadn't enjoyed having him inside her at all.

The only reason he hadn't divorced her was the scandal such an act would have created. There had never been a divorce in the Winslow family, and his papa had told him before he died that there would never be one.

Zach had been the only decent thing to come out of their union. Yet he knew he hadn't been the best role model for his son. But even if he'd wanted to, he hadn't had a chance. He'd been upstaged by Marian from the get-go.

"You've gone too far this time, Taylor," Marian said, piercing the lengthy silence. Her face was taut.

Taylor tossed the damp towel he still held back onto the sideboard and in an insolent drawl said, "As usual, it's you who's gone too far. But just for the sake of humoring you, what the hell are you talking about?"

Marian's hazel eyes blazed at him with an almost maniacal glare. "You know very well what I'm talking about. Your latest little whore."

Taylor's features froze into lines of fury. "If I were you, I'd be careful. I won't have you interfering in my business."

"Your whores *are* my business," she spat out coldly.

He could feel his body heat. The fury seethed. "I don't have to listen to this shit. I'm going to take a shower."

"You were seen with her, Taylor. The bottle has made you careless."

Taylor's eyes narrowed to tiny slits. "What did you say?"

"You heard me." Clutching her robe at the neck, Marian stepped forward, the color high in her face. "I won't have you flaunting your affairs in public. Even if you don't care about me, think of your son.''

"Goddammit, leave Zach out of this!"

"You fool, Zach is what this is all about! He's getting married and making a life for himself in Shawnee. I refuse to stand by and let you bring shame on him and Beth.''

"You're full of shit if you think I'm going to let you threaten me.''

"What do you think your friends, especially those at the church, will think when they find out you're unfaithful?'' Her lips curled into a sneer. "And your cronies at the bank? What will they think when they find out what a drunkard you've become?''

Taylor's face and neck flushed red. "Just how are they going to find out?''

"I'm going to tell them, that's how. I'll tell your son that you're screwing a woman his age.'' Marian's eyes burned savagely in the morning light, ironically making her more attractive than ever. "Do you think he'd have any respect for you then? Or ever let you touch your grandchild?''

His ears roared at the same time that his eyes glittered with demonic rage. "I'll see you in hell first!''

Marian laughed, but the sound held no mirth. "At one time I would have cringed had you said that to me, but no longer. What you think of me no longer matters. All I care about is Zach. And make no mistake, I'll do whatever I have to do to protect him.''

Her calm hazel eyes seemed to see right through him. It was as if she could tell that he was squirming inside because, for the first time since that day long ago when he'd struck her, she had crossed him. And was actually calling his bluff.

"Get rid of her, Taylor. Today.''

Without waiting for his reply, she turned and walked out of the room.

Should he take her seriously? Yes, dammit, he should. Suddenly Taylor felt sweat pop out on his forehead and his upper lip. His hands trembled. His gut was on fire. Damn her to hell. He reached for the whiskey bottle and fastened his lips around it.

The potent liquid didn't help. His mind raced as he wiped his mouth with the back of his hand. He knew he would have to watch himself. He wasn't prepared to give up Carolyn just yet, so he would have to make sure they weren't seen. But he wouldn't forget this incident.

His face closed into a rigid coldness. No one squeezed Taylor Winslow's balls and got away with it. That went for his partner, too. It was time they had a talk. In fact, it was long overdue.

Taylor eyed the phone mounted on the side of the cabinet. Slowly he ambled toward it, loud hiccups punctuating each step he took. It was only after he had dialed the Melbourne number that he remembered Foster had gone out of town for the day, something to do with those horses of his.

Swearing under his breath, he slammed down the receiver and headed toward the stairs, pausing in his unsteady progress long enough to take another swig out of the Kentucky bourbon bottle.

Five

"**W**hy do birds suddenly appear..." The throaty strains of the popular song eased through Beth's lips as she tossed the damp bath towel aside and grabbed the box of powder on the corner of the lavatory. Continuing to hum, she doused herself liberally with the haunting fragrance of Shalimar, only to suddenly cough when the fumes rose like wildfire and burned her nose.

"Way to go," she muttered, struggling for a clear breath. Disgusted, she finally dropped the puff and replaced the lid. If she wasn't careful, there wouldn't be any left for her wedding day.

Not that she couldn't get more where that came from, but it wouldn't be the same. The powder had been a surprise gift from Zach, and though he was generous to a fault in many ways, unsuspected gifts were not his forte.

As always, thinking about Zach prompted her heart to race. While the wedding day was near, she'd seen very little of him during the past week, though they had talked on the phone each evening.

Because of their planned honeymoon jaunt to New Orleans, Zach was working extra hours at the mill, trying, he'd stressed, to make his presence felt. She couldn't complain, because she, too, had been busy with parties and last-minute preparations for the big day. By evening she was exhausted.

Still, she missed Zach, missed feeling his arms around her, missed their long, intimate conversations about their future, and missed his hot, eager lips against hers. Soon, though, that would be rectified, because he was due in an hour. They were going out to eat and to a movie.

Realizing she needed to hurry if she was going to be ready on time, Beth snatched the long cotton robe off the knob on the back of the door and slipped it on, belting it securely around her waist.

While the song broke once again from her lips, she padded barefoot into her bedroom. For a moment she paused and looked around.

Not only would she miss the house itself, she would miss this room. It was lovely, a typical teenager's room, she thought with thankfulness toward her grandmother for helping her decorate it.

Peach-colored drapes with sheers covered the two ceiling-to-floor windows. However, nothing covered the French doors that opened onto the veranda skirting the entire back of the house.

Momentarily distracted, Beth breathed deeply, as if to inhale the rich scent that would float inside if she were to open the doors onto the sultry night. Planter boxes, lining the balcony, were ablaze year-round with a variety of luscious flowers. Suddenly she smiled whimsically as she heard the chirp of a cricket trying his best to outdo the sound of a katydid.

With an abrupt shake of her head, she refocused her attention. But instead of making her way to the chest where she kept her underwear, Beth let her eyes make another sweep around the room.

A magnificent white wicker canopied bed, covered with a thick polished cotton comforter and duster—both the color of peaches—dominated one wall. Adding to its effect were dozens of pillows splattered across the comforter in different sizes and shapes.

The plush carpet, the étagère with her collection of china cups and saucers, the paintings on the walls, the bulletin board littered with dried corsages and other school memorabilia, and vases of fresh flowers added to the room's charm.

It was almost as if she was cataloging every object, committing it to memory, as if she would never see this room again, which was, of course, ridiculous. When she and Zach spent the night here at Cottonwood, they would sleep in this room.

For as long as she could remember, this had been her sanctuary, her refuge in time of trouble, a place where her heart, no matter how battered or burdened, never failed to find a measure of peace.

Yes, it was her retreat and hers alone, very feminine, very romantic, especially with her mother's wedding dress hanging in all its splendor on the closet door. The years had been kind to it. In fact, the dress had been so well preserved that it could have passed for new. Made of ivory lace combined with silk taffeta, it looked too delicate to touch.

The headpiece, which enhanced the gown's perfection, hung on the same rack. Lace flowers on tiers of ivory created an illusion that would fall softly over her shoulders.

Beth never tired of looking at the ensemble. The fact that it had belonged to her mother made it even more special.

Her heart skipped a beat. Her mother. Kathleen Perry Melbourne. A beautiful woman. A perfect mother. Beth had been devastated when she had died. And resentful.

Suddenly she shook her head violently, trying to ward off the onrush of old regrets that tugged at her from the depths of her soul.

She had only been six years old when Kathleen died, and at that impressionable age she had been certain it was somehow her fault. While her daddy and grandmother had explained to her that it was no one's fault that her mother had gone to heaven to be with the angels, Beth hadn't been able to comprehend such a thing. She kept thinking she'd done something wrong.

During the days leading up to the funeral, she'd cried over and over that her mamma wasn't dead, that she would never leave her.

After seeking advice from the family doctor, Foster, accompanied by her grandmother, had finally taken her to the funeral home, hoping to convince her that her mother was indeed dead.

Her grandmother had grasped Beth's hand tightly in hers and walked with her to the casket. Beth had stared at her mother long and hard, thinking she looked so pretty and alive. Following a gasp, she peered up at her grandmother, her eyes bright with joy.

"Gran, Mamma's not dead, she's just sleeping...."

"Beth...honey...don't."

Ignoring Grace Childress's broken plea, Beth had whipped around and cried, "Daddy, Daddy, come quick! Mamma's only asleep."

"No, baby, no," Foster had sobbed.

Beth had met him halfway and yanked on his hand. "Don't cry, Daddy," she'd said in her grown-up voice. "Let's wake her so she can come home with us."

She would never forget the pain that had racked her tiny body when they wouldn't let her wake her mother. She'd sobbed as if her heart were broken, which indeed it had been.

Though she'd never blamed Trent for her mother's death, as Foster unwittingly did, she did resent being left alone without a mother. It had set her apart, made her different. Her friends hadn't known what to say or do when they found out that her mother couldn't car pool or make brownies for the local PTA.

Beth had survived those years only because she'd had a doting father and grandmother. But the scars were there, and they were deep and sensitive.

Maybe Trent had been on target when he'd accused her of being possessive of their daddy. Maybe she did selfishly bask in knowing that she was the fair-haired daughter, the chosen one.

If so, she couldn't apologize, realizing it stemmed from the very human desire to cling to something or someone you loved at all cost. Trent had never had a mother, so she reasoned that what he hadn't known he couldn't miss. That was absurd, of course, and while Beth hated herself for thinking such thoughts, she couldn't erase them. The feeling of wanting to possess and be possessed was as much a part of her makeup as breathing.

Thank God Zach didn't resent her possessiveness; instead, he seemed to thrive on it, telling her that he felt the same way about her.

A heartfelt sigh escaped her lips, but it was the wetness on her cheeks that jolted her back to the moment at hand. Following a mental kick in the seat for dallying, she hurried to the dressing table and sat down.

With accustomed ease, Beth reached for the moisturizer bottle and felt the lid give way beneath the tug of her fingers. After squeezing a dab on the ends of two fingers, she began massaging the cream into her face. Instead of concentrating on what she was doing, her eyes strayed once again toward the closet and the dress.

What was wrong with her? Why was she feeling so depressed all of a sudden? Those days of heartache and loneliness were for the most part only memories she had pushed to the dark place in her mind. Rarely did she allow them to escape. Was her swing in moods because she was getting married? That had to be it. It was unfair that her mamma wasn't here to share this time with her, to help her prepare.

Her grandmother and Rachel had more than done their part, but it wasn't the same. Zach's mother had been willing, as well. Beth had rebuffed her efforts, though not without just cause. Still, the rejection of Marian Winslow's help had annoyed Zach, and he had questioned her about it.

"You hurt Mother's feelings about the wedding, you know," he'd said one evening shortly after they had become engaged and were in the midst of making wedding plans.

Only minutes before, they had left the movie theater. Once they were mobile, Zach had headed straight for their favorite parking place, a used car lot on the edge of town. No cop in his right mind would think to look for them there, Zach had told her many times, his grin well in place.

Beth longed to snuggle against his hard chest, eager for the hot kisses she knew would be forthcoming. But she hadn't, having detected a certain hard note in his voice.

She stared at him, her brown eyes wide and troubled. "It's . . . it's because she hurt mine first."

Zach's lips tightened.

"You don't believe me, do you?" Beth's words were barely audible.

"Of course I believe you, but . . ."

"She tried to take over, Zach. Honestly, she did. You can ask Gran."

"I don't need to ask your grandmother. Anyway, that's not the point. She wants to be a part of things, and up until now you haven't let her."

"Did she tell you that?"

"No."

"Then how do you—"

"Because every time the wedding's mentioned, she gets a hurt look on her face. . . ." Zach paused, as if he couldn't find the right words.

Beth backed slightly away and sighed, knowing all too well that put-upon look that never failed to exploit Zach's tender side. "At first I welcomed her input, only she couldn't be content with that. She wanted to take over, to do everything her way."

"I know she likes to have her way...."

Beth's laugh rang hollow. "You can say that again."

"Cut her a little slack, will ya? Just for me?" Zach grinned, and his tongue circled his pearl white teeth.

That little gesture caused her heart to pound and he damn well knew it, Beth thought. He knew how to get to her, how to dig beneath her stubbornness and get what he wanted.

"After all," he went on, his grin deepening, "her only son is getting married. She's bound to be uptight."

Uptight was a mild word for what his mother was, but Beth saw no reason to add insult to injury. Her inability to share a rapport with Marian was as much her fault as the older woman's. They were both stubborn to the point of bullheadedness, and they were both possessive of Zach.

Yet Marian was okay. She would be more than okay, however, if and when she stopped thinking and feeling as if she was better than three fourths of the population of Shawnee.

"So," Zach prodded, tweaking her nose, "what's the verdict? Are you going to stop acting like the spoiled brat you are and be kind to my mamma?"

"All right, you win," she said, shaking her head, causing her hair to shimmer in the moonlight. "I'll do better. I promise."

"Come here."

Zach's sudden husky tone sent chills through her. "You come and get me," she whispered, angling her head to one side.

"You'll pay if I do."

She giggled. "I sure hope so."

The memory of what had followed caused the blood to rush into Beth's cheeks. She realized suddenly that she wouldn't need to wear any blush; both cheeks were burning.

Following a few choice words at her continued dalliance, she finished doing her face in record time.

It was only after she'd opened her closet door that she heard the doorbell. Zach? Already? An hour early? Thinking that he was as eager to see her as she was to see him, she giggled to herself. Knowing that Jessie would greet him, she made no effort to race downstairs.

With a grin still on her face, she reached for the paisley backless sundress and jerked it off the hanger. However, when the insistent peal showed no signs of letting up Beth slung the dress across the bed and frowned.

Where on earth was Jess? she asked herself, her frown deepening, then remembered. Jess had the evening off; she was seeing her sister, who was visiting from up north. Simultaneously, it dawned on Beth that she had the house to herself, because her daddy was still out of town, and her brother was at a friend's house studying.

Wondering why Zach didn't just come on in, she dashed out the door and bounced down the stairs, her hands caressing the graceful wood as they slid down the banister. By the time she reached the door, her robe was gaping and she was out of breath.

Without a second thought, Beth grabbed the brass handle and pulled, grinning broadly. "Oh, Zach, I'm so glad you're early," she said, only to suddenly feel her hand freeze around the handle and her smile collapse.

Taylor Winslow's red-streaked eyes moved slowly over her. "Hello, honey," he slurred. "Sorry to disappoint you."

He wasn't sorry at all, Beth thought, stepping back and clutching her robe around her. "What . . . do you want?" She heard the quaver in her voice and hated herself for it.

Taylor swayed toward her. "Now is that any way to talk to your future father-in-law?"

Beth reeled away from his foul breath. For a moment she was tempted to slam the door in his face. Choosing instead to step farther back, she stammered, "My—my daddy's not here."

A light flared in Taylor's eyes. "Ah, that's too bad."

"I'll . . . be glad to give him a message."

"Mmm, I was sure hopin' to talk to him myself."

Beth licked her suddenly dry lips, and her eyes moved from his. "Well, I'll . . . uh . . . tell him you came by. Now, if you'll excuse me . . ." she added, beginning to push the door shut.

Taylor braced a hand against it. "Not so fast, honey," he said in a throaty whisper.

Beth's eyes widened, an unknown fear stealing her breath.

"I think I'll come in and wait." He winked. "And you and I can have a little chat."

Six

The color fled from Beth's face as he all but forced his way across the threshold. She had no choice except to stand aside. But her mind was in an uproar. The last thing she wanted was to have a "little chat" with Taylor Winslow. To her knowledge, they didn't have anything to chat about. Even if they did, she would prefer it to take place when someone else was around and he hadn't been drinking.

Feeling his beady eyes on her, Beth edged the lapels of her robe up around her throat. Something close to fear darted through her as she tried to interpret his look.

"I—I wish I had time to visit with you, Mr. Winslow—"

"Don't you think it's about time you called me Taylor?" he asked slyly, continuing to scrutinize her closely, as though he could see through her clothes.

Beth drew back, his hot, soured breath making her nauseated. That combined with his strong cologne made her head pound with jackhammer force.

"Look, Mr. Winslow—" she emphasized the *mister* "—Zach's supposed to be here any moment to pick me up. You're welcome to wait for Daddy in the living room, but you really must excuse me."

Taylor smiled a knowing smile. "No hurry. Zach'll be late."

Beth swallowed hard. "Well . . . I need to get ready, anyway."

"I told you, there's no need to rush. Zach just got in from the mill."

Repelled by his leering smile and soft coaxing tone, Beth backed up, trying to think what to do next, trying to be calm. She couldn't. She was both repulsed and jittery.

As if sensing her fear, Taylor softened his tone even more. "You can't run away from me forever, you know, honey." His eyes glinted. "Don't forget, you'll soon be living under my roof."

Heightened fear washed through Beth in waves. She couldn't speak. Her mouth felt dry as cotton. What was that remark supposed to mean? Why was he behaving like this? Granted, she had never felt comfortable around him, but this weird behavior, these insinuations...

Forcing herself to take deep, calming breaths, she tried again to think, to make sense out of what was happening. He hadn't done anything except talk, and it wasn't in her nature to be rude. Besides, her daddy would never forgive her if she was rude to his partner without just cause. Too, she didn't want to start off her marriage by completely alienating her future father-in-law. Therefore, she had no choice but to give him the benefit of the doubt.

Still, she couldn't quite forget that she was alone in the house, and that she was naked underneath her robe. Nor could she forget that her unwanted visitor had been drinking, though to what extent she didn't know.

Maybe she should take a different approach, act more sure of herself. "If you'd like to sit down," she suggested with cool politeness, "I'll get you a cup of coffee."

"Thanks, but no, thanks." Taylor patted his breast pocket and grinned. "I got the only upper I need right here."

Beth heard the clink of his signet ring against the liquor flask, and again her confidence faltered. Not knowing what else to do, she unwillingly forced her unsteady legs to move toward the formal living room. The instant she stepped inside she switched on the lamp that was just beyond the door. The soft light gave the lovely room a sudden comforting glow and offered her a greater sense of security.

Aware that Taylor was close behind her, she crossed to the massive glazed-stone fireplace, determined to put as much distance between them as possible. She propped herself against one corner of the brick hearth, feeling somewhat more in command of the situation.

But instead of sitting down as she'd thought he would, Taylor swaggered toward her. "Yeah, my boy's a lucky man," he said. "But then, you're one helluva lovely girl." He paused and lowered his whiskey-inflected voice, while his eyes slid over her. "Or should I say woman?"

Beth suddenly felt chilled all over, yet drops of perspiration popped out on her skin and gathered between her breasts. Her heart hammered against her ribs. She was suffocating in her own fear. Just like that.

He was getting much too personal. What did he want from her? Surely not what she was thinking. Such a thing was not only ludicrous, it was also unbelievable. This man was Zach's father, for heaven's sake. Her daddy's business partner!

She needed to get hold of herself.

"Thank . . . thank you," Beth stammered at last, careful not to antagonize him or show her fear. But she couldn't control the nervous tremor that gave her own voice a raspy edge.

"Yeah, my boy's a lucky man," Taylor repeated, having moved within touching distance of her, where once again his rank breath assaulted her senses.

"I'm—I'm glad you think so, Mr. Winslow."

"Call me Taylor, I said."

Beth's eyes were stark, dilated. "I . . . can't."

"Sure you can, honey," he whispered urgently. "I want to hear you say my name."

"Please . . . Mr. Winslow," she wailed, "why are you doing this?"

"Doing what, honey?" he whispered again.

In terror, her mind searched for a way to sidestep him. "My . . . my daddy will be here any minute now."

"All we *need* is a minute." Taylor reached out then and ran a finger along the curve of her neck.

Beth cringed. "Don't! Don't do that."

His finger didn't waver. "Don't do what, honey? Touch you like this? Jesus, your skin's like satin."

"Stop it!" Beth cried, giving her head a violent shake. "Get away from me!"

His features turned ugly. "You think you're better than me, don't you?"

Beth shook her head again. This time her hair tumbled over her face, hiding it. "Please . . ."

"Yeah, you think you're too good." He kept on touching her.

"No! I . . ." Beth couldn't get the words past her frozen lips.

"Zach won't ever know about this, you hear?"

Zach! Oh, Zach . . . please . . . please come on! Help me!

"You hear?" Taylor pressed, his eyes taking on a wild glint.

"I'll tell . . . tell Daddy," Beth sobbed, mashing herself against the fireplace, feeling the stone dig into her back.

Taylor trailed that same finger down until he parted the robe at the neck and found the creamy curve of her breast. "Go ahead, tell your daddy."

Her whole body was shaking, besieged by tremors.

"Trust me," Taylor said. "He won't say a word. He owes me."

Beth's eyes sparked. "That's crazy! My daddy doesn't owe you anything, except maybe a spit in the eye."

Taylor grabbed her and jerked her hard against his chest. "I have the power to ruin your daddy, girlie, and the Melbourne name to boot."

"Let go of me!" Beth shrieked, her fingernails sinking into his forearms.

"Not until I'm ready. So you'd best settle down."

"You're crazy! My daddy—"

Taylor sneered. "Your daddy won't do shit. He doesn't have a pot to piss in or a window to throw it out of."

"What?"

"You don't know, do you? That's why I came to talk to your old man. He's got his balls in the cutter, and without me they'll damn well stay there."

"I don't believe you!" Beth shoved at his shoulders, trying to free herself. "You're just making this up!"

Taylor laughed harshly. "Then why is your lower lip trembling? And why are your eyes wild like a young filly's?"

Were his accusations true? Oh, God, was her daddy in debt to this scumbag? No. That was impossible. Foster was a good businessman. Their finances were sound. Or were they? She had no way of knowing either way. Still, no matter how convincing Taylor sounded, she didn't believe him. After all, he'd been drinking. It had to be the booze talking.

"Let go of me!" Beth cried again. "And get the hell out of my house. I don't intend to listen to any more of your lies!"

"Oh, you'll listen, all right!" he cracked. "You'll listen to any and everything I have to say."

Beth wanted more than anything to spit in his face, but fear of what he might do killed that notion. Instead she snapped, "You pervert! Zach'll kill you!"

"Why, you little bitch," he countered, jerking open her robe and exposing her breasts. "You can't threaten me with my own son. I think it's time someone taught you some respect."

"No!" Beth tried to wrestle out of his grasp yet again, but she could not, stunned at how strong he was. Then, before she could rebound, he lifted her bodily by the arms and thrust her against the flat wall next to the fireplace with such force that she lost her breath.

"You'll pay for this!" Though she heard her heartbeat pounding in her ears and the taste of fear was like vinegar in her mouth, she struggled to free herself.

"Oh, no, you don't, you little wildcat," he taunted, shoving her hard against the wall again.

This time when Beth looked into his eyes, ice-cold terror rendered her motionless. He looked like a madman.

"Please . . . stop." Her voice trembled, and tears blinded her, as she sensed his hatred and resentment of her.

Taylor leered at her. "No way, honey. I've been itching to touch you for a long time, to show you how it feels to have a real man."

Beth opened her mouth to scream, but a sweaty hand prevented that. "It'll do you no good to scream," he said, his hot breath searing her skin.

A muffled wail escaped her. She was going to be sick. Gasping, she gulped down the bitter bile filling her throat. Her mind raced. What to do? She had to do something. Anything. Unwittingly she sagged against him.

"So you're finally coming to your senses, huh?" Taylor whispered, nuzzling his day-old beard against her neck, but not before he loosened his grip and uncovered her mouth.

Suddenly Beth pushed against him with all the energy she could muster.

"Oh, no, you don't." He laughed, grabbing a handful of her hair and jerking her back against him. "Why, you *are* a regular little filly. Yessirree, I like 'em frisky."

"You pig!" she screamed, just as he twisted her around and ground his lips into hers.

She strained against him, but to no avail. With his lips still locked on hers, he manhandled her backward until she felt the edge of the sofa graze the backs of her legs. Then, pulling his mouth away, he trapped her wrists in one hand and with the other reached for his zipper.

Horrified at the sight of his erection, Beth felt another surge of bile fill her throat. This couldn't be happening. Not to her. But it was. Oh, God, it was.

She wouldn't give up without a fight. Her face deathly white, she kicked at his shins. "Let me go, you bastard! You'll never get away with this."

Beth's cries were in vain. In spite of Taylor's inebriated state, she could not dent his brute strength. He shoved her down onto the sofa and climbed on top of her.

Sobbing, she beat at his back with her fists, her chest rising and falling in spasms. "Get off me, you bastard!"

Clapping one hand over her mouth, he groped and fumbled with the other until her robe was even more thoroughly parted.

"So pretty," he rasped, his greedy eyes ravishing her flesh. Then his hands were all over her breasts, stomach, thighs, while he was grinding himself against her, smashing, driving his tongue between her teeth.

Beth clawed his back again repeatedly, even slapped his ears, but he didn't move off her. He simply clutched another hank of her long hair and yanked it until tears of pain seeped from her eyes.

"I'll make you feel real good," he whispered. "Don't fight me."

"No!" Her heart convulsed. Her chest tightened. Scream! Scream! She opened her mouth to scream, but only broken whimpers came as she realized in sudden horror what was about to happen.

Lifting his buttocks, Taylor wedged a hand between their bodies and parted her robe the rest of the way. She went rigid. Why couldn't she scream? She ached to, but her mind refused to obey her. Her body wouldn't obey, either. It felt like a slab of steel.

Then, suddenly, when he opened her legs and she felt his probing flesh, she screamed and bit him hard on the neck.

He grunted, then continued.

No! Zach! Daddy! Anybody! Oh, God! Please, not me! Don't let this happen to me! She felt herself slipping into unconsciousness, as if she was falling into a deep, dark, black abyss. Time passed in slow motion, like a dream. Somewhere she heard breathing. And soft cries. They sounded far away.

Then the pressure lifted. She whimpered and lay without moving.

Taylor stood and peered down at her while he straightened his clothes. "You forget all about this, you hear? You tell Zach and he won't believe you. You got what you asked for. We both know that, don't we?"

With that, Taylor turned, walked out of the room and then out the front door.

Beth's nausea rose instantly, and her skin crawled. She had to get to her room. Somehow she had to get up the stairs. Zach couldn't find her like this. She gasped for air, feeling as if her lungs were going to burst. Oh, Zach, she cried silently. Oh, Zach, Zach, Zach.

It seemed like hours before she could move. Jagged sobs tore from her throat as the horror of what had happened hit her, something so hideous, so vile, that she knew she would never be the same again. She had been shamefully violated and betrayed.

Holding her hysterics at bay, ignoring the fact that her whole body ached and her head pounded, Beth forced herself to stand. She inched slowly out the door toward the stairs.

Only after she made it to the first step did she hear the sound. A door had opened. Or had it shut?

"Zach?" she cried. No answer. "Daddy?" Again no answer. Nothing but silence and her thundering heart.

She turned and crawled on her hands and knees up the stairs.

Beth didn't know how long she'd been lying in the fetal position in the middle of her bed, a pillow clutched in her arms.

The first thing she had done when she reached her room was run to the bathroom, where she'd hung her head over the commode. Nothing came up. She was empty of everything, as if the blood had been drained from her body.

Moments later she had climbed into the shower and scrubbed herself until she was certain she'd scrubbed the top layer of skin off. Then, as if she were outside herself looking in, she methodically slipped into a pair of jeans, a cotton shirt and tennis shoes.

Now, as she remained folded over like a question mark, dry-eyed and numb, she tried to piece together her feelings. That was impossible. Nothing seemed real. It was as if she was hallucinating.

She began to tremble. Her teeth banged together, and the saliva dried in her mouth. She felt a violent tingling start at the top of her head, then spread the entire length of her body.

She had been raped! The emptiness inside her screamed. How was she ever going to face another human again?

Especially when a vital part of her had just died.

Seven

Foster Melbourne sank heavily into the padded chair and made a pretense of mopping the sweat off his forehead and mustache. He merely wasted good energy, because as soon as he lowered his handkerchief the fine mist popped right back out.

He should be at Cottonwood, he knew. Instead he had felt the need to stop by the mill, to pull himself together before he faced his family. It hadn't been a good day. The anticipated sale of some horses had not gone according to plan. The bottom line was that he hadn't gotten nearly the money he should have. But when a man was down, like he was, others took advantage.

But he wasn't just down. He was in trouble up to his eyeballs. But he'd been in trouble before and gotten out of it; maybe he could again. Though this ruckus couldn't have come at a worse time, he thought, lunging out of the chair and pacing the floor.

He wished Beth was already married. Once that happened, he would feel better. Meanwhile, he had to think of a way to soothe Richard Walsh, his wishy-washy banker friend, who was turning out not to be a friend after all.

Too bad he couldn't turn to Taylor and the mill as he had so many times before. But that route was out of the question. The well had run dry. The unvarnished truth was that he and Taylor barely tolerated each other now. Hopefully, though, if and when he got out of this latest mess, he could make amends with his partner, for Beth's sake if nothing else.

Unexpectedly the phone rang. Foster stopped and eyed it long and hard, telling himself not to answer it. But he was afraid not to; it could be Beth or Trent.

He stalked to his desk and yanked the receiver off the hook.

"Melbourne."

As he listened to the voice on the other end of the line, the color drained from his face until it was pasty white.

"I'll see you in hell first," he shouted a few seconds later, than slammed the receiver down.

He had no choice now but to do what he should have done long ago. He had to tell Beth. And Zach. Because of Beth, Zach would help him.

With his shoulders back, Foster walked to the door, flipped off the light and walked out, leaving the darkness behind him.

Near the stairs Beth heard voices. She recognized her daddy's and Trent's. Was that Zach? Was he there, too? She couldn't separate the voices, couldn't make out what they were saying. It didn't matter, though. Nothing mattered. Inside her, everything was numb.

But hovering under that numbness was a black pain lying in wait to overcome her as soon as her body adjusted to the shock.

Unwilling to move from the middle of the bed, Beth ground her jaws together so hard that her ears roared, louder and louder. She felt ashamed, used, violated. As she placed her hands over her ears, fresh tears burned her face and eyes.

Oh, please, she didn't want to see anyone. Please don't let anyone find me, she prayed, most of all Zach.

Zach! Blindly she rocked against the pillow, a new fear burgeoning. No longer was it the terror of her own private hell that reared up at her. Zach was a new terror.

Should she tell him his daddy had raped her? Beth whimpered like a child and tried to think, but it was so hard. Her thoughts were so jumbled, her feelings so savage, she didn't know how she felt, what she thought.

She had to deal with Zach. If she told him, would he believe her? And if he did, would he still want her? Or would he think she was sordid? Dirty? Eyes wild, hair matted and tangled, face streaked with tears, Beth bolted upright, a new wave of terror running through her.

What if he blamed her? What if he thought she was somehow to blame? No! He wouldn't, *couldn't,* think that of her. He loved her. She covered her mouth to keep from crying out loud. Even if he didn't think any of those things, he must never know. As abhorrent as it was, Taylor was right. Knowledge of what Taylor had done would destroy Zach. It would destroy her to have to tell him.

Not only could she not tell Zach, she couldn't tell anyone. She simply couldn't bear it. If only she had fought harder... if only... if only...

Beth hugged herself and rocked some more. What was she going to do? Maybe if she pretended it hadn't happened, the pain would simply go away. She sank her teeth into the back of her hand. Or maybe the Lord would take mercy on her and make her die now.

"Beth, I'd like to talk to you. Open the door, sugar?"

Her daddy! She didn't want to see him. *Couldn't* see him. Not now.

"I'm... I'm getting dressed," she managed to say through stiff, parched lips.

"Are you all right?" A pause. "You sound funny."

"I'm... I'm fine, Daddy." Go away, she wanted to scream. Leave me alone!

"Your brother said he saw you at the top of the stairs bent over double like you were sick."

"I'm . . . I'm fine," she said again, feeling as if her skin was crawling under her clothes. Her legs were clamped together so tightly they quivered.

Foster rapped his knuckles against the wood. "You damn sure don't sound fine. Are you decent?"

"No!"

"Get decent," Foster ordered. "I told you, I want to talk to you."

"Please . . . Daddy . . . not now," Beth sobbed.

"Are you sure you're all right, sugar?"

No, of course I'm not all right! I'll never be all right again. I've changed. My life has changed. It's over.

"Go . . . away . . . Daddy." Her entire body throbbed now. She mustn't give in to it.

"What do you mean, go away? I'll give you two minutes, young lady, to put something on, then I'm coming in."

Beth's teeth began knocking together so hard she couldn't speak to tell him to leave her alone. Closing her eyes, she willed her daddy to go away.

He didn't. In less than two minutes he made good on his promise, pushed open the door and walked in.

Beth felt his shock rather than saw it.

"Good Lord, child, you look awful!"

Beth's eyes opened, and she looked at him as though she had never seen him before, then she silently began to sob.

Muttering a curse, Foster hurried to the bed, sweat glistening on his forehead. The instant his robust frame sank onto the mattress, he reached for her. For a second Beth went rigid in his arms.

He looked stunned, then whispered roughly, "What's the matter? What happened?"

"Oh, Daddy . . . Daddy!" she cried and didn't fight him when he pulled her into his chest.

"It's all right, sweetheart. Whatever it is, it's all right...."

The air conditioner flipped on suddenly, sending cool air swirling through the room. Neither noticed the sound or the change in the climate. Beth clung to her daddy as if she would never let him go, while Foster continued to hold her tightly, a troubled frown on his face.

"Shh, stop crying. Daddy's here." He began patting her awkwardly on the head. "You can tell me all about it and everything will be all right."

Think! Beth told herself, taking great gulps of air. You have to think. Only she *couldn't think!* "No, it's not...it's not...he..." She couldn't go on. Taylor's evil face jumped before her eyes in full-blown color, and at the same time his threat pierced her soul. Choking on her sobs, she buried her face back against Foster's chest.

"Now, now, child, you've got to stop crying. Did you and Zach have a fight? Is that what this is all about?"

Beth raised glazed eyes. "Please...there's nothing you...you can do. I want to be by myself." Huge tears trickled down her face.

Foster looked at her, at a loss as to how to deal with the situation. His eyes darkened, and his mustache twitched above his mouth.

"I'm not leaving until you talk to me, even if it takes all night. So, if you and Zach didn't have a fight..."

Again Beth shook her head violently.

"If it's not Zach, then what the hell's got you so upset?" He paused and gave a deep sigh. "Are...you pregnant?" Fear punctuated each word.

Pregnant! Oh, God! She hadn't even thought of that. Could Taylor have... No! She felt as if she were going to throw up again. Frantically she tore out of Foster's arms and took several more deep, gulping breaths.

"Sugar...what?" Foster's voice shook.

Beth ignored him, her mind scrambling to come to terms with reality. As quickly as the panic had swamped her, it receded. Of course she wasn't pregnant. She couldn't be. She was on the pill. Her mind was simply so shattered that for a moment she hadn't been able to think straight.

"If you won't talk to me, will you talk to your grandmother? Or Rachel?" Foster sounded desperate now.

"Oh, Daddy," Beth sobbed, clutching at his shirt.

He caught her wrists, and when he did, she flinched.

"What...?" he began, looking down at her hands. "Your arms and wrists—why, they're red and swollen."

Beth tried to draw them away.

"Oh, no, you don't." Foster kept them trapped between his hamlike hands.

"Please, Daddy, don't ask—" Her voice broke.

"What the hell do you mean, don't ask? I go out of town for one day and come home to find my daughter holed up in her room, hysterical. Not to mention all bruised up."

Foster stood abruptly, but he never took his eyes off Beth's ravaged face. "Who did this to you?"

Sucking her bottom lip between her teeth to keep it from trembling, Beth averted her eyes, stalling for time. She had to get him to go away before she found herself telling the truth. She had never been able to lie to him about anything.

"Who did this to you?" Foster asked again. Although his voice was still gentle, his eyes weren't. They were ice-cold. When she continued to hesitate, his tone changed. "Dammit, talk to me, girl."

"I...can't!" she wailed, knowing that by refusing to talk to him she was making matters worse. When her daddy wanted something, he was like a tenacious bulldog. He didn't know when to let go.

"Then I have no choice."

She straightened, her head reeling. "What...do you mean?"

"I mean, I'm going to talk to Zach."

"No!" she cried. "Don't! You can't..." Beth's voice faded into a sob.

A muscle worked in Foster's jaw. "Then tell me, or Zach it is."

Think! Beth told herself again. Zach couldn't see her like this. First, though, she had to pacify her daddy. Lie! Tell him you fell off your horse. That's it. He'd believe that. After all, Pretty Boy had thrown her before.

"Pretty Boy...threw me."

"I'm not buying that."

Tears rolled relentlessly down Beth's cheeks. "Daddy...I..."

"The truth, Beth." This time his tone brooked no argument. "The truth. Only the truth will do."

Suddenly she realized she was aching to do just that, to pour out the nightmarish events of a little while ago, to expel them from her soul. If she didn't, she feared her insides might explode. Dare she risk it? Dare she tell him the truth? She opened her mouth, but words failed her. She couldn't do it.

"Beth!"

Her mind groped. In order to make him go away, she had to tell him something, something that he would believe. She had to be careful, so very careful.

With her head lowered, she whispered, "Mr. Winslow..." The second she spoke his name, her face crumpled. "He..."

"Taylor!" Foster Melbourne looked horrified. "He did this to you?"

She felt the hysteria rise to the surface once again as Foster loomed over her, breathing hard. "Jesus. But why? I mean...Jesus," he said again.

"No, Daddy, you're wrong...."

Foster's eyes glinted with suppressed violence. "Was he here? In this house?"

"He . . . he was drinking, and when . . . when he started saying awful things about you and I told him to leave, he . . . grabbed my wrists. . . ."

"Why that sorry— When I get through with him, he'll rue the day he was ever born. Did he . . ." Foster paused and swallowed hard, as if he was searching for the words to say what he had to say. "Did he touch you? I mean . . ." Again he trailed off, his voice cracking, while sweat oozed from his forehead.

"No," Beth choked out.

"I'll kill him! That's what I'll do!" Foster ranted, the veins in his neck standing out like taut strings on a violin. "Yes, sir, that son of a bitch's ass is mine." Foster took several backward steps. "When I get back, I'm taking you to the doctor, you hear? You be ready."

"Daddy!" Beth held out unsteady hands. "Where are you going?"

He paid her no heed, just kept edging slowly backward, his face still wearing that horrified, twisted look.

"Daddy, no!" she cried again, forcing her heavy legs to move and scrambling to the edge of the bed. "Don't go. He didn't hurt me. . . . I swear . . . he didn't hurt me. . . ."

"It's all right, sugar," he said in a voice Beth hardly recognized. "Daddy will take care of everything. You just sit tight."

The words had no more left his mouth when it happened. Without warning he went rigid, raising a hand toward his heart.

"Daddy?" The word came out a mere whisper.

Foster opened his mouth to speak, but only gasps came out. He stared at her, then fell facedown on the floor.

Beth screamed and lunged off the bed.

By the time she reached his side, Foster was parchment white and still as death itself. Visions of her mother danced before her eyes, and she screamed again, a bloodcurdling scream like that of a trapped and wounded animal.

"Daddy, Daddy, talk to me," she begged, nestling his head in the crook of her arm. When she got no answer she screamed again.

Trent burst through the door and cried, "Beth, what's wrong?"

"Trent, call for help!"

Trent couldn't seem to move. His face was ashen, and he stood as if frozen.

"Don't just stand there!" Beth shouted.

Still Trent didn't move.

"Trent!"

He bolted then, like a frightened rabbit, and ran toward the phone.

"Hurry. Oh, hurry," Beth whispered, rocking her daddy in her arms.

Eight

As the ambulance sped through the streets, making its way toward the small hospital on the other side of town, the siren screamed.

Beth was hardly cognizant of the offensive sound; she was hardly cognizant of anything at all. The blessed numbness had returned. If she wasn't in shock, she was very close to it. To keep her teeth from chattering together she bit down hard on her lower lip. Letting go of her daddy's hand, she pulled her sweater tighter around her.

The evening was hot and sultry, but she had deliberately grabbed a sweater while the medics were loading Foster into the ambulance. The marks on her wrists had to be covered. Besides, she'd been cold. From the moment her daddy had collapsed on the floor and she had scrambled into the rear of the ambulance along with Trent, she had not stopped shaking.

"He's—he's going to die, isn't he?" a pale-faced Trent asked, his voice sounding small and forlorn.

Beth felt her heart turn over. They were sitting on one side of Foster, a medic on the other. Beth turned toward Trent, searching for the words of reassurance that he longed to hear. None were forthcoming, because she was experiencing the same fear, the same uncertainty.

Finally she whispered, "All we can do is hope and pray."

Although Trent nodded and continued to sit reed straight, Beth saw his lower lip tremble. She had to fight the urge to put her arms around his shoulders, and pull his thin body next to her. But she sensed he wouldn't appreciate her calling attention to his weakness. He was trying so hard to be grown up.

"I—I called Gran," he said, his gaze focused on Foster's face, now partially covered by an oxygen mask.

"She'll meet us at the hospital." It was a statement, not a question.

Trent nodded in confirmation.

Another silence fell between them. Beth peered into Foster's face, fighting back the tears. When the paramedics had arrived on the scene she had been certain her daddy was dead. They had assured her, however, that he was still breathing.

Beth lifted her head as if she were drowning, unable to bear looking at Foster's inert figure. Even though she could see only a small portion of his face, due to the oxygen mask, it was gray against the white pillowcase. An IV was inserted in one arm, while the other was hooked to a mechanical attachment of some sort. What did it mean?

"We're doing everything we can, Ms. Melbourne," the baby-faced attendant said, as if reading her mind.

"I know...and we appreciate it," Beth responded softly, glancing in Trent's direction. She hoped her brother would be encouraged by the man's calm words of assurance, but he wasn't. He continued to sit stoically silent.

How much more could she take? Beth asked herself, the memories of the past hour crashing down on her once again. For a moment she couldn't breathe. The pain was so excruciating she feared her heart might burst.

On her way back downstairs after she'd retrieved her sweater, she had paused outside the door of the living room. She hadn't meant to, of course. She hadn't even been aware that she had stopped until she realized her legs were no longer moving and that her eyes were fixed on the couch.

She had shivered. The room seemed defiled. Never would she be able to enter it again without remembering it was there that her life as she knew it had been destroyed.

Beth closed her eyes and tried to fight off the memory of those pain-filled moments, but it wouldn't go away. She had intentionally not thought of Zach, although when she'd gone to her room she had called and told the Winslows' housekeeper to tell him that she was on her way to the hospital.

Reaching for her daddy's hand again, she cradled it against her damp cheek. I'm so sorry, Daddy, she cried silently. She blamed herself. If only she hadn't said anything. *If only I hadn't mentioned Taylor's name.* There were so many regrets that she couldn't begin to name them. The bottom line was that in trying to protect Zach, she had sacrificed her daddy.

A scream tried to claw its way from Beth's throat. She wished she could slither off and die. But she couldn't. Now was not the time to think about herself and the hideous trauma she had just lived through. That would come later. And Zach. Thoughts about him, about them, would also come later. Her beloved daddy needed her now. She wouldn't let him down. Thank God he was still alive. He had to pull through. He just had to. She couldn't imagine life without him.

She remembered all the things he had done for her: the time he'd taken out of his busy schedule to come to the school play in which she'd had the leading role, the times when he'd been her friend and confidant. Though he'd never been a demonstrative father, he'd been kind, making up in many ways for her lack of a mother.

She loved him so much, even though she didn't see him as often as she would have liked. Now she felt like a little girl again, recalling the sound of his footsteps clicking against the hardwood announcing his presence, the sound of his booming voice, so loud in the house, giving her confidence and making her laugh.

God wouldn't take him from her, not yet....

"We're here, Ms. Melbourne," the attendant said softly.

Blinking, Beth stood and watched as they lifted her daddy from the ambulance. Then, with Trent at her side, she followed behind the stretcher into the hospital.

"Are you on your way out?"

Zach removed his hand from the doorknob and walked toward the voice. Marian Winslow sat behind a small antique secretary in her office adjacent to the kitchen.

Zach had always been partial to this room. It reflected his mother's taste, not that of the highbrow decorator who had redone Wimberly. The walls were solid glass, offering a breathtaking view of the grounds, which were now scattered with luscious flowers.

Filled with nothing but antique furniture, the room had a coziness the rest of the house lacked. It belonged exclusively to his mother.

When she was at home, this was where she was most often found. It was here that he had come as a child when he'd hurt himself and wanted attention.

He smiled, thinking that his mother looked especially nice this evening. The purple dress she had on highlighted her still-creamy skin and set off her perfectly coiffured hair.

On closer observation, however, he noticed the circles under her eyes. Was she ill? Or simply worried about something? His daddy, most likely, he thought, tightening his lips.

Suddenly Zach felt the need to remove that tense look from her face. "You look pretty, Mamma."

Marian appeared flustered but pleased. "Why, thank you, Zachery. What a nice thing to say."

He grinned mischievously. "I aim to please."

"I know you do," she said seriously. "That's why I'm proud of you."

"Mamma, is something wrong?" He paused and waited for her answer. When none came, he went on, "Is it Daddy?"

Marian smiled and turned away, but not before he'd seen a flicker of pain cross her face. "Everything's... everything's fine."

Zach knew better. Everything was not fine. Things had never been fine. But he would never get either of them to admit it, he thought bitterly. He was tempted to ask if his daddy had added another woman to his list and flaunted that fact in her face. But it wouldn't do any good to confront her; she would just deny it.

If they chose to live this way, then so be it. He had stopped worrying about their relationship long ago, except when it affected him.

"What about you?" she asked, filling the deep silence.

Zach countered with a question. "What about me?"

"You and your father." She tapped a long nail on the desk. "I understand you told him you wanted to be a partner."

"That's right," Zach said flatly.

"And if he didn't make you one you were going to leave."

"Right again." Zach's tone was clipped.

Marian drew her brows together. "You didn't mean that, surely."

"I damn well did mean it."

"Zach, please, don't swear."

Zach rolled his eyes. "All right, Mamma."

"Where would you go? If you left, I mean." Her voice held fear. "What would you do?"

"I'd find something." Zach stuffed a hand into his jeans pocket and shifted his feet. "I can't just stand by and watch the mill disintegrate before my eyes."

"And that's what it's doing?"

"Yes."

"And you think walking out is the answer?"

"No, I don't, but if it'll get Daddy to wake up, then I'm willing to do it."

Marian sighed. "What about Beth?"

"What about her?"

"Would she leave Shawnee? Her family?"

He thought for a moment. "Yes, I think she would."

"Well, we both know it won't come to that," Marian said with confidence.

Zach shrugged. "Daddy can be awfully stubborn. But then, I don't need to tell you that, do I?" he added pointedly.

Again Marian couldn't quite meet his eye. "No, you don't need to tell me that."

"So he told you about our conversation?" Actually, Zach found that hard to believe. He knew it was his daddy's policy to keep his mother in the dark about his affairs, especially the mill. What had happened to change that?

"Zach, please give him time." Marian's eyes were pleading, as was her voice. "Now that you're back home and about to be married, I can't stand the thought of you leaving again." She paused and took a deep, quivering breath.

He wanted to tell her that everything was going to be all right and that he loved her, but the words lodged in his throat. Why couldn't he say them, particularly now, when they were so needed? He did love his mother—everybody loved their mother, didn't they? But it seemed so phony to say it now. He felt sorry for her, but he didn't respect her.

"I don't want to leave, either," Zach said at last.

"Then be patient. This is your home. The mill is your inheritance. Just be patient," she repeated. "I promise, in the end you'll get what you want."

Zach sighed and rubbed the back of his neck. "All right, Mamma, I'll cool my heels for a while and see what happens."

"Zach."

At the sound of the unexpected voice, Zach spun around, then grinned. "Hi, Carmen. What's up?"

For once Carmen Marsh, the Winslows' housekeeper, didn't respond to Zach's smile. Instead, her eyes were wide and nervous.

"Is something the matter, Carmen?" Marian asked, standing up and moving from behind the desk.

Carmen had eyes only for Zach. "That phone call. It was Beth...."

An alarm went off in Zach's head. "Has something happened?"

"Not to Beth, but her father...they're on the way to the hospital with him."

"Oh, no," Marian whispered, staring at Zach. "That poor girl."

Zach didn't say a word. He clenched his jaw, then spun on his heel and dashed out the door, slamming it behind him.

Nine

The instant he saw her in the waiting room, looking so empty, so lonely, so unapproachable, yet so beautiful, Zach halted. Her hair was pulled straight back into a ponytail, leaving her profile in full view, a profile that bespoke such extraordinary beauty that for an instant Zach was literally stunned. But then, Beth had always affected him that way.

Shaking himself mentally, he made his way toward her. As if sensing his approach, Beth swung around. Their eyes met and held, hers wide and haunted, his narrowed and troubled.

"Are you all right?" he asked.

She didn't respond.

Zach caught his breath at the pain ravaging her face to such a degree she appeared almost ethereal. For an idiotic moment he was afraid that if he touched her, she might disappear.

"Beth," he whispered before closing the distance between them and putting his arms around her.

"Don't!" She jerked away, her eyes wide. "Please ... don't."

Zach dropped his hands as if he'd been stung, but he didn't take offense. He knew, looking into her upturned face, that she was crazy with worry. Again he was struck by the hollow emptiness he saw reflected there. "How is he?"

Beth swallowed hard. "We—we don't know, actually. We're waiting for the doctor."

Looking to see who "we" were, Zach's gaze scanned the room. No one was there.

"Are Trent and Gran with you?"

Beth nodded. "They've gone to get something to drink." She paused, and Zach felt the tension return. "The doctor... told us it would be a while before he'd know anything definite."

"Why don't we sit down, before you fall on your face?" Zach's eyes darkened with concern. "You look like if your throat was cut, you wouldn't bleed a drop."

Beth didn't reply. Instead, she crossed her arms on her chest and turned her gaze out the window.

Sighing, Zach did likewise. From high on the fourteenth floor, where the intensive care unit was housed, the scattered lights of Shawnee twinkled like a heaven full of stars on a clear night. Protected from the noises of the street below, it was almost as if they were cocooned in a vacuum.

But they weren't. Far from it. The sounds around them, the sounds of a well-run hospital, made them very much aware of where they were.

"What happened, baby?" Zach asked after a moment, hoping that by encouraging her to confide in him he could erase the look of lethargic hopelessness that her eyes still held.

"He—he either had a heart attack or a stroke."

"When?"

"Just before I called Wimberly."

Zach frowned and leaned one shoulder against the window to get a better view of her. Why was he having to pull every scrap of information out of her? It wasn't like her to be so uncommunicative, even when things were at their worst.

Swallowing a sigh of frustration, he tried again. "Had he been feeling bad? Where was he when it happened?"

"No, he hadn't been sick, not that I know of, anyway."

Her tone was emotionless, as if she was talking to a complete stranger. Again Zach curbed his frustration, though he had to dig for patience. Finally he said, "Go on."

"Daddy...he came to my room and we—we were talk-ing—" Beth's voice caught on a half sob.

"Shh," Zach whispered, circling her shoulder with an arm and drawing her close against him. Though she stiff-ened again, she didn't pull away. Resting his chin on top of her head, he inhaled the fresh scent of her hair. Then, in his most soothing voice, he asked, "What were you talking about?"

She was silent for so long that he didn't think she was going to answer him.

"We—we were just talking," she said at length, the tremor still noticeable in her voice. "Nothing special."

Zach slid his arm down her back. She moved away. Cursing silently, he watched her, while in the recesses of his mind a warning sounded. He felt a wave of unexplained fear. He had learned long ago never to ignore his instincts. They had gotten him out of more jams than he cared to re-call. Now they were working overtime. Something was wrong. Her peculiar behavior had the same effect as wav-ing a red flag in front of his face.

He knew Beth Melbourne better than she knew herself. Granted, she should be upset. Foster Melbourne was her mainstay, her anchor. Most parents were. Because he had been her *only* parent, he'd been even more so. Besides, your parents were immortal; they were supposed to live forever.

Still, something wasn't right; he would swear to it. But what?

"It—it was awful," Beth was saying, her eyes lowered. "Daddy...was talking to me one minute, then the next, he was lying on the floor."

Zach breathed an inward sigh of relief. At least she was opening up a little. Maybe his imagination had been playing tricks on him. "Hey, I know it was awful. But you've got to believe he's going to be all right. He has a lot going for him. Physically he's in good condition. You said so yourself."

"Oh, Zachery, I'm so glad you're here," a woman's voice said from behind.

Suddenly aware that they were no longer alone, both Zach and Beth swung around.

Zach's eyes met those of Grace Childress, Beth's maternal grandmother. In her late sixties, she was a thin, fragile-looking woman whose face was etched with both beauty and strength. When she spoke, her deep black eyes never failed to blaze with life, except now, when they were uncharacteristically subdued.

"Hello, Gran," Zach said and hugged her.

Beside her stood Trent, whose taut features brightened when he saw Zach.

"Hello, buddy." Zach's mouth curved into a shadow of a smile. "You okay?"

Trent nodded, then stuffed his hands into the pockets of his cutoffs and stared at the floor.

Zach reached over and tousled his straight dark hair.

"No word from the doctor?" Grace asked, her gaze focused on her granddaughter.

"Not yet." Beth's voice sounded strained, as if it was difficult for her to even talk.

Gran forced a smile. "Either of you care for something to drink?" She held up a cardboard tray. "Trent and I bought an extra Coke and a coffee."

Zach turned to Beth. "How 'bout it?" Sensing she was going to refuse, he added, "It might make you feel better."

"I'm . . . fine. But you go ahead."

Zach's eyes sought Grace's. A troubled frown drew her thinning white brows closer together. Then, wordlessly, she shook her head as if to say, I don't know what to do with her, either.

"I'll stay here with you," Zach said after a moment. "I'm not thirsty, anyway."

The silence continued long after Grace and Trent had made their way to a long sofa on the other side of the room.

When the silence began pulling at his gut, Zach reached out and gently turned Beth around, then began kneading the muscles at the base of her neck. "Maybe this'll make you feel better."

She pulled away. "I'm fine."

A cold pain filled his chest. "No, you're not. What's wrong? I know you're worried about your daddy, but..." His voice faded. Then, after a moment, his lips stretched into an angry line. "Do you want me to go? Is that it?"

Suddenly her eyes widened and she appeared frightened. When she spoke, her tone was even. "No, of course I don't want you to go. Why would you think that?"

He almost choked. "Why the hell wouldn't I, after the way you're acting?"

Following that outburst he fell silent, but his body, tense and charged, could not be still. He paced to the other side of the window.

She followed him. "Zach?"

"What?"

"Is Daddy in trouble?"

Bingo. His instincts were about to pay off. Alert now, Zach straightened. "What do you mean?"

"Financial, maybe?"

Zach moved to her side. "Could be. I don't know."

Beth's face went blank. "Your...your daddy... Taylor..."

"When did you see my daddy?" Zach's tone registered shock.

She tilted her head, as if wincing. "Earlier...this evening. He...came to the house."

"What for?"

"To see . . . Daddy. Only he—he wasn't home."

"So are you saying my *daddy* discussed finances with you?" The thought astounded him, and it showed.

Beth averted her gaze. "Not . . . not in so many words."

He had a bad feeling, and he didn't like it. "Beth, you're driving me nuts! Just spit it out. Are you saying money had something to do with Foster's stroke?"

"Yes . . . no! . . . I don't know!"

"Yes, you do." His tone quickened. "You know a damn sight more than you're telling."

"No!"

He stared at her in disbelief, watching that mutinous look he knew so well slide over her face. God, but she was stubborn to a fault. Once she made up her mind, hell could freeze over before she'd change it.

"Beth, look—" Zach got no further. From the corner of his eye he saw a large man, with a ruddy face that gleamed as if freshly shaven, enter the room. He recognized him immediately: Dr. Ben Aimsley, Shawnee's one and only heart doctor.

"Beth, the doctor just walked in."

With a start, Beth whirled around and hurried forward. By the time Zach reached her side, both Grace and Trent were already there.

"Is he going to be all right, Doctor?" Beth asked without preamble.

Dr. Aimsley reached for Beth's hand and squeezed it, but his eyes encompassed them all. "It's too early to tell. He's in a coma—"

"Oh, no!" Beth cried.

"Now, now, my dear," the doctor cautioned soothingly. "The news is not all bad. His vital signs are good, and he's breathing on his own."

"Was it a heart attack, Doctor?" Grace asked, slipping an arm around each grandchild.

"No, ma'am. It was a stroke."

Zach peered down at Beth, who looked as if a paltry puff of wind could blow her away. He wanted to hold her, make her pain go away, but he knew he couldn't. For now, he seemed to be on the outside looking in.

There *was* something he *could* do, though. He could talk to Taylor, find out the part he had played in all this. It was useless to try to get anything else out of Beth.

"Is he—is he paralyzed?" Beth was asking.

Dr. Aimsley rubbed his neck. "Yes, he is. His whole left side is affected."

"And his mind?" Grace put in softly.

Dr. Aimsley sighed. "At this stage we just don't know. It could be serious."

"Are you saying he could be a vegetable?"

Zach was stopped short by the terror in Beth's voice.

Dr. Aimsley's eyes were gentle. "I'm sorry, but that's a possibility."

Beth seemed to search deeply for air. She began shaking. "No! That's impossible. He—" Without warning, her body folded like a rag doll.

"Zach!" Gran cried.

He grabbed Beth just before she crumpled to the floor.

The following day Zach walked into Taylor's office at the mill with only a perfunctory nod at the blue-eyed blonde who occupied the secretarial chair.

He had wanted to confront his daddy yesterday, but he'd been afraid to leave Beth. When she had fainted, his own heart had almost stopped beating. With Dr. Aimsley in command, however, she had come to shortly. The doctor had given her something to calm her nerves and sent her home to get a good night's sleep, stressing the fact that there was nothing any of them could do, that if there were changes, he would call.

Trent had gone home with his grandmother, while Zach had taken Beth to Cottonwood. She had gone immediately upstairs and sprawled across her bed. He figured her head had no more than touched the pillow before she was asleep.

Unwilling to disturb her, Zach had left her clothes on and lain down beside her. This morning, after she'd showered and changed clothes, she'd insisted on going back to the hospital.

Now, as Zach eyed his daddy sitting behind his desk, he leaned against one corner of it.

"I guess you're looking forward to the big day, eh?" Zach switched his attention to the man who'd spoken: Lucas Ambrose, the mill's business manager. He flashed Zach a knowing grin before standing and holding out his hand.

Zach eased off the desk and towered over the short, overweight, heavy-featured man, who stood straight, chin slightly raised, as if to squeeze every inch of height out of what God had given him.

"Yeah, it won't be long now," Zach said with as much politeness as he could muster. He didn't like Ambrose, never had. He couldn't understand why Taylor had hired him; he wasn't competent. In fact, he was downright incompetent. "Only there might not be a big day if Foster doesn't improve," Zach added, almost as an afterthought.

Lucas's grin faded. "Damned shame. I was both shocked and sorry."

"Is there any change in Foster's condition?" Taylor asked. "Lucas and I were just talking about him."

Zach leaned back against the desk and faced Taylor. He smelled the liquor on his daddy's breath. Not bothering to hide his disgust, he muttered, "There's no change."

Taylor lit a cigarette and took two strong puffs. "How's Beth holding up?"

"Okay, I guess."

"Your mother's awfully worried."

"What about you?" Zach asked pointedly and thought he saw a spark of fear spring into Taylor's eyes. But then they narrowed, and he couldn't be sure.

"What kind of question is that?" Taylor demanded, grinding out his cigarette.

"Look, Daddy, I want to talk to you alone." Zach's tone stopped just shy of being rude.

"I don't have any secrets from Lucas," Taylor said, turning away. "Especially if it concerns the mill."

"But I do."

Lucas held up his hands. "Hey, no problem, boss. I have a lot to do, anyway."

"On second thought, maybe it is a good idea if you stay," Zach said suddenly.

"What's gotten into you, boy?" Taylor asked heatedly.

Ambrose shrugged, then looked at Taylor.

"Sit down, Lucas."

The room was quiet for a moment, with only the sounds from outside relieving the sudden tension. Somewhere in the distance a whistle blew, followed by a diesel engine springing to life.

"Let's get on with it, shall we?" Taylor said, slurring his words.

Zach could feel his temper rising. Even if Taylor wasn't drunk, he'd been drinking a sight more than he should have been, especially at this hour of the morning.

"What kind of financial trouble is Foster in? And why the hell did you mention it to Beth?"

"Did Beth tell you that?"

Again that flicker of fear. This time Zach knew he wasn't mistaken.

"Well, did she?" Taylor demanded when Zach didn't respond right off.

Zach set his jaw. "Quit stalling, Daddy. Just answer my questions."

Taylor reached for another cigarette and lit it, sending a cloud of gray smoke through the air like a smoke signal. "What else did Beth . . . tell you?"

"Nothing. That's the problem."

Taylor suddenly seemed to relax, and when he spoke, his voice was strong. "All right, I went to talk to Foster. It was a visit I couldn't put off any longer."

"Well, whatever you said to Beth, she repeated it to him." Hard eyes locked on Taylor and held him pinned.

"Are you suggesting I caused his stroke?" Taylor asked in a huffy tone, but he was squirming in his seat nonetheless.

Ambrose coughed suddenly as his eyes darted from father to son.

Ignoring Ambrose for now, Zach asked his father, "Well, did you?"

"I never meant to say anything to Beth. It was all a misunderstanding," Taylor finished lamely.

"Misunderstanding, my ass." Zach was seething. "You'd been drinking when you went over there, hadn't you? That's why you spouted your big mouth off and upset her!"

Taylor's eyes came alive. "Now, see here, boy, I don't have to sit here and be grilled by you."

For a long moment father and son glared at each other.

"That's right, you don't," Zach said, reining in his temper. "So let's stick to the facts." The anger still simmered, but he would have to be careful. If he antagonized Taylor much more, he'd never get the truth.

"Tell him, Lucas. Tell my son the facts."

"Well, uh, Zach, Mr. Melbourne's in debt to the company." Ambrose's false teeth clicked as he talked. "And we're not talking small bucks, either."

"Borrowed against his shares, right?" Zach's tone was brisk.

"Right," Ambrose echoed. "He bet the money on horses."

Zach sucked in his breath, then let it out slowly, his mind littered with chaotic thoughts of how this news would affect Beth.

A satisfied look crossed Taylor's face, as if he had enjoyed shocking Zach. "Now you know why I went to see Foster."

"To tell him what?" Zach demanded.

Taylor snorted. "Why, I thought that'd be obvious. But since you want it spelled out, I was going to tell him he couldn't take any more out of the till."

"Don't you think you left it a little late?" Zach demanded sarcastically.

Taylor slammed a fist down on the desk. "You think you have all the answers, don't you? Well, you damn sure don't. Times are hard and getting harder, especially with all this Watergate shit." Taylor waved a heavily ringed hand through the air. "Ah, but what do you know? You're just a twenty-two-year-old kid, spoiled—"

Zach leaned into his face. "I know, all right!" he said, his voice shaking with suppressed anger. "Remember, I'm the one—this twenty-two-year-old kid—who told you you needed to get your act together and get this mill back on its feet."

Ambrose cleared his throat, as if trying to defuse the tension in the room.

Zach backed away, but he wasn't through. "So you had a right to confront Foster, but not Beth. You upset her. Then, when Foster came home, she upset him." His anger flamed anew.

"*Are* you accusing me of causing Foster's collapse?"

Zach rubbed the back of his neck. "Of course not," he muttered.

"Good. Now, can we get on with the rest of the story?"

Zach stopped short. "You mean there's more?"

"Foster also owes the bank." Again Taylor's tone sounded almost gleeful.

Zach struggled to take it all in. "So what's the bottom line here?"

"You're smart, you figure it out," Taylor said, pulling another cigarette out of the nearby pack and lighting it.

Zach glanced at Lucas, then back to his daddy. Taylor was puffing overtime on his cigarette.

Zach blinked against the offensive smoke and asked, "Is Foster Melbourne broke?"

"He's been broke, Zach, for a long time," Lucas put in, his false teeth still clicking.

"So what does all this mean?" Confusion added a rough edge to Zach's voice.

Another silence, this time prolonged.

Lucas coughed.

Taylor rose from behind the desk and pinned Zach with a hard stare. "You'd best have a seat, 'cause you're not going to like what I'm about to say."

Ten

"You won't tell me who attacked you?"

"No," Beth said, the tiny word sounding as if it had been scraped from her throat.

"There's nothing I can say that will change your mind?"

Tightening her lips, Beth shook her head.

Reverend Paul Broussard came from behind his desk, walked silently to the couch and sat next to Beth.

In his late sixties, he was a man who could best be described as average: average height, average weight, average features. His eyes were the one exception. They were the kindest, most caring eyes Beth had ever seen. *He* was the kindest, most caring man she knew.

When she was in grade school he had come to Shawnee's First Baptist Church as an assistant pastor. She hadn't known it then, but he'd recently buried his wife of only one year, who had been killed in a freak car accident. To date, he had never remarried, making the church and its members the center of his existence.

After the head minister had moved on to a larger church, Reverend Broussard had taken his place. During the following years he had become a close and dear friend to the Melbourne family, a friend to whom they had turned for help on many occasions. Today was no exception.

It hadn't been easy to approach him, to admit that she'd been raped. In fact, it had been the hardest thing Beth had ever done in her short lifetime. But she'd had to tell someone. The burden had become too heavy to bear alone. Guilt, remorse and shame had dogged her relentlessly, until she'd feared she might lose her mind.

This morning, following two sleepless nights at her grandmother's, Beth had gotten up early, showered, dressed and gone to the hospital, where she found her daddy's condition unchanged.

She had stood beside his bed in the intensive care unit and stared down at his unmoving body. Foster's face had been as white as the uniform of the nurse who whisked in and out. Finally, feeling a scream building inside her, she'd known she had to get out before she made a complete fool of herself.

Leaning over and resting her cheek against his, she'd whispered, "Oh, Daddy, I'm so sorry, so sorry for everything." It was only after she'd lifted her head that she had realized she was crying. Her daddy's face had been wet with tears.

From the hospital she had driven straight here. The instant she'd walked into the parsonage, this unpretentious brick house with its hodgepodge of furniture and memorabilia scattered about, she'd known she had made the right decision. Its warmth had enveloped her as if she were a lost loved one come home at last.

When Paul had ushered her inside his study, words hadn't been necessary. As both a friend and a minister, he had already spent hours at the hospital boosting her family's spirits.

But when she'd started crying and told him why she'd come, he'd been stunned speechless. He'd recovered quickly and in his gentle way had begun asking for details. She had adamantly refused to give any, telling him only that she had been attacked in her own home by someone she knew.

"All right, my dear," he said, bridging the long silence. "I won't ask you again." He paused again, the worry lines around his eyes reflecting his concern. "I want you to seek professional help. It's a *must*. You have no choice."

Beth couldn't have felt more drained than if she had just run five miles uphill. Her lower lip began to tremble, and her entire face bore the tracks of fresh tears. "But that's why I came to see you, Uncle Paul," she wailed.

"Talk to me, then. Tell me how you really feel," he encouraged, his tone warm and soothing. "How you feel inside."

"I . . . don't know if I can."

"Try," Paul pleaded. "Please try."

Beth shuddered. "Most . . . most of the time I feel dirty, like I'll never be clean again."

"Go on."

"And there's . . . there's this awful thing inside me that wants to explode whenever I breathe. Oh, God, it hurts so bad. I tell myself I was raped." She wiped the tears from her eyes, then beat on her chest. "Me. Beth Melbourne. I was raped. But it couldn't have happened to me. Things like that happen to other people. Only it *did* happen to *me!*" She sobbed, her shoulders heaving. "And I hate myself, and I feel so terrible, so . . . scared."

"Of what?"

Her hand shot to her mouth to try to control her sobs. "Of everything."

"Shh, you'll make yourself sick," Paul cautioned gently. "But you're doing fine. Getting this all out in the open is the first step toward healing. You need to go farther, only I can't take you there. I'm not qualified. I can only listen. I can't offer you the kind of help you need."

"Uncle Paul, please," Beth wailed again, toying with the Kleenex in her hand until it was in shreds. "I can't bear the thought of anyone else knowing."

"I can understand that, my dear, but telling a trained doctor is like telling me. It would go no farther. I can give you the name of a clinic—"

Beth stood suddenly and jammed her hands into the side pockets on her skirt. "No! I just…can't take the chance." She fought back the urge to burst into tears again. "You— you don't know how close I came to not even coming here."

"Beth, please, sit back down."

When she was beside him again, he went on in a firm but gentle tone. "Listen to me. We're talking about the rest of your life. In order for you to come out of this without any lasting scars, you need to spend time with someone who knows how to deal with this type of trauma."

Beth shuddered inwardly. Although what he said made sense, she simply couldn't do it. Talking about the rape out loud had been almost as bad as experiencing it. She never wanted to go through that again.

Yet Reverend Paul had been wonderful, had made her feel almost human again. She was grateful. She had needed to tell her story, to hear herself tell it. But she could never tell anyone else.

The obstinate set of Beth's features spoke for her. After sighing deeply, he said, "Don't misunderstand me, I'm not giving up on trying to persuade you to follow my advice. But in the meantime, I want you to promise me something."

"If I can."

"Promise me you'll remember that none of this was your fault, not the attack and not your daddy's stroke. You are *not* the guilty party, you're the victim."

Beth reached for another tissue from the box on the table beside her. "If only I hadn't said anything to Daddy—"

"Stop it, my dear. Stop torturing yourself. You did what anyone else would have done. He didn't give you any choice. After all, you're still a child."

Beth almost smiled. "I'm eighteen, Uncle Paul. That's hardly a child."

"To me you're still a child. Anyway, you did what you had to do."

"I . . . I don't know." Her voice was lifeless.

Paul plowed his fingers through his hair. "I know I promised I wouldn't ask this again, but I have to, for my own peace of mind, if nothing else. Won't you please tell me who did this to you? Charges should be pressed against him."

Startled, Beth looked up, a tiny flame of panic in her eyes. "Oh, no, no. I . . . could never do that."

"I hate having to ask this . . ." Again the reverend paused and cleared his throat. "But I have to. Is there a chance you might be . . ." Again he paused.

Beth sat silently for a long time, rehashing her pain, her humiliation, and staring at the man who was trying so hard to help her glue her life back together. At last she whispered, "No, there's . . . no chance."

Paul closed his eyes for a brief moment. "Thank God."

"Do—do you think Daddy's going to be all right?"

He didn't speak for a moment. While she waited for his reassurance, Beth stared through the miniblinds. It was shaping up to be another hot summer day, perfect for donning a bathing suit and taking a leisurely swim, then lounging in the sun. Her heart wrenched. Would she ever enjoy such simple pleasures again? She doubted it.

"All we can do is pray, my dear. Even though he's in a coma, he's not dead. We have to cling to that fact."

"I'm trying to, but it's so hard."

"I know." Paul watched her closely for another moment, then asked, "Would you like something to drink? Lemonade, maybe?"

Beth pushed a lock of hair behind her ear. "Lemonade sounds good."

Paul smiled before getting up. "I'll be right back."

Beth had just eased her head back onto the cushions and closed her eyes, willing her tight nerves to relax, when he came back into the room with a glass in one hand and a cup in the other.

They sipped their drinks in silence. A minute or two later, Paul leaned over and placed his cup on the coffee table in front of him. Angling his head, he asked, "What about Zachery?"

Though he spoke softly, his words had the impact of a bullet hitting plate glass. Beth flinched, then suddenly hung her head and crossed her arms tightly, as though giving herself a hug she felt she needed.

Since her father's stroke, Zach had been her shadow, which hadn't helped. He'd only this morning gone back to work at the mill, leaving her on her own. She couldn't have asked for anyone to be more thoughtful. He'd sensed her continued withdrawal—she'd seen it in his eyes, heard it in his tone. Yet he hadn't condemned her or questioned her, certain her standoffish attitude had to do with the trauma over her daddy and that soon she would come to grips with it.

As for their wedding and their future—well, she had kept those things in cold storage. But she knew she couldn't put off thinking about them for much longer.

"I don't know." Beth's voice trembled as she spoke, and her throat swelled, trapping her tears in her throat.

Reverend Broussard dragged the back of his hand across his forehead. "Well, there's still time to make a decision."

"Not much." Beth rubbed her right temple. "But I can't seem to think anymore."

"I know you won't believe me now. But you *can* and *will* get through this time in your life. You're made of strong stuff, Beth Melbourne."

Suddenly Beth felt her throat ease, releasing the tears. They streamed down her face. Gently Reverend Paul put his arm around her and held her close. Her shoulders shook.

"Atta girl. Go ahead and cry. Get it all out. This may sound corny—isn't that the word you kids use?—especially coming from an old fuddy-duddy like me." He smiled. "But my mamma used to tell my sister, 'Think of tears as a safety valve releasing pressure on the heart.'"

Beth cried until she couldn't cry anymore. It didn't help.

When she finally walked out to her car she felt as though chains still shackled her feet.

A short time later Beth turned into the driveway at Cottonwood. Rachel's car was sitting in the circular driveway. Beth's heart sank. Then she panicked, purposely steering the car into the garage at the rear of the house. She would rather die than let herself be seen in this state.

After doing what she could to repair her makeup, she got out and made her way back toward the front of the house. Rachel was out of her car and leaning against it.

"Hi," Beth said, trying to put some life into her voice.

If the look on Rachel's face was any indication, she had failed miserably. "No change in your daddy, huh?"

"None. He's still in a coma."

Rachel made a face. "That's awful."

"Why didn't you go inside?" Beth asked, changing the subject. "Jessie's there."

Rachel pushed herself away from her car. "I just got here."

"I meant to call you, but . . ."

"Hey, don't worry about it," Rachel said. "Believe me, I understand. Have you been at the hospital?"

"Part of the morning," Beth said evasively. She would have to be careful.

When Beth didn't expand on that, Rachel said, "Mamma sends her love."

"I appreciate that."

A gentle breeze teased the tops of the huge oak and cypress trees and for a moment filled the silence.

Rachel shielded her eyes from the harsh sun that even the thick branches couldn't filter and peered directly at Beth. "You can tell me to mind my own business if you want to, but I have to ask, what about the wedding? Is it still on?"

"I don't know," Beth said in a faltering voice. "I haven't been able to deal with anything other than Daddy." And my own heartbreak, she added silently.

"But you have to deal with it soon," Rachel pointed out, though her tone was warm and sympathetic.

Beth clasped her cold hands together and stared at Rachel through wide, wounded eyes. "I will, only not now. Maybe tomorrow."

Rachel looked as if she wanted to press the issue, but she didn't. "Is there anything you need?" she asked instead. "Anything special I can do?"

Beth's gaze focused on her once again. "Yes."

"Name it."

"Just hug me."

Eleven

"Gran, how's Trent?"

Grace Childress's sigh filtered through the phone lines. "He's confused, of course, and worried. But he's going to be fine. I'll see to him. You just take care of Foster."

Beth sat down on the couch in the library and, after banking the phone against her shoulder, willed herself to relax. She couldn't; she had been uptight for too many days now. It was almost as if it had become a new way of life for her.

Toying with the phone cord, she listened as her grandmother went into detail about Trent's activities. Her gaze drifted to an open window. Evening shadows were slowly edging out the sun. She couldn't believe the day was nearly gone.

After Rachel had left, Jessie had fixed Beth some lunch. Then Beth had gone back to the hospital and sat with her daddy until an hour ago. When she'd gotten back home, she had showered and called her grandmother.

"Then he's not giving you any trouble?" Beth asked, seeking further assurance. "When Trent gets upset, he's at his worst."

"You just stop worrying about your brother," Gran said soothingly. "Remember, I know him about as well as anyone, including yourself. We have an understanding, and we're getting along just fine."

"He's not balking about going to summer school, is he? That's important to Daddy, you know, especially since he had to pull strings to get Trent back in. He'd have a hissy fit if he thought Trent stayed out because of him."

"No, he's doing fine there." Grace chuckled. "As I said before, we have an understanding, like the one *we* had when you were his age. Remember?"

A brief smile altered Beth's lips. "I remember. For such a small lady, you always were one tough cookie. As I recall, you'd only tell me once to do something, then there was hell to pay if I didn't."

"You don't have to swear, my dear."

Beth smiled again. "Oh, Gran, you're priceless, and I do love you."

"And I love you." Grace paused, and when she spoke again her tone was sober. "That's why I'm worried about you."

It was all Beth could do to speak past the lump that suddenly rose in her throat. "Don't be. I'm . . . all right."

Although she had ached to run to her grandmother with the truth, to seek comfort in her fragile but strong arms, she hadn't. She'd been afraid of what the shock would do to her. Besides, Gran was totally responsible for Trent. She couldn't stand the idea of adding to that burden.

"You're not all right, and we both know it."

"Well, I'm coping. How's that?"

"There's something else bothering you." It wasn't a question but a flat statement.

Beth squirmed uncomfortably. Like Rachel, her grandmother was far too perceptive. If she wasn't careful, she'd be telling Gran everything, in spite of her vow not to. If only she was better at hiding her feelings. She had to get better, that was all there was to it. Zach would be the hardest one to fool. He was biding his time, she knew, until he could ask her questions, questions she wouldn't answer.

"Beth, honey," Grace chided in her genteel voice, her concern evident.

"Sorry, Gran." Beth forced a lightness into her voice. "It's Daddy. Really. I'm...afraid he's not going to get well. And, too, I think he...may be in some kind of financial trouble."

"Oh, dear, no. Surely not."

Beth had her mouth open and was about to reply when the doorbell chimed. Although Jessie would answer it, she didn't want to be caught downstairs in her robe.

"Gotta go now, Gran. Someone's at the door. I'll talk to you later."

"You don't need to hurry on my account."

Startled, Beth gasped, then scrambled to her feet. Zach stood in the doorway, propped against the doorjamb.

She shouldn't have been surprised, but she was. He almost always called first.

He had one thumb hooked in a belt loop at his waist, while the other hand hung loosely at his side. His stance was firm on the oak-planked floor underneath, but it was not the floor that garnered her attention. Nor was it his apple red T-shirt or his tight jeans, washed so many times their color was no longer evident.

It was his eyes. They were filled with uncertainty and something else, an emotion she couldn't quite identify. Fear, maybe? A trace of vulnerability?

While her mind churned, he continued to stand there silently. Then slowly, deliberately, he started toward her. She wanted to flee, to disappear, but she knew that was impossible. She had dreaded this moment, but now that it was here she had no choice but to face it—and him.

She didn't know how she felt. A heavy swirl of emotions engulfed her. While she knew deep down that she still loved him—that would never change—the thought of making love with him was frightening. God help her, but she was confused. One wrong move on her part could shatter their future. No matter what happened, though, her heart had been coated with a grime that no amount of happiness could ever scrub entirely away.

"Beth." He sounded as if he'd swallowed sandpaper.

Their eyes met and held for an eternity.

Lowering her head, Beth felt breathless, felt an expanded sensation in her chest.

Zach closed the distance between them and tipped her chin. He was standing so close now that she could see the tiny flecks of gold mixed with the green of his eyes, the faint lines that flagged their corners, see the gleam of sweat. But most of all, she inhaled his scent.

"I—I wasn't expecting you," she stammered, dry mouthed.

"Yes, you were."

A hand came up to her cheek. Long fingers traced the shape of her face, her lips, her eyelids.

"It seems so long since I've touched you."

Before she could respond she was in his arms and he was kissing her. For a moment she kissed him back, and they spoke with their bodies what no words could have expressed.

But when he touched her breasts, Beth stiffened and pulled away. "Don't, Zach," she murmured, backing up.

Zach winced as if she'd hit him in the gut.

"Okay, let's have it. Something's wrong, and I want to know what it is."

"Nothing's wrong."

He clenched his hand in a fist. "You're driving me nuts!"

Turning her back, Beth walked to the French doors. The yards of hot pink silk whispered against her bare legs. Once there, she stared outside, watching as the shadows finished gobbling up the sun.

The silence stretched.

"You didn't come just to see me, did you?" They had been wordless for so long, her own voice sounded rusty. "I can sense you have something to tell me. Something bad."

"Look at me, Beth."

She slowly turned around.

"I want an answer to *my* question first. What's bothering you?"

She watched his neck, the way the tendons stood out, and she knew that he was hanging on to his temper by a thread. His voice, if not exactly threatening, had taken on a steely edge. She couldn't get by without answering him.

"It's . . . it's just that I'm exhausted. And worried about Daddy." She couldn't quite meet his gaze. "But you should know that. He's all I can think about right now."

Zach's eyes probed hers. "Are you sure that's all?"

"I'm sure."

He looked as if he wanted to argue. Beth held her breath.

"Okay, I'll give you the benefit of the doubt. For now."

"So now it's your turn," Beth said.

He didn't pretend to misunderstand her. "You're right, I do have something to tell you, and I hate like hell—"

"It's okay," Beth interrupted. "I can take it. You asked . . . Taylor about Daddy's finances, didn't you?"

"Yes."

"It's . . . it's not good." In spite of herself, her voice quivered.

"No."

"So tell me."

"Your daddy's in debt up to his neck, both at the mill and at the bank."

She stared at him and he stared back, their eyes holding the same look of misery. It was as if they were looking into the same mirror.

"Why? I mean . . ." Beth's heart thudded wildly.

"He's been gambling heavily at the racetracks."

"How much money are we talking about?"

"I don't have the exact figure, but it's a big chunk of change."

"I . . . can't believe it."

"I'm afraid that's not all."

Beth's only reaction was that the remaining color drained from her face. "Go on."

"Foster used Cottonwood as collateral at the bank."

Beth feared what was coming, and though she couldn't bear the thought of hearing it, she couldn't stop herself from asking, either. "Does that mean what I think it does?" Her words were a whisper.

Zach raised his hands to the back of his neck, and when he did she could see his muscles tighten and the agitated rise and fall of his chest. "You could lose Cottonwood."

She cried out, clutched at her breasts as if she were having a heart attack. No! Impossible! It just couldn't happen. On top of everything else that had happened to her, she couldn't lose Cottonwood, too.

"No! I don't believe you. Daddy wouldn't do a thing like that. He—he loves Cottonwood more than anything else in the world."

Zach stared at her through dark, serious eyes. It was that look, which never wavered, that convinced Beth he was telling the truth.

She whimpered, then slumped against the windowsill.

Zach closed the distance between them with breathtaking suddenness. But when he reached to take her into his arms, she stepped back.

"How could he do something so stupid as that?" she cried, her head tilted up just slightly, as if she were treading deep water and trying not to sink.

Zach's face was as pale as hers. "Beats the shit out of me."

"But—but I could've sworn he loved Cottonwood more than anything. More than me, more than Trent!"

"Not more than his horses and gambling, apparently."

"Oh, Zach," she whispered brokenly, "what am I going to do?"

"Hey, you're not alone in this. You've got me. You know I'll do everything possible to see that you don't lose Cottonwood. So will Daddy." He paused, then added, "I know this isn't the time to talk about the wedding, but under the circumstances, why don't we scrap the big church affair and—"

"I don't think we should get married right now."

"*What?*" His question came wrapped in disbelief.

Beth wet her lips. "I need time."

"That's crazy, Beth. You don't mean that."

"I mean it," she whispered, suddenly unable to tear her eyes away from him.

"You're just upset. My God, you've gone through enough to drive you crazy. I understand that. But you can't let it come between us." He was clenching his fists, and she could see the cords in his neck pulsing from the strain.

"So much has happened so quickly that I can't sort it all out." Tears darkened Beth's eyes. "My whole life has been turned upside down. I just need some time."

"You don't need time, you need me, goddamn it!"

"Zach, please, try to understand."

Switchblade quick, he stepped up to her again. "Understand! What is there to understand?"

She stared back at him defiantly. "I just explained—"

"Oh, really?" he interrupted. "Well, that's just not good enough."

She forced herself to look at him coldly. "You're making too big a deal of this."

"Don't do this to me." Zach's face was livid with helpless anger. "Don't do this to *us.*"

She hardened her heart against the pleading note in his voice. "I have no choice. I have my daddy to see to. And Cottonwood." She spread her hands. "I have other obligations."

"Fuck those obligations!" he exploded.

Her teeth ground together, and to her relief she felt a surge of anger replace the pain. "I'll pretend you didn't say that, because I know you didn't mean it. I can't turn my back on my family or my home, and you know that."

"We can get through this together."

"You don't understand, Zach." She spoke so softly that he had to bend his head to hear her.

"Then help me understand. Don't shut me out."

She looked at him, her agony of the past few days showing in her eyes.

"Beth," he said thickly.

She passed her tongue over her dry lips, then whispered raggedly, "Zach, don't . . ."

"Don't what? Don't tell you that I love you?"

She stood motionless, the ache in his voice stabbing at her heart. Then finally, painfully, she forced herself to shake her head. "Please, just go." It was barely more than a whisper. "I want to be by myself."

"All right, I'll go." There was fire in his eyes. "But this discussion is not over, not by a long shot!"

Twelve

Zach slipped one leg into his jeans, then the other. Afterward, bare chested and barefoot, he left the loft bedroom and made his way very gingerly down the stairs. He was on the bottom step before it dawned on him that the cabin had been remodeled and refurbished.

Had he been that drunk? Yes. Even now, his head felt like it was going to burst. Bracing his right hand against the wall, he lowered himself until his rear made contact with the hardwood.

Through bleary red eyes Zach continued his perusal of the place. The living area had loft-high ceilings and windows. A Naugahyde couch and chairs, a desk and an entertainment center swam before his eyes. Still, in the large space they did little to shrink the size of the room.

Off to the left was a kitchen with a bright orange countertop. A huge fan whirled above his head, while a floor lamp burned unobtrusively in one corner. The bathroom was to his right, down a short hall, and next to it was another bedroom.

Another sharp pain shot through his head, and he winced. Served him right, he thought, staring squint-eyed at the nearly empty bourbon bottle on the table beside the recliner.

After he had stormed out of Cottonwood he had jumped into his car and started driving. It was only when he found himself near the coast that he stopped at a phone booth and called Charlie Bentley, asking if he could borrow his cabin.

Not only was Charlie one of his best friends from high school, but he was one hell of a mill hand. He'd started working there after graduation. When it came to paper-making, Charlie was like him; he had a special knack for the job. And once he was put in charge, he aimed to see that Charlie got a promotion.

Once his friend had given him the go-ahead, telling him where the key was stashed, he'd reasoned that the mill could do without him for a few days. Anyway, he had work with him that needed to be done in uninterrupted quiet, quiet that he found hard to come by at the office.

Before leaving the phone booth he had called home and left a message as to his whereabouts. Maybe if he stayed away from Beth, he had told himself, she would come to her senses.

Despite the fact that she had dismissed him like a naughty child—he paused in his thoughts, a grimace alter-ing his face—it had taken every ounce of self-discipline he could muster to walk away. He hadn't wanted to leave her; instead, he'd wanted to jerk her into his arms, crush her fragile body against his and kiss her soft lips until she begged him not to leave her.

That rejection had hurt; it had hurt like hell. Not only that, but he had felt out of control, as if he'd been tossed out to sea without a life jacket.

The minute he had arrived at the cabin he'd felt the urge to put on his Nike running shoes and run on the beach, lis-tening to the surf pound in his ears. He hadn't. He'd walked through the door and headed straight to the liquor cabinet. By the time he'd crawled upstairs around four o'clock in the morning, he'd been blind, stinking drunk. He'd been drunk off and on since.

Now, as he continued to stare at the bottle, he felt the urge to guzzle the rest of it down.

Why not? Anything was preferable to what he was feeling. The mere thought of Beth triggered disturbances and contradictions that turned his body into a war zone. The image of her looking so fragile, so alone, before he had walked out, recurred repeatedly, like bouts of fever.

His feelings concerning her changed by the hour. He ached for her, detested her stubbornness, pitied her vulnerability, loved her, and wanted to yank up her skirt and paddle her behind.

More than anything, he was frightened. Fear was beating against the walls of his chest like an insistent but unwanted guest, fear that he was losing her, that she was slowly slipping away from him.

Yet he couldn't conceive of that happening. She had sent him away because she'd been distraught. Just as she'd told him, her secure little world had come crashing down on her head. He could understand that.

But why hadn't she let him help her? That was something he couldn't understand. She had never turned away from him before. Never. When something went wrong, she wouldn't run to her daddy or her grandmother. She would run to him.

Why now, when they were about to be married in three weeks, was she refusing to lean on him? It didn't make sense. What did make sense was his loneliness. He could hardly stand it.

But he didn't want to upset her further by pushing. He simply hurt from the need to be with her. He didn't know what to do. He couldn't make himself believe that it was his fault, that he'd said and done all the wrong things.

He got up and ambled toward the bottle. After putting it to his lips, he guzzled down the remaining contents.

"Caught you in the act, my friend."

Zach jerked his head around, then muttered a curse.

"Scared you, huh?" Charlie Bentley sauntered farther into the room, a grin taking up his whole face.

He was a huge man with a beard, and blue eyes that twinkled when everything was going his way. But when they weren't, those blue eyes turned to ice.

Wordlessly Zach glared at him.

Charlie chuckled and angled his head. "No wonder you didn't hear me. You're drunker than a skunk."

"*Was* drunker than a skunk. Right now, I'm stone-ass sober."

"Yeah, and I'm Batman, too."

Zach sneered and turned away.

Charlie chuckled; then his features sobered. "What the hell's going on, Zach? You know, man, this cabin's yours any time you want it, but why hole up here now?"

Even though his head was still banging, Zach answered him. "When Beth's daddy's in a coma? Is that what you're asking?"

"Guess so," Charlie drawled.

"Well, the truth is, my fiancée told me to go fuck myself."

Charlie didn't flinch. He merely narrowed his eyes. "Not in those words."

"Nope, but that's what she meant."

A silence fell over the room as a weak sun peered through overcast skies and an aggressive wind whistled against the windows.

Charlie sighed. "I doubt that. You know how girls are when they get uptight. She's probably having her period or something."

"I wish. This mess with her daddy has freaked her out."

"Yeah, I heard about that."

Zach cursed. "You mean tongues are already wagging?"

"'Fraid so. Word has it that Melbourne's dead broke."

Zach rubbed his grizzled jaw. "I hate to admit it, but it's true. Foster's run up a debt that would choke a horse, both at the bank and at the mill."

Charlie whistled. "No wonder Beth's bent out of shape."

"She wants to postpone the wedding."

Charlie's jaw dropped. "You're kiddin' me!"

"Do I look like I'm kidding?" Zach's drawl had a weary, sardonic cast.

"No. What you look like is shit."

"If it's any consolation, I feel like it, too, only worse."

Charlie grinned. "The warmed-over kind, huh?"

"You got it."

"Well, postponing it isn't the same as calling it off," Charlie said consolingly.

"But I'm afraid that's next. In fact, I'm just waiting for the other shoe to fall."

Charlie shook his head. "Naw, she wouldn't do that. Why, Beth's crazy about you, always has been."

Another silence fell.

Finally Charlie said, "Sit tight. I'll make some coffee."

"Don't want any coffee," Zach muttered churlishly.

Charlie's stride didn't falter. "Too bad. You're gonna drink a cup anyway. I didn't drive all the way down here on no social call."

His curiosity piqued in spite of himself, Zach stood, only to find himself gulping for air in order to fight the dizziness that assailed him. A few seconds passed before he followed Charlie into the kitchen.

"So why *did* you drive down here?"

"Taylor sent me."

"He can go to hell, too."

"Well, if it's all the same to you," Charlie drawled sarcastically, "I'll let you tell him that."

"What does he want?"

Charlie scratched his head. "Don't know. Maybe he just wanted to make sure you were all right. Anyhow, I volunteered to check on you."

"Hey, I don't need a nursemaid."

"Couldn't prove it by me."

"Go to hell."

Charlie merely laughed, then filled a cup with coffee and handed it to Zach.

Zach nodded his thanks and sat down in the nearest chair, careful not to jar his head.

"Aw, man, why don't you shower, get dressed and go home?" Charlie asked. "You know Beth is probably going crazy wondering where you are."

The thought cheered Zach, and he grinned. "Reckon?"

"I'd bet on it."

"Well, she might as well be," Zach said with sudden determination, "'cause I'm not going to let her renege on this wedding, even if I have to hog-tie her and haul her down the aisle."

Beth peered once again into the rearview mirror of her Mustang, more for reassurance than anything else. Though her features were paler than usual, she knew she looked her best, having erased the dark circles under her eyes with concealer. In order to look more mature and businesslike, she had parted her hair down the middle, pulled it back into a ponytail at the nape of her neck and fastened it with a navy clip.

She had chosen a navy linen dress that, when she stood, struck her above the knees. Completing her outfit were navy pumps and a paisley belt. Her only jewelry was a set of diamond studs, a gift from her daddy on her sixteenth birthday.

After giving each cheek a tiny squeeze with her fingers, Beth got out of the car and, standing beside it, faced the bank.

Here goes, she thought. For three days now she had spent her time alternating between bleak thoughts of Zach and Richard Walsh.

Walsh proved easier to think about, since he stirred far less emotion and no stomach spasms at all.

Still, facing her daddy's banker would be no easy feat. But something had to be done, and she was the only one who could do it. She refused to lose Cottonwood.

Realizing that she was merely stalling for time, Beth hurried up to the front door, determined to remain cool and in control. But by the time she reached Richard Walsh's office on the second floor, her heart was beating out of sync. She stood before his attractive but aloof secretary and forced a smile.

"Mr. Walsh is expecting you, Ms. Melbourne. Go right in."

Beth nodded her thanks. The door to his office was partially open. Beth squared her shoulders and crossed the threshold.

Richard Walsh came out from behind his desk, a hand outstretched. "Nice to see you, Beth," he said cordially.

Beth wished she could feel the same, but she couldn't. Close to her daddy in age, he was a ruddy-faced man with curly gray hair cut close to his skull. His medium-sized body, perfectly groomed in a brown suit, was thick around the chest, as if he lifted weights.

"Same here, Mr. Walsh," Beth said, her tone sounding far too husky. She cleared her throat before taking his hand.

When the brief handshake came to an end he indicated with the sweep of a hand that she should take the plush chair closest to his desk.

While he made his way back behind his massive desk, Beth tried to control her still-erratic heartbeat by looking around. The room was opulently but tastefully furnished in period pieces of walnut. Even the carpet was thick and expensive, in a sea foam green. There were several leather chairs about. On the wall behind him hung a Clementine Hunter painting Beth recognized as rare.

"I'm so sorry about Foster," Walsh was saying, leaning back in his chair like a king on his throne. "I pray that he'll make a full recovery."

"Thank you," Beth replied politely.

"Has there been any change?"

Beth crossed her legs at the ankles. "No, he's—he's still in a coma."

Walsh sighed and shook his head.

"About Daddy's debt to the bank, Mr. Walsh—"

"I figured that was why you wanted to see me. But you needn't worry your pretty little head, you hear?"

Beth's fingers curled up and closed. His attitude grated; he was treating her as if she were a flighty teenager without enough sense to get in out of a good hard rain.

"Someone has to," Beth said in a voice that had become chilly.

He raked his hair with carefully manicured fingernails. "Now see here, young lady, this is men's business. And your daddy wouldn't cotton to you interfering."

"Mr. Walsh, please!" she said, outraged. "Don't patronize me." She frowned and made an obvious effort to get hold of herself. "My daddy," she added in a raised, controlled voice, "is in no condition to make decisions. He may never—" she paused and swallowed hard "—be again."

"Still, I don't feel comfortable discussing this with you." That air of impatience clung to Walsh. "We'll think positive that your daddy'll get back on his feet."

"And what happens in the meantime?" Tears threatened; Beth blinked furiously.

"Why, you just concentrate on that wedding of yours—"

"While you take Cottonwood." Her voice shook. "Is that it? Isn't that what you have in mind, Mr. Walsh?"

He seemed momentarily caught off guard. His face filled with color. "Now, honey, who told you a thing like that?"

"It doesn't matter," she said with a drip of acid. "Whether you admit it or not, I know. What I don't know, though, is how much my daddy borrowed against Cottonwood and what it will take to make it right."

Silence filled the room for long, heavy seconds.

Finally Richard Walsh stood and crossed his arms over his barrel chest. "I'm afraid it's too late."

Her breath stopped for a moment. "What? What did you say?"

"You didn't misunderstand me," Walsh said in a note of triumph.

Beth forced herself to get out of the chair and back toward the door. "I won't let you take my home." Hot tears stung her eyes, and her lower lip quivered. "You hear me? I won't!"

Later, after she was back in her car, Beth began to cry, even though she had promised herself that she wouldn't. She put her head down on the steering wheel and sobbed.

When the tirade ended, Beth dried her eyes. Then, switching on the engine, she drove off, her lips stretched in a tight line.

The instant the door closed behind Beth, Walsh calmly reached into his right-hand desk drawer and took out a pipe and pouch of tobacco.

After packing it tightly, he lit it, then settled back in his chair and puffed, basking in his success. He hadn't felt this good about things in a long time.

His private line jangled suddenly. With that satisfied smile still intact, he lifted the receiver.

"Walsh here."

He listened for a moment, his smile burgeoning into a full-fledged grin. "I was just about to call you, old friend."

While the voice on the other end monopolized the conversation, Walsh watched the smoke from his pipe curl through the air. Finally he got his chance to speak, smiling with confidence. "No, you didn't misunderstand. It's as simple as that. So if you're still interested, it's a go."

Thirteen

Beth sat straight up in the bed as if she'd been shot. Clutching at her thudding heart, she tried to swallow. There was no saliva; her mouth was as dry as cotton.

Wild-eyed, she turned and stared at the empty space next to her on the bed. She had been dreaming that Zach was next to her, caressing her, entering her pliant flesh with his strength, his hot mouth whispering assurances that he was hers for all eternity.

But she hadn't seen Zach since she had told him she wanted to postpone the wedding. Now she had this awful feeling that he was lost to her forever, just as her beloved Cottonwood was. Feeling a bout of nausea coming on, she took several deep breaths.

Nothing, however, could stave off the terrible trembling that was rattling her bones.

Had it been only yesterday when Richard Walsh had told her the bank was seizing her home? It didn't seem possible. She was sure a lifetime must have passed, though for the most part she had existed in a stupor. She had eaten, but only enough to keep from getting sick. She had slept, but only enough to function coherently.

Beside her bed the clock ticked. She stared at it sightlessly, still clutching herself. The numbness was ebbing slowly, harsh reality taking its place.

After leaving the bank she had made her way to the office of her daddy's longtime friend and attorney, Andrew

Sullivan. As luck would have it, he'd been able to see her immediately. The second after she was seated in his comfortable but unpretentious office, she explained what had transpired between Walsh and her.

"My dear, what did you hope to accomplish by going to the bank alone? No way could you hold your own against the likes of Richard Walsh."

The dapper attorney was a slightly built, soft-spoken man whose unremarkable features masked a ruthless intelligence. But Beth had always liked him. More important, her daddy liked him and trusted him. The only pretentious thing about him was the gaudy diamond ring on his little finger.

"I thought I could handle it alone." Beth gave a hollow laugh. "Now I know how stupid that was. But I have some money in trust from my grandmother, and I thought it might be enough to cover Daddy's debt at the bank, only—" Her voice broke on a note of despair.

"Only it wasn't a drop in the bucket compared to what your daddy owes."

"Right." She managed to force out the word.

For a long moment the room was silent.

"I knew Foster was digging himself into a hole with his gambling." Concern deepened Sullivan's already gruff voice. "I tried to talk some sense into him, warn him that he was getting in too deep, but he wouldn't listen."

"What am I going to do, Mr. Sullivan?" Beth touched her throat and stared at him in a glazed way. "There's...no money." She shook her head. "I—I keep thinking I'll wake up and this will all be a dream."

"I know," he said gently, reaching over and giving her hand a squeeze.

"What am I going to do?" she asked again, her eyes round, terror stricken. "Daddy—Daddy owes so much money. Not only did he borrow money for his gambling debts, but he invested in several risky ventures that turned sour."

Sullivan leaned against his desk and crossed his arms. "Well, the house and land, of course, will take care of his debt at the bank."

"But there's the mill." Beth's tone turned fierce. "That debt has to be paid back, too. I won't let anything jeopardize those shares."

"And don't forget you have Foster's long-term care facing you, over and above what the insurance will pay. If he doesn't get well," he added kindly, "you'll have to put him in a nursing home."

"I feel so helpless, so…confused." Beth's voice cracked.

"I have to admit, you've had a heavy load dumped on you. Most teenagers couldn't even begin to respond to this kind of pressure." He paused and cocked his head. "But then, you're not like most teenagers, are you?"

"I guess not. Gran said I was born grown up."

Sullivan chuckled.

"Right now I feel ancient."

"That's understandable, under the circumstances. But it's not the end of the world."

"Yes, it is," Beth wailed, digging in her purse for a tissue.

Sullivan rubbed his forehead. "You know I'll do what I can. Your daddy and I go back a long way. I'm beholden to him for a lot."

"I appreciate that more than you'll ever know." Beth's eyes were wide and intense. "But what can *I* do? There must be something."

"There is."

She scooted to the edge of her chair. "What?"

"I suggest you have an auction on the grounds of Cottonwood, sell off the priceless treasures that have been in the Melbourne family for generations. They will generate lots of cash, cash that you desperately need."

"Auction." Her voice, sharp and strangled, seemed to come from some other throat. "You mean sell our personal things out of the house? Oh, I couldn't—" She moaned like a lost soul.

"I don't see where you have much choice, my dear."

In the end, she didn't....

Taking a deep breath to ease the pressure inside her, Beth tossed back the covers and got out of bed. She made it to the bathroom, only to realize her head was banging. She deserved worse, she told herself, for silently rehashing that conversation with Sullivan. She had a bottle of aspirin half open when the phone rang.

Zach? She dropped the bottle. The thought of talking to him made her weak. She splayed her hand against the woodwork for support. He was still upset, she knew, because he hadn't called. She couldn't blame him, though, not after the way she had behaved. Dashing to grab the phone before Jessie did, she lifted the receiver.

"Hello."

"Ms. Melbourne, this is the hospital."

Beth's stomach felt as though it were an elevator that had stopped too quickly. She gripped the receiver. "Yes."

"We wanted you to know that your father opened his eyes earlier this morning."

Beth gasped.

"But before we could call you," the voice went on hurriedly, "he drifted back—"

"That's wonderful!" Beth cried, interrupting her. "I'll be right there."

Fifteen minutes later she had showered and was slipping into a turquoise cotton skirt and blouse. Later, Beth couldn't have said how she'd managed to dress in such record time, because her hands were shaking out of control.

What did it mean? Was her daddy going to be all right? The ramifications of such a thought made her giddy, despite the nurse having reemphasized just before she hung up that Foster was no longer alert.

Jessie stood at the foot of the stairs when she raced down them.

"Lordy, child, what's your hurry?"

"Oh, Jessie, Daddy opened his eyes!" She grinned and planted a firm kiss on the housekeeper's round face.

Jessie clamped her hands together. "Praise the Lord, child. That *is* good news. Have you told your grand-mother and brother?"

"No, not yet. See you later."

"I'll be praying, honey," Jessie called to her back.

Beth got halfway down the driveway, only to suddenly crunch down on the brake. Zach's GTO was heading up the driveway. With her heart in her throat, she sat paralyzed until he stopped, but not before their vehicles literally bumped noses.

She watched as he came toward her, a chaotic mixture of emotions raging inside her. She wanted to run, yet she wanted to fling her arms around him, too.

He had on jeans, a green shirt that exactly matched his eyes, and boots. Sunlight rippled over the tanned muscles of his arms, calling attention to their strength. God, he looked good.

When he reached the car he leaned against it and peered inside.

"Hi."

His cologne surrounded her like a heady mist, making the urge to touch him that much greater. "Hi yourself."

"I couldn't stay away." His voice sounded strangled.

"How've you been?"

Something trembled between them.

"Do you have to ask?"

She circled her lips with her tongue. "No. You...look like hell." His mouth had a tightness that hadn't been there before, as if smiling didn't come easily these days. He needed a haircut; his hair was shaggier than she'd ever seen it.

"So do you. Dark circles and all."

She didn't take offense, because she knew he spoke the truth. "I know," she whispered.

"God, I miss you."

Her insides twisted. "I miss you, too."

"So why aren't we together?"

"Zach, please. This is not a good time."

"When *is* a good time?" Pain sharpened his tone.

"Later. I'm on my way to the hospital—"

"No! I want to talk now."

Conscious of Zach's hand gripping her arm, Beth stared at him and felt a sharp shiver go through her.

Silence hung between them.

His eyes were dark and luminous at close range, while pain swam in their depths as if trapped.

"Oh, Zach..." She ached to tell him that she was sorry, that she loved him, but she couldn't. Her lips moved, but nothing came out. She feared she might choke on all the unsaid words.

"There's no way I'm going to stand by and let you walk out of my life." His voice sounded abnormally harsh. "That's just not gonna happen, you hear?"

She turned away, her heart beating in her chest like a hammer on an anvil.

"Look at me...please! You owe me that, at least."

When Beth turned back around, he went on. "I've been patient, you'll have to admit that. But my patience is running out. I know you went to see Richard, and that he told you the bank was foreclosing."

"Of course you know," Beth said dully. "I'm sure everyone in town knows."

"So what! They're not important. But I am. I wanted to hear it from you. Why didn't you come to me first?" He beat on his chest in an exaggerated fashion. "Me, your fiancé. I would've gone with you to the bank and to see Sullivan.''

"I . . . did what I thought best.''

"Are you sure about that? Really sure?''

Her breath came back in burning spurts, allowing her to speak. "I don't have to stay here and explain myself to you—''

"Don't go . . . please. I'm sorry. It's just that I'm . . . Oh, hell, I don't know what I am.'' Although the corners of his mouth were still white with tension, his tone when he spoke again was edged with pain. "Have you told Gran and Trent?''

"Yes.''

"How about Jessie?''

Tears sprang into her eyes, and she could only shake her head.

Zach swore softly. "Back to Sullivan. What did he advise you to do?''

"Auction off the furniture for cash,'' she said bitterly.

He drew a shocked breath. "There's got to be another way.''

"Well, there isn't.'' She gripped the steering wheel at the same time that she soaked up his rugged features, his tall, firm body, as if for the last time. "I've got to go, Zach,'' she said, not bothering to disguise the panic in her voice.

Without warning she jerked the gear into reverse.

Zach jumped back, but he didn't say anything. He stood with his shoulders hunched, his face an expressionless mask.

She tore her eyes away, thinking her heart was literally breaking. She could feel it. It was only after she reached the end of the driveway that she looked into the rearview mirror. Zach's back was to her, and he was staring at Cottonwood.

* * *

The seconds and minutes ticked by while Zach remained still, except for his mind. It journeyed back to a day long ago. . . .

"I'll race you to the house!"

Zach threw back his head and laughed. "You're crazy! Why, that won't even be a contest. I'll win hands down."

Beth, dressed in shorts and a halter top, stopped in her tracks and whipped around, her nose tilted. "Oh, is that so?"

They were on the back lawn of Cottonwood on a lazy spring afternoon, having just come from a trek through the woods.

"Yeah, that's so."

"I almost beat you the other day, smarty-pants."

Zach jammed his hands into the pockets of his athletic shorts and grinned. "Only because I let you."

"Why, you rat."

He shrugged, his grin widening. "What can I say?"

"Nothing. How 'bout putting your money where your mouth is?"

Zach grinned. "You're on."

"All right." Beth placed her hands on her hips. "I'll bet you a milk shake."

"A milk shake! Shucks, that's peanuts."

"Okay, dinner, then."

Before Zach could reply, Beth took off. "You can't catch me!" she shrieked, her laughter ringing through the air.

"Ha! That's where you're wrong!" Digging in his heels, Zach raced after her.

With her hair flying behind her like silk, Beth scrambled up the hill, around the pool, then inside the house.

"You're not playing fair," Zach shouted, charging up the stairs behind her, following her laughter.

He caught up with her in her bedroom.

"See, I told you I could beat you!" she cried, her breath coming in jerky spurts.

He edged forward, a leering grin on his face.

She edged backward. "You . . . you stay away from me."

"You cheated, and I'm gonna make you pay."

"How?"

"Guess," he whispered, trapping her against the back wall with his body.

"Zach!"

"Zach, what?" His throaty laughter turned into a muttered groan as he slowly untied her top.

She raked him with her aroused eyes. "What...what are you going to do?"

"Make love to you."

"Here?" The word came out in a shriek.

"Here."

"What about Jessie?"

"She won't come in."

"Daddy'll kill us both."

"He won't know," Zach whispered against her parted lips.

Zach shook his head, aching to erase the memory from his mind. It refused to fade. Beth's laughter, the mental picture of him sliding her up the wall, then back down onto his hard arousal, wouldn't let go.

The sun had peered through the French doors and surrounded them in its warmth while he nibbled on her neck, then her mouth. God, it had tasted like the sweetest of nectar.

He thought about her breasts, the sweet plucking sensation of his lips on her nipple. And the purring groan she made in the back of her throat when he had made her come.

"Zach? You're welcome to come inside."

The sound of his name jolted him out of the past, but it did nothing to relieve the tension inside him. Jessie was standing on the steps. He stared at her, feeling as if a giant hand were pressing against his lungs so that he had difficulty breathing and speaking.

"No, Jessie, but thanks, anyway," he finally said.

He watched her disappear, and still he stood and stared at the lovely old home. It was untenable that Beth's laughter would no longer filter down its halls.

It was only after he turned and headed back to his car that he realized his face was wet with tears.

Fourteen

"I'm sorry, Beth, but there's been no further sign of response."

Beth's gaze drifted from Dr. Aimsley back to her daddy's figure on the bed. "If only I'd gotten here sooner—" Her voice broke. If only she hadn't let Zach detain her. If only...

"It wouldn't have made any difference, I'm afraid." The doctor spoke kindly. "Even if he had been awake, chances are he wouldn't have recognized you."

Without taking her eyes off her daddy, she asked, "What are you saying?"

Dr. Aimsley sighed, and there was a reluctance in his voice when he explained. "The stroke caused considerable brain damage. Even if he regains consciousness, he'll be both mentally and physically impaired. He'll never be the same man he once was."

"Never?"

"Never. I know I'm painting a gloomy picture, but that doesn't mean you should give up hope. In my business, miracles happen every day." He paused. "Still, I want you to know what you're facing—long months and even years of rehabilitation."

"Please, Doctor, if you don't mind, I'd like to be alone."

"Sure." He smiled sadly. "I understand. Call if you need anything."

The moment the door closed, Beth sank wearily into the chair beside Foster's bed. For the longest time she simply stared at him. Then, lifting his cold hand, she laid the back of it against her wet cheek.

"Oh, Daddy," she whispered, tears streaming down her face into her mouth. "I don't know what to do. I'm so scared. So much has happened to me, and none of it is good. I—"

A new onslaught of tears jammed her throat, and for a minute she couldn't go on. "I can't stand the thought of losing Cottonwood. It's killing me. Why, Daddy? Why?" She sniffed noisily. "I'm trying not to be bitter and angry, but I am. It's not fair. It's just not fair."

Continuing to cling to Foster's hand, she lowered her head over onto the side of the bed and sobbed until exhaustion claimed her.

Later, feeling drained to the bone, she let go of his hand, stood and walked to the window of the private room he now occupied.

The sky was clear, with only a few clouds to mar its beauty. But Shawnee needed rain, as did all of southern Louisiana. The heat, coupled with the humidity, was stifling. The minute you stepped outside, both took your breath away.

The weather, however, was the least of Beth's worries. Turning slightly, she fastened her troubled gaze on her daddy again. She hadn't been surprised when Dr. Aimsley had told her he wouldn't get well. Deep inside she had known his chances of recovery were almost nil. Still, when she actually heard it spoken aloud the blow had been severe, as if he'd come up behind her and karate chopped her in the back of the knees.

She dreaded telling Gran and Trent. Though she knew they would be upset, they wouldn't be shocked, as they had been when she told them about Cottonwood. Beth suddenly went cold all over, thinking about that encounter.

"No!" Grace Childress had cried, the color spilling from her face. "That's . . . not possible."

"You mean we have to move?" Trent had chimed in incredulously.

Ignoring the sad heaviness inside her, Beth had gone on. "Yes, Trent, honey, I'm afraid we do."

"But—but what about me?" Panic flared in his eyes. "Where—where will I live?"

"With me, of course," Gran said quietly.

"Daddy...he gambled everything away," Beth said, her hands spread helplessly. "We . . . there's no money."

"I—I can't believe it." Grace eased into the nearest chair, as if her legs were no longer capable of supporting her.

"You're lying!" Trent's chin wobbled as he glared at Beth. "You're just saying that. We—we've always been rich."

"Oh, Trent," Beth cried, "it is true! We're broke."

"You know you're welcome to what little money I have," Grace said, her voice sounding odd, as if she were in shock.

Beth sighed, her tense shoulders drooping. "I couldn't take your money, Gran, even if it would make a difference, which it won't. It's all so complicated."

"Suppose you tell us what you know," Grace said. Then, turning to her grandson, she added, "Trent, honey, come on and sit with me. It's going to be all right. We'll face this together."

When Beth finished telling them about her trip to the bank and then to the lawyer, the room fell as silent as death.

"There's something else," Beth said, finally breaking the silence.

"This stinks," Trent said suddenly, bitterly.

Trying her best to ignore her brother and his outburst, Beth swallowed hard and added, "We—we have to have an auction."

"Auction!" Grace was horrified. "You mean . . . ?"

Beth nodded. "That's exactly what I mean."

"Oh, my Lord," Grace whispered.

"Oh, Gran, I don't have any choice." Beth squeezed back the tears. "The money from the auction will pay off Daddy's debt at the mill. And there's the possibility that Daddy will have to be put in a...a nursing home."

"And insurance won't cover all of that," Grace responded gravely. It was a statement, not a question.

"Right."

"I'm never going to school again," Trent said, his eyes flashing angrily.

Stunned by his outburst, Beth faced him. "Why on earth not?"

"Because—because everybody'll make fun of me, that's why."

Beth looked at Gran, who was staring at her grandson with pain in her eyes. "Oh, Trent, maybe not."

His lower lip trembled. "Yes, they will."

Although both she and Gran had talked to him, trying to explain that he didn't have anything to be ashamed of, that this bad time in his life would pass, their words had fallen on deaf, childish ears. Trent had been inconsolable.

She couldn't blame him. As she had pointed out to Zach, the Melbournes were the talk of the town, despite the prayers of concern from friends and employees alike, and despite the flood of flowers and get-well cards sent to the hospital. Tongues were wagging, and she abhorred it.

She felt that same way now as she walked back to her daddy's side and brushed an errant strand of hair gently off his forehead. But life went on, and you had to do what you had to do. There were no free rides—she was simply learning that much sooner than most.

"Don't worry, Daddy," she whispered. "I'll make it all right somehow." She leaned over and kissed his cheek. "I love you, and I'll take care of you. I promise."

* * *

"I have forty-five hundred for this lovely Clementine Hunter painting in pristine condition. It's been in the Melbourne family for generations. Do I hear five?"

A gentleman stood and called out loudly, "Five thousand."

"Five thousand for the Clementine. Do I hear fifty-five hundred?"

For a moment the crowd was silent.

"Five thousand going once, twice..." The auctioneer pounded his gavel. "Sold to the gentleman in the blue suit for five thousand."

Each time the gavel sounded and another item went to the highest bidder, Beth flinched inwardly, feeling as if a part of herself was being auctioned off with it.

But to the outside world looking on, Beth was taking everything in stride, as were her grandmother and her brother. Together they sat in lawn chairs off to the side and looked on in stoic silence while the painful process took place.

A week had passed since Sullivan had advised her to have an auction. She had thrown all her energy into planning it. Of course, she hadn't done it alone. Friends had joined in and helped, especially Rachel and her mother.

The auction had been scheduled to begin at eleven o'clock. But by ten o'clock the house and grounds were teeming with people, giving it a circuslike atmosphere.

To her dismay, cars clogged every available parking space and some that were not. Dressed in a simple pink linen dress and white pumps, she had walked outside and stopped in horror, aghast at what she saw.

People were milling around the large yard, thoughtlessly tramping over Jessie's flower beds and grinding their heels into the lawn. Some had stood in small clusters merely gawking, while others had battled the crowd like hungry piranhas in a feeding frenzy.

Most of the action had centered around the long display tables that covered the patio and lawn, holding the items that were shortly to be auctioned off.

Now, as Beth continued to sit beside her family, she felt perspiration trickle down her face and saturate her underarms. Only after she reached for a Kleenex did she realize she was being watched. She twisted her head and peered from under the screen of her lashes. Zach's eyes bored into hers. He was using a huge oak tree as a prop, looking pale and gaunt, as if he, too, had been gutted.

It came to her then. She couldn't marry Zach. For a second she was stunned by her own thoughts. Not marry Zach? Impossible. Zach was a part of her already. Without him, she wouldn't be whole. She couldn't leave him. She would never survive.

But to stay, to become his wife, would be equally devastating, if not more so. She simply couldn't chance it. If she failed to tell him the truth, how could she handle the pain in his eyes when he wanted to make love and she refused him?

Pain as sharp and biting as a hot knife sliced through her, bending her double. He deserved better than half a woman; he deserved a whole one who could meet his needs both physically and mentally. She could do neither. She was merely a shell of her former self.

Only because she loved him could she let him go. That love would provide her with the strength to do the right thing. But could she truly survive the final, ultimate pain of parting? She had to. The die had already been cast.

Shuddering, she turned her attention back to the auctioneer. But not for long. Unable to bear Zach's close scrutiny another minute, Beth leaned toward her grandmother and whispered, "I'll be right back."

"Are you all right, dear?"

"No, Gran, I'm not," Beth answered honestly. "I don't think I'll ever be all right again."

With her head down, Beth made her way through the people, trying to block out the voices around her. She couldn't. Conversations followed her.

"Y'all look at that handmade quilt! Why, it's simply marvelous."

"Yeah, no telling how long it's been in the family."

"And those dishes. Wow, I just have to have them...."

Dear Lord, I can't stand this, Beth cried silently, upping her pace in order to escape the naked greed.

I want it! I've gotta have it! was the order of the morning as Shawnee's well-heeled salivated over the Melbournes' treasures.

When Beth would have stumbled, strong arms grabbed her. "Hey, missy, what's your hurry?"

She didn't have to look up to know who had his hands on her. His foul breath would have told her, even if his voice hadn't. Beth jerked away as if she'd been burned.

"Don't—" She caught herself just as Marian walked up and stood beside her husband. Although she didn't say anything, Marian stared at them both, a perplexed frown marring her forehead, as if she were trying to figure out what was going on.

Before anyone had a chance to relieve the menacing silence, Zach strolled up and draped an arm around Beth's shoulders. For a brief moment she leaned against him, glad of the support.

"Something wrong here?" Zach asked easily. Beth wasn't fooled. She could see the muscles in his jaw twitching. Underneath that cool, pleasant tone she heard the cold displeasure. How much had he seen?

"No," Taylor said with a polished smile. "We came to offer Beth our support," he added, rubbing one grizzled cheek. "We couldn't let her go through this alone. Could we, Marian?"

"Of course we couldn't," Marian responded gently.

Beth scarcely heard her. She was too busy trying to control the brilliant red anger charging through her. *You bastard! You drunken pervert!* How dare he do this to her? How dare he act completely innocent? If it hadn't been for Zach, she would have had him thrown off her property.

"Beth, are you all right?" Zach asked, his gaze hooded.

"I'm—I'm fine, but I need to go. I have things to do."

His eyes were warm. "Will I see you later?"

"I . . . okay."

When she would have walked off, Taylor stopped her. "Oh, before you go, I thought I'd mention the note to the mill . . . ."

"Daddy, not now!" Zach seethed. "Can't—"

Beth interrupted. "Don't worry, Mr. Winslow, the mill will get back every dime my daddy owes." Her voice cut the elder Winslow with the clean precision of a finely honed knife. "Plus interest."

Zach looked from one to the other, then back to Beth. "Trust me here," Zach pleaded. "You don't have to worry about that."

Beth's denial was abrupt. "Yes, I do, Zach. Not only do I intend to pay the money back, I intend to hold on to my daddy's shares, as well. So if either of you has any plans to buy him out, forget it!"

"Jeez, Beth! You know better than that." Then, whipping around, Zach focused his attention on Taylor. "Right, Daddy?"

Taylor cleared his throat and again kept his gaze off Beth. "Well . . . uh . . . sure. But I was thinking that Beth might want to trade her shares in lieu of the debt."

"No!" Beth's chest heaved with fury. "Absolutely not."

"Calm down, honey," Zach said to Beth, glaring at his daddy. Then, turning back to Beth, he added, "Nothing's going to happen to your stock. Trust me on that."

"As soon as I know what the auction brings in, I'll be able to pay some of the debt. I'll sign a promissory note for the rest."

"Whatever you want is okay by me," Zach said gently, staring at her with his heart in his eyes.

For a moment she held his gaze.

Marian coughed discreetly.

"I have to go now," Beth finally said in a husky voice.

"Oh, Beth," Marian added, "if there's anything you need until the wedding, please let me know." Though her eyes were filled with concern, she appeared ill at ease. "I'm so sorry about Foster... about all of this."

"I know, Mrs. Winslow, and—"

"Please, don't you think it's about time you called me Marian?"

"All right, Marian. I... appreciate your concern." Beth paused, then muttered, "See you later."

The instant Beth was out of hearing range, Zach turned back to his father, his face livid. "What was that all about?"

Marian placed a hand on Zach's arm. "Son, please, not now," she chastised, her gaze taking in the milling crowd around them.

Zach shrugged off her hand. "Answer me, Daddy. When did you decide you wanted Foster's shares?"

"What good are they going to do him?" Taylor's eyes were hard. "Answer me that. Why, he's nothing but a vegetable—"

"God," Zach cut in, "you make me puke."

"Hold up, Ms. Melbourne."

Beth stopped suddenly and felt her heart sink. Not again, she thought, hating to turn around. First Taylor Winslow, now Richard Walsh.

She turned slowly. "Yes, Mr. Walsh?"

"My, my, but this is some shindig you've put together."

Bypassing his sugar-coated dig, she said coldly, "What did you want to see me about?"

He flushed at her rudeness, and when he spoke his tone was equally cold. "I thought you'd like to know we have a buyer for Cottonwood."

"Wonderful."

Flushing under her sarcasm, his lips tightened. "Is that all you have to say?"

"What would you like me to say?" She smiled tightly. "You think I should be jumping for joy at losing my home?"

"I'd watch that sharp tongue if I were you, missy."

"Is that all, Mr. Walsh?"

"Don't you want to know any of the details?"

"No," Beth said sharply. "I don't want to know who bought it."

Walsh brushed the air with his hand. "Suit yourself."

Beth watched as he sauntered off, thinking what a pompous asshole he was.

Minutes later, after she'd been inside the house to check on the refreshments, Beth forced herself to return to the auction site. But in order to keep from running into Zach or his family, she went the back way and quietly reclaimed her seat.

Her grandmother leaned over and gave her arm a squeeze. "It'll soon be over."

Without saying a word, Beth stared at the auctioneer and listened as he enthusiastically continued to auction off pieces of her heart.

Fifteen

Overnight the rain had fallen gently, bathing the earth in its sweet-smelling freshness.

Beth ran a hand through her hair, ruffling it as she continued to stare out the window, unable to bear the hollow sound of the near-empty house.

The auction had taken place three days ago, but already Cottonwood had been stripped to the bones. Only the pieces of furniture she had kept remained. And, of course, her and Zach's wedding presents. They were boxed in another room.

While she waited for the moving van, Beth's thoughts turned to the auction. In terms of money, it had been a success. But in terms of her mental and physical well-being, it had been disastrous. She was still reeling from the impact of losing virtually everything.

Trent's personal belongings had been packed first thing. Then he, along with Jessie, had gone to Grace's, where they were now situated. Thank God Grace had had room for Jessie. Nevertheless, Beth had cried like a baby when Jessie had hugged her close just before getting into Gran's car.

Jessie had scolded her, saying, "Hush up. Dry those tears. As soon as you get settled, I'm coming to take care of you."

While that promise had been comforting, Beth knew it would be a long time before she was settled enough to take care of Jessie. Of paramount importance was picking up the pieces of her shattered life and putting them back together. And Gran had been there to help. Beth had leaned on her, grateful for her support. Still, it hadn't been easy to tell Gran her decision concerning Zach.

"Oh, Beth, are you sure?"

"I'm ... I'm sure."

"Well, whatever you decide, darling," Gran had said, tears clustered in her eyes, "I'm with you. All I've ever wanted is for you and Trent to be happy."

Now, as Beth continued to stare into the bright sunlight, dressed in a yellow cotton jumpsuit and sandals, she watched as Zach parked his Pontiac in the driveway and got out.

She had called him at the mill and told him that they needed to talk. "I'll be right there," he'd said and hung up.

With her heart in her throat, Beth turned and waited for him. Within seconds she heard his footsteps ring hollowly on the tile floor.

"Beth, where are you?"

"In the living room." Her slightly raised voice seemed to echo off the walls in the deserted house.

He crossed the threshold, only to suddenly halt. Then he smiled that endless smile of his. In the space of a heartbeat, her thinly veiled control almost deserted her.

"Mornin'," he drawled.

"Morning." Her voice quivered.

He stepped closer, his smile still intact. "I'd kiss you if I didn't smell like a swamp rat."

It was obvious that she had interrupted him working, because he was dressed in a pair of faded jeans that barely clung to his hips and an old T-shirt with the logo of Louisiana State University scrawled across the front. Perspiration glistened on his forehead and above his lip, while the sun streaming through the French doors highlighted the damp ends of his hair.

Their eyes held for another long moment; then Beth said, "I'm . . . sorry if I pulled you off the job."

"Don't be. I'm not."

"What—what were you doing?"

He sighed as if impatient, but his eyes never strayed from hers. "Working on the number one machine. The SOB went crazy again."

Beth almost smiled. "And you were the only one who could fix it, right?"

He gave her a sheepish grin. "Naw, but you know me. I can just take that office for so long, then I go nuts."

"I know," she said softly. Then, reaching inside her pocket, Beth pulled out a folded piece of paper and held it out to him.

"What is it?"

"Can't you tell?"

"Looks like a check."

"It is."

Two long steps put him close enough to take it from her. Silently he glanced down at it. "In spite of what you think, this isn't necessary," he said, lifting his head.

"Yes, it is."

"Look, the money your daddy owes the mill isn't going to make or break us, so if you—"

Beth shook her head, cutting him off. "Take it," she said tersely. "As soon as I can, I'll start paying off the rest of it."

Zach rocked forward on the balls of his feet. "But that's not why you called me, is it, to give me this money?"

She swallowed against the swelling in her throat. "No."

He waited. The silence seemed to scream at them.

Suddenly Zach was within a hairbreadth of her. "This is crazy, Beth. We're dancing around each other like two strangers, when all I give a damn about is kissing you until you beg me to stop."

He slapped his thigh. "But what am I doing? I'm standing here treading on eggshells like some wimp, afraid of saying the wrong thing. Now, is that priceless, or what?" He paused, as if to get his second wind. "Especially when we're about to get married." He paused again. "We *are* going to get married, *aren't we?*"

Beth's stomach rolled, reflecting the tension inside her. Yet she'd known that this moment, so long postponed, like a trip to the dentist, had to be faced.

"No, Zach, we're not."

The words hung in the air, stark, ugly.

Beth wet her lips. "I can't . . . I won't marry you." Dear Lord, she'd actually said the words. Somehow they had gotten past her convulsing throat and through her stiff lips. But the hard part was still to come. She had to convince Zach that she meant what she said.

"I won't let you do this to me, Beth!" His voice rose, lean and razor sharp, as if to defend himself from another invisible attack. "I won't let you walk out on me. Not now! Not ever!"

Before Beth realized his intention, he grabbed her and mashed his mouth against hers. She moaned and pushed at his chest until their lack of breath forced him to let her go.

Though thoroughly shaken, icy numbness settled around her heart. "You have no choice."

"The hell I don't! Can't we at least talk about it? You know, like mature adults. Maybe I'm wrong, but when you're in love aren't you supposed to discuss things before you make any major decisions?"

"There's nothing to discuss."

He sucked in his breath while the air between them seemed to turn to stone.

"It's over between us, Zach."

The moment was fragile, as if everything revolved around this one point.

"What's happened to you?" he whispered raggedly. "I can't remember when I didn't know you, and in—"

"Zach—"

"Let me finish. And in all that time, all those years, I've never seen you like this. It's almost as if I don't know you anymore."

"That's because pieces of me are missing, Zach."

"What are you talking about?"

Realizing she'd said too much, Beth tried to backtrack. "Daddy—"

He exploded before she finished. "Daddy! He'll always come first with you, won't he?"

"Please, let *me* finish," she said quietly, her throat hammering painfully, her voice almost lost. "Daddy's stroke, the loss of Cottonwood—I'm still trying to come to grips with all that."

Zach looked at her with anguish in his eyes. "Believe me, I understand. I want to help make it better." His voice seemed not to be his own. "If you'll let me," he added softly, "I can heal you."

Beth felt as though the heavy air of a moment ago had been sucked from the room; it was so difficult to think, to breathe. "It's...over, Zach," she said again.

"No," he said, his voice sounding scratchy. "It will never be over, not between us. And you know it."

Beth's round, haunted eyes gazed back at him. "Zach, don't.... Let it go. Let *me* go."

He flinched visibly, as if each word Beth said inflicted a wound deep inside him.

"What is it? Why are you doing this?" His voice was flat and harsh, like winter. "I know there's more to this than your daddy and losing this house, though God knows that's enough."

"You're wrong," she lied with strength.

"No, I'm not wrong, and you know that, too," he said, so gently and tenderly that her heart knocked frantically from the pain of it.

"Zach . . ."

"God, Beth, I love you so much it hurts. I ache all over."

"Don't . . ."

"Don't what? Don't love you, is that it?" When she didn't answer, he went on. "Please, don't do this! I can't think anymore. You're making me think crazy things, like everything we feel is wrong, when I know it's not."

Beth closed her eyes against his words. "I'm leaving Shawnee, Zach. I'm going to Northwestern in Natchitoches—I think I may even have a scholarship. With the money Mother left me, along with a part-time job, I can make it."

Suddenly she turned away. She could no longer trust herself to look at his white, agonized face, at his eyes, which were no longer green but dark wells of pain.

"Beth," he croaked. "Look at me."

She turned back around. "I want us to be friends. . . ."

"Friends!" He looked at her as if she were mad. Then he pitched back his head and laughed, a grating, hollow laugh. "That's priceless. Friends, huh?"

She nodded wordlessly.

His voice lowered, and a nasty edge came into it. "Well, let me tell you what *I* want. I want to wake up every morning with you beside me and fuck you till you're senseless!"

The silence in the room was like a deafening roar.

"Nothing you can say, no matter how crude or how shocking, is going to make me change my mind." Beth paused and closed her eyes for a second, feeling as if her breath was being choked out of her. "I think it's the best thing to do, for both our sakes."

"Oh, no, you don't," he muttered harshly. "Where do you get off saying what's best for me? Obviously you don't know anymore, or you just don't give a sweet goddamn. Which is it?''

Beth covered her eyes with her hands and willed herself not to cry.

''Beth,'' he whispered, the sting having gone out of his voice, leaving it weak and soft. ''Do you want me to beg? Is that it?''

''Don't...don't do this...please!'' she cried, feeling dizzy.

''Hearts do break, you know. And you're breaking mine.''

His words were almost her undoing. For an impulsive moment she wanted to run to him, catch him to her heart and beg him never to let her go.

But then the image of Taylor Winslow's face flashed before her eyes, as did the imagined horror and condemnation she would see in Zach's face were she to tell him the truth.

Bracing herself, Beth lifted her gaze to Zach's and said steadily, ''Has the thought ever crossed your mind that I might have stopped loving you?''

''And have you?'' he asked, the bones beneath his skin seeming to take on new prominence.

''Yes.''

Outwardly he showed no emotion. ''All right, Beth,'' he said at last in a tired voice. ''You win. You do what you feel you have to do. I won't bother you anymore. You have my word on that.''

She stood rooted to the spot as he walked to the door. ''Zach...''

He swung around, his face cold and set.

She held out her hands to him, palms up, her eyes reflecting her soul. ''Please...don't hate me.''

For a moment he hesitated, as if debating something. Then he shrugged. ''Save it, Beth. Nothing you could say or do now would make any difference. To paraphrase Rhett Butler, I suddenly don't give a damn."

Beth held herself reed straight, certain her heart was literally breaking; she could feel it tear loose. It wasn't until she heard his footsteps die away that the rest of her broke loose, too.

She sank into a heap on the bare hardwood floor, buried her face in her hands and cried harsh, bitter tears.

"Zach . . . Zach! My precious love. Zach! I can't bear it. I want to die. Oh, God, please, let me die. What will I do? How will I live?"

Beth braked the car in the driveway of Cottonwood and stared through the glass at the graceful lines of the lovely old home.

She hadn't intended to come here. Somehow, though, she'd found herself doing just that, as if her mind needed respite from the pain of saying so many goodbyes.

She had just left the nursing home, where she'd kissed her daddy. An hour before, she'd embraced her grandmother and her brother. And yesterday she'd told Rachel goodbye.

"Leave? What on earth are you talking about?" Rachel had cried, looking stunned. "You can't leave. You're getting married!"

Rachel had just gotten in from shopping and was in her bedroom, changing clothes. Beth sat down on the edge of Rachel's bed, her legs threatening to give way beneath her.

"I called off the wedding."

"You what?"

"Even all the wedding presents have been returned," Beth went on in a dull, methodical voice.

Rachel stared at her with her mouth open. "You're not serious!"

"I'm dead serious."

"But—but why?" Rachel shook her head as if to clear it. "Is it all this mess with your daddy?"

Beth nodded mutely.

"Jeez, it just blew your mind, right?"

Again Beth nodded.

"Well, it's blown mine, too." Rachel paused and sat beside Beth on the bed. "What—what about Zach? How did he take it?"

"Guess," Beth whispered.

"Bad, huh?"

"Worse than bad. He—he hates me, Rach."

"Naw, he doesn't," Rachel said, looping an arm around Beth's shoulders. "He's just hurt. He'll get over it."

Beth's lips twisted. "No, you're wrong. He'll never get over it."

"And from the looks of you, I'd say you're having second thoughts."

"Oh, Rachel!" Beth wailed. "I still love him, but I had to break it off. I just couldn't handle getting married right now." Beth wrapped her arms around herself. "After...after everything that's happened, there's no way I can make Zach happy."

"What are you going to do?"

Beth told her. Afterward, they hugged and declared pledges of friendship to last a lifetime....

Now, at last, Beth had come to bid farewell to her beloved home. Oddly, there were no tears gathered in her throat. Maybe it was because her heart had toughened into armor.

Then images of Zach's distorted face flashed before her eyes. She trembled.

Two days ago, when she'd told him it was over, she hadn't thought she'd survive. But she had. And out of the ashes of that survival had risen a heartbroken yet determined young woman. One day, when she was whole again, she would return to Shawnee and to Cottonwood.

After all, she had a score to settle.

Part II

Sixteen

Fall, 1983

The weak rays of the morning sun drew Beth to the window. She stood there for a long time.

At seven o'clock the city of Natchitoches, Louisiana, was quiet, but not as quiet as her condo had been, or as quiet as her office was now. She took a deep breath and found it helped. Her slender hands were still shaking, but they were no longer uncontrollable.

She had to go to Shawnee. As always, she was dreading it. Days before she was to make the three-hour trip, her insides turned into a bundle of nerves. It never failed, despite the fact that it had been ten years since she'd left home. Since she'd left Zach.

Those years had made a marked difference in Beth. Before tragedy struck, she had been outgoing, lighthearted, at times outrageous—secure, happy, full of hope.

Now she was less talkative, more serious. The laughter of those bygone days showed only in fleeting glimpses in her eyes. At twenty-eight she still looked eighteen and sometimes sixteen—defenseless, untouched, fragile. But there was something more. No matter how dazzling her smile, how warm her eyes, there was a loneliness about her, a loneliness that tore at the soul.

Out of the corner of one eye Beth could see the mess strewn across her desk. If stacked neatly, the sketch pads and catalogs would make a tiny mountain. Most of the time the onslaught of work made her feel alive; the challenge gave her a reason for getting up every morning.

The In-Look, the name she'd given to the chain of clothing boutiques of which she was the proud owner, was her life. But the success she enjoyed had not come without sacrifices. Specifically, it had cost her a personal life.

Once she had enrolled in Northwestern State University here in Natchitoches, she'd found a much-needed part-time job in a boutique.

As it turned out, the small, privately owned shop had been a godsend. She'd been working there only a month when she learned she had a flair for fashion. The older woman who owned the shop spotted that right away and taught Beth everything she knew.

Yet the years had been difficult. Time hadn't allowed her a social life, even if she had wanted one, which she hadn't. Her days had been long and tiresome, and by their end, she wanted only to go to her dorm and fall into bed. Many a night she wasn't able to do that for having to work on finances. She would pull her little black ledger out of the drawer and sit for hours, jockeying her money. But with her trust fund, her job, her scholarship and her frugality, she had made it, even managing to pay small sums on the remaining note at the mill.

During those times Beth had also returned home regularly to check on her family. Her daddy finally came out of his coma, but, as the doctor had predicted, he existed in a vegetablelike state. Her brother, under the close supervision of her grandmother, had managed to make it through school, though at times Beth hadn't been sure she or Gran would survive his teenage years.

In addition to her monetary and family problems, there had been her emotional problems to cope with. She soon learned that leaving Shawnee couldn't erase the trauma she had been through. Just as Reverend Broussard had told her, it would take professional help and guidance to bring that about.

Beth fought against giving in, telling herself again that if she pretended she hadn't been raped, the pain and the memories would go away. But they hadn't. In the end she realized she couldn't beat them on her own. Attending a counseling group for rape victims had been a trauma in itself. She had done it, though, not fudging on one meeting.

When the sessions had come to an end, it had become clear that she'd done the right thing. The group had taught her that there was indeed life after rape.

That newfound trust in herself had been severely tested every time she returned to Shawnee. She always made it a point to see Rachel, but never Zach, if it could be avoided. However, she hadn't been able to avoid him or Taylor at the mill's board meetings.

In spite of her renewed faith in herself, facing her nemesis never failed to shake her confidence. While she hadn't come out unscathed, she'd managed to hold her own, finding that hate and a thirst for revenge went a long way in preserving one's facade.

It had been those encounters with Zach that were the most devastating. The pain of regret seared her like a hot knife. Nonetheless, she had worked around the hole in her heart and made a life for herself apart from Shawnee, apart from Zach.

A year before her scheduled graduation, the owner of the boutique had told Beth she was going to sell the store, or, if she couldn't sell it, she was going to close it. Beth had been devastated, not because she feared she wouldn't be able to get another job, but because she loved the small specialty shop and had come to know and enjoy its customers.

"Oh, Nellie," she'd cried, "why would you even think about selling?"

Nellie Burkett, a tiny, birdlike woman, had smiled sadly and said, "Doctor's orders, I'm afraid. Those chest pains I thought were indigestion were my ticker. He told me to slow down if I want to live to see sixty."

"Why didn't you tell me you hadn't been feeling well?" Beth asked, her eyes wide with shock.

"I didn't want to worry you. Anyway, like I said, I thought it was indigestion."

"So—so when do you plan to...?" Tears clogged Beth's throat, and she couldn't go on.

"Oh, please, don't cry." Nellie paused with a smile. "Listen, I've been thinking. Would you like to buy the shop?"

Aghast, Beth stared at her. "I'd buy it in a heartbeat, only it's impossible. There—there's no way. I have to pinch pennies as it is."

Nellie grinned. "What if I financed it? I'd be willing to let you pay only what you could afford until you got on your feet."

It was an offer Beth hadn't been able to pass up. After taking over the shop and applying the ideas she had learned through her marketing major, she had, within months, doubled the volume of business.

Success had been a huge motivator. Five years later she had paid Nellie off and planned a new store at the same time. Now she owned eight In-Looks throughout the state.

She had recently renovated the original store and added offices.

Beth shifted her gaze off the near-bare trees in the park across the street and back to the clutter on her desk. She had far more to do than stand there and feel sorry for herself. Suppressing a sigh, she walked to the nearby filing cabinet, opened it and pulled out a folder. She shoved the drawer closed, only to feel a stab of pain in her right hand.

"Damn," she muttered before quickly reopening the drawer and rescuing her little finger. She immediately slipped it between her lips and sucked on it until the pain subsided. She mustn't let her emotions have free rein. She had to return to Shawnee, and that was that. If she saw Zach—well, she would just have to make the best of a bad situation.

Beth crossed to her desk, sat down and, as she did every morning, took a moment to survey her domain. In everything, she saw colors, shapes and textures. This morning was no exception. The office was warm and vibrant with its apricot-colored carpet and soft green fabric coverings on the couch and chairs. Adding to its warmth were the carefully positioned worktable in one corner and the ceiling-to-floor shelves packed with the latest fashion magazines and books in another.

Beyond, jutting off from a short hallway, were three other rooms, which finished out the suite of offices in the rear of the shop. One belonged to her assistant and buyer. The other two were workrooms.

Beth's eyes then wandered to the tall, handcrafted file cabinet, her latest indulgence, crammed full of sketches, clippings and notes, as well as names of satisfied customers and their tastes.

The In-Look specialized in play clothes for women, both expensive and moderately priced. Her choice of styles was only a small part of what kept her shops thriving. The personal service they offered was the key. Beth made it her business to know each of her regular customers by name and find out something personal about each of them.

Though she no longer worked the floor on a steady basis, her employees carried out her policies to the letter. As a result, The In-Look had continued to flourish when other dress shops hadn't.

Eventually Beth intended to design a line of costume jewelry and name it "Exclusively by Beth." She had envisioned that idea for years. Soon, she promised herself, she would turn that dream into reality. Meanwhile, she continued to open new stores.

Beth was proud of her accomplishments. Because of them, another dream was closer to coming true, the dream of returning Cottonwood to its rightful owners—the Melbournes. The debt to the mill had been paid off, and she had managed to build a nice savings account.

Deciding that a cup of coffee was what she needed to get her started, she got up, crossed to the tiny bar and refilled her cup. She had taken her first sip when she heard movement near the door.

Her assistant, Tracy Wadsworth, stood on the threshold. "Good morning," she said cheerfully.

Beth looked down at her watch, then raised her eyebrows. "Isn't this a bit early for you?"

Tracy grinned. "Surprised, huh? Well, I knew you wanted to unpack all that freight we got in late yesterday, so I forced my body out of bed and here I am."

"Thanks, I appreciate that," Beth responded warmly.

Although she had employees who took care of such mundane matters, there were days when Beth loved to handle the merchandise herself. Today was one of those days. While she enjoyed seeking out sites for future stores and going to market, she missed the daily hands-on routine that she used to enjoy when she worked the front alone.

"You want me to start on the freight right away?" Tracy asked.

Beth thought for a moment longer. "No, it'll have to wait. Apparently you've forgotten the style show. It's looming closer."

Tracy rolled her eyes. "Don't you ever slow down for one minute? Nothing like being a workaholic."

Beth grinned. "Guilty as charged."

Tracy made a face.

Beth's grin widened. "Want some coffee?"

"In the worst way," Tracy said.

Beth poured a cup and handed it to her.

While Tracy took a sip, Beth watched her with admiration. Tracy, in her early twenties, was quite attractive. Her naturally curly brown hair highlighted her petite features and large green eyes, eyes that were covered by glasses when her contacts were out, which was most of the time.

She had come to work for Beth shortly after she bought the shop. Tracy had wanted the job as much for the opportunity to learn the rag business as for the money. Tracy was gifted, with a God-given sense of style.

The In-Look, Beth knew, had worked its spell on Tracy, too. It was a main interest in Tracy's life as surely as it was the *only* interest in hers. Not only was Tracy an excellent assistant, but a deep affection had developed between them. Neither made friends easily. Tracy was warm and charming, yet surprisingly shy with strangers.

As for Beth, there was still a certain part of herself she kept isolated, which made it difficult to put forth the extra degree of closeness that turned an acquaintance into a friend. Because of that, Tracy's friendship was extra special.

"By the way, that outfit looks great," Tracy said, putting her cup down on the corner of Beth's desk.

"You think so?" Beth asked anxiously.

She had on a long-sleeved orange jumpsuit with a bright turquoise-and-orange waistband from the newest line they had chosen to carry. To date, few stores had the style in stock. The fabric was a soft cotton knit, and it didn't constrict her anywhere. The effect was astonishing. She had seen the line at market and been immediately excited, her trained eye telling her she'd stumbled on something hot.

"Are you fishing for a compliment, by any chance?" Tracy's eyes twinkled.

Beth looked sheepish. "Well, maybe I am. What about our women? Think they'll like it?"

"You bet. These outfits'll be the talk of the town. You wait and see."

"Hope you're right, because we've spent an awful lot of money here, my friend."

Tracy angled her head. "I know this is changing the subject, but your hair's different, isn't it?"

"I had it cut a little more yesterday," Beth responded with an inward wince. Every time she made a trip to the beauty shop, she thought of Zach and felt guilty. Gone was the long, straight mass he used to delight in running his hands through and touching his lips to.

Though still the same butterscotch color, Beth now wore it swept away from her face in a short, stylish pageboy. Zach, she knew, would hate it.

"Something wrong?"

The cloud lifted from Beth's face instantly. "No, why?"

Tracy shrugged. "You looked sorta funny for a minute, that's all."

Beth forced a laugh. "Maybe it's because I feel one of my bitchy moods coming on."

Tracy made a gesture with her hand. "Pooh. You know better than that. You're never bitchy. Why, you're the only person I know who rarely complains about anything. No matter what happens, you just handle it."

"That's called surviving, my friend. I'm a pro at it. And while we're on this deep, dark subject, as soon as we get the details of the show worked out, I have to make a fast trip home."

"Your daddy." It was more of a statement than a question.

Beth nodded. "The nursing home he's in now has been sold, and they're threatening to close it, saying it's not turning a profit."

"You believe that?"

"No, not at the prices they charge."

"Why don't you take Michael with you?"

Beth smiled for real this time. "Still trying to play cupid, huh?"

"I just don't understand how someone with as much on the ball as you could have stayed single all these years. The men around here must be blind."

Beth forced a lightness into her tone. "It's a long story, and one you definitely don't want to hear."

"You could do much worse than Michael, you know," Tracy said in the same light tone, as if sensing she had struck a raw nerve.

Beth sighed. "I won't deny that."

Two years ago she had met Michael Jumper at a political fund-raiser. Though several years her junior, he had worked his way up to a full partnership in a prestigious law firm in Natchitoches. He was handsome, divorced and sought after by half the single women in town. Yet he wanted Beth. She wanted him, too, but only as a friend.

For the longest time, even after the months of counseling, she'd flinched when it appeared a man might touch her. But it hadn't been the rape rearing its ugly head; it had been her feelings for Zach. They had never died.

She had been honest with Michael from the outset, telling him she wasn't interested in making a commitment. To date he hadn't pushed her, though she knew he must see other women, in spite of his denial.

"So?"

Beth blinked. "So what?"

"So why don't you take him with you? He could keep you company."

"Tracy, at this rate the freight will never get unpacked."

Tracy grinned. "In other words, don't press my luck, right?"

"Right."

"You're hopeless, you know," Tracy said on an exasperated note.

Beth winked. "I know."

Seventeen

Beth left the shop as twilight was battling the weakening sun for supremacy. In conjunction with the purring engine of her car, her stomach gurgled. It dawned on her then that she hadn't eaten since breakfast. Only when she was nervous did she think of food. Then she used it as a panacea for her anxiety.

Rather than take the time to stop and get something at a fast-food restaurant, she decided to take her chances at home. Surely the fridge contained something edible, although it had been ages since she'd been grocery shopping.

The evening was lovely, she thought, easing the Riviera out of her parking place. The In-Look, located on Front Street facing the Cane River, was in a prime location. Many old buildings and antebellum homes remained along the river and side streets, thus bringing throngs of tourists to the area.

But there was a down side to this location. When she walked or drove through these now-quiet streets, bittersweet memories of Cottonwood haunted her. Still, she was content here, in this small town often referred to as a miniature New Orleans.

During the Christmas season Natchitoches would be teeming with sightseers wending their way through a fairyland of thousands of lights. Streets, buildings, homes, riverbanks and bridges would soon be ablaze with them. The city was known throughout the South for its spectacular display of the Christmas spirit.

She always looked forward to that time of the year because business soared. When the tourists came to see the lights, they came with full pocketbooks.

Even though her condo was on the opposite side of town, Beth reached it in record time. However, she paused outside the door, reluctant as always to enter the house, a house where emptiness greeted her like a slap in the face.

It seemed to take delight in waiting for her every evening, that cold emptiness, hiding on the other side of the door, ready to devour her the minute she walked in and switched on the lights. It would rush at her in the same way the sounds of the moss-covered trees swaying in the wind rushed at her. She would find herself standing mute, like a small child afraid of the dark, unable to move.

As ridiculous as it was, she was afraid of her own house.

This evening offered no respite, though she refused to give in to the paranoia. Squaring her shoulders, Beth charged inside, where a large living area, furnished in wicker and warm colors, welcomed her. While her home was a far cry from Cottonwood, it was nevertheless adequate for her needs and should have acted as a soothing balm; only it didn't. She knew why. The mansion that graced the rich land of Shawnee was home. No other house, no matter where or how luxurious, would ever take its place.

After dropping her purse and briefcase onto the nearest chair, Beth headed for the kitchen, her feet sinking into the plush cinnamon carpet. Unfortunately it offered no relief to her aching feet and tired muscles.

She grabbed a Lean Cuisine from the freezer and popped it into the microwave. A few minutes later, as she ate, Beth found herself thinking about her impending visit to Shawnee.

"Leave it alone," she muttered aloud, jabbing her fork into the chicken breast.

Maybe Tracy was right; maybe she should consider marrying Michael. Anything was preferable to what she was going through now. She had to admit she ached for the things so many other women had: a home, children. But that was as far as it went. Old pains, old scars, always rose to the surface and snuffed out those longings.

Disgusted with her train of thought, Beth pushed her chair away from the table and made her way into the bedroom. She turned on the nearest lamp and paused to stretch tired muscles. Minutes later she was prepared for bed, only to have the idea suddenly lose its appeal.

Convinced she wouldn't be able to sleep, Beth walked outside to the patio. She immediately breathed in the cool night air. It shocked her system. Shivering slightly, she belted her cream-colored robe tighter around her and sat down.

Moonlight streamed across the tiny yard, illuminating the few leaves left on the trees. She could hear the wind atop the trees, moaning. Another norther was due to blow in; she assumed this was it. Somewhere close, a cricket chirped. The air smelled good, like leaves burning.

She closed her eyes and tried to empty her mind, willing herself to relax. But there were moments, like now, when the dry rattle of the past marched through her mind full force, sweeping everything aside, forcing her to dwell on that awful day when she had pushed Zach out of her life.

Without fail, the pain hit her with unbearable force. She wanted to sink to her knees and sob her eyes out. Although she regretted many things that had happened that day, she'd never regretted keeping the truth from Zach. For comfort she recalled the Bible story about the two women who claimed the same child and the king who said he would cut him in two and give one part to each. The one who really loved the child said no.

The truth would have cut Zach in half, destroyed him. What she did regret was her inability to let Zach go, to admit that he would never share her life again.

While the desire to regain possession of Cottonwood and avenge her rape still burned like a silent flame within her, another desire burned equally bright, if not more so—her love for Zach.

Once she'd healed in both body and spirit, she'd realized how much she still wanted him. And because he had never married, she often fantasized that they would get back together.

Those fantasies, however, had been short-lived. She could count on her fingers the times she'd seen Zach in the intervening years. With each encounter he'd left no doubt as to how he felt about her. He hated her.

Those cold green eyes had looked through her as if she no longer existed. *Don't hate me!* her heart had cried. *What I did, I did out of love.*

Each time she left Shawnee, she would plead with herself to let go of the past, let go of Zach. She had clung to her dreams for too long, knowing that sometimes pain was a crutch to hold on to when the alternative was no better.

Another shiver ran through her. At the same time the phone rang.

Quickly she went back into the living room and reached for the phone on a table at one end of the couch.

''Hello.''

''What'cha doin'?''

Recognizing her brother's voice immediately, Beth sank onto the couch, her legs suddenly unable to support her. ''Is something wrong?''

''Does something always have to be wrong for me to call?'' The whine in Trent's voice carried through the line.

''Either that or you want something.'' She tried to temper her sharp tone, but failed. ''Which is it this time?''

"You never change, do you? Too damned bad I'm not perfect like you."

"Trent...please," she said softly, painfully, his digs never failing to hit their mark.

Although Trent was twenty-two, he behaved most of the time as if he were sixteen. He was selfish and spoiled and had caused Beth more than one sleepless night. Yet he'd managed to stay off drugs and out of jail. For that Beth was thankful.

The years, however, had done little to eradicate Trent's resentment toward her. But then, they hadn't lessened her guilt toward him, either.

For the most part, her grandmother and Zach had borne the responsibility for her brother. In spite of his feelings for her, Zach hadn't reneged on his promise of long ago to help Trent. When Trent refused to go to college, Zach had put him to work in the mill.

Nothing, though, had quelled that wild and restless streak in Trent, a streak that over the years had been another bone of contention between them.

"Beth, are you still there?" Trent asked when the silence stretched.

"I'm still here."

"You're right, I do need something."

"Money."

"Yeah."

"How much?" Even to her own ears, her voice sounded hollow.

"Two hundred dollars."

"Two hundred! What on earth for?"

"Oh, for chrissake, don't make such a big deal out of it. I'll pay you back."

"That's not the point."

"That's the *only* point," Trent stressed in a cold tone. "Don't forget, I'm grown. I don't have to listen to any more lectures from you."

"And I don't have to lend you any money, either," Beth countered hotly.

"Aw, just forget it, then. I shoulda known better than to call you. I'll ask Zach."

"No! Don't you dare ask Zach for money." Beth struggled for a decent breath. "I'll send it to you. But when I get home, we're going to have a talk."

"I'm not a kid!"

"Then stop acting like one."

With that, Beth replaced the receiver, only to have it ring again, seconds later.

"Damn," she muttered under her breath. Enough of Trent was enough.

"Hello," she snapped.

"Beth?"

"Oh, hello, Michael," she murmured, momentarily disconcerted.

"Did I catch you at a bad time?"

He sounded so calm, so sane, so sweet that tears welled up in her eyes. "No, not at all."

"You sure?"

"I'm sure."

He didn't sound convinced. "I know it's late, but I wanted to talk to you."

"Is something wrong?"

"No. I just wanted to hear your voice."

Beth forced herself to relax. "That's nice."

"Are you all right?"

She was tempted to unburden herself on him, but she couldn't. It wouldn't be fair to him.

"Beth?"

"I'm—I'm glad you called," she said finally with a brave smile, trying to convince herself that she *could* settle for second best.

Eighteen

Beth lay against him. He could no more disentangle himself from her than he could still his pulse.

Her flesh was pliant and damp. Her nails sank into his back, while her tongue licked the flesh on his shoulder. She whimpered, then trembled against him as his hand made contact with the warm wetness at her thighs.

Abruptly, thunder broke apart the sky.

Beth brushed his hand away and, twisting, put her hot mouth on him, engulfing him. Needles of ecstasy jabbed him as he gave in to the mindless pleasure her lips and tongue were bringing him.

Thunder crackled again; rain slammed against the windowpane.

With a muted cry, Zach reached for her and lifted her atop him. Beth gasped. He convulsed and poured into her. . . .

With his heart hammering and sweat oozing out of every pore on his body, Zach sat straight up in bed as if he'd been shot from a cannon.

Had it been a pounding on his door that had awakened him from his dream, or had it been his pounding heart? While trying to control his trembling insides, he lay still and listened. Only the rain splintering against the window greeted him.

How did she do it? How was it possible, after all this time, for Beth to reduce him to scarcely more than a psychotic, babbling idiot? Again Zach felt the hard pangs of panic pressing on his chest. She had moved like a sorceress through his dreams, forcing his suppressed desires to the surface.

If the flesh-and-blood Beth were to walk into the room at this moment, he could deny her nothing. These dreams left his body yearning for her as if she were the food, drink and oxygen he required to live.

"Let it go, Winslow!" he muttered, leaning over and jerking open the drawer of his bedside table. Hands still shaking, he fumbled around until he found what he was looking for. Then, with another muttered curse, Zach latched onto a package of cigarettes and, before he had time to think, hung one between his lips and lit it. Only after he leaned back on the pillow did he take a long, deep puff, hoping it would ease the pounding in his head.

It didn't. It made him feel nauseated because he hadn't smoked in years. Still, he kept a pack near him just to prove that he was strong enough to leave them alone. Just as he had proved himself strong enough to leave Beth alone.

With only the glow from the lightning outside, Zach rummaged through the drawer again until he found an ashtray. He flicked the ashes from the butt into it, then ground it out unnecessarily roughly.

That was when he heard the loud knock, followed by, "Hey, man, wake up and let me in. It's raining like hell out here."

Immediately recognizing his assistant's somewhat strained voice, Zach lunged out of bed, turned on the lamp, then struggled into his jeans. Seconds later, he opened the front door.

Seconds later Matt Thorne stepped inside and shook himself like a wet dog. "I thought sure I'd drown before you got your carcass to the door."

Matt was not only Zach's right-hand man at the mill but a good friend, as well. He was short and he had a receding hairline, though he wasn't much older than Zach. He wore horn-rimmed glasses, and his skin had a red hue to it, suggesting either good health or bad booze. Zach knew it wasn't the latter, as Matt was into physical fitness to such an extreme that he didn't even drink so much as a beer.

Any other time Zach would have found his friend's predicament amusing, along with his out-of-sorts mood. Not tonight. Zach would put his rotten mood up against anyone and win the contest hands down.

"My carcass, as you so quaintly put it, was in bed, where it's supposed to be."

Matt brushed the back of his sleeve across his eyes, then narrowed them. "You don't look like you were asleep. In fact, you look awful."

"Just get to the point," Zach said, grinding his teeth. "You didn't come over here in the middle of the goddamn night to check on my condition."

Matt grinned. "Nope, you're right, but maybe I should have. What's the matter, you tie one on tonight?"

"Since when did you get to be such a nosy bastard?"

Matt shrugged, but his grin got wider. "That's part of the reason why you keep me around."

"Well, I just might rectify that if you don't tell me why you're standing here at one o'clock in the morning dripping on my floor."

The grin slid from Matt's face. "I tried to call, but you didn't answer. George Anderson got hurt on number two."

Zach rammed all five fingers through his hair, making it stand on end. "How bad?" His tone was terse.

"Bad enough, but not critical."

"Think I oughta go to the hospital?"

Matt scratched his chin. "No. Everything that can be done is being done."

Zach motioned with his hand. "You may as well come on in."

They were silent until they reached the den; then Zach faced Matt again and asked, "Want a towel?"

"Naw, I'm fine."

"Sure? How 'bout coffee?"

Matt's tired features brightened. "Yeah, that sounds good."

"Hope you don't mind instant."

Matt's face fell. "Forget it."

"Sorry," Zach said with a half smile.

"Bet you don't have anything decent to eat, either."

Ignoring his barb, Zach asked, "What about the machine?"

"The crew's hard at work on that baby now. But I just wanted to warn you that we may have to shut her down."

Zach took a deep breath. "Thanks for letting me know."

Matt snorted. "You'd have had my ass for sure if I hadn't, right?"

"Right."

"So I'll keep you posted."

"One of these days, maybe we'll replace number two."

"It'd be nice, but I'm not holding my breath."

Zach's smile was devoid of humor. "Don't."

"Hope I don't have to disturb you any more tonight, boss. Go back to your dreaming."

"I'll pass," Zach muttered under his breath, watching as Matt slammed the door behind him.

Moments later Zach crawled back into bed, wondering what was going to happen next. After flipping off the light, he eased his head back onto the pillow, but he was too keyed up to sleep. He lifted his head and stared at the ceiling, watching in fascination as the lightning danced across it, creating humanlike shadows. He was afraid that if he closed his eyes the dreams would start all over again.

Making up his mind that was not going to happen, Zach steered his thoughts to the mill. While it was prospering, and had for years after Taylor had made him a full partner, there were still daily problems that had to be dealt with.

On the whole he was proud of the work he'd done. As he'd predicted, the mill's profits had shot up. Although there had been royal battles when it came to making changes he'd wanted, he hadn't budged.

Still, there was more to do and a long way to go before Southland produced to its full potential. Replacing the number two machine was as much a top priority now as replacing number one had been years ago, especially if they were to fight off another takeover threat.

Suddenly Zach felt the urge to try another cigarette, only to steel himself against giving in. He had started smoking after Beth had left him. Then, several years later, he'd quit the nasty things, swearing never to touch them again.

But he hated it when one of the men got hurt. If another suffered the same fate, the union would be all over him like a dog on a june bug.

Let 'em come, he thought. He loved the challenge associated with his work. He always had.

If it wasn't for the dreams that pounced on him at the most unexpected times, like a thief waiting in the dark to clobber him, he could brag that he had not only won the important battles in his life but the wars, as well.

Yet it took only one of these gut-wrenching sexual fantasies to prove that he still belonged to the human race and that he, like other mortals, had a definite chink in his well-oiled armor.

Well, he would just have to work that much harder to repair the damage. He was hell-bent that one day Beth Melbourne would be purged from his mind forever, that when he saw her she wouldn't mean any more to him than the average woman on the street whom he'd never met and didn't care to.

He hated her. That hate had been his salvation, his anchor against the rage, the humiliation, the fear and the pain that had kept him raw and bleeding on the inside.

So where was the ultimate peace that such clarity of emotion should have brought him? Why was hatred failing him now? Why had it let these dreams sink their teeth into him again, recreating that excruciating pain?

Even now he could feel rage in his gut like a hot poker. With that feeling came the memories. For a moment Zach allowed the bitterness of long ago to touch him again.

Though Beth had rejected him, he hadn't felt the impact of that rejection until he'd gotten behind the wheel of his GTO. It had hit him then with the shock of an unexpected blow to the gut. The nightmare that had begun with Foster's stroke had come to an end. But not for him. The indisputable fact that it was over between them had plunged him into a nightmare of his own, more terrifying than anything he could ever have imagined. He had lost Beth. She no longer loved him. She had broken his frigging heart.

Afterward, he merely existed in a dark void. The light had gone out of his life. He ate; he slept; he worked. In fact, he'd never worked harder in his life than he had worked those first months and years.

The nights—God, they had been unbearable. They turned him into a crazed man. Beer, whiskey, anything he could get his hands on, had been his constant companion. And women. He had gone through a stable of women that would have made the hottest male heartthrob green with envy.

None, however, had brought the relief he'd sought. They had only increased the void, intensified the ache. In the end, his work, not the hate raging inside him, had saved him.

His family hadn't had that luxury. His parents had been certain their reputation was ruined for life.

His mother had cried, "Oh, Zachery, how could she do a thing like that? Why, we'll be the laughingstock of Shawnee."

"Goddamn it, she'll marry you if I have to drag her down that aisle," Taylor had bellowed.

"Forget it, Daddy. It's over." Zach's face had twisted. "If she got on her knees and begged, I wouldn't take her back." Surprisingly, it had been Beth's grandmother who had helped him the most. Even though Grace hadn't totally understood her granddaughter's sudden but irrevocable decision, she had sympathized with him, had been there for him when he thought he couldn't make it through another day.

Although he'd known Beth had returned to Shawnee numerous times, it was a year after their breakup before he saw her. At that, it had been by accident, an accident that was another jolt to his system, almost as traumatic as the first had been.

He had been to the nursing home to check on Foster, as he did at least once a week, if not more. Those weekly visits had started after Beth's departure. No one held a gun to his head. It had just seemed the right thing to do.

He'd been halfway down the walkway when he'd looked up and stopped in his tracks, while his breath congealed in his lungs.

He stepped back then, as if pushed by a giant, invisible hand. His eyes widened, and his lips parted.

"No!"

The whispered word came out sounding like a scream.

The past was staring him in the face again, making a mockery of his life. Blood rushed in his ears. Pain settled in his lungs and what was left of his heart. He had known this day would come, but he'd thought he was prepared. Only he wasn't. Oh, God, he wasn't.

In retrospect, he'd been convinced his imagination was overactive. Beth couldn't be that beautiful, that perfect.

But she was. She was every bit as beautiful as he'd imagined, if not more so. The jutting breasts, the softly rounded hips, the willowy legs that peeped from under her kelly green skirt, were all there.

Dear Lord, despite the hell she'd dragged him through, he felt the old attraction rear its ugly head. He groaned silently, felt his body tense, as if arched for flight. But fear and confusion rendered him motionless.

"Hello . . . Zach," Beth whispered haltingly.

His eyes traced the delicate line of an artery pulsing in her neck as if trying to pump life back into her suddenly bloodless complexion.

She was just as stunned by this unexpected meeting as he was, he thought with a twinge of brutal satisfaction.

When he didn't answer, she spoke again. "What—what are you doing here?"

The soft, summer voice poured into his bloodstream, and his heart constricted. "I came to see Foster."

"That's kind of you."

His lips were cotton dry, and he had to try twice before he could speak successfully. "Yeah." It was a harsh taunt.

She stepped closer, and when she did the fragrance of her hair filled the air around him.

"I—I want to thank you, too, for seeing about Trent and Gran."

Again her presence, her scent, seemed to mesmerize him, heightening his deep-seated fear of the sexual power she still wielded over him.

His face hardened, and he moved back. Even with the open space between them, they were still standing much too close.

"Look, you don't owe me a thing." His voice was curt and grating. "Let's just leave it at that."

There was anguish on her face. "You . . . won't even let me thank you?"

''Let's just cut the crap, all right? I can't think of one good reason to continue this conversation. As far as I'm concerned, we don't have anything to say to each other.''

She sucked in her breath and blinked twice, as if to resist any threat of tears. ''Don't . . . Zach. I . . . thought after all this time, we could at least be—''

He cut her off. ''No, we can't!''

Beth jerked, as if his words had hit her like a whiplash. ''You didn't even let me finish.''

''Didn't have to. I know what you were going to say.'' He folded his arms across his chest with rocklike immobility. ''I told you already, we can never be friends.''

''My God,'' she whispered. ''When did you become so cynical, so hard?''

He laughed bitterly. ''You're something, you know that? You're really something.''

He could see the tiny pulse at the base of her throat beating overtime, the same pulse that he had touched in passion. . . . Cursing silently, he tore his eyes away.

''You've changed. You're not—''

''You're right, I'm not!'' His voice shook with anger. ''I'm not the same chump you kicked in the gut a year ago. If I were you, I'd remember that.''

''Zach . . .''

Ignoring her plea, he hammered on. ''I know we have to see each other because of the mill. But in the meantime, you stay the hell out of my way, you hear? Just stay the hell away!''

Now, as Zach struggled to wipe that violent memory aside, he sat on the edge of the bed again and dropped his face into his hands. He didn't try to fight the awful feeling of hopelessness that washed through him.

Finally he lifted his head and stared into space. Was the hole in his heart one that even time itself could not heal?

Nineteen

The wind howled through the leafless trees like a lost baby crying for its mother. The sun hid behind a cloud, contributing to the growing chill in the air.

The couple in the car, tightly embracing, were oblivious to the weather. They were too intent on arousing each other.

Trent Melbourne tore his mouth away from the bottle-blonde's lips and sucked much-needed air into his lungs.

"Oh, Vicki, Vicki, I'm crazy about you."

Vicki Fairchild lifted her baby blue eyes to Trent and grinned, exposing a slightly crooked front tooth. That minor imperfection failed to detract from the young woman's freckle-faced beauty. If that wasn't enough, she had the body to go with the face. When standing, she was as tall as Trent, who measured just under six feet. But she wasn't gangly. Her curves were in all the right places.

She had recently graduated from college in Natchitoches and was staying with her parents in Shawnee until she decided whether she wanted to go back to school for a masters or get a job.

"I bet you tell that to everybody you date," she said, a husky but teasing tremor in her voice.

Trent grinned. "Why, honey, that's not true. Anyway, you're the only one I'm seeing. When are you going to start trustin' me?" he asked in a drawl at the same time that he slipped a hand inside her bra and tweaked a nipple.

Vicki rolled her head and moaned. "Please . . . don't."

"What do you mean, please don't?" His hand now surrounded the entire breast.

Vicki opened her eyes and looked around. "I ...mean ... we shouldn't ...not with your friend coming."

Trent grimaced. "Bill Glass is no friend of mine. He's a muscle man sent to collect. But don't worry about him now," Trent added, removing his hand from her breast and easing it down her flat stomach. "He'll be late to his own funeral. Let's move to the back seat." His hand dipped lower. "And take care of pressing business."

Vicki placed her hand over his. "Trent ... please," she pleaded again. "I don't want to be doing it when Bill comes."

"Aw, baby, come on. We'll hear him when he drives up."

Trent's souped-up Mustang was parked on a deserted road at the edge of town, where there was little if any traffic.

"It's broad daylight." Vicki's eyes darted toward the back window. "Someone else might see us."

Trent scowled and pulled back. "Not in this godforsaken hole in the road, they won't." He paused and looked at her through narrowed eyes. "You tryin' to tell me somethin', honey?"

"No, of course not," Vicki responded quickly. "It's just that I don't like to have to rush when ...when we do it."

Trent's face lightened somewhat. "Now that you put it like that, it makes sense. Guess I'll have another beer."

Vicki lifted a strand of long hair and twirled it around a finger. "Haven't you had enough?" Her tone was hesitant.

"Hey, you're not my keeper." His face clouded with anger. "Nobody tells me what to do."

"Maybe they should," Vicki said without rancor, her voice barely audible.

Trent's temper flared anew, and bitterness shone from his eyes. "I've been doing what I damn well pleased since I was twelve years old, when my old man had a crippling stroke and my sister hauled ass and left me with my grandmother.''

Vicki gulped visibly. "Sorry, I didn't mean to say that. It's just that you're driving."

"So fucking what?"

Vicki's lower lip began to tremble, and she stared at him wide-eyed. "Don't be mad at me. I didn't mean to sound bossy."

"Ah, shucks, honey, when you look at me like that I can't stay mad at you."

She smiled. "Good."

Grinning, Trent reached into the back seat and pulled two beers out of a foam cooler. He popped both tops, then handed one can to her.

For a minute they sipped in silence, the wind whipping around the vehicle, playing havoc with it.

Finally Vicki spoke. "Did you have any trouble getting the money?"

Trent took another swig of beer, then wiped his mouth with the back of his hand. "How'd you know about that?"

She flashed him a puzzled look. "You told me, remember?"

He shrugged. "Yeah, I do now. That was the night I got lit and Bill hit me up for the money. Right?"

Vicki nodded.

Trent turned away from her and stared out the window into the sunlight. "I had to ask my sister for it."

"Bet you hated that."

"Had no other choice," he said sullenly, one hand tightening around the steering wheel. His knuckles turned white. "I couldn't ask Zach for another advance on my check. He'd have told me to take a flying leap. Didn't dare ask Gran, either." Trent was silent for a moment. "There just never seems to be enough money."

"And Bill wouldn't let you wait to pay him back?"

"Are you kiddin'? That son of a bitch told me to have it today or he'd break both my legs."

Vicki clutched at his arm. "Are you serious?"

"Damn straight I'm serious."

"Trent, please, promise me you'll stay away from the tracks. I'm really scared this time."

He shrugged off her hand. "'Fraid I can't do that. The track is in my blood the same as it was in my old man's." He fell silent again and stared into the distance. "That's what ruined us, you know."

"I know."

Trent smirked. "It's been years since we lost everything, and people still talk about the fall of the mighty Melbournes like it was yesterday."

"You can't let that bother you."

He harrumphed. "That's easy for you to say." Suddenly he looked into the rearview mirror. "Ah, here's Bill. Sit tight. I'll be right back."

True to his word, he climbed back into the Mustang five minutes later.

Vicki's eyes shot him a wordless query.

"No problem," Trent said, cranking the engine. "Reach me another beer, will ya, honey?"

He guzzled down half of it before pulling out onto the highway.

"Where to?" Vicki asked, watching as he anchored the can between his legs.

He flashed her a leering grin. "My place, of course."

A silence fell between them as Vicki nestled close to his side, resting her head against his shoulder.

"Damn!"

Vicki's head popped up. "What's wrong?"

"Guess."

"Cops?"

"Righto."

"Are—are they after us?"

"Since the dude's lights are flashing and we're the only ones around, I'd say that's a safe bet."

"What—what are you going to do?" Vicki's voice held fear.

"What do you think?"

Vicki laid a trembling hand on Trent's arm. "Pull over, I hope."

"No way, baby, no way."

Beth slowly steered her car through Shawnee's early-evening traffic. Having just left the nursing home, she knew she must look a sight. Traces of tears still marked her cheeks. Her appearance was of little consequence, though, as she was going to her grandmother's and no place else.

No matter how often she saw her daddy sitting in his wheelchair, either in his room or on the lawn, the cowlick on the top of his head sticking straight up, she wanted to scream her pain for all the world to hear.

She had learned to endure, if not accept, his inability to move, to communicate. But the vacant look in his eyes proved her undoing every time. It tore at her heart and reawakened the guilt that lay dormant inside her.

From somewhere she found the strength to cope, to pull herself together so that her facade dared anyone to pity her for the scandal that had robbed the Melbournes of their good name and fortune.

That facade had been carefully in place when she'd confronted the nursing-home administrator. However, the news she had received had been good. She had learned that the deal to sell the home had fallen through. So until the owners found another buyer, the home would continue as it was. Still, the trauma of eventually having to search for a new facility loomed like a thundercloud.

Above-average facilities that cared for the elderly as well as the incapacitated were rare. Beth had thought long and hard about moving Foster to Natchitoches, but she had

never been able to take that drastic a step. Besides, with
nine shops to oversee, she was gone too much. In Shawnee, Trent, Gran and her father's friends were there to see
about him. And Zach. She couldn't forget him. He had remained faithful in visiting Foster, for which she was grateful.

Guilt weighed heavily on her for not coming home
sooner. But now that she was here, she was looking forward to Gran and Jessie pampering her. The past few
months had been hectic. She had been to market in both
Dallas and New York. Also, she'd spent two months
working in the Houston store while she searched for a new
manager.

The only dark spot on an otherwise favorable horizon
was her upcoming chat with her brother. She intended to
find out what he had needed two hundred dollars for,
whether he liked it or not.

In addition, she had Rachel on the agenda. She couldn't
wait to see her, especially after the way her friend had
sounded on the phone yesterday.

"Oh, Beth, I can't wait to see you!" she had cried.

"Same here, Rach."

"Can we have lunch?"

"I don't see why not. I'm planning to stay a few days."

"Terrific."

"You sound higher than a kite. What's up?"

"Oh, Beth, I'm so happy, I'm afraid I just might burst a
blood vessel."

Beth laughed knowingly. "It wouldn't have anything to
do with a man, now, would it?"

"Well . . ."

"You devil, stop tormenting me. Tell me."

"No."

"No! What do you mean, 'no'?" Beth practically
shouted into the receiver.

Rachel chuckled as if enjoying herself. "Not over the phone. This is look-you-in-the-eye kind of news."

"I'm going to strangle you when I see you."

"Promise you'll be happy for me instead." Rachel's tone had turned serious.

"Silly, why wouldn't I be? After Rory, you deserve a break."

"Call me the minute you hit town."

"Will do."

As her thoughts continued to dwell on Rachel, Beth was delighted that her friend had found someone deserving of her. When Rachel's marriage had broken up two years ago, she had thought her life was over. During those first terrible months, she had come often to Natchitoches, using Beth as a sounding board.

Beth hadn't minded. That was what friends were for, she told Rachel whenever she would apologize. Too, it had given Beth a chance to repay a long-standing debt. If it hadn't been for Rachel's support when Foster had had his stroke, Beth wouldn't be sane today.

Following her divorce, Rachel had moved back to Shawnee and gotten a job as a secretary for a local realtor. While Beth knew Rachel had never lacked for men friends, she'd had no idea she had gotten serious about someone. She was thrilled by the sudden turn of events and looking forward to their lunch date.

It wasn't until Beth braked at the red light adjacent to the local drive-in that the old familiar lump appeared in her throat. She and Zach, and Rachel, too, had spent many hours cruising this area.

Suddenly she found herself fighting off a feeling of nostalgia. Some things never changed. Thank God Shawnee was one of them. It was still the same small, laid-back Southern town it had been when she left.

The train still whistled down the tracks that paralleled the only main street. Spanish moss still draped the huge oak trees. The proud old houses and brick sidewalks still heralded the quieter, gentler living of the past.

Minutes later, when Beth pulled into the driveway of her grandmother's modest but comfortable home, she noticed that Trent's car was not in the garage. She shouldn't have been surprised. It was Friday evening. More than likely he was with friends—or a girl.

Beth let herself in the front door, then immediately paused and shed her plum-colored gabardine jacket, hanging it on the hall-tree.

Her grandmother's house had always been a second home to her. The interior seemed to be without walls. The living room became the dining room, which sort of blended into the kitchen and so on. Polished hardwood floors and antique furniture brightened with cushions made for a cozy and warm atmosphere.

"Gran? Jessie?"

"Beth, honey, is that you?"

"Where are you, Gran?"

"In the kitchen."

Before Beth could take a step, Grace Childress rushed toward her, her arms outstretched, her face radiant.

Wordlessly they embraced; then Beth pulled back and said, "Oh, Gran, you look wonderful, as usual."

And she did. Even though she was in her late seventies, Grace didn't look it, nor did she act it. She remained one of the most beautiful women Beth had ever seen, both inside and out.

"Well, I can't say the same for you, child," Grace said, her piercing black eyes scrutinizing Beth. "Why, you're much too pale, and I do believe you've lost more weight."

Beth grinned. "Well, I'm sure that gumbo I smell will put several pounds on me."

Grace answered her grin. "You noticed, huh?"

"Jessie knows my favorite."

"I'll have you know Jessie didn't fix it this time."

"Oh?" Beth's brows came together. "By the way, where is Jess?"

"She's sitting with an ill friend. She hated to miss you, but it couldn't be helped. Her friend had no one else."

"I'm sorry, but I understand."

Grace grabbed Beth's hand and swung it. "We can eat whenever you're ready. We don't have to wait for Trent."

"Speaking of my brother, where is he?"

For an instant Grace frowned, putting stress on her delicate, crepelike skin. "With friends, I'm sure. But before we discuss Trent, why don't you slip into something more comfortable?"

A short time later Beth strode back into the kitchen wearing a pair of tight-legged jeans and a blue sweater.

"Feel better?" Grace asked from where she stood in front of the stove.

"Actually, I feel like a new woman, so much so that I'm not going to let you wait on me."

"You'll do as you're told, young lady." Another radiant smile took the sting out of Grace's words. "Now, you have a seat and leave everything to me."

Beth was about to do exactly that when the doorbell rang.

"Expecting company?" she asked, raising her eyebrows.

Grace shook her head. "No, but that doesn't mean anything. It's probably someone hunting Trent. This place is like Grand Central Station."

Beth shrugged before padding sock-footed toward the door. When she was halfway there the bell rang again.

"I'm coming, I'm coming," she muttered.

Without bothering to check the peephole, Beth jerked open the door.

Zach stood on the porch.

"Oh," she said breathlessly, feeling the bottom drop out of her stomach.

Zach didn't say a word; he merely stared at her as if she were a ghost.

She circled her lips with her tongue. "What—what are you doing here?"

"I came to see your grandmother." He paused and drew a harsh breath. "Trent's been arrested."

Twenty

Beth stared at him, a stupefied expression on her face, and while she wanted to respond, she could not. Nor could she move. Not only was she having trouble comprehending what Zach had just told her, but she was having trouble with the undisputed fact that he was standing in front of her in the flesh.

Despite such unexpected and bizarre conditions, she had the irrational urge to fling herself into his arms. Every time she saw him, the years seemed to disappear until they were once again together.

But nothing could be further from the truth. Zach himself was testimony to that. He had recovered from his apparent shock at seeing her. His face was blank. Only his eyes were alive; they glittered like pinpoints of steel.

Pain jabbed Beth in the heart so fiercely that she had to say something or scream. But before she could get the words out, her grandmother rounded the corner.

"Beth, honey—" Grace began, only to stop, then break into a smile. "Why, Zach, what a nice surprise."

"Hello, Gran," he said in a slightly rough but warm voice.

Still smiling, as if oblivious to the suffocating tension in the air, Grace swung her gaze back to Beth. "Where's your manners, child? Y'all should be in the living room where it's comfortable, not standing here with the door wide open."

With that, Grace walked away. Apparently sensing she wasn't being followed, she hesitated, then turned back around, a frown reshaping her carefully arched brows. Quickly she looked from Beth to Zach.

"What's wrong?" she asked. "Has something happened?"

A flush replaced Zach's pallor. His eyes sought Beth's as if to say, please, help me out here.

Beth dragged her gaze away and faced her grandmother, whose pallor had become more pronounced.

"It's Trent, Gran."

Grace lifted a hand to her heart. "Oh, no," she whispered. "Is he—?"

"No, Gran," Beth said, rushing to her side and placing an arm around her shoulders. "He's—he's not hurt, if that's what you were about to say." After feeling her grandmother relax against her, she went on, "He's been arrested, that's all."

"That's all!" What little color was left in Grace's face swiftly disappeared.

"He's in jail, actually," Zach put in, shifting from one foot to the other.

"In jail," Grace repeated dumbly. "What—what did he do?"

"Why don't you sit down?" Zach said. "Then we'll talk."

It was clear from the expression on his face and his sympathetic tone that he feared the older woman was about to faint, or worse.

Beth's arm tightened around Grace's shoulders. "Come on, Gran, do as he says. You're trembling all over."

No one said a word until they reached the comfort of the small living room, where a fire burned softly and unobtrusively in the fireplace.

"What happened, Zach?" Beth asked, sinking onto the couch beside her grandmother.

Zach had positioned himself by the fireplace and was resting an arm on the mantel. He stared at a point beyond her shoulder when he spoke. "He tried to outrun the cops."

Both women gasped.

Then Grace asked, "Oh, dear me, Lord, why would he do a thing like that? Surely he knew he couldn't get by with it." She reached into her pocket and pulled out a tissue. "Is—is he all right? I mean . . ."

Zach pinched the bridge of his nose. "He's fine. A little shaken up, of course."

Tears gathered in Grace's eyes, and her chin began to quiver. "Will you and Zach see about him?" she asked, clutching Beth's hand. "Should—should we call Andrew?"

Without looking at Zach, Beth brushed a stray hair off Grace's damp cheek. "If I . . . if we promise to take care of things, will you go to your room and lie down?"

"Oh, but I couldn't. . . ."

"Beth's right, you know," Zach put in quietly. "You rest and leave everything to us."

Zach's calm tone and take-charge attitude seemed to be the tonic Grace needed. With Beth's help she rose, then gave him a tentative but thankful smile.

"Gran, do you want me to come with you?" Beth asked anxiously, standing with her hands clenched in front of her.

"No, dear. I'll be fine. You just take care of your brother."

Once Beth and Zach were alone, silence filled the room.

Finally Zach turned to her, his features tight and unrelenting. Gone was the softness that had been there a moment ago when he'd dealt with the older woman.

Despair filled Beth as she sat down on the comfortably upholstered sofa. Not only did she have to deal with the stunt Trent had pulled, but she had to deal with Zach's uncompromising attitude toward her, as well. Both were bitter pills to swallow.

"I screwed up, didn't I?" Zach's voice was hard.

"What do you mean?"

Without answering, he twisted around, grabbed the poker next to him and punched the fire until the flames rose higher.

For one stolen moment Beth thrust aside the reason he was there and simply looked at him.

The years since their breakup had made a marked difference in Zach, even more than in herself, she thought.

There were lines around his mouth and eyes that hadn't been there before. She could tell that they weren't marks of age, but of pain. He seemed larger, too; not heavier, but more muscular through the chest and shoulders. And his forehead creased in a way she didn't remember.

The most significant change was that he was all grown up. He was a man now, a man with brains who could think on his feet and shoot straight. He had developed a quickness and strength that helped him beat the union boys at hardball.

But the sparkle in his eyes was no longer visible, nor was the smile that had once so vividly curved his lips. Rather, he looked as if he never smiled.

Had she done that to him?

Still, he had more power than any man she knew. Men feared him; women loved him. Dressed now in a charcoal jacket and tight gray pants, he looked wonderful. His dark hair, dashed with gray, grazed the collar of his white shirt, unbuttoned enough to hint at the hairy mat beneath.

"I should never have come here."

His voice jolted Beth out of her thoughts. "Gran had to know," she finally said, battling the sad heaviness inside her.

"I'm not so sure."

"Trust me, you did the right thing."

"I thought your grandmother was stronger."

"She is, except where Trent's concerned."

"That figures."

"Was he drunk?"

A frown slashed Zach's face. "No, but he'd sure as hell been drinking. The alcohol level in his blood was high."

"It's serious, isn't it?"

"Very."

"Prison?" Beth had trouble getting the ugly word past her lips.

"Maybe not, since it's his first offense."

"Thank God for that."

"He wasn't alone, you know."

Beth's stomach revolted. "Who—who was with him?"

"A young woman by the name of Vicki Fairchild."

"Is she okay?"

"She's fine. If it hadn't been for her, though, they both might well have been a statistic. She talked Trent into stopping."

"You saw her?"

"Yeah, I came straight here from the jail."

"Trent? What about him?"

"I only saw him for a minute."

Beth lunged off the sofa and began pacing the floor. "If only I'd been around more," she lamented. "I feel like I've failed him."

"But you weren't and you did," Zach said flatly.

Beth stopped midstride, his hurtful words causing a painful, aching trembling that choked off her breathing. "I did what I had to do, Zach," she said softly.

"Sure." His top lip curled backward.

"Are you saying I'm to blame for Trent's actions?"

He shrugged. "If the shoe fits, wear it."

"That's a terrible thing to say!"

"It's the truth, isn't it?" He paused and rubbed the back of his neck. "How could I have been so wrong about you? When your daddy had that stroke and you lost everything, you couldn't cope. Your grandmother wasn't enough. Trent wasn't enough. And I damn sure wasn't.''

His criticism stuck her like a hot needle. "How dare you sit in judgment of me!''

His eyes flamed as he quickly closed the gap between them. "Oh, I dare, all right. I dare to do and say any damn thing I please.''

"Oh, I forgot. No one crosses the mighty Zachery Graham Winslow and gets by with it.'' Sarcasm dripped like acid from her lips.

A muscle jerked in his jaw. "If I were you, I wouldn't push my luck.''

"What are you going to do, hit me?''

"I just might,'' he ground out with suppressed violence. "Lord knows I've thought about it long and hard enough.''

Suddenly the fight went out of Beth and she felt sick. Still she couldn't move, even though everything about him affected her, from the heat of his body to the height that forced her eyes up to meet his. He was devastatingly sensual. And dangerous. Her nerves felt as if they were prickling through her skin.

"Why do we do this to each other?'' she whispered, her throat throbbing painfully, her voice almost gone.

He gazed down at her for a few moments longer, then turned away abruptly, as if he'd been stung.

"The past is over, Zach,'' she whispered to his back.

He spun around, looking hollow, as if there were nothing inside him. "Is it, Beth? Is it really?''

She laughed, but without humor. "Oh, I get it. It'll never be over until you exact your pound of flesh. Right?''

"Wrong. As a matter of fact, I couldn't give a sweet goddamn one way or the other.''

Again his cruelty cut her deeply. Whimpering, she placed a hand against her mouth and stepped back.

Zach cursed, then released a deep, shaky breath, as if he, too, felt the effects of their verbal skirmish.

When the silence became unbearable, he said, "We'd better get down to the jail."

Although his tone was even, Beth thought she detected a sliver of panic. Good. She wanted him to suffer just as he'd made her suffer. "Will . . . you call Andrew?"

"I already have."

"Well, if you're going to give me the third degree, let's get it over with." Trent's surly words were directed at Beth.

They were back at their grandmother's. Beth, however, was still shaken by her visit to the police station. Andrew had met them there and assured them that Trent would soon be released.

Beth had questioned the attorney as to Vicki Fairchild's whereabouts. He had told her that the girl's mother had come to the station and picked her up. Beth would have questioned Andrew further, but Trent's appearance had forestalled her.

Soon afterward they left the jail and headed back to the house. Expecting Zach to simply let them out and drive off, Beth had been disconcerted when he shoved the car in park and followed them inside.

Now, as she watched Zach turn a sharp look on Trent, her alarm was renewing itself.

"I'd be careful how I spoke to my sister, if I were you," Zach said, a warning in his voice for all to hear.

Trent glared at Zach, but he didn't say anything. Instead, he poked the floor with the toe of one shoe.

"Trent," Beth said softly. "Look at me."

His eyes were defiant. "If you think I'm going to bend over like a child and let you spank my ass, you can forget it!"

Zach took a step toward him. "You'd best watch your mouth, boy!"

"Sorry," Trent muttered, stealing a glance at Beth from under his long lashes.

"What is it you want, Trent?" Beth could hear the pleading note in her own voice, but she was desperate to find out what was driving her brother toward self-destruction. "You have so much to offer, so much potential. You're just wasting it."

Trent inhaled sharply. "Save the psychology, will ya? It's wasted on me. Anyway, how the hell would you know? You're never around."

"Oh, Trent!" Beth cried. "That's not fair. I've been working for your future as well as mine."

"Yeah," he sneered.

Unable to stand the thought of seeing the I-told-you-so look in Zach's eyes, Beth kept her face averted.

"I didn't do anything but drink a few beers," Trent mumbled into the lengthening silence.

"And get your butt hauled to jail," Zach finished for him. "You call that nothing?"

Trent grimaced. "It won't happen again."

"Well, it damn sure better not." Zach paused. "Not if you want to continue to work at the mill, that is."

Trent straightened angrily. "You can't fire me. Don't forget, we still own part of the mill."

"Stop it, Trent!" Beth cried. "Stop it right now. Think about what you're saying!"

"Your sister's right. You'd best start thinking. I'm not your enemy here. Neither is Beth. We're on your side. But what you did this evening is serious shit. And unless you get your head on straight, the judge is liable to use you as an example."

Zach's words seemed to have a sobering effect on Trent, because when he spoke, his voice shook slightly. "You're right." Then, switching his gaze to Beth, he said, "I'm tired. Mind if I hit the sack?"

Beth sighed. "Stop in and see your grandmother first."

Trent walked to the door, his shoulders slumped dejectedly.

"Haven't you forgotten something?" Beth asked.

Trent pulled up short and pivoted on his heels, his face flushed. "Er... thanks, Zach."

"Any time."

"You're right, things have totally gotten out of hand," Beth said the instant Trent was out of hearing range. "He's gotten...completely impossible. Gran..." Beth shook her head. "I had no idea."

"Ah, hell, he'll be all right. He's no worse than any other twenty-two-year-old."

"I wish I could believe that." Beth toyed with her lower lip. "He's got so much hate and anger inside him, so much more than I ever imagined."

"He's going to have to grow up sooner or later. Sure, he's had a rough go of it, but so have a lot of others."

"I know, but he... just needs to be loved," she said through a full throat. "I...thought leaving him with Gran was the answer."

"Love isn't all he needs right now."

Not pretending to misunderstand him, she smiled on one side of her mouth. "I agree. A good swift kick in the backside probably wouldn't hurt." The smile reached the other side of her mouth.

Suddenly Zach's eyes softened and he took a step toward her, as if her smile had suddenly unfrozen his heart. But then he stopped.

Their eyes collided urgently, then locked together.

Beth felt as though all the air inside her had been siphoned out; it was impossible to think, to see, to breathe.

Zach cleared his throat. "Look, I gotta go."

Beth nodded, unable to speak.

It seemed as if he had something more he wanted to say. She waited with her heart in her throat, but the moment passed.

"Later," he muttered brusquely, then turned and stamped toward the door.

''Zach.''

He spun around, his eyes suddenly vacant.

''Thanks for—''

He waved a hand, cutting her off.

The silence that followed his departure brought the tears that had been threatening all evening to Beth's eyes. Using the door for support, she leaned against it and let them fall unchecked.

Twenty-One

Zach stalked down the steps and jerked open the door to his car. Once behind the wheel, he sat there for a while, then, swearing, he slammed the door and jammed the key into the ignition.

A light sheen of perspiration broke out across his upper lip. His nerves were as tightly strung as a rubber band.

He muttered another expletive before steering the Cadillac onto the street, purposely thrusting all thoughts of Beth and those huge doe eyes out of his mind.

The gods refused to smile on him. No matter how hard he tried, he couldn't erase the vision of Beth's beautiful, grief-stricken face from his mind. His thoughts were flying faster than the wheels of his vehicle.

Her face was on the windshield before him, on the pavement ahead of him, speeding with him along the dark road.

"No!" The tiny word came out sounding as if it had been dug from the depths of his soul. He'd made a new life for himself, one that didn't include Beth. He would be damned if he'd let her sink her tentacles into him again.

He was worrying needlessly, wasn't he? After all, he no longer loved her. But she had made a fool of him, and for that he had never forgiven her. She had been like a sickness inside him, or at least, that was the way a friend had described it. He had never stopped to analyze the feeling. He just knew it was there, driving him every day of his life, that all-consuming desire to even the score with Beth.

Given that, what he couldn't understand was why he had reacted so strongly to her this evening. Granted, this was the first time they had actually said more than a few words to each other. Mostly they had passed like ships in the night. So was it the sudden and close proximity of this evening that had brought to life buried desires and longings?

Maybe, maybe not. Either way, he was in a heap of trouble.

Though it galled him he had to admit that, for a second, he'd been tempted to haul her into his arms, smash his lips against hers, rip her clothes off and satisfy an almost animal ferocity that was tearing his guts to shreds.

That weakness within himself infuriated him. He could feel it like a lump sitting in the center of his chest. She had gotten too close; she had found cracks in his defenses that he was unprepared for. But next time, he would be prepared.

Beth was the past. New plans were in the offing for the future, and nothing—and no *one*—was going to upset them.

By the time Zach swung the car into his parking place at the mill, his entire body was drenched with sweat. Without pausing, he threaded his way through the office proper until he reached a small anteroom that contained nothing but weights.

He shed his jacket immediately, raised his arms and peeled off his shirt. Seconds later he was down to his briefs and eyeing the weights in front of him.

When he finished his workout, Beth would be crammed back into the dark recesses of his mind where she belonged, nothing but a bittersweet memory.

"You're looking exceptionally lovely this morning, my dear."

Hoping to buoy her spirits as well as dress for lunch with Rachel, Beth had put on a rust-colored skirt and oversize sweater.

Beth smiled at her grandmother. "You like my outfit, huh? It's from the shop. We just got it in."

"That's your color, no doubt about it."

Changing the subject, Beth asked, "So how do you feel?"

She had joined Grace earlier in the breakfast nook for cereal and sweet rolls. They had just pushed their empty plates away and were enjoying their second cup of coffee.

Although Grace smiled, there were shadows lurking behind that smile. Again Beth had the urge to throttle her brother for causing her grandmother unnecessary pain.

"Now that Trent is out of that awful place, I feel fine."

Beth tilted her head. "You really had Zach and me worried last night."

"I was worried, too, only not about myself. Wasn't it kind of Zach to do what he did?"

Beth sighed. "I don't know why he keeps putting up with Trent. Thank God he does, though. Speaking of my brother, how was he feeling this morning?"

When she'd gotten up at seven-thirty, he had already left for the mill. A part of her had been glad, because she dreaded another face-to-face confrontation. Still, shirking her duty wasn't the answer, either.

"A bit subdued, actually," Grace was saying. "And humble."

"Good. Maybe this has taught him a lesson."

"What—what's going to happen to him?" Grace's eyes suddenly filled with tears. "I...you don't suppose he'll go to...?"

"Prison. I hope not, but more for your sake than his."

Gran's eyes implored her. "Oh, please, don't say that."

Beth drained the last of her coffee, then pushed her empty cup aside. "I don't mean it. You know that. But something needs to make him grow up."

"I'm putting my faith in Zach."

Beth's hand moved in a silent gesture of protest. "Oh, Gran, don't do that. It's not his place."

"I beg to differ with you, my dear. For years now, Zach has tried hard to include Trent in the mill. And well he should. After all, half of it belongs to you and Trent." Grace paused and sipped on her coffee. "Since Foster's unable to carry on, the responsibility lies with your brother. Besides, Zach *wants* to help Trent. He's exactly the influence the boy needs."

"Trent's not a boy any longer, Gran. He's a twenty-two-year-old man."

Gran's features softened, and she went on as if Beth hadn't interrupted. "Zach's doing it because of you."

Beth looked blank. "Me?"

"Don't play dumb with me, young lady." Grace's tone was mildly chastising. "He's taking Trent under his wing because of you."

"You couldn't be more wrong."

Again Grace seemed to ignore Beth. "If only you and Zach..."

"Please, don't," Beth said sharply, more sharply than she had intended, especially when she saw her grandmother flinch. "There's no point in resurrecting old bones," she added in a gentler tone, "or getting your hopes up."

"You're right, of course, only—"

Beth cut her off. "How did we get onto this subject, anyway? We were talking about Trent."

"Ah, yes, my grandson. Did you know he's moving into an apartment?"

Beth raised her eyebrows. "No, but I'm all for it. But how do you feel about it?"

"I'll miss him, of course. But I think he has a girl now that he cares about, so maybe it's the best thing."

"Vicki Fairchild?"

"How did you know?"

"She was with him when he got arrested."

"Oh, my."

"I was hoping to meet her, but she'd already left when Zach and I got down to the station."

"I've met her once, and from what I could tell she's crazy about Trent. Hopefully, she'll give him the love he needs."

"Oh, Gran, why is it that no one thinks *I* love him? You of all people should know better."

Grace reached across the table and covered one of Beth's hands and squeezed it. "Of course I know better, but . . ."

"But what?" Beth pressed, feeling the need to further defend herself. "How could I have done things any differently? Even if I could have taken him with me, he would have been miserable. He's always resented me. You know that. But I love him, and I want him to be a responsible person, have a home, a family and an important place in the mill. And someday Cottonwood," she added quietly.

"Are you sure that's not *your* dream you're trying to push off on him?" Grace asked, her tone unaccusing but troubled.

"Maybe," Beth responded defensively. "What's wrong with that?"

Before Grace could answer, the phone rang. Beth scooted her chair back and reached for it.

A few seconds later Beth said, "Rach, is that you?"

"Yes," came the croaking voice on the other end.

"Heavens, you sound awful."

"I feel awful," Rachel wailed. "I've got a dilly of a case of the flu."

"Gosh, I'm sorry. Is there anything I can do?"

"Well, you can take the shot in the rear that the doctor's sure to give me."

Rachel was deathly afraid of needles and always had been. Beth smiled. "I'd do most anything for you, my friend, but that one I'll pass on."

"Chicken," Rachel chided.

Beth laughed and winked at her grandmother.

"I'm sorry about lunch."

"Me, too, but there's always another time, even though I'm dying to hear your news."

"We'll make it a point to get together before you leave."

"I'll call you tomorrow. You take care of yourself, you hear?"

When Beth hung up, Grace had cleared the table and was frowning. "I hate to go off and leave you, especially now that your date fell through."

Beth held up her hand. "You go ahead with your club friends. This tour has been planned for months, and I wouldn't think of letting you cancel."

"You could come with us." Grace sounded wistful.

Beth shook her head. "Look, don't worry about me. I'll probably spend most of the day with Daddy."

Reverend Paul Broussard gave the swing another push. His gray hair stood on end as he laughed along with the child. Beth, having pulled alongside the curb moments before, watched from inside her car. Foster sat beside her.

After her grandmother had left, Beth had slipped out of her sweater and skirt and put on a long-sleeved cotton blouse and jeans. As a precaution against the October chill she had looped a cardigan around her neck and driven to the nursing home.

The various and sundry chores that she liked to do for her daddy, like trim his nails, cut his hair and replenish his wardrobe, had taken the biggest part of the morning. The hands-on contact made her feel closer to her daddy.

Once she was finished, she'd had two attendants lift Foster into the front seat of her car. Although Foster couldn't get out of the vehicle, he could enjoy the ride, or at least that was what she told herself.

The park was their first stop. Beth leaned over and kissed her daddy on the cheek. "I'll be right back, okay?"

The reverend was still swinging the child when she approached.

"Hello, Uncle Paul," she said, easing up beside him and slipping an arm through his.

He turned abruptly. "Why, Beth, what a nice surprise." A wide grin made the tired lines around his mouth completely disappear.

"I see you haven't changed. Still going all out for the underprivileged."

He shrugged. "Someone has to."

"So how are you?"

"Just right," he said, beaming.

Beth smiled.

"Can you spare an old man a moment?"

"Sure."

While Beth looked on, Paul stopped the swing and lifted the small, pixie-faced girl onto the ground. "Meg, honey, you run along and play with the others. We'll swing again later."

The child stared up at Beth with unbridled curiosity.

Beth smiled and squatted so that they were eye level. "Hello, Meg."

"Who are you?"

Paul laughed. "Ah, the bluntness of children."

Beth tweaked a dark curl. "I'm Beth. How old are you?"

"Four."

"Are you going to get all dressed up and go trick-or-treating soon? Get lots of candy?"

Meg's lower lip protruded and she hung her head.

Realizing something was wrong, Beth raised troubled eyes to Paul.

He ruffled Meg's curls. "Tell her of course you are."
When Meg didn't respond, he added, "Why don't you say
bye to the nice lady and go play with the others? I'll be
along shortly."

Meg looked at Beth for a moment longer, then scampered off.

"What a delightful child," Beth said, standing up. "Only
I put my foot in my mouth, didn't I?"

Paul gazed at her soberly. "Two years ago several of the
parishes got together and started a home for abused women
and children."

"Is Meg one of those children?"

"I'm afraid so. Her mother recently took Meg and her
sister out of an intolerable situation. But the other side of
that coin is they're now destitute. Halloween costumes are
mostly just wishful dreams. The shelter does what it can,
but..." His voice trailed off.

For an instant Beth couldn't speak, her throat too full of
emotion. Then at last she said, "Will you promise me
something, Uncle Paul?"

"Name it."

"If I send you a check, will you see that Meg and her
sister have Halloween costumes and later Christmas presents? While I'm at it, I'll write you another check for the
shelter. Can you use it?"

A look of relief crossed his face. "It would be a godsend."

"Consider it done."

He smiled. "Mere thanks is not enough."

"Forget it. I owe you, remember?"

Although she had seen him numerous times over the
years, they had never mentioned the day when she had
come to him, her life in shambles.

They were quiet for another moment; then Paul looked
down at Beth. "So how are you?" he asked pointedly.

Without warning, Beth felt her face drain of color.

"I'm sorry," Paul said gently. "I didn't mean to upset you."

Beth smiled a shaky smile. "You didn't. It's just that those memories don't resurface very often, but when they do, it's like someone sucker-punched me in the stomach."

"Don't ever feel you have to apologize to me for your feelings."

"I don't. For the most part, I'm all right. If it hadn't been for your advice to seek counseling, I doubt I'd be where I am today. For the most part I've managed to glue myself back together."

"I can't tell you how hard I've prayed that sunlight would once again fill *all* the dark corners in your heart."

She smiled sweetly. "That hasn't happened yet, but who knows? Someday..." Her voice trailed off, and again they fell silent.

"I understand you're doing well with your business."

Beth's face brightened. "I love what I do. It's my life."

"There's more to life than work, my child. You should have a home, children of your own."

Beth averted her gaze. "You sound like Gran."

"Your daddy would want that for you, too."

Beth squinted against the blast of sunlight that suddenly appeared through the clouds. "Speaking of my daddy, he's with me. You want to say hi?"

"You bet."

Arm in arm, they made their way toward the car.

Cottonwood.

Sometimes she dreamed the house was no longer there, that someone had played a cruel trick and set it afire, burning it to the ground. Always, when she had that dream, Beth felt compelled to rush home to Shawnee to reassure herself that all was well with her beloved home.

Though the nightmare hadn't plagued her in a while, she had still felt a longing to come here today. After she'd taken

Foster back to the nursing home, she'd been too restless to go back to Gran's empty house.

Now, as she sat in her car a short distance away from the house itself, she didn't feel the calm, the sense of peace, that always followed such a visit.

Was it because she was no longer content to look and not touch? She experienced an urge to rush inside, rush through the large airy rooms, slide down the banister. The urge was so strong that she felt sick.

What was wrong with her? She had come too far to sink into despair now. With the exception of her two newest shops, business was booming, enabling her to add to her savings account. Soon she would be able to make an offer on Cottonwood. The fact that it was still standing vacant was all the more reason to rejoice. Suddenly a numbing, breathless fear threatened to choke off her breathing. What if the owners refused to sell?

She wouldn't think about that now. She wouldn't think about that *period*.

Was this restlessness inside her related to Zach? Of course. Being with him last night had set her heart back years.

Zach. Forever Zach. "Oh, Zach, my darling," she whispered aloud, leaning her head back against the seat and closing her eyes.

Strands of hair fluttered against her cheek, aroused by the breeze caressing her face. She felt its chill as twilight fell.

Involuntarily she sighed, a small, breathy sound from the bottom of her soul. It startled her. The ache for Zach was so physical that she crossed her arms over her chest and rocked slowly in the seat.

Beth refused to let her mind dwell on what she was doing until she had eased the car into the parking space next to Zach's.

She was nervous; her heart was racing so hard she thought she might faint. It took every ounce of courage she could muster to walk through the doors of the mill. Since it was after business hours, the outer office was deserted. But there were signs of occupancy in the whirring of the ceiling fans and the faint light coming from Zach's office beyond.

He was sitting on the corner of his desk, rummaging through some papers. His power of concentration was such that he hadn't heard her come in. She moved closer.

The sight of him made her feel boneless. Her breath came in quick and shallow spurts. How she loved him! She was struck anew by the force of it. Seeing him again this way forced that secret emotion out in the open. She trembled with longing even while her eyes soaked him up with spongelike greediness.

She took delight in drawing this moment out as long as possible, selfishly not wanting it to end. Her pulse beat erratically as her eyes lingered, taking in his strength, his intensity.

Then he looked up.

She slowly closed the door behind her and leaned against it. "Zach, I . . . er . . ."

He waited, his face deathly white.

Twenty-Two

"Zach...I..." Beth's voice trailed off, words failing her.

He said nothing, continuing to stare at her as if she were a mirage.

"I want to talk to you," she said finally, breathlessly.

He still didn't say anything. He stood, crossed his arms over his chest and leaned his buttocks against the desk, using it as a prop.

Beth tried to smile, realizing that now that she was here she didn't know what to say. She hadn't thought about it beforehand; she had been too panicked to think clearly.

She knew she'd had to come; she couldn't have stood it otherwise. She shivered, feeling the connection between them, as delicate as a candle's flame trying to survive in the wind. She held her breath, hearing only her booming heartbeat to measure the seconds.

Her longing for him, the certainty that she couldn't walk away, the utter fragility of the moment, terrified her. He hadn't sent her away. Yet. What if he did? she wondered wildly. She would survive, of course. But would she want to?

He looked so fit, so dear, in a pair of faded jeans and a T-shirt that showed every muscle in his well-honed body. It was uncanny how he could melt her heart just by being in the same room.

When the silence seemed without end, Beth sought his eyes for clues and saw a stirring there. Her throat constricted, and she moved, drawn inexorably toward him.

"Why did you come here, Beth?" His voice sounded hoarse.

She sank her nails into her palms. She could hardly breathe, she was so charged.

"I . . . I wanted to thank you for helping with Trent."

"You could've called."

"I know," she said, faltering again, her eyes large and luminous.

"Then why didn't you?"

He never raised his voice, not so much as a decibel. Maybe that was what unnerved her. He was too calm, too steady, sending danger signals through her.

"I can understand how you feel," she whispered, knowing they were no longer talking about Trent.

He gave a bitter laugh. "Can you, now?"

"Yes." Her voice had turned throaty, as if her troubled emotions were jammed into that one tiny word.

His eyes flashed contempt, and at the same time he uncoiled his arms and walked toward her. "If you live to be a hundred and ten, you couldn't possibly know how I felt."

Oh, God, this had been a mistake. She saw that now. But she was trapped, trapped by her own smoldering yearnings and desires.

"You're wrong, so very wrong!" she cried. Tears came into her eyes.

"Like I told you before," he stressed in a tired but cold voice, "it doesn't matter."

"I don't believe that. I saw the look in your eyes last night."

Zach sucked in his breath loudly. "Damn you."

"I tried to stay away. I thought I could never see you again like this, that you were out of my life forever."

He was looming over her now; she could sense that he was furious, could see how he was straining to control himself. The fan turned slowly overhead; air fanned their faces.

"Don't you understand?" he hissed, watching her, watching as jewel-like tears spilled from beneath her thick lashes. "I don't want you here. The sight of you makes me sick!"

Beth cried out and took a step back, then another, feeling her heart split a little more with each move.

He opened his mouth and said "Beth" so softly that, had she not been looking at him, she would not have known he'd spoken.

She stopped, then started to cry.

Zach fought for control. His pulse beat hard in his temples, and he felt a sudden surge of blood into his head. He ached so much to touch her, to crush her against him. But he couldn't. Something hard and unyielding inside him could not erase what she had done to him—the misery, the pain he had endured at her hands.

Beth bent over, her shoulders shaking.

"Don't!" he cried from the depths of his soul. He could stand anything but her gut-wrenching sobs.

"I—" The remainder of her words tangled in another sob.

Zach reached out suddenly, grabbed her by the shoulders and yanked her against him. Then, with the weight of his body trapping her, he framed her face in his hands, his eyes blazing into hers.

She opened her mouth as if to speak.

His mouth ground into hers, reducing any sound she tried to make to little more than a whimper.

Controlling her head with his kiss, he let his hands roam freely. They toured her neck roughly, surrounded her breasts, lingered, then continued downward. With every touch she seemed to grow hotter, yet she pushed against him, but to no avail. He was relentless in his pursuit.

His hand delved beneath the waistband of her jeans and found the warm wetness between her thighs, while his hot lips closed around the tip of one breast.

"No," she breathed. Then, placing her hands on either side of his head, she pushed his sucking mouth from her flesh.

"Christ, this is madness!" Zach's breathing was fierce, his eyes demented.

Beth's heart hammered violently. "No...not like this...not in anger."

"It's too late," he whispered raggedly, his hold on her tightening.

"Please, Zach...not like this," she said again, her voice pleading.

His lips curled. "Yes, damn it, like this! You just couldn't let it go, could you? You just kept shoving until you pushed me over the edge."

"Zach!"

"Just shut up!"

His lips sank hungrily against hers again. She turned pliable against him and clung. Suddenly all his outrage, bitterness and regrets vanished. Nothing mattered except their desperate need for each other in a world turned upside down.

As if their legs were no longer capable of holding them upright, they sank as one to the carpeted floor, its softness buffering their knees.

He held her in his arms as tremors attacked his muscles, jolting like a tiny earthquake. His eyes drank her in, the high-cheekboned face, the long graceful neck, the ripeness of her lower lip, and he knew with a pang that she had managed to puncture the concrete that had shielded his heart.

The years rolled away as if they had never been.

"Beth," he groaned against her neck, feeling her hammering pulse through the soft skin.

Her fingers rubbed the back of his neck, twisted through his hair. He felt her against him, felt her quiver like a jolt down his spine.

Her scent was powerful and sweet, prying loose the memories from deep inside him. He remembered how to please her as they drifted flat on the floor. His lips trailed downward, nibbling, licking the saltiness of her skin, while her head bobbed and her eyes fluttered closed.

Greedily his lips returned to hers, their sweetness an intoxicant. He sucked at them with the hunger of an infant.

She reached for the zipper on his jeans, her breath coming in great gulps.

"Not yet," he whispered. When her eyes questioned him, he kissed her, his fingers busy removing her shirt.

His hot tongue made delicious circles around her breasts. He nursed them with his lips until she arched against him, her nipples sharp points that speared him. Their peaks were flushed a hot pink, as if on fire.

Quickly he raised her buttocks off the floor and stripped her jeans down her legs. He raised her thighs, hearing her delicate sigh like a murmur of her heart. His hands reached up to tease her nipples while his head inched down until the sweetness of her was against his lips.

Beth shuddered, then moaned beneath him. He felt her stiffen when he left her dampness to take her nipples back into his mouth.

"Zach, ohhhhhhh..."

He loved the sounds she made. He never wanted the moment to end. He heard every breath she took until, with a whispering moan, she jerked, then wilted.

When she was coherent again, she whispered, "Darling, my darling." Her fingertips traced the outline of him, hot and hard as steel beneath the limits of his clothes.

"Take your pants off," she pleaded, peeling the zipper open.

With unsteady hands he did as she ordered, then lay back beside her again, skin against skin.

Moonlight punched a hole through the window, then passed over them as if they weren't there.

Beth had eased her body down so that her lips were close to his quivering length. Her fingers stroked his hardness languorously.

The instant her mouth replaced her hands, Zach felt his heart knock so hard against his chest he feared his flesh would burst open. Cords inside his thighs rippled, then tensed into a kind of pleasurable pain that as yet had no outlet.

"No more!" he cried at last. "No more!"

He moved against her, probing, then penetrated her in one long, slow, heated glide that brought tiny tears to the corners of her eyes.

"Oh, yes," she sighed, grasping his buttocks fiercely as he pumped into her. She met him thrust for thrust.

"Beth," he whispered hoarsely. "Beth..."

They lost all sense of time and space as they climaxed simultaneously. He was aware of nothing except Beth, who brought him pleasure like the hot lick of the sun against their damp flesh.

For a while neither one of them moved. Neither spoke. They simply breathed and grappled to come to terms with what had happened.

Zach was the first to disentangle himself and stumble to his feet. Keeping his face averted, he climbed into his jeans.

Beth's eyes were questioning. "Zach..." Her lungs seemed unwilling to perform their function. "Please...tell me you're not sorry."

"Put your clothes on," he said in a dull, quiet voice, giving in to the reality that reached out of nowhere and jabbed hard, cold fingers into his heart. She had played him for a fool again. But the most disgusting part was that he had let her.

Trembling visibly, Beth got to her feet and reached for her clothes. She stared up at him, the hurt and bewilderment clear in her eyes.

Cursing, he turned away.

"Zach?" she whispered again.

Her voice sounded broken. For a moment he couldn't bring himself to face her again.

Finally he turned.

Beth flinched visibly at what she saw in his eyes. The color seeped from her face.

"Don't look at me like that!" Zach muttered savagely.

"You're sorry, aren't you?" Her voice was lifeless, dull. "But why? I thought..."

"Go on." The words came out a sneer. "You thought what?"

Red washed Beth's face. "I thought that we...that maybe we...could begin again." She paused and swallowed. "Since you...never married..."

"Funny you should mention marriage," he said with deceptive mildness.

"I don't understand." Beth's voice was tremulous, as if she were about to cry.

The time had come at last. Payday was here. He could hurt her now as badly as she had once hurt him.

"No, I'm sure you don't. But you're about to."

"What do you mean?"

"Rachel and I are getting married."

Time seemed to tick by in slow motion.

"*No!*" Beth squeezed the word out, her eyes wide with horror. "No, no, no!"

Before he could answer she whipped around and bolted for the door. Without looking back she slammed it behind her.

Zach stood still, his chest heaving, his mouth dry, his pulse thundering, tasting the bitter bile that rushed upward into his throat.

With a thunderous growl he pivoted and in one swoop cleared everything off his desk. The noise rocked the room like a cannon shot.

All at once his body began to shake uncontrollably, and he felt cold inside.

"Beth," he whispered to an empty room.

The chill in the evening air hit her square in the face when she bolted out of the building. But it did nothing to stop the hot bile that surged up at the back of her throat. It caught her halfway, forcing her to stop and choke down the wretched stuff. By the time she jerked open the car door and slid behind the wheel sobs like tiny avalanches assaulted her body.

Blinded by both pain and humiliation, Beth wrapped her fingers around the steering wheel so hard that her nails sank into her palms and pierced her skin. But that pain was minor compared to what was taking place inside her. Suddenly her insides rebelled, and she yanked on the door handle. After leaning over, she emptied her stomach. When she was spent and could lift her head, she curled into a ball on the seat, reminiscent of the time she'd been raped.

Zach and Rachel. No! Impossible! But she knew in her heart of hearts it was true. Rachel had been going to tell her, but fate had interfered, and Zach had been the one to deliver the bombshell.

It wouldn't have made any difference. Either way, the pain, the shock, the sense of betrayal, would have been the same.

"Oh, God, why do you hate me?" she sobbed, pounding on the seat. "What have I done to deserve this? I hate them both! Oh, God, I can't stand it! I can't stand the thought of Zach and Rachel..."

The idea of Zach making love to Rachel, touching her body with his lips, his tongue, the way he'd just now touched her, made her want to scream.

"Nooooo!" she cried instead, covering her ears with her hands.

She wanted to hate him, swore she did hate him. How could he do this to her? How could he be so cruel? The damage he had inflicted on her was beyond repair. When he'd been inside her like a second heartbeat, she had come alive. She had never wanted that feeling to end. But it had, abruptly and sadistically....

She never knew how long she remained in that position. With darkness enveloping her like a cloak, time ceased to mean anything.

How much more blood would she be required to give? she asked herself once her head had cleared somewhat. Whatever it was, she would give it. Survival had become second nature for her.

Forcing herself upright, she mopped the tears from her face and started the engine. She turned the car onto the street, pretending she wasn't headed home to a house that was as empty and cold as her heart.

Twenty-Three

"Hey, I'm talking to you."

Beth spun around. Tracy was standing in the door of her office, a worried expression on her face.

"Sorry." Beth sighed. "My mind was a million miles away."

"You're telling me," Tracy said. Though her tone held a hint of censure, her smile tempered it.

Beth sighed again. "I know I've been like an old bear with a sore paw for the last few weeks, but I..." Her voice faded. Now was not the time to indulge in her personal problems. Their work load was too heavy. Anyway, Tracy wasn't privy to the bone-crushing pain that constantly pressed on her heart.

"No apologies necessary," Tracy said, smiling. "We all have our days. But I'll admit you've had more than your share." She paused as if to consider what she was about to say. "If you want to talk, you know I'm here."

Beth forced a smile. "Thanks, but this is something I have to work out myself."

When Tracy spoke again, she changed the subject. "By the way, Michael called."

"Oh?" Beth's face didn't brighten.

"He asked me to remind you about your dinner date tonight."

Beth tapped a long nail on the desk. "I'd forgotten all about that. With the show, I don't see how I can make it.

Do me a favor, will you? Call him back and cancel, then tell him I'll talk to him later.''

Tracy pulled a face. "Poor Michael. He'll be crushed."

"He'll live," Beth said dryly.

Tracy shook her head and laughed. "Everything's set up out front, if you'd like to take a look-see."

"Everything but the food, right?"

"Right. It's much too early for that."

Beth glanced down at her watch. "But not too early for Sal Ventura. Even as we speak, he should be here setting up shop."

"My thoughts exactly, only he's not."

"Oh Tracy, would you believe I have butterflies?"

"Yep." Tracy pushed her glasses higher on the bridge of her nose, then pursed her lips. "Me, too, and the fact that I have four eyes today doesn't help."

Beth chuckled. "Contacts out of order again, huh?"

"I told my doctor he was dead meat if he didn't find me some I could wear that wouldn't cause me to sniffle like a baby." She shrugged. "You see how much weight my threat carried."

"You look just fine, granny," Beth teased.

Tracy's answering grin suddenly faded, and her eyes became serious. "It's good to see you smile again."

"You've earned a medal for putting up with me."

"No apologies necessary," Tracy said airily. "I told you that. While you may have been in a funk, your work hasn't suffered."

"Speaking of work, we'd best get busy. If I know our ladies, some of them will be here an hour ahead of time."

Beth got up from behind her desk and followed Tracy into the shop area. Once there, she paused and looked around. A sense of pride darted through her as she took in the peach-colored walls hung with garments in all colors, sizes and shapes. The mint green carpeted floor held racks filled with more of the same, while two large glass cases sparkled with costume jewelry and other accessories.

Today the shop looked better than it ever had. Potpourri, mixed with the scent of flowers, permeated the air. A feeling of magic, of anticipation, prevailed.

The racks had been pushed close together to make room for the decorated table soon to be laden with goodies and champagne. But the cramped effect did nothing to distract from the partylike atmosphere. It enhanced it, Beth thought, her gaze sharp as she continued to scrutinize the premises, making sure everything was in order down to the last detail.

Having a trunk show had never interested her before. Having a representative of a company show his merchandise directly to her was not her way of doing business. Her confidence had always been in herself. She went to market, along with her buyer, chose the clothes for her stores, then taught her managers how to sell them to individual customers. That strategy had always worked well for her.

But then she met Sal Ventura, the merchandising representative from T.J. Collectibles, a line that, in her estimation, rivaled that of Howard Wolf in its consistency and quality.

Not only was the line Sal peddled sheer dynamite, but so was the man himself. In her mind's eye she could see him and his ever-present grin. Dark haired and dark complexioned, he was as round as he was tall. But you forgot that he wasn't handsome, that his nose was too big, his mouth too wide. When he smiled and talked about fabric and styles, you forgot everything else. You were immediately captivated.

Beth had been immediately caught up in his magic. Like her, he loved what he did, and it showed. Another thing in Sal's favor was that his trunk shows were different. He brought live models to show off his clothes, if the customer so desired.

Now, as Beth threaded her way through the shop, she envisioned what the table would look like in a few hours. A bowl filled with champagne punch would occupy one end, while plates of hors d'oeuvres would grace the middle. A catering service would serve the refreshments, leaving Beth and her clerks free to mingle. She had mailed a hundred invitations, and if anywhere near that number came, the shop would be bulging.

Turning slightly, Beth got a glimpse of herself in the mirror. Her features were marred by dark circles under her eyes, as livid as bruises, and worry lines from lack of sleep. Nonetheless, her outfit went a long way toward not only camouflaging her weight loss but keeping anyone from noticing that she was not at her best.

"Hey, boss," Tracy said, interrupting Beth's reverie, "Sal's here."

"So how do you think it went?" Tracy asked hours later.

"Fantastic. I couldn't have been more pleased."

Tracy smiled. "Or shocked."

"That, too." Beth removed an earring and massaged her earlobe. "If I had known how profitable it was going to be, I would have done this a long time ago."

Tracy slipped out of her heels. "Well, we live and learn, thank goodness. And speaking of learning, I guess I'm never going to get it through my thick skull that I can't wear heels all day and remain human."

"Go ahead, get out of here. Take your sore feet home. I don't even want to see you tomorrow. You've earned the day off."

"Really?"

"Really. You're the one who organized everything." Beth's eyes twinkled. "I hold you entirely responsible for the day's success."

"Pooh. You worked just as hard as I did."

"No, I did not. Now get out of here. Scat."

"What about you? You're dead on your feet, too."

"I'm going home just as soon as I load my briefcase."

"Well, I'll say good-night, then."

When Beth was finally alone she did as Tracy had just done. She took off her shoes. For a moment she did nothing but wiggle her toes, making sure they were still part of her body.

She was tired. Yet it was a pleasant tiredness. Hopefully, when she got home and crawled into bed, she would sleep like a baby, which was something she hadn't done since Zach had carved another chunk from her heart.

A month had passed since that awful night. But time and distance hadn't helped. She had replayed every word they had spoken, every touch she and Zach had shared, until she'd nearly driven herself crazy.

Beth had thought she was an emotionally strong person, that nothing could ever hurt her as badly as losing Zach the first time. But when he'd told her that he was going to marry her best friend, she had fallen again. As she looked back on it now, the pain she'd suffered at Taylor's hands paled in comparison.

The entire scenario that Zach's words had evoked was as vivid this minute as it had been that day—visions of Zach's hands roaming Rachel's body. . . .

It was in those moments that she was positive she couldn't stand it. But she had. She stood it, as she'd stood so many things before. Her work had once again been her salvation, making her days at least tolerable. Nights were the hardest. Most of them had been spent in a chair in the living room, reading, because she was unable to sleep.

Now, as she fought to shift her mind onto something else, she couldn't. Another onslaught of pain hit her, so intense it electrified her nerve endings, doubling her over like a question mark. Finally the feeling passed, but she was so weak she couldn't move. The sound of her heartbeat was like thunder in her ears.

Since that night she hadn't seen Zach or Rachel. She'd been afraid, though, that she might run into both of them when she returned to Shawnee for Trent's court appearance. Thank heavens Zach had been out of town.

And Rachel . . . well, she'd assumed that because of the engagement her friend simply couldn't face her, which had been a blessing in disguise. Trent's troubles had demanded her full attention and energy.

Before Trent's case came up, Grace had introduced her to Vicki Fairchild. Beth had been impressed, thinking that if anyone could straighten her brother out, it was this girl.

Trent, because it was his first offense, had been given probation. But he hadn't gotten off scot-free. He'd been fined and instructed to do quite a few hours of community service.

Once they had reached Grace's house, Beth's sense of well-being had faded as she and Trent got into another verbal skirmish.

"Are you all right?" she'd asked after Grace and Vicki had gone to the kitchen to prepare lunch.

"I guess," he'd muttered, his eyes hooded.

Beth touched him on the arm. "You won't ever do anything like that again, will you?"

He pulled away from her. "Jeez, don't start on me."

"I have no intention of starting on you," Beth said patiently, "but I must have your word. Even if you don't care about me, think about Gran."

Instead of reassuring her, Trent cocked his head to one side and said, "I want to sell Daddy's share in the mill."

"What?"

"You heard me."

Beth gasped; then hurt and anger turned her voice cold. "Even if I could, I wouldn't. Stop and think about what you're saying. That's your inheritance, for God's sake."

"So?"

"Is that all you can say?" Beth wanted to shake him till his teeth rattled. "I suppose you don't care about your roots, either?"

"I suppose you're talking about Cottonwood?" he drawled.

"That's exactly what I'm talking about!" Beth countered hotly.

Trent, equally angry, glared at her. "Oh, it's easy for you to talk about roots. You don't have to live here, where people still point a finger at you because of what Daddy did. I hate this town, and I'd like nothing better than to leave and never come back. And in case you've forgotten, Cottonwood doesn't belong to us anymore and it never will again. Why won't you accept that?"

"I'll tell you why!" Beth was practically shouting now. "Without our home, without our land, we're nothing! We're nothing," she repeated. "Nothing!"

"We're nothing anyway," he said matter-of-factly.

"I don't believe that for one minute. But right now, that's not the point." She paused. "I have to think it's in our favor that Cottonwood's still unoccupied, despite the fact that it's been sold."

Beth had given that fact a great deal of thought, asking herself why someone would invest in a home like Cottonwood, keep up the repairs on it for years and never live in it. But even though she'd never been able to come up with an answer, as she'd pointed out to Trent she saw the house's emptiness as a plus. She wasn't about to look a gift horse in the mouth.

"Well, you just go ahead and play your little mind games with that relic, but I intend to face facts."

"Is that all you have to say?" Beth's tone was as brittle as ice.

"No," Trent muttered sullenly. "I'm tired of not having any money."

"That's your own fault. If you'd stay away from the racetracks and the bookies, you wouldn't have that problem. You make good money at the mill."

Trent scoffed. "That reminds me. What about the dividends on our shares? Now that the mill's turning a profit again, they should be rolling in."

"Half of the money keeps Daddy in the nursing home and the other goes into savings."

"Why?"

Beth lifted her chin. "I'm determined that Cottonwood is going to belong to us again."

"Who wants that albatross, anyway? I certainly don't."

"Trent!"

For a moment they both fell silent, breathing heavily, as if they were suddenly aware that they were creating a breach they might not be able to close.

"I mean it, Beth," Trent said at last, but with less venom. "As soon as the old man finally keels over, I'm going to dump my shares and kiss this hole goodbye."

Following those words he stormed out, leaving her feeling both drained and furious.

Of course, nothing had been settled. She had left Shawnee, rationalized that Trent hadn't meant half the things he'd said, that when—not if—she got Cottonwood back, he would be happy, and eventually settle there and rear a family.

As to shares, no way was she going to let them out of family hands.

Now, as she readied herself to leave, Beth slipped back into her shoes, opened her briefcase and stuffed papers into it.

A few minutes later she locked the door behind her and walked out into the cool night air.

Twenty-Four

The November afternoon was crisp, with a hint of frost in the air.

Beth sat next to Michael on a park bench near a small pond and watched several ducks flap their wings. They were fascinating creatures, she thought, as well as beautiful. And their lives were so simple. For a crazy moment she almost envied them.

Michael had picked her up earlier, and they'd gone to Sunday brunch at a new restaurant. The food had been delicious, but she had eaten very little, even though she knew she couldn't afford to lose any more weight. Lately it seemed she didn't have much time for the small pleasures in life, such as relishing a good meal. Work had consumed her.

Suddenly a blast of wind found its way down to them. Its bite went through her. Shivering, Beth pulled her jacket together.

"Cold?" Michael asked, his smooth voice shattering the quiet silence.

She turned toward him and smiled into his almost breathtakingly handsome face. A deep tan was the backdrop for thick blond hair and blue-gray eyes. Despite his taste for life's amenities, his tall, lean body had retained its suave, muscular look.

"It's a little chilly," she finally admitted, "but I'm not ready to go."

Michael reached for her hand. "Did I tell you that you look exceptionally lovely today?"

His tone was smooth and polished, as was everything about him. For some reason that irritated Beth. Maybe it was because he always seemed to know exactly what to say.

"No," she said, staring down at their clasped hands, wondering why she didn't withdraw hers. She felt nothing, no catch in the area of her heart, no erratic pulse beat. Nothing like what she felt when Zach...

Suddenly she withdrew her hand and stood. The light had just gone out of her day. "Let's walk, shall we?"

Michael didn't budge. Instead he stared up at her. "Is my touch that repulsive to you?" His mouth was drawn into a thin line.

"No, of course not," she lied, feeling her face grow uncomfortably warm.

He stared at her for a second longer, then sighed and got to his feet. "You're a hard one to figure, Beth Melbourne."

"How's that?" she asked, more for conversational purposes than anything else.

They began strolling along the sidewalk that would eventually lead to a gazebo nestled in the midst of huge, bare-limbed pecan trees.

"Oh, I don't know, exactly." His eyes searched her face. "Or maybe I do. One minute I think I've penetrated that shield you keep around you, and the next I feel I haven't even made a dent."

"Sounds like you've given that a lot of thought," Beth said lightly, reaching into her shoulder bag and pulling out her sunglasses. She plunked them on the bridge of her nose.

The sun that had been playing hide-and-seek with the clouds finally won the battle. Its warming force felt comforting.

"I have, and I'd give it more if I thought it would do me any good," he said pointedly.

Beth shivered again, this time from agitation rather than cold.

Michael, misinterpreting, said, "Come on, let's go to the car. We can talk there."

"Oh, but I'm—"

"Don't argue, okay? Just come on."

Beth shrugged. "All right."

They were silent until they reached the close confines of Michael's Lincoln. Immediately he started the engine and revved up the heat. Then, facing Beth, he said, "Better?"

"Much." She smiled. "I guess I was colder than I thought."

"See, I do know what's best for you sometimes."

"Michael . . ."

"I recently took on a big case," he said as if she hadn't spoken. "The biggest of my life, in fact, and won it."

Beth blinked against the sudden switch in conversation. "That's—that's wonderful, but . . ."

"You're wondering what that has to do with you, with us, aren't you?"

Beth nodded, shifting in the seat until she was facing him.

"I'm getting around to that. Anyway, I'm thinking about going into private practice, starting my own firm."

"I think that's great." Beth smiled. "I know you'll make a go of it."

Michael's features were somber, but his eyes were warm. "I want you to be a part of this new venture." He paused. "I want you to marry me."

Beth opened her mouth, then shut it. She shouldn't have been shocked, but she was.

"You're shocked, aren't you?"

Her thoughts were chaotic. "Am I that easy to read?"

"In this instance, yes."

"I didn't think marriage was in your vocabulary."

He smiled and angled his head. "Would you have lived with me, if I'd asked?"

"No."

"So, there's your answer."

This time it was Beth who reached out and took his hand and linked it with hers. "You know I care...."

"Please, spare me the standard line." He drew a deep, pensive breath. "And don't say no till you've at least thought about it. We'd make a good team, you know. We're both devoted to our careers. We both like to travel. Neither of us particularly cares about having any kids. Right?"

Wrong. Beth wanted children, all right. Zach's children. Since that was never going to happen, she tried not to think about it. It hurt too much. But she had no intention of explaining any of that to Michael. Still, she didn't want to hurt him.

"I'm flattered that you asked—"

His eyes flared. "Don't be flattered, just say yes."

"I'm sorry, Michael, I . . . can't."

"I know you're not in love with me. I can handle that." His mouth quirked. "Anyway, love isn't all it's cracked up to be. You wouldn't be sorry you married me, I promise you that."

"Oh, Michael," Beth said, her brows drawn together in a frown. "It's obvious you don't know me. For a while I thought maybe I could settle for second best, but I know now I can't."

Zach was lost to her forever. She knew that. But after being with him again she couldn't bear the thought of another man being inside her, touching her in the secret places that only Zach's hands and lips had touched.

"Ah, so there is someone?"

"No," she said dully.

"Don't lie, Beth."

She flushed.

"That son of a bitch, whoever he is, hurt you badly, didn't he?"

"Don't press it, Michael. Please. We can never be more than friends. If you're willing to settle for that..." Her voice trailed off, but her meaning was clear.

"All right, Beth, you've made your point. For now. But I'm not giving up."

"Please, if you don't mind, I'd like to go home."

Beth locked the door, turned off the lights and made her way to her bedroom, a cup of mocha in hand. She didn't care that it was too early to go to bed. She intended to read until sleep overtook her.

Outside her bedroom door Beth paused, fighting down a gust of panic as she thought about the emptiness that waited for her on the other side. You'd better get used to it, she told herself, opening the door and charging across the threshold.

After taking off her clothes she cracked a window so that she could enjoy the fresh chilly air. Once the miniblinds were adjusted, she rolled down the flowered comforter and slid between the crisp sheets. She had just propped her back against the pillow and taken a sip of her coffee when the doorbell rang.

"Great," she muttered, setting her cup down on the bedside table. She reached for her robe at the foot of the bed, slipped into it and hurried into the front room.

When the phone rang at night, it frightened her; she was always certain it would be bad news from home. But when the doorbell rang at night, it always angered her. Unexpected company was not to her liking.

Keeping the chain lock intact, Beth eased open the door and peered out.

"Hello, Beth."

The bottom dropped out of her stomach. *"Rachel!"* Beth wasn't sure if she spoke aloud or merely made a tiny sound in the back of her throat.

"Are . . . you going to invite me in?"

Even in her own agitated state Beth heard the slight tremor in Rachel's voice, as if her friend were on the verge of tears.

She had known she couldn't avoid Rachel forever, but when the confrontation did take place she had wanted it to be on her own terms. Not like this. Oh, dear Lord, not like this, not when she was so unprepared, so vulnerable.

"Of course." Beth stepped aside, the paralysis suddenly wearing off.

Rachel stepped into the middle of the living room and swung around, her pale complexion offering little contrast to the white sweater she was wearing.

"Why don't you sit down?" Beth said, avoiding Rachel's intent gaze. "I'll—I'll get you some mocha."

Rachel shook her head. "No, please, I don't want anything."

"Are you sure? It's delicious. I was just—"

"Stop it, Beth." Rachel's eyes were wide and pain filled. "Stop acting like you're talking to a stranger."

A silence, suffocating in its intensity, forced them both to breathe hard.

Beth reached the nearest chair and sank into it, her jellylike legs no longer able to support her. "You're right, small talk was never our thing."

"I—I wasn't sure if this was a good idea." Rachel's voice was thin and anxious. "Coming here, I mean."

"We're friends, Rachel," Beth said, though her expression was pained.

"I was hoping you'd say that."

Beth blinked, her eyes burning. "Rachel . . ."

"I wanted to tell you, honestly I did. Only . . . I got sick, and then Zach told me he had told you."

What else did he tell you? Beth cried silently. *Did he tell you that we made love until we were wrung out to the very core?* How could they—how could *Zach*—have done such a thing?

Rage. Suddenly that red-hot emotion threatened to consume Beth. Then, like a healing calm in the aftermath of a storm, she gathered her courage about her. Rage became her inner strength, warming her, buffering her wounds and, to some extent, her pain.

Rachel toyed with the gold chain around her neck. "But I had to see you." She paused, the skin on her face tightening. "I had to make sure you—you no longer cared."

Beth closed her eyes; she could hear her own breath. "It's over between Zach and me." She gritted her teeth. "It has been for a long time."

Rachel wilted visibly. "I thought so, but sometimes, when the two of you are together, I get the feeling it will never be over. That's when I get really scared."

"You ... have nothing to fear from me."

"You know I've always loved him." Rachel's eyes were blurred with tears.

"I know," Beth said in a voice brimming with the emotions she was holding in check.

"Will you come to the wedding, be my maid of honor? The date is set for January the seventh, a Saturday."

"No." The sharp little word was out before Beth knew it. It hung in the air, diminishing all the other shadows that hovered over the room.

The tears finally spilled from Rachel's eyes. "Why?"

"I ... can't."

"Oh, Beth, are we reduced to lying to each other now?"

Matching tears welled up in Beth's eyes. "As God is my witness, I'll be at a show that weekend, in Paris."

"You can't get out of it?"

"No, no matter how much I want to."

"Will you come see me? Us?"

"Of course." Beth could barely get the words out. "Of course I will."

Again the silence was long and heavy with unspoken emotions.

"Well, I guess I'd better get going," Rachel said uneasily. "Mother's waiting for me to pick her up at a friend's. Anyway, I need to let you get back to bed. You look like you had a rough day."

Beth tried to smile. "Every day is rough."

"Can I have a hug?" Rachel asked softly, narrowing her eyes as if trying to read Beth's soul.

"You better believe it," Beth cried and flew into her arms. "Be happy and God bless."

Following Rachel's departure, Beth methodically switched off the light in the living room and walked back to her bedroom. Instead of climbing into bed, she sat down on the edge and dropped her head into her hands.

"Don't you cry, Beth Melbourne." Her breath was sawing in her throat. "Don't you dare!"

It was time to put the past where it belonged, behind her once and for all. Let it go! *Let Zach go.* Could she? Her mind said yes, while her heart screamed no.

The latter won. Not only had she lived with pain inside her heart for so long, she had lived with Zach inside her soul for even longer. Now she feared neither raw place would ever heal.

But then she remembered what her grandmother had told her recently, and suddenly those words made all the sense in the world.

"Beth, honey, it's time you filled those empty places in your life that cause you so much pain."

Maybe at last she could fill *one* of those empty places, the one where Zach had been, and get on with her life.

Was it possible?

Fear clutched at Beth with icy fingers, making her shiver. She didn't know the answer to that question. But she had to try.

In order to keep living, she had to try.

Twenty-Five

Spring, 1987

"Good morning, darling."

Zach didn't respond to his wife's cheery words of greeting. His back to her, he continued to stand in front of the wide windows that overlooked a stand of rain-washed oaks, their limbs coated with thick green leaves, a sure sign of spring.

In the distance the profile of Cottonwood seemed to wink at him through the rich sunlight.

"Zach?"

He spun around. Rachel, his wife of three years, was staring at him with a perplexed frown on her face.

"Sorry, Rach. I guess my mind was wandering."

She smiled a knowing smile. "I bet no farther than the mill, though, huh?"

Zach answered her smile as he left the window and sauntered to the table where Rachel was sitting. After leaning over and pecking her on the cheek, he sat beside her.

"You're right. I *was* thinking about the mill."

The dining room in their private apartment at Wimberly, designed for no more than eight people, had walls covered with woven paper that enhanced its ambience of understated elegance. Impervious to the old silver, glittering crystal chandelier, delicate glassware and fine linen,

Zach enjoyed a moment of quiet here every morning before he began his hectic day. Over several cups of coffee, he devoured the morning paper.

"Want to talk about it?" Rachel asked softly, her eyes perusing him warmly.

Zach reached for his cup and raised it to his lips. Over the rim he returned his wife's gaze. "I just wish to hell I knew what to do."

Rachel's eyes crinkled a bit at the corners. "I gather you had no luck in postponing the meeting?"

"Nope. The Cox boys want a decision, and they want it now, or at least within the next couple of days. Far as I'm concerned, it might as well be now."

"Has Taylor given you a definite yes or no?"

"About what?"

At the sound of the gruff, unexpected voice, they both turned around.

Taylor Winslow stood on the threshold, one corner of his mouth lifted in what could be labeled a smile, though whatever it was it failed to ease the lines around his mouth or the heavy booze-bags under his eyes.

Still, the years had been relatively kind to Taylor, Zach thought, even if he did hate to admit it. No matter how much he or his mother harped, his daddy refused to quit drinking.

"Didn't hear you knock, Daddy," Zach said pointedly.

Taylor shrugged. "Aw, I tapped. Same thing."

"How do you figure that?"

Rachel stood suddenly, as if to stop an argument that was about to take place. "How 'bout breakfast, Taylor? Emma can fix you some hotcakes."

"Hell, no," Taylor drawled, his gaze now on his daughter-in-law. "I'd just as soon eat a sack of candy. All that syrup and butter doesn't set well with me."

Rachel laughed and rubbed her stomach. "Mmm, that's what makes 'em so good."

"And fattening," Zach chimed in with a grin.

Rachel thrust out her lower lip in a pout. "I thought you didn't care if I was slightly on the, er, chubby side."

Taylor walked farther into the room, grabbed a chair and sat down. Then, winking at Rachel, he said, "You pay him no mind, you hear? You look just fine the way you are."

"Why, thank you," Rachel responded heartily, throwing Zach an I-told-you-so look. "At least someone appreciates me."

Zach pushed the paper aside. "I was teasing, and you know it."

"You'd better be, 'cause you're stuck with me." Rachel placed her hands on her hips. "Anyway, I have an excuse for the extra pounds."

"Yeah, and where is that grandson of mine?" Taylor asked. "His grandma sent me to check on him."

Zach cut Taylor a quick glance. "Yeah, I bet. Wild horses couldn't have kept you away, regardless of what Mamma wanted."

"Well, you can rest easy, Granddaddy Taylor," Rachel said, her face aglow. "Randall's cold is better. And he slept through the night, which is more than I can say for your son." She turned her eyes to Zach. "You were up and down half the night."

Zach feigned innocence. "Who, me?"

"Yes, you."

"Sorry, guess I had a lot on my mind."

Suddenly a loud cry rang through the air.

Taylor's crusty features lit up like a light. "Ah, that's my boy. Always seems to know when his granddaddy's around."

Zach rolled his eyes.

Rachel grinned.

"Want me to get him, Rachel?" Taylor asked.

"Thanks, but I'd better do it. He's probably wet. I'll be right back."

A few minutes later she was back, carrying eight-month-old Randall Zachery Winslow in her arms. "All dry and squeaky clean now, aren't you, my darlin'?"

Taylor lunged to his feet. "Lemme have that boy."

Obediently Rachel handed the baby over to Taylor. He sat down immediately and began tickling Randall's chin and making cooing noises. The baby grinned and kicked his feet in rapid succession.

Zach looked at Rachel and smiled.

She had just blown him a kiss when Taylor looked up and said, "What's the latest word on the pending deal?"

Zach's smile faded. "That's what we were talking about when you came in."

"I assumed it was."

"In fact," Rachel said, "I had just asked Zach whether you had given a definite yea or nay."

"Hell, I told him to sign the papers. I'm all for the merger."

"It's just not that simple, Daddy, and you know it."

"Sure is. Only you won't accept that."

Zach dragged a hand through his hair. "I'm still not convinced it's the best for the employees or for Shawnee, when you get right down to it."

"Listen, boy, you're worrying about the wrong thing. The bottom line here is money. And the Cox outfit is offering us a hell of a lot of cash."

Zach's face was set in impatient lines. "In this case, money's not everything."

"Well, I'll be damned. Never thought I'd live to hear you say that." Taylor's voice rose. "Since when did you come to that conclusion?"

The baby whimpered.

"Granddaddy's sorry," Taylor said suddenly, once again bending his head over the baby, who was lying in the crook of his arm, staring wide-eyed at the ceiling.

"Want me to take him?" Rachel asked, her gaze soft on her baby.

Taylor's head popped back up. "Naw, he's fine."

"I've gone over all the angles in my mind and on paper," Zach said, picking up the conversation where they'd left off, "and I'm still not convinced that Cox is on the up-and-up, if you get my drift." His tone turned brisk. "There's something about the offer that just doesn't sit well with me. But I've been over those papers with a fine-tooth comb, and I can't find a thing."

"So sign 'em."

"I can't."

Taylor swore softly, then gave Rachel an apologetic look. "He's got a head like a piece of granite. I just wonder how you put up with him."

Rachel glanced at Zach. "I sometimes wonder that myself."

The lines on Zach's face relaxed a little, and he actually smiled. For a moment the tension eased.

"Either of you care for another cup of coffee?" Rachel's eyes darted between them. "Emma made a fresh pot."

"No more for me, hon," Zach said, pushing back his chair and getting to his feet. He walked over to the window again and looked out.

"Me, either," Taylor said, turning his gaze from the baby to his son. "So what's it gonna be?"

Zach swung around with a curt jerk of his head. "I don't know. The Coxes say they want me to continue to run things, but my gut instinct tells me it won't happen that way. Oh, for a while it'll be all right, but then..." His voice trailed off.

A frown slipped across Taylor's face. "So the bottom line is a no vote from you?"

"Yes."

There was a drawn-out silence.

"What about you, Taylor?" Rachel asked quietly. "Are you going to support Zach?"

"Yeah, Daddy, what about it?"

Although Taylor was retired now and had relinquished all control of the day-to-day running of the mill to Zach, he still had his shares and therefore had voting privileges.

"You know I will, even though I think it's a mistake. If we merged, at least we wouldn't have to fight the union alone. These last few years, they've gotten too big for their britches, if you ask me. A real pain in the royal rear."

The baby stirred, and Rachel held out her arms. "Here, let me have him. I'm sure your arm's numb by now." She smiled. "Besides, he's sound asleep."

Zach watched as Rachel took the child and cuddled him against her. For a fleeting moment the mill and all its troubles slipped from his mind as he thought about his son, about the countless joys he had brought him. Randall was his lifeline. When he thought he couldn't make it another day, he would focus his mind on Randall, and everything would fall back into place.

"I gotta agree with you about the union." Zach swung around. "But you'll have to admit I've managed to handle them. So far, that is," he qualified quickly.

"Yeah, but for how much longer?"

"As long as it takes."

"Oh, honey," Rachel put in, "if you merged, wouldn't it cut down your work load?" She paused and looked down at her son. "The way things are now, you hardly get to spend any time with Randall."

A dart of pain needled him. "You're right. That part about it I hate. But still, in good faith, I can't let the mill go."

"When's the meeting?" Taylor asked.

Zach exhaled slowly. "Soon."

"What about Trent? Is he going to be in on the negotiations?"

Zach's green eyes swept Taylor. "I think that's only fair, don't you? Especially since I've been training him for an executive position."

"One that you'll have to create, though," Taylor challenged.

"So?" Zach's face was closed.

Taylor came back with a question. "Do you think that's wise?"

"In the long haul it'll pay off."

Taylor made an aggravated noise in his throat. "Let's hope you're right. But I'll tell you this, you've got more faith in that boy than I do."

"Well, he's sharp, and he has a real knack for the job. But most important, he does his job. He leaves his personal problems at home." Zach paused. "Don't forget, too, he'll own part of the mill one day."

"Does he know about your plans for him?"

"No. I've started him at the bottom, forcing him to learn from the ground up."

Taylor's eyes narrowed. "What about Beth? Has she been notified?"

At the mention of Beth's name Zach's mood turned sour, like his stomach. But his face showed nothing. "I called and left word with her secretary."

It galled him that the mere mention of Beth's name could still affect him. But he knew why. That night with Beth, prior to his marrying Rachel, never should have happened. But, like a fool, he'd let his hard cock overrule his sound judgment. He was still paying for that stolen night. He'd felt both guilt and contempt—guilt because he had betrayed Rachel, contempt because he hadn't been strong enough not to touch Beth in the first place.

Her presence never failed to spring loose the emotions inside him. As a result, he dreaded each time mill business brought her to Shawnee.

Rachel, however, had no such reservations. She and Beth had remained friends and kept in touch. When he was out of town they would often meet for lunch.

Even as his thoughts were roiling inside him, Rachel was singing Beth's praises. "I can't wait to see her and hear all about the new store she's opening. In fact, I badgered her on the phone last week until she finally promised to spend at least one day with Randall and me."

Zach felt something in his throat, something that was hard to swallow. He couldn't say a word.

"I'd just as soon she stayed the hell away from Wimberly, myself." Anger brought a flush to Taylor's face. "She's not welcome here."

"What's with you two?" Zach demanded coldly. "Every time y'all are in the same room, you're at each other's throats or you're giving each other the cold shoulder. You're worse than two children. Beats me why you have your stinger out for her."

An odd expression crossed Taylor's face; then something hard replaced it. "Why, boy, that oughta be obvious. After all, she left you standing at the goddamn altar!"

Rachel gasped.

Blood rushed to Zach's ears like a battle cry. "Yeah, that's right! It was me she left, not you!" He pounded on his chest as if to reiterate that point. Then, with a disgusted snort, he turned away, deeply rocked by the violence he felt.

Tension hung in the air like a thick, smothering fog.

"Well," Taylor spluttered at last, "she...she made the entire family look bad, made us the laughingstock of Shawnee. You know that as well as I do." His face wrinkled like a prune. "And I'll never forgive her."

"Oh, Taylor, that's an awful thing to say!" Rachel cried. "And after all this time, too."

"Can't help it," he said in a tight voice. "It's the truth."

Rachel opened her mouth, only to shut it just as quickly.

Zach sliced a hand through the air. "Why the hell are we discussing this, anyway?" His sharp tongue was deadly, like an open razor in the hands of a child.

Only silence met his blast of fury.

Twenty-Six

"Reverend Jim Bakker, one of the country's most popular television evangelists, resigned his ministry today after admitting to an extramarital sexual encounter seven years ago.

"Bakker charged that he had been blackmailed subsequently as part of a 'diabolical plot' to gain control of his PTL Club, which reported revenues of 129 million in 1986...."

Disgusted with the turn the news had taken, Beth twisted the knob on the radio to Off. Immediately silence filled the car, offering a blessed relief. Only the thrum of the wheels gliding across the pavement could be heard.

Lord knows she was distracted enough as it was without having to endure the trials and tribulations of Jim and Tammy Faye Bakker.

This particular trip home couldn't have come at a worse time, she thought, wrapping her slender fingers more tightly around the steering wheel. But it couldn't be avoided. Her vote on the merger was imperative.

Still, she had been reluctant to leave the new boutique that she'd recently opened in Arlington, Texas, especially as new business ventures were a bit risky these days. Because of the oil crisis, both Louisiana and Texas had suffered financially, their economies struggling to survive.

She was confident, though, in her own ability to beat the odds. It was the element of risk that had spurred her on.

Nothing was predictable. There were no guarantees; you either made it or you didn't, and each new day, each new venture, presented a whole new set of challenges.

Once Zach and Rachel had married, such challenges had enabled Beth to gather the pieces of her life together yet again and rebuild them into something she could live with.

She had done a good job of it, too, she reminded herself, though there had been plenty of rough spots along the way. But she'd had Tracy to depend on, and the other woman hadn't let her down. And there was Michael. When he finally realized she wasn't going to marry him, he'd turned into a true friend.

At the moment, though, neither her work nor her friends could temper the side effects of this particular trip home. Eight months ago, when a baby boy had been born to Zach and Rachel, the walls of her cardboard house of security had been severely shaken.

Again she tightened her fingers around the wheel. The thought of Zach and Rachel creating a baby, a baby that by all rights should have been hers, was like a bitter taste in her mouth.

She hadn't been back since the baby was born and, God help her, she didn't want to go back now. But no matter how much she dreaded it, her obligations couldn't be shirked.

During the past three years her daddy's situation had changed very little. He was still in the same nursing home, and while his physical condition hadn't improved, it hadn't deteriorated, either. Though Foster remained a worry, it was her grandmother who now garnered the majority of her concern.

Recently Grace had suffered a mild heart attack, but the doctor had assured Beth that there had been no permanent damage. She believed him, yet she couldn't stop worrying. She'd made it a point to call Gran every day, if for no other reason than to reassure herself.

Not only did she have that burden to contend with, she had Trent, as well. He remained a constant source of heartache. He had moved in with Vicki Fairchild soon after he'd been placed on probation. To date they were still living together without benefit of clergy, much to Gran's regret.

"Why, your mother's probably turning over in her grave right now," Gran had said after Trent broke the news to her.

"Let us pray not," Beth had replied, trying to hide a smile.

Grace hadn't thought it amusing then, nor did she now. And Beth had to agree with her feelings about Trent and Vicki. If she'd had her way, she would have preferred to see them get married. But she hadn't voiced her opinion, knowing that Trent would not welcome it.

At times she felt she was making headway with Trent, only to have that progress undermined by another unexpected altercation. At such times she realized that he resented her as much now as he ever had. One of her greatest fears was that he would never change, never forgive her for being Foster's favorite child.

Still, he did have one thing in his favor. He seemed to be doing his job at the mill and doing it well. Today, however, her troubles with Trent were not top priority, nor was the upcoming visit with Rachel, where she would be introduced to Randall for the first time, traumatic as that would be. Top priority was bracing herself for yet another face-to-face encounter with Zach. And Taylor.

Beth realized with a start that she'd entered the city limits of Shawnee. Quickly glancing at the clock on the dash, she noted it was almost nine-thirty. She had hoped to get here in time to stop by both her grandmother's and the nursing home before the meeting, but with it set for ten o'clock, she didn't have time to do either.

She turned onto the road that led to the mill and tried to ignore her rapidly increasing heartbeat.

"What's wrong?"

Trent laced his hands behind his head and stared at the ceiling instead of Vicki, who lay beside him.

"Nothing," he said curtly.

With a resounding sigh, Vicki flopped on her side and slung a leg across his body, trapping him.

"Oh, no, you don't," she said. "You're not going to shut me out again. Something's bothering you, and I'm not letting you up until you tell me what it is."

He turned his head slightly and grinned. "Mmm, now that sounds like a good idea."

Vicki punched him playfully on the arm. "I'm serious." Her eyes suddenly took on a troubled glaze. "Have you been to the racetrack again?"

Trent's lips thinned, and he averted his gaze.

"Oh, Trent," Vicki wailed, "you promised you wouldn't."

Trent pulled her closer to his side, suddenly needing to feel the warmth of her naked body against him. "I know I did, baby, but—"

"No!" Vicki placed her hands over both ears. "I don't want to hear any more excuses."

A mutinous expression rearranged Trent's features. "We needed the money."

"But you didn't win, did you?" Her tone had a defeated edge.

"No."

Tears surfaced in her eyes. "Damn you, Trent!"

He disentangled himself and lunged into a sitting position, turning his back to her. "If you can't handle it, you're free to get out any time you like."

"Do—do you mean that?" Vicki whispered.

He twisted his head and looked at her out of the corner of one eye. "No."

"You know I don't want that, either," she said tremulously.

His shoulders slumped in defeat.

Vicki exhaled loudly, as if trying to find the courage to say what she had to. "Every time your sister is due in town, you pull one of these stunts."

"That's bullshit!" He stood.

Vicki scrambled to her knees. "No, it's not bullshit." Her eyes were wide and anxious. "It's the truth. You go to the track on purpose, and I think you lose on purpose."

He spat a curse. "That's the craziest thing I ever heard."

"No, it isn't. It's the truth, only you won't face it, just like you won't face a lot of other things."

"Such as?" he responded snidely.

She lowered her eyes. "For starters, you won't face the fact that you actually enjoy working at the mill."

"Since when did you get so full of wisdom?" A coat of sarcasm surrounded each word.

"Go ahead, make fun. I don't care."

Trent's laugh was short, biting.

"This problem with Beth just won't go away, you know."

"I don't want to talk about her."

"Why do you let her get to you like this? Why do you care what she thinks?"

"I don't care. She can go take a flying leap as far as I'm concerned."

"Ha! That's another bald-faced lie. You care, all right, only you won't admit that, either." Vicki bolted off the bed and looked him in the eye. "I've never been able to figure out what makes you two tick. It's obvious she cares about you—"

"Wrong! All she ever cared about was Cottonwood and my daddy. They were a team."

"I'm sure your daddy loved you, too."

For the longest time Trent didn't respond. The room was quiet, but outside, birds chirped merrily, as if they didn't have a care in the world.

A muscle twitched in his bristled jaw. "He didn't even like me, Vick."

The silence stretched for another long, heavy second.

Vicki reached up and brushed the hair off his forehead, then kissed him gently on the lips. "Well, I like you. I like you a lot. Will that do?"

"Yeah, that'll do," he said hoarsely.

Their eyes held while she caressed his cheek with the back of her hand. Then, wordlessly, they sat back down on the bed, where the lines on his face suddenly tightened. "And then there was Zach."

"Zach?" Vicki frowned. "What are you talking about?"

"Beth and Zach." He smiled a humorless smile. "At one time, I think old Zach squeezed out my old man."

"Really? What happened?"

He looked away nervously. "I don't know. It was a long time ago. I don't even know why I brought it up."

"Beth cares about you," Vicki said softly. "I see the way she looks at you."

"Believe what you want. I just wish she'd sell Daddy's shares in the mill to Zach and give me my portion of the money. We'd be outta this town so fast it'd make their heads swim."

"Do you think that'll ever happen?"

"Nope."

"How do you think she'll vote on the merger?"

"Against it."

"You sound so sure."

"I am," Trent said flatly. "She's not about to let go of the mill. It's part of our 'roots.'" He mimicked Beth's tone, and Vicki giggled. His lips relaxed into a brief smile.

"You'd really like to see the mill sold?" Her tone held disbelief.

"Yes." He avoided her intent gaze. "Hell, yes."

"Whatever you say. Only I think you're lying to yourself."

"That's your prerogative."

Vicki sighed. "So where does all this leave you?"

"Out in the cold, where I've always been."

Vicki patted his back lovingly. "Maybe if you told your sister how you felt...?"

"Oh, she knows, all right, but since she holds the old man's power of attorney, she can do anything she damn well pleases." Trent's eyes turned dark. "And what hacks me off even more is that Zach won't give me any responsibility. He treats me like I'm some fucking idiot off the street. I've worked my butt off, but do you think he or my sister appreciates it? Hell, no."

Vicki leaned over and brushed her lips against his shoulder. "I appreciate it, but then when you go to the racetrack and blow your money, I get steamed."

"I know, Vick," he said wearily. "I get mad at myself, too. Most of the time I hate myself."

"Well, just as long as you don't hate me."

"I could never do that," he said simply.

She stirred restlessly. "I... hate it when we fight."

He turned so that he was facing her, his eyes brooding and uncertain. "You're not going to leave me, are you? Sometimes I can't believe that you love me, that you're still here."

"I'm not going anywhere, you big dummy," she teased. "I love you." Vicki tightened her arms around him as he bent his head to kiss her. It was a tentative kiss, as if he were afraid.

Suddenly desperate to love her, Trent deepened the kiss, blocking out everything but her eager mouth and hands as she clung to him.

"Vicki, Vicki," he muttered, their harsh breaths mingling.

She arched her body against him until he could feel her throbbing and ready.

"I want you," she whispered urgently.

"You got me."

He kissed her again, hotly, and she clung to him with a sigh before he tore his lips from hers and fastened them on her breast.

"Ahhh!" Vicki cried with her eyes closed, while her hands explored his body as he explored hers.

But when she wrapped her hand around his jutting hardness, Trent fluttered wildly in her grasp and released her nipple with a moan.

"Now!" he muttered frantically and parted her legs. With a long breath he thrust into her full force, lowering himself until his cheek pressed against hers. He moved slowly, heard her moan, felt her fingers dig into his buttocks.

When the explosion came, it rocked them so hard that all they could do was wilt against each other and fight for breath.

"Trent?" she murmured after a little while.

"Mmm?"

"If I ask you to marry me, would you?"

He stiffened, then pulled back and looked down at her with an incredulous expression on his face. "You're asking me?"

"No."

"What's this all about, then?"

Color touched Vicki's face. "I—I just wondered what you'd say if I did."

Trent sucked in his still-laboring breath and for a moment didn't respond. But his hesitation, fleeting as it was, was enough to bring a pained look to Vicki's face. He cursed himself silently. Marriage? That was the last thing on his mind at the moment.

"What's wrong with the way things are now? I love you, and you love me. Why mess with it?"

"Forget it," she whispered, dropping her gaze.

He tilted her chin back up. "Hey, don't do this to me, please, not now. You know I've got to be at that meeting."

"So you're going?"

"You better know it." He stared off into space. "I wouldn't miss it for anything."

Vicki lowered her head and smiled.

Twenty-Seven

During the recession of the early eighties and the oil crash of the late eighties, Southland Paper had managed to keep its head above water. The company had avoided massive layoffs, thus hanging on to its place in the area.

Zach's firm hand and expertise had gone a long way toward making that possible, Beth reminded herself.

With Foster inept, Taylor relinquishing control and her own absenteeism, it had been left up to Zach to call the shots. And call them he had, with a vigor and vitality that had brought results. When he'd been given the CEO mandate, the changes had started to show.

Now, as Beth parked her car in the plant's lot and got out, she tried to ease the tension building inside her by taking several deep breaths.

Once inside, she threaded her way through the front offices, nodding and speaking to the various employees. Out of the corner of her eye she caught a glimpse of her reflection in a round mirror that hung above the couch in the cozy waiting area. She'd been determined to look her best and hoped she'd reached her goal. A deep fuchsia raw silk skirt and matching blouse hinted at the fill curves beneath, in addition to creating the perfect foil for her butterscotch-colored hair.

Finally, after reaching her destination, the small boardroom that was an appendage of Zach's office, she found she could no longer control her hammering heart.

Why did she dread this meeting so? It was no different from the others she had attended through the years. Of course, she'd dreaded them, too, but today seemed worse. Maybe it was partly due to Taylor. She knew he would be present, and being polite to him for any length of time was untenable.

If anything positive could be gleaned from seeing him, it was to remind herself with whiplash force that she owed the bastard, that someday he would get his comeuppance for what he'd done to her.

As a rule, Beth would attend the meeting, take care of her family obligations, then leave town. But not this trip. In the morning another emotional shock faced her. The promised day with Rachel and her tiny son loomed large.

"Oh, good morning, Ms. Melbourne," Zach's secretary said.

Bracing herself, Beth smiled. "How are you, Sarah?"

"Good, thanks. Mr. Winslow's expecting you."

Beth nodded and, before she could give in to the urge to take flight, crossed to Zach's door. Thinking that some of the others would already be present gave her the courage to turn the knob.

When she stepped across the threshold she saw no one—except Zach. He was busy digging through a filing cabinet that was next to the window. He didn't bother to look up.

For a moment Beth allowed herself the simple privilege of studying him. She never tired of that. He'd improved with age. At thirty-six he was better looking than he'd been at twenty-two, especially now that his hair was more silver than black. The sunlight streamed through the window and picked up the wiry threads, highlighting them.

There was no order to them; as usual, they looked mussed, as if he'd combed them on the run. A fleeting smile touched her lips. As always, his hair scraped the collar of what he was wearing. Today it was a pin-striped gray suit that fit his hard-toned body to perfection. Some things never change, she thought. He still had a butt like a high-school quarterback.

For an instant she imagined his body without the clothes, standing unabashed before her, his eyes and mouth hot with passion as he thrust into her again and again.

Realizing the train her thoughts had taken, Beth felt heat flood her face, scorching it. She must have whimpered, too, for Zach's head came up suddenly.

He stared at her. The moment was airless, thick, impenetrable. The floor seemed to shift under her feet.

"Beth."

It was a sandpaper cry. She heard her name, but she could not recognize his voice.

Finally, after a moment in which they were held frozen in the heat of the room, Zach stepped toward her, his expression now closed, unreadable.

"I didn't hear you come in."

He was her best friend's husband. Yet a moment ago she hadn't been able to stop looking at him, hadn't been able to stop her insides from melting. Now her stomach knotted with a different kind of anxiety. What if he knew what she'd been thinking? She wasn't proud of herself. But she couldn't control her feelings where Zach was concerned.

Beth clutched the straps of her purse as if they were a lifeline. "Sorry," she said a trifle breathlessly. "I guess I should've knocked, but—"

"Forget it," he said, their eyes meeting again.

She was wrong. He had changed. A grim line circled his mouth, as if he were in permanent pain. Her heart twisted. Was he unhappy? Were he and Rachel having trouble? Despite the fact that he was lost to her, she wanted him to be happy. Until now, she'd thought he was.

Beth swallowed hard. "I—I haven't seen you since Randall was born."

At the mention of his son, Zach's eyes brightened, and he smiled. She tried to ignore the jealousy that pierced her heart, but she couldn't. It was overwhelming in its intensity. But pride, prodded by sheer force of will, came to her rescue. It enabled her to school her features so that none of her torrid emotions showed.

"Ah, yes, my son. He and Rachel have changed my life." Zach's words were pointed. "I'm happier than I've ever been."

Beth felt the pulse in her throat and fought the urge to flee again, but, like a trapped animal, she stood frozen, her eyes wide. So much for her thoughts of a moment ago, she told herself, feeling nauseated. She'd obviously misinterpreted those pain lines around his mouth. Or maybe, deep down, she'd been fooling herself. Maybe she'd hoped he was unhappily married.

In the charged silence, Beth forced herself to say, "Congratulations."

"Thanks." Again his voice sounded brittle, as if he had lost the faculty of easy speech.

"You're welcome."

There was an unnatural silence.

Dear Lord, why did it have to be this way every time they met? Why couldn't she bury the past, or rise above it? Why did she have to feel as if she were in the dentist's chair and her teeth were being extracted without any novocaine?

"I understand you're setting the world on fire."

She lifted her face, and the sunlight brought her features back to life.

Zach cleared his throat and stepped back.

His putting more distance between them didn't escape Beth's notice. She sighed, and her face clouded over. "Hardly, but I am doing well."

"Rachel tells me it's more than that." He stuffed his hands into his pockets and hunched his shoulders.

In spite of herself, Beth smiled. "Rachel's prejudiced."

"And a little jealous, too."

"I doubt that." Pain lent an edge to Beth's voice. "She's got everything she ever wanted."

Zach's eyes filled with an unnameable emotion. Then he turned away, but not before Beth heard him swear.

When she would have responded, the door burst open.

Abruptly Zach's eyes swung back around and he stared beyond her shoulder, a relieved look flooding his face. Beth thought he looked as if he'd just been saved from the electric chair. Her breath caught in her throat. Damn him, she cried silently, and wished she meant it.

Zach's long stride took him to the door. Beth didn't move.

Soon the room would be filled, the players all in their places, she thought ironically, telling herself she *would* get through the ordeal.

Leading the way, and the first to acknowledge her, was Lucas Ambrose. She hadn't seen the short, heavy-featured business manager in a while. He hadn't changed; he still wore a look of ruthless intelligence.

"It's nice to see you, Beth," he said, flashing her a sincere smile.

"Same here, Lucas," she responded politely, watching as he walked into the other room and pulled out a chair at the round table.

While she waited for her brother and Taylor, both of whom were standing by the secretary's desk talking to her, Beth gazed about the room, though she was careful to keep her eyes away from Zach.

His office fitted him. Contrasting with the luxury that had surrounded him all his life, his workplace was just the opposite. It was almost austere in its practicality and nononsense approach. There was a large walnut desk, two padded chairs, a metal file cabinet, an IBM computer and three oversize plants scattered about the room. The only personal touch was the picture on his desk of a smiling Rachel and Randall, a picture that Beth had purposely not looked at.

Zach's voice pulled her back to the moment at hand. "Hi, Trent," he was saying. "I'm glad you could make it."

"I wouldn't have missed it," Trent said before focusing on Beth. "When did you hit town?" he asked.

Instead of hugging him the way she ached to do, Beth smiled. "A little while ago."

Trent had grown up to be a handsome young man. Her gaze perused him critically. With his dark, naturally curly hair, blue eyes and sullen fullness to his lower lip, he was a heart stopper. Too bad he didn't always behave as well as he looked.

Yet she'd been reassured that he was doing well at the mill. Gran had told her that Zach was proud of him and the progress he'd made. She wasn't surprised. Trent had inherited a feel for papermaking from Foster, just as Zach had from Taylor. Beth often wondered what Trent could have accomplished if only he'd taken an interest early on and applied himself. But all he ever talked about was selling the shares in the mill so he could split.

"How're Gran and Daddy?" she finally asked for his ears only, hoping to remove that sullen look from his face.

"Gran's fair and Daddy—" Trent broke off with a shrug. "I haven't seen him lately."

Beth opened her mouth, only to close it abruptly. Now was not the time to ream him out for not going to the nursing home more often. Besides, even if it *was* the right time, it wouldn't do any good.

"Nothing like bringing up the rear, I always say," a voice boomed from behind her.

"Close the door, will you, Daddy?" Zach said tightly from his position just inside the boardroom. "And get a move on. We're running late."

Beth stiffened.

"I'll talk to you later," Trent mumbled, then sauntered off to join Zach.

Beth forced herself to turn around and face the man she hated more than she'd ever hated anyone or anything in her life. "Taylor," she said coldly, a moment of triumphant reward surging through her.

He looked terrible. The whites of his eyes were filled with red spiderweb lines, and his face was a pasty gray color. Booze. It was going to be the death of him yet, and she couldn't wait. God was going to get him, she told herself without a flicker of conscience.

"Hello, little lady." Taylor's laugh had a scoffing edge. "Didn't think you'd show up."

"Go to hell, Taylor," she said softly—so softly that, for a moment, she wasn't sure he'd heard her. But then she knew he had, because unnatural color flooded his face and his mouth twisted in an ugly fashion.

"I see you haven't changed."

"Not when it comes to you," she countered with a syrupy smile that never reached her eyes. Without waiting for his reply she walked off and left him. When she reached a chair in the boardroom she felt all eyes on her, especially Zach's. Had he heard her exchange with Taylor? She didn't think so, but she couldn't be certain. She steeled herself against looking at him.

Taylor took a seat across from her. Once seated, he pulled a pipe out of his pocket. "Anyone mind?" Then, as if he didn't care whether they minded or not, he opened a pouch and began poking tobacco into the small hole. "I've always wanted to smoke a pipe," he said into the silence. "Figured it's not as lethal as cigarettes."

Beth continued to watch him sink his finger into the tobacco, feeling a revulsion she was hard-pressed to control.

"Not much difference," Trent drawled. "Personally, I'd rather not breathe the crap, if you don't mind."

"Me, either," Beth added, disgust beating against the walls of her chest.

Red faced, Taylor opened his mouth as if to argue.

"Put it away," Zach said. His tone brooked no argument.

Though Taylor's mouth stretched into a grim line, he crammed his paraphernalia back into his pocket. But there was a murderous glint in his eyes when he looked at Beth.

Following a moment of silence, Zach took charge. "First Lucas is going to give us the financial report."

Beth listened carefully. The mill, as predicted, was in sound financial shape, growing every year. After Lucas finished they discussed other pertinent business, such as acquiring more land for timber, and the price of newsprint and an upcoming audit. Following the voting on appropriate measures, a silence filled the room.

Zach broke it. "Now, for the real purpose of this meeting." His gaze sought Beth. Though his features grayed a little, his eyes never left hers. "Lucas, if you would, please hand Beth a copy of the proposal."

She took it from Lucas and immediately thumbed through the pages. But without guidance, it looked and sounded like Greek. "Tell me in simple terms what it says," she said to Zach.

When he finished, her eyes widened.

"Whaddaya know about that," Trent mumbled next to her.

Finally Beth found her voice. "I thought they wanted to merge, not buy us out."

"That's what I thought, too. But when we met again, they said they were prepared to go either way."

"They must want Southland rather badly to offer us this much money."

"You're right, they do," Zach said flatly. "Only I'm not prepared to sell or merge. Nor is Taylor."

Again all eyes turned to Beth.

She straightened in the chair. "That makes it unanimous. I don't want to sell or merge, either."

Zach's face broke into a wide grin. "We'll tell them thanks, but no thanks."

Beth caught her breath, feeling as if a ray of sunshine had just poked through the dark clouds. How long had it been since she'd seen him smile like that? She couldn't remember.

"How do you feel about it?" Zach asked Trent.

"What difference does it make what I think?" Trent angled his head toward Beth. "She has the final say-so."

"She's protecting your inheritance."

"That's what I've been trying to tell him," Beth put in evenly.

Zach lifted his eyebrows. "Is there a problem here that I should know about?"

"No problem," Trent said, his face white.

"I know I've made it tough on you, Trent, made you learn from the ground up." Zach paused with another broad smile. "Even made you empty a few wastepaper baskets along the way, right?"

"Yeah, right. A lot of wastepaper baskets," Trent mumbled, looking a bit perplexed, as if he couldn't quite figure out where this conversation was leading.

Beth wondered, too, but she kept quiet, content to sit back and listen.

Zach chewed on the corner of his lip for a second, then spoke quickly, as if now that he had made up his mind he couldn't wait to get the words out. "I think you're just the man I'm looking for." He paused again, only this time he didn't smile. "Yep, I think you'll make a fine assistant mill manager."

Trent jumped up, his mouth open, his eyes on fire. "You do?"

Without answering, Zach turned to Beth. "What about you? Think it's a good idea?"

Beth grinned. "Why, I think it's a wonderful idea."

Trent swung his gaze to Beth, a dumbfounded look replacing the shocked one of a second ago. "You do?"

"Is that all you can say?" Zach asked, clearly amused.

Trent gulped. "Well . . . no. I mean . . ."

"Hey, boy," Taylor said in his bourbon-scratched voice. "Cat got your tongue?"

Trent, having recovered now, rolled his eyes, then laughed sheepishly, as if embarrassed by all the attention.

God, but her brother's laughter sounded good, Beth thought, thanksgiving welling up inside her. If anything would turn him around, this would. She had Zach to thank. But when she turned and caught his eye, his face closed to a rigid coldness.

Beth winced as if he'd struck her, then turned away. Her heart felt old and swollen. Several minutes passed before she pulled herself together enough to get up, the meeting having been adjourned.

Without saying a word to anyone, she stood and made her way to the door.

"Hey, wait up. Where you going in such a hurry, sis?"

Beth stopped, turned and looked at her brother through a maze of unshed tears. He had never called her sis. She smiled. Now that was a good sign, a very good sign indeed.

Twenty-Eight

Zach massaged his forehead while his eyes scanned the report on his desk. He couldn't believe he was just getting around to apprising himself of what had taken place yesterday in the various departments. After his rounds each morning, poring over the reports always followed.

But not this morning. Since he'd arrived at seven o'clock he hadn't stopped. He'd not only had the all-important meeting to prepare for, but the head of the union, Wade Griffin, had cornered him. Griffin was on his goddamn back. He'd had no choice but to look over the suggestions the man had thrust at him.

Zach paused in his thoughts, a bitter smile turning his lips into a smirk. Suggestions, hell, they were ultimatums.

Griffin thought he was smart, though. Or maybe he thought Zach was stupid. Well, he had news for him. He wasn't stupid, nor was he going to knuckle under to the union's outlandish demands. The sooner Griffin realized that, the better off he would be.

Zach increased the pressure on his forehead. His power of concentration was broken. Disgusted, he thrust aside the report. If it hadn't been for the positive outcome of the meeting this morning, he would have thrown up his hands in frustration, said to hell with it, put on a hard hat and gone to the wood yard. Nothing like hard labor to jerk the kinks out of your mind and body. For a moment he was tempted to do just that. Then he remembered that Matt

Thorne was due any minute with information that Zach had asked for.

As if on cue, Matt poked his head around the door.

"Get your ass in here on the double," Zach said, standing. While Matt lumbered across the room, Zach wrestled with the button beneath his tie. As soon as he removed both the tie and his coat, he tossed them onto the nearest chair.

Matt grinned. "Been waitin' long?"

Zach sat back down. "No."

"You're not busy?"

The lines around Zach's mouth betrayed the pressure he was feeling. "Yeah, busy trying to decide if I want to chuck it now or later."

Matt quirked an eyebrow. "Meeting must've turned sour, huh?"

"Hell, no. Beth sided with us."

"Well, you oughta be celebrating instead of crying in your booze."

"Oh, I'm celebrating, all right. But I never really thought she'd go along with the deal in the first place. Unless it was to spite me, that is."

Matt fiddled with the rim of his glasses. "What would you have done if she had?"

"That would've been grounds for murder."

"I do believe you're serious."

Zach didn't say anything.

Matt looked at him strangely for a second, then said, "Well, I'm glad things turned out okay."

Zach sighed. "Thanks."

"Something's bothering you. Let's hear it."

"Griffin's on my ass again."

Matt didn't respond immediately. Instead he walked around Zach's desk, laid down a folder, then eased back into a chair. "He *is* an ass. You know, God's bound to get that guy."

Zach grinned darkly. "Not if we get him first."

"Any ideas?"

"No, but I'm working on it. In the meantime, God may get me."

Matt gave an answering grin and leaned forward. "Naw, if he hasn't already, he ain't gonna."

Zach grinned, lifting one side of his mouth. "Don't be too sure of that." Then he fell silent and watched as the sunlight called attention to Matt's receding hairline. "Aw, hell, it'll all work out somehow." His features cleared. "So, what'cha got?"

"The figures you asked for," Matt said. "They look promising, too." He leaned back in his chair and stretched his legs out in front of him. "Take a quick look-see."

"Want some coffee?"

"Yeah, don't mind if I do."

After reading for a little while Zach raised his eyes and grinned at Matt, who was in the process of blowing on his coffee to cool it. "I had no idea the schools used that much construction paper."

"Well, I did. I have two kids who seem to go through the stuff by the ton." He took a sip of coffee and grinned. "Wait till Randall gets to school. You'll see."

Zach smiled. "Can't wait."

"So, how should we proceed on this?"

Zach scanned the figures one more time. "Quickly. As in now. Someone's already making that stuff. We might as well get in on the action." He paused. "I don't have to tell you that competition's getting tougher every day. In order to survive, we're going to have to continue to branch out. Newsprint alone just won't cut it anymore."

"I hear you, boss," Matt said, tossing his empty cup in the wastebasket.

"Oh, and while you're at it, check on that fax-machine paper. My gut instinct tells me those things are going to skyrocket. Why not get in on the action?"

"No reason. I'll get on it pronto. Anything else?" Matt rose to his feet.

Zach followed suit. "Yeah, matter of fact, there is."

Matt lifted both eyebrows. "Shoot."

"Have Charlie meet me here in the morning. I'm finally going to give him some help."

"Trent?"

"Yeah. You think it'll work?" Zach watched his assistant carefully.

"Sure do," Matt drawled and rubbed his chin. "I know he can be a pain in the ass, but that boy knows his stuff. He's a chip off the old block, all right. Foster Melbourne damn well knew what he was doing."

"Trent's nose for the job is instinctive, which makes it even better."

"Well," Matt said, "we'll keep our fingers crossed that he'll work out."

When Matt closed the door behind him there was no sound in the room except Zach's own heart beating. He listened to it for a second, then went to the coffeepot and filled a cup.

His intentions were to finish reading the reports so he could clear them off his desk. But after sitting back down he found he still couldn't concentrate, at least not on business.

Stealing a look out the window, he noticed that the sun had finally won the war over the clouds, thus turning what had started out to be a cool, gray day into a mild and beautiful one. The kind of day when you said adios to work, grabbed a picnic lunch and a pole, and headed for the woods. And spent the afternoon eating, fishing and making love—like he and Beth used to do....

Zach uttered a sound like a wounded beast, then lunged to his feet, knocking over his cup of coffee, which spilled everywhere.

''Way to go, Winslow,'' he grunted, watching the dark stain spread across the papers. Instead of mopping up the mess, Zach turned, stomped to the window and stood there, a myriad of emotions boiling inside, ranging from rage to guilt and back to rage.

She did it to him every time. Just being in the same room with her wrung him inside out.

What the hell was the matter with him? He had it all. What more could he want? He was doing what he loved. He was married to a wonderful woman, who had mended his heart after Beth had broken it. Not only that, but she had given him the greatest gift of all, the son that he loved with all his heart.

So what was his problem? Why did he let Beth get to him? She made him ache, that was why.

The minute she entered the room, looking as if she'd just stepped out of the latest *Vogue,* the ache began. He'd watched her and felt a piercing sadness growing like cancer cells inside him, striking him to the bone.

His face had remained impassive. He'd made sure of that, having become a master at deception. Still, he had been nearly desperate for the meeting to come to an end. Every gesture, every move, every smile, had ripped open the sealed memories of another time, another place.

It was those memories that were making him crazy now. Was he doomed to remember for a lifetime every sound, every smell, every taste of her? He felt something jump in his gut. Dear God, he prayed. As it was, he was wondering how he could go home and explain to Rachel what he was thinking and feeling.

''Hey, good-lookin','' a voice purred from behind, ''you got a minute?''

Rachel! Guilt charged through Zach with such force that for a second he was too weak to turn around. Finally he swung around and grinned. ''Well, now, lemme see. Maybe I could find a second to spare.''

Rachel giggled and came toward him. He met her half-way, grabbed her, held her tightly against him, then kissed her long and hard.

When they were both gasping for air he let her go. She pulled back and stared up at him, amazement written across her flushed face. "Goodness," she whispered, clearly flustered. "I'll have to make a habit of surprising you more often."

He tweaked her on the nose. "I'm going to hold you to that."

She cocked her head and stared at him. "Hey, is there something you're not telling me?"

A pain of a different kind stabbed him, and again he kissed her. She deserved better than him. "Now, where's that good-lookin' son of mine?"

"Outside with your good-lookin' secretary," Rachel teased breathlessly.

"How 'bout I take you two to lunch?"

"Me and your secretary, or Randall?"

Zach swatted her on the rear. "Watch your mouth, woman."

"Ah, now I know. The meeting went well."

Zach felt another twinge of guilt. He'd meant to call her, only... "It went great."

She squeezed his hand. "I knew it would."

"Come on," he said, placing an arm around her waist. "Let's get our son, and I'll tell you all about it."

Twenty-Nine

Ruby Carrington was an attractive, strong-featured woman with dyed black hair and dark brown eyes that were oftentimes cool and shuttered.

Beth had always felt that Rachel's mother didn't like her, that she merely tolerated her because of who she was. That thought alone had always disgusted Beth and saddened her for Rachel. In many ways Ruby was as big a snob as Marian Winslow, only Ruby didn't have anything to be snobbish about. Not until her daughter married a Winslow, at least. Afterward, it seemed as if Ruby was sure she had the right to tilt her nose and act as if she, too, were better than the average mortal.

When Beth was eighteen she had known that Rachel's mother wanted Rachel to marry Zach, but not because she was putting her daughter's happiness above anything else. It was Ruby's own happiness, *her* standing in the community, that she was concerned about. Rachel was merely a tool.

Now, as Beth watched Ruby cuddle her grandson in her arms in the living room of Rachel and Zach's private apartment, she couldn't help but wonder if her attachment to her grandson was for show as well, then felt ashamed of her thoughts.

Who was she to sit in judgment of anyone? As the old adage went, she was the pot calling the kettle black.

She had dressed casually but trendily in a pair of pleated jeans, an oversize cotton sweater with shoulder pads and dangling earrings. She'd felt the need to buoy her sagging spirits.

While Beth wanted to see Rachel and spend time with her, she had dreaded coming here to Wimberly. At first she didn't know which she feared seeing the most, Zach or Taylor, but the latter finally won. The thought of coming face-to-face with Taylor again was abhorrent. Yesterday's encounter would suffice for a lifetime.

She'd been relieved that when she'd phoned Rachel to confirm their plans, her friend had casually volunteered the information that both Zach and Taylor would be out of town all day.

Still, Beth had mixed emotions. The prospect of seeing Rachel with her baby was tantamount to suffering a slow, painful death. But she'd known she would have to face them sooner or later, and it might as well be sooner. She had made her choice long ago, and there was no turning back.

But instead of having Rachel to herself, she'd been disappointed when Ruby Carrington had arrived after she had. They had visited politely over coffee until Randall had cried out. Rachel had gone and gotten him out of his crib and brought him back with her. Since then, Ruby hadn't had much to say. She'd merely held Randall and rocked him.

"Well?"

Beth ceased her woolgathering and gave Rachel an innocent smile. "Well, what?"

Rachel made a face, then stuck out her tongue at Beth. "You're bad, you know that?"

Beth smiled, kicked off her shoes, lifted her feet off the floor and tucked them under her. "Uh-huh."

"If you don't tell me my son's the most beautiful baby you've ever seen, I'm going to mark you off my friend list." She grinned.

Beth held up her hands in mock fear. "I surrender. He's the most beautiful baby I've ever seen."

"Really?"

Beth's gaze softened on the baby, sleeping peacefully in his grandmother's arms. "Really," she whispered.

"He looks like me," Rachel said matter-of-factly but with pride.

Beth scrutinized the tiny face. "Exactly." She had noticed that the minute Rachel placed the baby in her arms and she'd gazed into his sweet, round face.

Before Rachel could respond, Ruby stood. "I hate to leave such good company, but I have an appointment. And I'm already late." She paused and handed Randall to Rachel. "It was nice seeing you again, Beth," she added politely. "As usual, you look wonderful."

Beth stood and smiled, more amused than offended by the insincerity she heard in Ruby's voice. "Thanks, Ruby," she said lightly.

After kissing both Rachel and Randall on the cheek, Ruby lifted her purse off the back of the rocker and made her way toward the door.

"Bye, Mamma," Rachel said. "I'll see you later."

"Take care of my grandson."

"Yes, Mamma."

After the door slammed, Rachel looked at Beth and rolled her eyes. "She thinks I don't have the sense God gave a billy goat."

Beth laughed.

"Hold on a second. I'm gonna put this ton of bricks down, then I'll make us a fresh pot of coffee."

"Need any help?" Beth asked.

"Nah, I'll only be a minute."

While Beth waited for Rachel her eyes scanned the room. This was to have been her and Zach's home, she thought with a sharp pang. More than likely she would have decorated it much the same way Rachel had.

The green, peach and white area rug went with the pale peach walls and white trim. An expensive painting hung above the marble fireplace, a gift she was certain had come from the Winslows.

Through an open archway she could see the kitchen. The color scheme had been carried out in there, as well. Overall, the apartment spoke of a cozy but quiet elegance.

"You've done a fantastic job with this place," Beth said when Rachel walked back into the room.

Rachel didn't respond, busy worrying with the zipper on her paisley slacks.

Beth smiled. "What's wrong?"

Rachel frowned. "Fat. That's what's wrong."

"You're not fat."

"Well, I'm sure not skinny, either."

"No, but you're a long way from being fat. Anyway, you have an excuse, you've just had a baby."

"Are you forgetting that Randall's eight months old? I should've been rid of this blubber months ago."

"You'll get it off."

"I know, that's what I keep telling myself, only—"

"Only what?"

"When I look at you, I feel like a blimp."

Beth gave an unladylike snort. "Come on, you're being too hard on yourself."

"Maybe so." Rachel shrugged. "At least Zach says he doesn't care."

"And that's all that counts," Beth said softly, trying to ignore the jab of pain in her heart.

"So you like the way I've done the apartment, huh?" Rachel asked, changing the subject.

"I told you I did."

"Wanna see the rest of it?" she asked, leading Beth into the kitchen.

"Yes, but later. Right now, I'm dying for a cup of that fresh coffee."

"How 'bout some breakfast to go with it?"

"Thanks, but no thanks." Beth grinned and sat down at the round oak table. "Still can't abide an egg winking at me in the morning."

Rachel laughed.

"But go ahead and fix yourself something."

"Are you kidding? I ate long ago, right after I fed Randall. No ten o'clock eating time around here, except maybe on Sundays."

"With a baby, I guess not."

"Rest assured, they make a difference. Just in the eight months since he's been here, this place has turned into Grand Central Station."

Beth chuckled. "I'm not surprised. Babies have a tendency to do that, or so I'm told."

"Taylor's the worst."

Beth blinked in surprise. "Taylor."

"Yep. He stops by every morning and plays with Randall."

Beth turned her gaze toward a window and watched a squirrel as it jumped from one moss-covered limb to another. "So he dotes on his grandson? That's good."

"I know you don't care for Taylor, but he's been good to me."

Beth had often wondered how Taylor and Marian honestly felt about Rachel. She had feared that they both, but especially Marian, would hold it against Rachel because her family lacked the "correct" ancestry.

Marian could tolerate "poor white trash" only as long as they knew their rightful place. She believed that success belonged to those who could trace their lineage back hundreds of years.

But maybe Taylor was so thankful that Zach hadn't married her, and even that he had married at all, that he had embraced Rachel with open arms.

"I'm glad," Beth finally said, forcing herself to face Rachel once again. "Grandparents are important. I can't imagine life without Gran."

"My mother's another one." Rachel paused, poured two cups full of coffee and brought them to the table. After handing one to Beth, she sat opposite her. "If she doesn't come by, she calls."

"Your mother's devotion doesn't surprise me."

"Not only is she crazy about Randall, she's crazy about Zach, as well."

"That's great," Beth said for lack of anything better to say.

Rachel looked at Beth over the rim of her cup. "That doesn't surprise you, either, does it?"

"No."

Rachel sighed. "Mother never hid the fact that she wanted me to be Mrs. Zachery Winslow."

Beth's knuckles whitened around the cup. "I know."

"Look...Beth," Rachel began, her eyes clearly troubled.

Beth reached out with her free hand and squeezed Rachel's. "Hey, it's all right, Rach. Really."

"Is it, Beth? Is it really?" She licked her lips as if they had suddenly gone dry.

"Don't," Beth pleaded, turning away. "Don't start again. I thought we'd settled all that."

Rachel withdrew her hand. "Sorry, I didn't mean to reopen old wounds."

"Oh, Rach, it's not that. It's just that there's no point in dragging it out again."

Rachel leaned her head to one side, her eyes intense. "Can I ask you something?"

"All right," Beth said hesitantly.

"Why didn't you marry Zach?"

"Rachel!"

Crimson color flooded Rachel's face. "Okay, okay. But please, just this once, humor me."

Beth smiled to cover her fears. "You know why."

"I know what you told me at the time, but—" Rachel broke off. "I guess what I'm trying to say is that I can't stand the thought of you being unhappy because I—" Her voice was thick with doubt and fear.

"Shh, don't say it," Beth pleaded. "Don't even think it. I made my choices a long time ago, and I still stand by them. The past is just that—the past." The lies came automatically to her lips. "You're married to Zach now, and you two have a life together, along with a wonderful baby."

Tears sprang into Rachel's eyes. "Oh, Beth, I love you."

"And I love you." Beth's eyes were also damp with tears. "Now see what you've done?"

Rachel giggled. "Just like old times, huh? We could both cry at the drop of a handkerchief."

"Yeah, we were something else, weren't we?" Beth asked, so relieved the tense moment had passed that she was almost giddy.

"Tell me what you've been up to. Anyone special in your life?"

Beth relaxed. "You mean a man?"

"Of course, silly."

"There was."

"Was?"

"I told him he was wasting his time."

"Grrr, sometimes I'd like to strangle you."

Beth gave her a lopsided grin. "I know. I'm hopeless."

"You must really like what you do."

"I love it. But is it ever a challenge. It seems as though I have to be on my toes twenty-four hours a day."

"That's obvious," Rachel said drolly. "You're as skinny as a matchstick. Don't you know that all work and no play makes you a d-u-l-l person?"

Beth laughed. "That's me."

"And Cottonwood?"

Like quicksilver, Beth's face changed. "What about it?"

"You still want it back?"

"More than ever." The determination in her voice was unmistakable.

"Well, I—" Rachel got no further. The phone rang. She grimaced. "Probably someone wanting to sell me aluminum siding."

Beth shook her head and smiled, then turned toward the window again, trying not to eavesdrop on the conversation. But when Rachel wailed, "You mean this afternoon?" Beth found herself listening and watching without apology as Rachel's face sobered and her shoulders sagged. "The morning won't do?"

Rachel listened for a few more moments, then said, "I see. All right. I'll be there."

When she hung up the phone she stared at Beth, a troubled frown on her face.

"What on earth, Rach?"

"Well, to make a long story short, the doctor is insisting I come in this afternoon. At two-thirty, to be exact. He insists on talking to me about one of my test results."

Beth's heart skipped a beat. "Are you sick? I mean—"

"No. At least, I don't think so. I've just had a little discomfort in my pelvic area, and some vaginal bleeding, since Randall was born. Dr. Faircloth ran extensive tests."

"Well, I'm sure it's nothing serious, but by all means you should go and talk to him."

"What about you?" Rachel's lips curved downward into a pout. "I hate to cut our visit short."

"Maybe we won't have to. How 'bout this? Why don't I baby-sit Randall? That way I'd be here when you got back. Then we could visit some more."

The cloud lifted from Rachel's face. "You wouldn't mind?"

"I'd love it."

"In the meantime," Rachel said, "why don't we pack a picnic lunch and go to the park? Randall loves to look at the animals."

"Fine by me."

The remainder of the morning sped by, and Beth couldn't remember having had such a fun, relaxed time in months. Randall was a delight; he grinned and cooed, and Beth fell promptly and hopelessly in love with him. During the times when he dozed, she and Rachel talked about her business. Rachel was fascinated by her work and wanted to hear all about it. On the way back to Rachel's, they stopped by the nursing home so Beth could see her daddy.

By the time they arrived at Wimberly, they were pleasantly tired.

"Why don't you take a nap with Randall?" Rachel suggested just before she walked out the door.

Beth gave her a quick hug. "I just might."

"Are you sure you want to do this?" Rachel's grin was teasing. "What if he tee-tees on you?"

Beth whacked her playfully on the arm. "Oh, for heaven's sake, I won't melt if he does. Go on, get out of here. We'll be just fine. If not, Marian's close. I'll call her."

"No, you won't. Marian's at one of her all-day club meetings."

"Well, then, I'll call your mother. But don't worry, we'll be fine."

Following Rachel's departure, Beth wandered aimlessly about for a while; then, deciding that Rachel's idea of a nap sounded good, she curled up on the sofa and laid her head back against the cushion. But sleep wouldn't come. She guessed she was too keyed up, as well as worried about Rachel. Although Rachel had downplayed this visit to the doctor, Beth knew she was concerned.

Too, now that it was a fait accompli, Beth felt uneasy being at Wimberly alone. What if Zach decided to come home early? Or, worse, what if Taylor dropped by?

She jumped up. No way was she going to ruin this day with morbid thoughts. It had been too perfect. Besides, it was time to check on Randall, although she'd been to his room at least a dozen times since Rachel left.

She stood over the crib and peered down at him. He was sleeping on his stomach, with his head facing the opposite wall.

"You're something else, Randall Zachery Winslow," she whispered. "Did you know that?"

He was too pretty, she thought, his beauty touching her heart. His tiny ears were perfect, as was his skin; it was rosy, like fresh peaches.

Tears clumped her lashes. Looking toward the ceiling, Beth blinked to keep them back. Her lower lip trembled. She looked back down and whispered again, "You should've been mine."

Swallowing the huge lump in her throat, Beth grabbed a Kleenex off the chest and wiped her eyes. She had to touch him. She had to feel his soft skin against her own, had to kiss that perfect ear.

She leaned over, only to suddenly stop midway. "Oh, my God! Randall!"

His tiny features were pinched in pain. He was choking.

In a panic, she picked him up and gently shook him. But he continued to gasp for breath.

What should she do? She didn't know! Common sense came to her rescue.

"Oh, please, dear God," Beth whimpered, quickly turning Randall upside down and patting him on the back. But that didn't revive him, either.

She put her finger in his mouth to see if there was an obstruction and found that his tongue had curled back into his throat, blocking the airway.

Desperate, she pressed her finger down on his tongue. "Breathe, please, Randall, breathe!"

It worked! He gasped, coughed and started to breathe.

"Thank God," Beth sobbed, removing her finger from his mouth and cuddling him close. His tiny but steady heartbeat against her own aroused such profound relief that she felt sick to her stomach.

Only after Randall began to whimper did she realize how tightly she was holding him. "Okay, young fellow, back down you go," she said, her voice quivering with the same intensity as her insides.

Even after he was once again in the bed and his diaper changed, Beth hovered anxiously, still reeling from the scare he'd given her. What on earth had happened? What had brought it on? Had this happened before and Rachel just hadn't mentioned it? Should she call 911?

That last unanswered question forced her to remain steadfast by his crib for what seemed an eternity, monitoring every move, every sound he made. When his chest hummed a steady rhythm and he was asleep, Beth finally decided she could leave him long enough to pour herself a much-needed cup of coffee.

The kitchen was quiet but she scarcely noticed, her rioting heart making its own noise. After quickly helping herself to the coffee, she leaned against the cabinet, glad of its support. She took two sips of the hot liquid and immediately felt better.

But what a freakish thing to happen, she thought. And such a close call, too. But she had come through, and she was proud of that.

But self-contragulation wasn't uppermost in her mind. Hurrying back to Randall was top priority. She didn't plan to budge, either, until Rachel returned.

She paused inside the door and smiled. Again she marveled at how perfect he was. Aching for a closer look, she
inched forward.

"Are you still sleeping, sweetheart?" she crooned,
bending her head over the crib.

That was when she noticed. He had started to turn blue
again.

"No! No. Not again!" Beth's voice reached the outer
limits of terror. "Breathe!"

She put her finger back on his tongue while she prayed
for a response. Nothing. Frantically her eyes searched the
room for a phone. There wasn't one. Holding him, she
raced into the living room. She found the phone, but she
couldn't dial. She was all thumbs. Her fingers shook; her
eyes blurred.

And Randall still wasn't breathing.

"Help me!" Beth cried, sucking in her own breath and
trying again.

She finally managed to complete the call. Only after a
grueling but short lesson on performing CPR did she receive reassurance that help was on the way.

"Please hurry!" she begged and slammed the receiver
down.

Beth then placed Randall on his back in her lap and
pressed two fingers into his sternum, all the while scared she
would break his ribs. He seemed as fragile as a china doll.

"Please, Randall honey, breathe."

With each word she spoke, Beth continued to press. His
fragile bones seemed to sway under her fingers.

She sat as if in a fog, and sobbed and pressed. And
soothed him, her words soft, like a lullaby she remembered from childhood.

Beth didn't look up until she heard voices. She didn't
recognize them. She didn't even realize that one was her
own, that she told them they should call Rachel at the doctor's office. But she knew she had. She must have.

"Are you all right, Ms. Melbourne?" one of the paramedics asked her when he got off the phone.

She couldn't answer him. All she could do was sit with her arms crossed over her body to protect herself. She kept shivering like a body in cold storage.

How long had it been since they'd taken Randall out of her arms and left her on the couch? Two minutes? Ten minutes? She had lost all concept of time. She couldn't remember how to read her watch.

Later a hand touched Beth on the shoulder. "Ms. Melbourne?"

She raised terrified eyes. "Is he...is he...all right?"

"No, I'm afraid he's not."

"But...but he will be, won't he?"

"I'm sorry. He's...dead."

Thirty

Flowers covered the tiny grave, and a pearl-like drizzle beaded their petals with a translucent beauty.

But Beth wasn't aware of any of it. She wasn't even aware that she was soaked to the skin. She wasn't aware of anything except that yesterday at ten o'clock Randall Zachery Winslow had been laid to rest in the cold, dark earth.

And she was to blame.

Her body wanted to fall into fragments. Her knees threatened to give way; her thoughts were chaotic. Her mind felt dislocated, almost as if she were in another person's body.

"Oh, Randall," she whispered brokenly. "I'm so sorry, so sorry."

Beth sank to the ground, her knees buried in the soggy grass. Her shoulders shook. She wept deep, raw tears that came straight from her soul.

She longed to get up, put her numb body back into the car and drive until she disappeared from the face of the earth.

But she knew she couldn't do that. Life wasn't that simple. Her only recourse was to return to Natchitoches, where she would no longer encounter the sympathetic but prying eyes of well-meaning friends.

More than that, she couldn't endure facing Zach and Rachel again. She doubted if she ever could.

When the paramedic had told her that Randall was dead, she had feared for her sanity. She remembered staring at him in horrified disbelief while a scream gained momentum in her lungs and terror built around her heart. She licked her lips, then slumped over. Her insides drew themselves into a hard, gripping knot.

"It's not your fault," the doctor had told her moments after he'd arrived and examined Randall.

She'd sat like a zombie on the couch, her face bloodless, her skin tight and white, and she'd looked right through him.

"Ms. Melbourne, I'm Dr. McKee. Do you understand what I just said?"

He had no more than gotten the words out when the front door burst open and Rachel charged across the threshold.

"Beth!" she cried, her frantic eyes searching the room until they found her friend. "Where's Randall? Where's my baby?"

Beth heaved herself to her feet and moved toward her friend, her eyes despairing. "Oh, Rachel..." Her voice failed. Rachel ignored Beth and ran toward the bedroom. Halfway there, the doctor caught her gently by the arm to stop her.

"Mrs. Winslow, don't. Please, let me talk to you."

"No!" Rachel wrenched her arm free. "Where's my baby? What have you done with my baby?"

"I'm sorry, Mrs. Winslow, but your baby's dead."

Rachel placed her hands over her ears and stepped back. "No!" she screeched. "You're lying to me!"

"Mrs. Winslow...please," Dr. McKee began, only to stop as the door opened again. This time it was Zach who walked in, his face twisted in alarm.

"Zach, oh, Zach!" Rachel ran to him and flung herself into his arms. "Our baby...our baby's dead!"

Zach reeled as if he'd been hit with an ax. *"What?"*

Tremor after tremor surged through Beth as she watched, helplessly locked in a prison of rage and guilt.

"My baby's dead. Dead. Dead!" Rachel screamed as she beat on Zach's chest with her fists.

He tried to restrain her, but in her grief-stricken state she was stronger than he was.

Beth stood motionless. Then she lowered her head and crossed her arms over her chest. Tears spilled onto her hands. When had she begun to cry?

Unwittingly she rushed to Zach's side to help him with Rachel. But when Rachel saw her, she screamed again, "Don't you dare touch me! It's all your fault. You let my baby die!"

Zach uttered a choking sound and stared at Beth, his eyes round in his white face.

Rachel moaned, then fell against him like a rag doll.

For a moment the very air seemed to hold its breath.

Finally Zach tore his eyes from Beth, looked down at the limp figure in his arms and cried, "Doctor!"

While the doctor hovered, Zach carried Rachel to the couch and laid her gently on it.

"Is she going to be all right?" he asked.

Dr. McKee's voice was soothing. "Your wife will be fine. She just fainted. When she comes to, I'm going to give her something to keep her quiet. She'll sleep.'

"My son, Doctor? Is it…true…?" Zach's voice sounded hollow, as if there was nothing inside him.

Beth tried to make sense out of what was happening, but she couldn't. She felt like a hunted animal that had had a net dropped over it. The more she struggled to be free, the tighter the net became.

The doctor patted Zach on the shoulder. "I'm sorry. It's true."

A cry tore from Zach's throat as his teeth clamped down on his lower lip and drew blood. His face bore the anguish of a man who had been to hell and back.

Beth averted her gaze, unable to watch him suffer.

The doctor patted him on the shoulder again and turned back to Rachel.

Zach walked over to where Beth stood. She forced herself to face him.

"My God, Beth," he whispered hoarsely, his eyes falling on her like a brick. "What happened?"

She wanted to say something; her brain screamed at her mouth, but the signals were intercepted. She simple stood there and stared at him.

He grabbed her by the arms and shook her. "Dammit, Beth, talk to me!"

His words cut through her like a sharp knife. When she still didn't answer, he shook her again. Her hair tumbled wildly around her cheeks and soaked up the tears.

"Go ahead," she challenged, "hurt me. I deserve it."

Zach froze, as if realizing what he was doing. With a tormented groan that came from deep within, he let go of her so quickly that she stumbled backward and almost lost her balance.

"Beth . . . !"

The pain in his voice seared her to the bone. She had to tell him. "I . . . was staying with Randall," she said, squeezing the words out, "while Rachel went to the doctor. I . . . I kept checking on him. The last time, I noticed he . . . he looked odd." Beth placed a hand over her mouth, as if she were about to throw up. "He . . . he was blue, and then he wasn't breathing. I . . . called for help, but it was too late." The last words were barely audible.

Zach turned to the doctor, who had walked up beside him. "Nothing could have been done?" he asked, his voice low and thin with grief.

"Probably not," Dr. McKee said kindly. "Although we'll know more later. The preliminary exam points to Sudden Infant Death Syndrome as the cause of death."

Zach uttered a choking sound. "Crib death?"

"Yes, Mr. Winslow."

"But how . . . ? I mean . . ."

"Unfortunately we don't have the answer to that yet. It's a cruel, mysterious killer that claims the lives of thousands of seemingly healthy infants each year."

"I can't . . . I don't believe it." Zach's voice was husky, scraping over the pain.

"Ms. Melbourne did everything there was to do," the doctor stressed. "She tried to save your baby's life, but he was too far gone."

A vein throbbed in Zach's left temple; otherwise, he might have been dead. "I'd like to see my . . . son now."

Beth's eyes followed Zach's back until he walked through the door into the bedroom and soundlessly shut the door. Moments later his sobs leaked through the cracks.

The sound was more than Beth could bear. Her legs folded under her like a collapsed chair. A paramedic's strong arms caught her and kept her from landing on the floor.

Wordlessly he helped her to the nearest seat.

"I'm . . . fine," Beth said at length. "I . . . think I should go home now." She closed her eyes while silent tears streamed down her face.

"Ms. Melbourne," Dr. McKee said, "you're in no shape to drive. Why not let one of the paramedics take you?"

Beth shook her head woodenly. "I'll be all right. Just give me a minute."

Dr. McKee looked as if he wanted to argue, but he didn't. "Here's something to take when you get settled." Treating her like an invalid, he lifted her hand and placed a small packet of pills in her palm. "If you need me, I'll be on call at the hospital."

What happened next passed in a blur. Beth was barely cognizant of breathing, much less functioning. When she got to her grandmother's, Grace consoled her as best she could. But Beth was inconsolable.

She decided later that it was her zombielike state that allowed her to get through the church service, though each word the minister spoke was like another spike of guilt being driven through her heart. The graveside service was even worse.

The sun showed no mercy.

The mourners, paying their last respects to Randall Zachery Winslow, squirmed under its relentless rays. There were plenty of mourners on hand, too. The death of the son of the town's oldest and most prestigious family was news, the type of tragic news that made for juicy gossip, especially in light of Beth and Zach's past relationship. So far the wagging tongues had been held to whispers behind closed doors, but that would soon change. Soon the whispers would burgeon into full-fledged voices, distorting the truth until no one recognized it, not even the ones who were spreading it.

Beth was conscious of that, and her best defense against the prying eyes was to hide behind a facade of dark glasses and stony silence.

With her peripheral vision, she could see Zach's stoic but brutalized features, and she could hear Rachel's quiet sobs. And then there were Taylor and Marian, who she knew blamed her. Especially Taylor. Although he hadn't spoken to her, she was aware of the venomous looks he cast her way. She could handle that, but what she couldn't handle was Rachel's blame. It crushed her, broke her heart.

When the service ended she and Gran made their way to the car. Halfway there, a voice stopped them.

"Beth?"

She pulled up short, then eased around. Zach and Rachel stood side by side, their faces ravaged with tears.

Her grandmother touched her on the arm. "I'll wait for you in the car, honey."

Rachel disentangled herself from Zach and held out her arms. "I'm so sorry, Beth," she whispered. "I...didn't mean what I said. I know you did all you could. Will you ever forgive me?''

"Oh, Rach," Beth sobbed, diving into her open arms. "I'd give anything if it had been me instead of Randall."

"I know, I know," Rachel whispered, then stepped back. "You take care now," she added, reaching for Zach's hand.

When Beth was home in bed that night, alone with her pain and heartache, all she could think about was that Zach had never said a word. He had simply looked at her with those vacant eyes.

Now, as she wrenched her tortured thoughts back to the task at hand, Beth forced her wobbly legs into a standing position. That was as far as she got. She didn't want to move. She didn't want to *live*. She hurt so badly, pain was a taste in her mouth.

Four days ago Randall was alive.

Now he was gone.

In a lonely hole.

She leaned over finally and placed a single rose at the foot of the grave.

"Taylor, just how long do you intend to drown your sorrows in the bottle?"

His wife's soft, accusing tone infuriated him. "As long as it takes, woman. Now get the hell out of my face and leave me alone."

"No, I won't leave you alone," Marian snapped, closing the distance between them and grabbing the empty bottle out of his hand. "Just look at you. You're disgusting. Dirty hair and dirty clothes. My God, you even smell."

Eyes blazing, Taylor lunged out of the easy chair in their bedroom and drew back his hand.

"Go ahead, hit me," Marian challenged, her own eyes afire. "Go ahead, if you think it'll make you more of a man," she spat, her lips curled back in contempt.

They glared at each other, both breathing heavily.

Eventually Taylor lowered his hand. "Aw, what the hell. Just get out of my sight."

Marian stood her ground. "Randall's been dead six months. It's time you came to terms with that."

"Who says?" he snarled.

Marian took a deep breath. "Do you love Zachery?"

"What does that have to do with it?"

Marian blinked in rapid succession. "You fool, it has everything to do with it. He needs your support, your love, right now. So does Rachel."

Taylor sneered. "You're wrong, as usual. He won't let me near him. And he sure as hell won't talk about Randall."

"That's because you're always half-cocked when you try."

"Ah, you don't understand. You didn't love the kid like I did."

Marian flinched as if he'd struck her. "How can you even think such a cruel thing, much less say it?" Tears pooled in her eyes. "Randall was my grandson, too. I loved him as much as you did. But I also love Zachery, and he and Rachel need us now. Both of us, damn you."

Taylor fell back into his chair and stared up at her with bleary eyes. "Why did she leave my grandson with *her?*"

"We've been over this a thousand times, Taylor. Let it go. For once, do something right. Sober up and support your son."

"Not until that bitch pays. She killed my grandson!"

"Oh, Taylor, you poor besotted fool." Marian shook her head sadly. "It wasn't her fault. Crib death is no one's fault."

"That's your opinion," he muttered. "I have mine, and I won't rest until she pays for what she did."

"If I were you, I'd be careful. One of these days you're going to mess with the wrong person and get what's coming to you."

Marian turned and marched out the door, slamming it behind her.

Taylor winced and cradled his throbbing head in the palm of his right hand. Damn her. Her threats didn't bother him. He could take care of himself; he always had.

He didn't intend to back down. He hated that bitch Beth Melbourne. But he would have to be more careful in the future. He saw that now. If he was to get even with Beth, he'd have to control the boiling rage that thundered through him every time she looked at him as if he were something less than human. He owed her for that, too.

He grinned smugly. But he'd shown her who had the upper hand years ago, hadn't he? There wasn't a reason in the world he couldn't do it again. He would bide his time, and victory would be his. The trump card was his to play, and when the opportunity presented itself, he'd play it.

Meanwhile he needed something to chase the pain, the burning sensation, from his gut. He didn't have to think long. He knew exactly the antidote. Carolyn. He pushed himself out of the chair and staggered toward the door. Taking her to bed, losing himself in her body, always made him forget.

For a while, anyway.

Thirty-One

The ax pierced the wood exactly on target, the sound shattering the silence of the warm November afternoon. But Zach was oblivious to the noise as he swung his arm high and continued abusing the piece of oak.

Since he'd long ago shed his shirt, sweat poured off his face onto his chest where it balled and glistened like early-morning drops of dew.

Before he'd attacked the firewood he had jogged three hard miles, getting his adrenaline flowing. He should have been at the mill. His desk was piled high, but he'd worked so much lately that he'd felt guilty. He needed to spend time with Rachel.

He stopped and let the ax fall to the ground, then reached for the towel dangling off the fence post behind him. Once he had mopped his face, he paused to get his breath. In the distance he could see several of his horses munching on the still-green grass. He almost smiled.

When the pain became too much to bear, he headed here to the uncleared thicket that was part of the Wimberly estate. Since he'd been old enough to swing an ax, gathering firewood for the three fireplaces had been his responsibility.

Along with jogging and working his horses, chopping wood was his therapy. Since Randall's death he'd spent more time here than ever on these therapeutic devices, much to Rachel's disapproval.

But then, Rachel didn't approve of anything he did these days. A heartfelt sigh split his lips. No matter how hard he tried, he couldn't please her. He didn't blame her; he was as much at fault as she was. He was hard to live with.

They were both grieving, but they couldn't comfort each other. Lord knows he'd tried, but he couldn't seem to let his own grief out in the open. He kept it bottled up inside until he feared he might explode. That was when he turned to physical exercise in hopes of easing the pain, the despair that sat like a lump of lead on top of his heart twenty-four hours a day, seven days a week.

Rachel remained indoors, virtually a recluse, refusing help from friends or family. When she wasn't crying she was begging him to let her adopt a baby. The fact that she couldn't get pregnant, after complications with Randall, made the situation even more devastating.

Still, the thought of another child made him sick, but he couldn't tell her that. He knew she missed Randall so much that a little more of her died each day. He could understand that. Even now, nine months after the tragedy, he felt the same way. Yet at times he still couldn't believe his son was gone. But to try to replace Randall with another child was unthinkable.

Zach's Adam's apple suddenly bobbed up and down, as if something too huge to swallow was lodged in his throat.

Starting a month ago, they had argued steadily about it. No common ground had been reached, and he feared they would never find that common ground. Their bickering merely created a deeper gulf between them.

"For chrissake, give it a rest!" he muttered, sending the ax crashing down on another fat log. He had come here to soothe his mind, to empty it of all thoughts. Instead he'd dwelled on his problems until he felt the acid once again burn his stomach.

"My, but I pity that poor log."

He stopped midaction and whirled. Rachel stood a safe distance behind him, hands in the pockets of her jeans. She looked awful, he thought, his heart twisting painfully. Although her hair was clean, it had no shine, even with the sun beating down on it. But then, nothing about Rachel shone anymore. Her blue eyes no longer sparkled. Her high cheekbones seemed fleshless. Her olive complexion was sallow. She was hurting, and he was powerless to do anything about it.

Was he wrong to deny her another child?

"Trent called," she said, shielding her eyes against the sun's rays.

Zach leaned on the ax handle and muttered a curse. "I don't need to ask what he wanted."

Rachel gave a sarcastic laugh. "I wouldn't think so."

"The mill's my job, Rachel," he said, trying to maintain a grip on his patience.

Her eyes suddenly flashed fire. "It's not your job," she spat. "It's your obsession."

"Don't start, Rachel. Just don't start. I'm not in the mood." A nerve in the side of his face was twitching, a sign anger was beginning to override his powers of reasoning. He felt hot and exhausted, and his head banged fiercely.

"You're never in the mood." Her voice was cold and raspy. "No wonder you don't want another child. It might take away from your precious time at the mill."

"That's hitting below the belt, and you know it!"

Her face crumpled. "Oh, Zach, I'm sorry. Believe it or not, I didn't come out here to fight with you. Honestly. It's just that when we're together—"

"All we do is fight. I know."

She nodded instead of speaking, loosening a tear from her eyes.

"Rach, don't." His voice had the pleading of the helpless.

Another tear trickled down her cheek.

Cursing silently, he deserted the ax and reached for her. She clung to him and buried her face in his neck.

He held her quivering body against his, all the while staring toward the sky, knowing that what he was about to say, about to do, might be the biggest mistake of his life. But at this point in his life he had no other choice. You did what you had to in order to survive.

"Rach," he said in a rough whisper, "if . . . if you want another baby, I won't stand in the way."

Her body seemed to shut down. She stopped crying. She stopped moving. She even stopped breathing. Then she pulled back and looked up at him and whispered, "Oh, Zach, darling, you won't regret it, I promise."

Everything was the same. Yet nothing was the same.

Beth climbed out of bed every morning, showered, dressed and went to the shop, either in Natchitoches or some other city. But every move she made was excruciatingly painful, both mentally and physically. She felt as if she were constantly treading water and getting nowhere. She no longer enjoyed her work or anything else. She simply existed.

After the funeral she'd been in shock. She knew that now. At the time, she hadn't. She had just walked around with a terrible emptiness inside her. On the rare occasions when she did feel something, it was guilt and self-loathing.

Though her mind told her that she wasn't to blame for Randall's death, her heart wouldn't accept it. No matter how hard she tried, she couldn't stop blaming herself.

Her friends had rallied behind her. Michael, her employees, special customers and Tracy had all tried to snap her out of her depression. Nothing had worked.

Not even Rachel's pitiful cry, "I . . . know you did all you could . . ." had been able to ease the self-loathing that had a death grip on her heart.

During the past nine months she had seen Rachel twice. Both times they had hugged, cried and remembered. Those get-togethers had been bittersweet. While Beth had enjoyed seeing her friend, she had come away more worried about Rachel than before, and more depressed herself. As for Zach, she hadn't seen him. Though she ached to, she had kept her distance, knowing how he felt about her.

"Beth, you busy?"

Beth looked up with a start. Tracy stood in the doorway.

"I should be, but I'm not. What's up?"

"Nothing. The girls just wanted you to see the front."

Beth stood behind her desk.

"If you get any thinner," Tracy said, staring at her through narrowed eyes, "you're going to turn into a spook."

Beth took umbrage. "Nothing like speaking your mind."

"Well, it's the truth. Just look at you. For months you haven't eaten enough to fill a thimble. If those circles under your eyes get any darker, you're going to have to use plaster of paris instead of makeup."

In spite of herself, Beth laughed.

Tracy slammed her hands together. "Well, I'll be damned. Wonders never cease. You actually smiled, and your face didn't crack."

Beth wrinkled her nose. "Okay, smarty, you've made your point."

"I doubt that," Tracy said drolly. "But it sounds good, anyway."

Beth shuddered, and she found herself sinking into the past once again.

Tracy looked at her for several seconds, then shook her head. "Beth, honey, you've got to let it go."

Beth didn't pretend to misunderstand. "I know. But how?"

"By absolving yourself of guilt."

Beth sat back down and stirred a paper clip on the desk blotter with a finger. "I wish it was that easy."

"It's not easy. I know that." Tracy's tone had a pleading edge to it. "But children die, Beth. Babies die. Every day. You did all you could, and you know it." She paused as if to let what she said penetrate. "The new year is coming up. I want you to promise you'll try harder to put the tragedy behind you."

"Everything you said makes sense. But it's so doggone hard." Beth took a deep breath and let it out. "Just don't expect too much too soon."

Tracy smiled. "I won't."

"So they've got the Christmas decorations up," Beth said, changing the subject.

"Yep, and wait'll you see what they've done, especially with the new shipment of party dresses we got yesterday."

"I'll be there shortly. Just give me another minute."

Tracy stopped at the door. "Oh, by the way, you want a tree in here?"

"No. In fact, I'm not even going to put one up at home."

Tracy raised an eyebrow. "You're going to Shawnee, then?"

"To Gran's. I'm taking Daddy out for the day, provided the weather cooperates."

Tracy's face held sympathy. "I don't know how you do it."

"I just do it."

"That same philosophy should apply to what we were just talking about."

"You're right again," Beth said softly, then smiled. "Now, go on and get out of here."

Tracy had been gone only a few minutes when she stuck her head around the door again. "Sorry, but there's someone here to see you." She lowered her voice. "I think it's your friend, Rachel Winslow."

Stunned, Beth stood, her heart racing. "Well, send her in."

A moment later Rachel walked into the office. Beth almost gasped aloud at the change in her. She looked like the Rachel of old. She absolutely glowed, dressed in a green suede suit, the rich color a perfect foil for her olive skin and dark hair.

What had brought on such a change? More to the point, what had brought Rachel to Natchitoches? Beth was intrigued.

"Hi," Rachel said.

Even as confused as her thoughts were, Beth heard the pleading note in Rachel's voice.

"Oh, Rach, it's so good to see you."

A smile broke across Rachel's face.

They met halfway and hugged. Beth pulled back to put her thoughts of a moment ago into words. "What on earth brings you to my fair city?"

"I came to see you, of course."

"Great. You look wonderful."

Rachel cleared her throat. "I can't say the same for you."

"Don't you start, too. Tracy's already been raking me over the coals about my weight."

"Good for her."

There was a short silence. Then Beth said quickly, "So, come on in and have a seat."

Rachel seemed suddenly less sure of herself. "Am I interrupting anything? I mean—"

"Of course you're not. And even if you were, it would be all right. Sit down and I'll get you some coffee. Or would you rather have a Coke?"

"Coffee'll be fine," Rachel said, sitting on the small sofa.

Beth crossed to the coffee maker behind her, poured two cups, then handed one to Rachel. "By any chance were

your ears burning?'' she asked, sitting beside Rachel on the
small sofa.

Rachel looked puzzled.

Beth's smile almost made it to her eyes. "Tracy and I
were just talking about you and..."

"Randall. You can say his name, Beth. It's all right."

"Oh, Rach," Beth whispered, reaching over and
squeezing one of her hands. "How...how are you doing?''

"Better. Much better, in fact. I think I just might make
it now."

"I'm so glad. I've been so worried. How's...Zach?"
Just saying his name aloud flooded Beth with unspeakable
despair.

Rachel avoided her eyes. "He's coping. Working all the
time, actually."

"So, are you planning to do some Christmas shopping
while you're here?" Beth said, switching the topic, hoping
to dispel the growing tension in the air.

"No, I came to see you, just as I said." Rachel couldn't
quite meet Beth's steady gaze. "Look, do you mind if we
shut the door?"

"No problem." Beth rose. Within seconds she was back,
sitting beside Rachel once again. "I told Tracy to hold all
calls, too."

Rachel smiled lamely. "Thanks."

"Oh, before I forget, what about your doctor's report?
How was your pap smear this time?"

The day Randall died, Rachel had learned that in addition to everything else, her pap smear had come back sus-
picious. In the wake of what had happened, Beth hadn't
found that out until weeks later. Since then she had kept a
close check on Rachel's health.

"I won't know for another week, but the doctor's still
not worried." Rachel smiled. "He just keeps a close watch
on the old bod."

"And you're not worried?"

"No, I'm really not."

"Good. So what's up?"

"I'm here to ask a favor." Rachel's smile turned into a grimace. "Actually, it's more than a favor."

"Anything. You know that."

Rachel's cheeks were white now, and a minute vein was beating in one eyelid. She opened her mouth, then quickly shut it.

"Rach?"

"I want another baby, Beth. But as you know, after Randall was born the doctor said I couldn't have any more."

"You can always adopt," Beth said gently.

Rachel clenched and unclenched her fingers. "I know, only I don't want to."

Beth frowned. "What are you getting at, Rach?"

"There's no way I can say this except to just come out with it." Rachel sucked in her breath, then suddenly pushed it back out. "I want you to consider being a surrogate mother." She ignored Beth's gasp and went on. "I want you to be impregnated with Zach's sperm. Have a child for me. For us."

Beth's mouth fell open, and she stared at Rachel with the shocked, empty expression of a person wakened from a terrifying nightmare. No way could her mind come to terms with what she'd just heard.

"Beth, please!" Rachel cried wildly. "Don't look at me like that."

Her mouth was so dry Beth placed her hand against her throat as if to help free the words. "Have—have you lost your mind?" A hysterical tone had entered her voice.

Rachel jumped up, her face contorted, her breast heaving. "You owe me, Beth! You owe me."

Beth felt the blow as if it had been physical. She fought off an attack of nausea and breathed in, slowly but deeply.

Surely she was dreaming. Surely she would awaken soon and find that this was indeed a hideous nightmare. But when she lifted her head and looked into Rachel's eyes she knew it was no dream. It was reality at its ugliest.

"I...I..." A sudden stutter afflicted Beth's speech. "I...thought you said you didn't blame me," she finally got out in a dull, listless tone.

"Oh, Beth," Rachel wailed, rushing back to the sofa and crouching on her knees. She peered up into Beth's face, her eyes pleading. "I'm sorry. I didn't mean that. It's just that I'm desperate."

The air was filled with total silence.

Rachel was the first to shatter it. "I've...thought about killing myself several times."

"Oh, God, Rachel. Oh, God," Beth cried in agony, then stood and rushed to the window. She looked out, searching for something familiar, something ordinary, something *sane*. The wind was blowing. She could see the dent it made in the few remaining leaves on the nearest oak tree.

Rachel came up behind her. "I probably *would* have, only Zach finally consented to get a baby."

Beth swung around. "You mean *Zach* consented to this?" Her voice squeaked with disbelief and rage.

"No. He knows nothing about this, about you, that is. Using you as the birth mother is my idea. He consented to a surrogate provided I took care of all the arrangements. He...he doesn't want any part of that."

"Oh, Rachel," Beth whispered brokenly, "why me? Is it because you really feel I owe you?" Tears overflowed her lashes.

"Because I can trust you, that's why."

Beth opened her mouth, but Rachel held up her hand and stopped her. "Please don't say anything else until you hear me out. If this baby can't be part of me, then I at least want it to be part of Zach."

"How can you be so insensitive?"

"I already told you," Rachel said, her face pinched, "I'm desperate." She paused as if to regroup. "Don't you see? You'd be perfect. You're young, healthy, and you're your own boss."

Beth merely shook her head and didn't even bother to stop the tears that flowed down her cheeks.

"Oh, Beth, please don't cry," Rachel begged. "I know this has been a shock, but..." Her voice played out as if she'd run out of steam. But when Beth remained silent she started over again. "I've been in consultation with a specialist our family doctor recommended. He assured me the procedure's no big deal."

"How long does the 'procedure' last?" Beth asked, staring at Rachel, her face masklike.

"There's no way to tell." Rachel's voice gathered strength, as if she sensed Beth might be weakening. "Sometimes it takes the first time. Dr. Hightower said that happens in a lot of cases."

"I see."

Rachel's brows furrowed. "There's some pain with it, though. I want you to know that."

Beth laughed bitterly. "The physical pain I can stand. But what about the emotional pain, Rachel? Have you thought about how I might feel about carrying a baby for nine months, then giving it up? What if...what if I changed my mind?"

Rachel turned pasty white. "But...but you don't want children," she stammered. "You...you wouldn't do that, not if you gave your word."

"What if I can't get pregnant?"

"I prefer to think positively."

Abruptly Beth skirted around Rachel and mumbled, "Excuse me." With that she turned and made her way out the door. She didn't stop until she reached the bathroom.

Within minutes she had lost everything in her stomach. Fighting to breathe, she struggled to her feet and over to the sink. She slapped cold water on her face, then rinsed her mouth.

Afterward she stood trembling and stared at her face in the mirror. "Dear Lord, this can't be happening," she whispered. She looked as if someone had slit her throat and drained all the blood out of her body. How much longer could she go on like this?

It was then that she knew what she was going to do. Maybe this was the answer she'd been seeking all this time. Maybe now she could look at herself in the mirror without wanting to die. Maybe now she would have something to live for.

The decision made, Beth repaired her face and walked back into the office.

Rachel stood and looked at her, her heart in her eyes.

"Does Zach have to know who the birth mother is?"

"No," Rachel said breathlessly. "In fact, he told me he doesn't want to know. Ever."

"You'd never tell him?"

"I swear I wouldn't."

Silence.

"Beth?" Rachel's voice sounded rusty.

Beth's lovely features twisted with sadness. "You win, Rachel. If God wills, I'll have your baby."

Thirty-Two

"Hurry, Trace, the baby's moving."

"I'm coming, I'm coming." Tracy tossed her purse, sweater and a sack onto the couch. "Don't you stop moving, you little bugger. You hear your auntie?"

Beth laughed, her hand splayed across her swollen abdomen. "He's listening, all right, 'cause he's still raising hell."

"Hey, what's this 'he' business?"

"I've always thought it was going to be a boy."

By the time Tracy made it to the window where Beth was standing, she was grinning in anticipation. "Well, we'll soon see, I guess."

"Here, give me your hand," Beth said. "Hurry."

When Beth placed Tracy's hand on the exact spot where the baby continued to raise a ruckus, Tracy's eyes widened and an awed look passed over her face. "Golly, that feels weird."

Beth half smiled. "It is weird."

"Does it hurt?"

This time Beth's mouth stretched into a full-blown smile. "Sometimes, especially like now, when he's using my rib cage as a punching bag."

"Feisty devil, isn't he?" Tracy quipped, finally moving her hand, only to stand back and watch. "Looks to me like he's ready to get outta there."

"Well, I wouldn't be surprised," Beth said with a sigh. "Before I came home I stopped by the doctor's office. Even though he still swears I'm only eight months pregnant, he warned me again the baby might come early."

"How early?" Tracy asked quickly.

"Possibly within the next two weeks."

"Jeez. That long? As big as you are, that must seem like an eternity."

Beth made a horrible face. "Are you saying I'm fat?"

Trace shrugged, then grinned. "Yeah, that's what I'm saying. It's all baby, though. Why, I bet you haven't gained an ounce—you remind me of a small but plump watermelon ready to be picked. But a perfect one," she added, her eyes twinkling.

"You better add a qualifier to that, my friend, or you're in big trouble."

"Oh, I'm not worried. You couldn't do it without me."

The laughter died in Beth's eyes. "How true. How true."

"Hey, don't get all maudlin on me now, you hear? You've done great so far."

"I have, haven't I?" Beth said, only to suddenly wince.

"What's wrong?" Tracy's voice was sharp with concern.

Beth took a deep breath. "Nothing, I hope. My tummy suddenly felt kinda funny, that's all. I guess I'm just tired."

"You look it. But you shouldn't be surprised. That flying trip to Houston was dumb." Tracy's eyes, from behind her glasses, were troubled. "You really should be horsewhipped, you know?"

"At least I had a chauffeur."

Tracy's expression said she wasn't impressed. "But you wouldn't have, if Lucy hadn't insisted on driving you."

"I do have a lot to be thankful for," Beth acknowledged. "Loyal employees are hard to come by."

"If you ask me, you're pushing your luck."

Beth held up her hands. "Please, no more lectures. Dr. Coburn told me no more traveling."

"It's about time he put his foot down. Now, why don't you go crawl in bed and rest? And I'll rustle us up another veggie to go with the butter beans and corn bread my mamma sent you."

"Mmm, that sounds delicious. Maybe my tummy's telling me I need to eat." Beth's smile was fragile. "Jessie used to fix butter beans all the time. They were Trent's and Daddy's favorite," she added in a small voice.

Tracy gave a tug-at-the-mouth smile at the same time that she caught Beth by the shoulders and turned her toward the hall. "Off you go. I'll holler when dinner's ready."

Although Beth lay down and pulled an afghan over her legs, she couldn't sleep. The ride home from Houston had seemed to take forever. Lucy had sensed that Beth was preoccupied and left her alone. But though she'd meant well, she hadn't done Beth a favor. Beth had kept thinking about the day Rachel would come and take the baby out of her arms and out of her life.

Desperate, Beth had finally forced those thoughts from her mind and asked Lucy to switch on the radio. Then, halfway home, her legs had started cramping.

All in all, it had been a long day. She hadn't been able to rid herself of the dire feeling of exhaustion that could sweep her so quickly now, rendering her almost helpless.

But the physical stress was nothing compared to what she was suffering mentally. Without warning her stomach heaved again, then subsided. She clamped her teeth together to keep them from shaking.

When Beth had agreed to Rachel's unorthodox request, she had thought she'd known what she was doing. She hadn't. The long-term effects hadn't been figured in to her decision. They hadn't hit her until after she had conceived and harbored the child within her body for months. Then they hit her like a ton of bricks.

The following months became the shortest, most excruciating of her life.

At the start of her fourth month, just before her pregnancy had begun to show, she'd returned to Shawnee to see her family, knowing she wouldn't see them again until after the baby was born. The thought of seeing Zach had never entered her mind. But that was exactly what happened.

They met by accident, as they had that day long ago at the nursing home. This time the bizarre happenstance had taken place at her grandmother's. She had learned later that Zach had stopped by to thank Grace for a cake she had made for him and Rachel.

Beth hadn't recognized his car, or she wasn't sure she would have stopped. She had been halfway up the steps when he walked out the front door, pulling it closed behind him.

They both froze and stared at each other for what seemed an interminable length of time, though in reality it was only a few seconds.

"Hello, Zach," Beth said in a strangled whisper.

It was the first time she'd seen him since Randall's death. As always, he looked mouth-wateringly handsome, dressed in a low-slung pair of worn jeans, a cotton shirt and scuffed boots. But the pain of losing a child was marked in his face and in his eyes. For once he looked older than his thirty-seven years.

"How've you been?" he asked.

Beth tilted her head, as if to keep it above water. The pines were tall and sharp against the sky.

"Do you really care, or are you just making polite conversation?" She hadn't planned on needling him. But when he looked at her with those detached eyes and spoke to her as if she were a distant acquaintance he'd met on the street, she'd wanted to jar that complacency any way she could.

For a wild moment she was tempted to scream, *How dare you treat me like this? I'm carrying your child inside me!*

His eyes darted back to her, and color replaced the pallor in his cheeks. "What do you want from me?" He spat out the question.

Tears collected in the corners of Beth's eyes, but she would not raise a finger to wipe them away. "Nothing," she whispered, hearing her own breathing. "Nothing."

Before she ran the risk of making a bigger fool of herself than she already had, she darted past him and ran up the steps.

His agonized cry fell on deaf ears as she jerked open the door and dived into her grandmother's arms.

A week later she packed her bags and left for Houston. There she rented an efficiency apartment and began searching for a suitable location for another boutique. Not only did she need a new challenge to keep her mind as well as her body busy, she'd needed to get away.

She hadn't wanted to broadcast her pregnancy. Actually, she hadn't been able to risk another encounter with Zach. Even with precautions, however, there was no way to completely safeguard her secret. She and Rachel had discussed what they would do if Zach found out, but had reached no decision. Both women simply prayed it wouldn't happen. Only those who had to know had been told, which amounted to her grandmother and Tracy. But it had been Tracy on whom she depended the most.

Though she'd kept up a grueling schedule, nothing had helped ease the pangs of loneliness that coming home to an empty apartment at the end of each day generated.

After-hours were the killers. The minute her head collided with the pillow, what she had done and what she was about to do settled heavily on her. She felt as if she was going to suffocate.

She would place her hands on the swollen lump that was her stomach and feel the baby move. Emotions she'd never felt before, or even hoped to feel, flowed sweetly through her.

After Zach had married Rachel, she'd known she would never marry, never have children. But when she'd walked into that strange office the lucky first time and Zach's sperm had been put inside her, a feeling like none she'd ever felt before had stolen over her. She hadn't been able to explain it then, nor could she now. Regardless of the outcome, the life she carried inside her had changed her life, changed *her.* She would never be the same again.

I'm going to have a baby! I'm going to have a baby— mine and Zach's, she would cry deep within her soul. But then, just as quickly, reality would slap her with the chilling force of ice water pitched in her face. *You poor misguided fool. It'll never be Zach's and your baby. Zach's, yes. Yours, no. Not now. Not ever.*

She had feared she would pass out, and yet in the midst of her pain, at the core, she'd experienced a desperate consciousness of reality. There was a question to which she must know the answer before she could take another breath. After giving up the tiny being inside her, how was she going to survive? She wouldn't give it up, she sometimes told herself fiercely. That was all there was to it.

But then the cold and brutal truth would rear its ugly head. She had no choice. She had given her word. Besides, she had a debt to pay. And then the pain and anger would drain out of her as though a gaping hole had been cut in her flesh.

If she hadn't had her work, she didn't know what she would have done. While she had worked on the new shop, Tracy had shuttled back and forth, overseeing the workings of the other shops.

Rachel, too, had done her part. On one of her visits they had spent time with the lawyer Rachel had hired to handle the adoption papers.

The day she had signed her name on the dotted line, her hand had trembled so badly that she could hardly write.

In the close confines of the stuffy law office, Rachel had gripped her hand and whispered, "You know you can see her any time you want to."

Beth felt like a drowning person sinking for the third and final time. "How... how do you know it's going to be a her?"

Rachel shrugged gently. "I don't know. I just do."

Beth nodded, her throat too full to speak.

Rachel squeezed her hand again before letting it go and turning back to the lawyer, who coughed, as if uncomfortable with the emotion-filled silence.

Two weeks ago Beth had finished up in Houston. A location for the new store had been chosen, the lease signed, a manager hired and the stock ordered.

Since returning to Natchitoches, she hadn't been to her office. For the most part she'd stayed at home, except for yesterday, when she'd gone back to Houston to tie up the loose ends. Tracy would take care of the store's opening next week.

Now Beth sucked in a breath, experiencing the same panicked sensation she'd felt a short while ago.

Heart racing, she shifted into an upright position and placed a hand over her heart, as if the gesture could stop the dreaded pressure. She could feel the blood rushing in and out of her heart, could hear its unsteady beat.

She could feel something else, too. An uneasy, queasy feeling in her stomach, much worse than when Tracy had sent her to her room. The thought of food made her turn green.

She was beginning to regret the trip. She should have listened to Tracy. But she'd been determined to be in control of *something*.

A stab of pain splintered through her lower back, the sensation so fierce she cried out. Instinctively she eased to her feet and made her way to the door.

"Tracy! Come quick." When Tracy reached her side she was breathing hard, as if she'd run up a long flight of stairs.

"My God, what's wrong?"

"Nothing's wrong. I think I'm about to have a baby."

"Now?" Tracy squeaked.

Beth whimpered and bent over, trying to catch her breath. "See what you have to look forward to," she said.

Tracy grabbed her waist. "What on earth are you talking about?"

"Having Wendall's baby," Beth muttered inanely. "If he ever asks you to marry him, that is."

"Holy cow, Beth!" Tracy cried, clearly rattled. "How can you talk so calmly about my love life when you can't even stand up?"

Beth grinned, only to suddenly have it turn into a grimace. She clutched at her stomach. "Oh, Trace . . . whoa . . . that one hurt."

Tracy's eyes were marble sized. "What—what should we do?"

"Do? Why, drive to the hospital."

The clock on the wall ticked off another minute.

"It's time, isn't it?" Beth asked, visibly tightening her hold on the sleeping bundle in her arms as if she would never let it go.

Tracy gazed at the clock, her expression bleak. "Rachel said she'd be here around three."

Beth was dry-eyed and controlled, but her body throbbed with the effort of maintaining her composure. "Well, it's five till."

"I don't think I've ever seen you looking more beautiful," Tracy said, a catch in her voice. "Or more sad."

Together they waited tensely in the bleak hospital room that overlooked the Cane River. It was a gem of a September day. The sun was dancing across the water, creating a rainbow of colors.

Beth sat in a high-backed chair next to the window, three days after she had given birth to a healthy baby girl. Despite the way it had begun, the delivery had turned out to be an easy one. By the time Tracy wheeled up to the emergency room entrance, Beth's water had broken. Several hours later she had awakened in her room to find a grinning Tracy by her side.

Now Tracy had come to drive Beth home from the hospital. But not before Rachel came for the baby.

"Thanks for doing my hair," Beth said, hoping that by talking she could relieve the awful pressure inside her.

She had washed and dried her hair earlier that morning. But Tracy had moussed it so that the curly blond mass haloed her face, complementing the gold caftan she had put on.

But nothing short of a miracle—and they both knew that wasn't going to happen—could remove the stark grief embedded in Beth's dark eyes.

"I just wish I could take the pain away," Tracy whispered, walking to the window and gazing out.

Beth bit down on her lower lip to hold it steady. She couldn't break down now. She *wouldn't*. Yet her sorrow was so complete, her hopelessness so total, they formed a tight band around her from which there was no escape. She dropped her head again, and her lips moved soundlessly.

While tragedy had walked with her through most of her adult life, to the point that she had even come to accept it as part of her life, this moment went far beyond that.

Beth raised her eyes. The slight movement shook loose the tears stuck to her lashes and sent them spilling over her cheeks. "Isn't she beautiful, Trace?"

Tracy swung around, her features softening. "That she is. In fact, she's the prettiest baby I ever saw." She reached over and opened one of the tiny fists. "Look, her fingers are perfect. I can tell right off she's going to have your beautiful hands. I bet she'll have your long nails, too."

"But she doesn't look like me, does she?"

"No, and from what you've told me about him, she doesn't look like Zach, either, if that's what you're asking."

In the explosive silence that followed, Beth leaned forward. "Oh, God, Tracy, what am I going to do?" Her voice trembled with hopelessness.

"Don't...please," Tracy pleaded, her own face pinched with misery. "I can't stand to see you cry."

The hot tears continued their trek down Beth's face. "I...I promised myself I was going to be brave when the time came to...give her up—" Beth's voice stopped in her throat.

Tracy leaned her head against the windowpane, and for a minute the hospital room, bare except for the flowers Tracy and Rachel had sent, was silent. Then Tracy turned around, wearing a belligerent expression.

"You don't have to let her go, you know. The pact between you and Rachel wasn't signed in blood."

"It might as well have been," Beth whispered from the heart. "It's just as binding."

Tracy stood straighter. "No, it's—"

"Please, Tracy...don't. It's...too late to turn back now." Beth's anger had left; she spoke in grief and fear of tomorrow.

"Beth, you're—"

A soft rap sounded against the door.

Beth's heart tripped.

Tracy let out a harsh breath and looked at Beth.

Beth didn't know what to do. Sit. Stand. Scream. Beg. *Die.* Maybe this time God would take pity on her and let her die.

The knock came again.

"Beth?"

Beth didn't hesitate a second time, afraid that her mounting sense of panic would send her over the edge. "Open it, please."

When Tracy reached the door she turned back around. "I'll leave you two alone."

Beth kissed the soft, plump cheek, then placed Amanda Elizabeth Winslow in Rachel's arms.

"Take care of her, Rach," Beth said brokenly, tears as hot as fire blurring her sight.

Rachel accepted the bundle as if she'd just been handed a piece of rare porcelain. "You know I will. She'll be the light of my life. And Zach's."

Beth turned away. The air in the room compressed until she was suffocating. "Please . . . take her. Take her . . . and go."

Gripping the bundle tightly in her arms, Rachel walked to the door, where she paused and swung around, tears in her eyes. "Beth . . . I . . . need your reassurance that you'll never tell Zach."

"You have it," Beth whispered, her voice quivering. "Please . . . just go."

The baby whimpered.

Beth moaned and bit down hard on her lip, hard enough to draw blood. The taste turned sour on her tongue, and she almost retched.

When the door clicked shut, the pain was so severe it took her breath away. Even though she remained standing, her legs were useless. Her stomach was empty. Her mouth was dry. Her throat was closed. Her eyes were holes in a mask. No! This wasn't happening to her. Her mind took a leap into nothingness.

She didn't know how long she stood there. It was only after she couldn't stand any longer that she fell back into the chair and instinctively placed a hand on her newly flat stomach.

Having a baby is the ultimate joy. It's inside you, a part of you! You feel it move; you smile when it gives you an unexpected kick. You feel its heart beating, feel it absorb you. And when it's no longer inside you, it's so vulnerable, so dependent on you to nourish it, love it....

"I wish you love, my precious daughter," Beth whispered. "I wish you love."

Thirty-Three

Beth bent and kissed her grandmother's cheek. "Talk to you tomorrow, love." She smiled. "Gotta run now."

Grace Childress clutched Beth's hand and clung to it. "I wish you didn't have to go."

"Oh, Gran," Beth said, straightening, though her hand was still tightly clasped in Grace's frail one. "I wish I didn't, either, but I promised Michael. I told you. Remember?"

This had been an unplanned and hurried trip to Shawnee. Grace's heart trouble had flared up again, and Jessie had called her, in a dither. Ordinarily Trent would have seen to Gran, but he was out of town on mill business.

Although her grandmother had insisted on the phone that she was all right, Beth had wanted to see for herself. After she had left work late yesterday evening, she'd driven here.

Grace sighed and leaned back on the couch. "Ah, yes, I'd forgotten."

Beth gave her grandmother's hand another gentle squeeze before standing. "Believe me, if there was a way I could get out of it, I would. But this is an important client Michael has to entertain, and he practically begged me to go." She let her voice play out, giving her slender shoulders a shrug.

Grace stood and smiled. "Why don't you put that poor fellow out of his misery and marry him?"

"Ah, Gran, he's a good man, only he's not for me."

"Only because you won't let him be," the old woman admonished with a smile.

"Maybe so, but that's the way it is."

Grace's smile vanished. "Did...you by any chance see Rachel?"

Beth reached out and removed an errant strand of white hair from Gran's cheek. "What you're really asking is did I see Amanda."

Grace nodded.

"The answer is no," Beth said softly.

"What about next week? Surely you're coming back for her birthday?"

Beth's eyes misted over. "I...can't believe she's a year old."

"Oh, Beth, honey, I can't stand—"

"Shh, Gran. Don't start. I really have to go." Then, realizing she had spoken more sharply than she'd intended, Beth drew much-needed air into her lungs and softened her tone. "Anyway, it...it's better if I don't see Mandy all that much."

"I know, darling, but..."

"Look, we'll talk about this later," Beth said quickly, a familiar pain sending icy fingers climbing up her spine.

"Oh, honey, I'm sorry." Grace's eyebrows puckered. "Please forgive me for being such a nosy ole busybody."

"You're no busybody."

"Yes, I am."

Beth embraced her grandmother again and for a moment clung to her. "Well, even if you are, I wouldn't have it any other way."

It was late when Beth got back to Natchitoches. For reasons that she was determined to ignore, the condo seemed lonelier than usual. Maybe it was her mood, Beth thought, going into the bedroom, where she immediately kicked off her flats. The remainder of her clothing followed.

Once she'd slipped into her robe, she reached for the outfit she planned on wearing tonight. The black-and-ivory rayon crepe was ideal for evening. Its slim silhouette was defined with padded shoulders, and the skirt grazed her knees. She wanted to look her best, as this client was crucial for Michael. Besides, she owed him; his friendship had proved invaluable. She was positive this Bill Blass number would do the trick.

Yet she dreaded the evening, dreaded having to be "on." It seemed that rare moments of total relaxation were few and far between. Still, most of the time she liked it that way, because it kept her from thinking.

After spreading the dress across the bed, Beth left the room and wandered into the kitchen. Moments later, a cup of mocha in her hand, she padded into the living room, sat on the couch and curled her feet under her.

Her gaze strayed to the fireplace. She stared at it with longing, envisioning cozy, cheerful flames crackling on the hearth. She wished she could stay right where she was for the rest of the evening.

A scoffing smile suddenly crossed her lips. Who was she kidding? Even if she stayed home she wouldn't relax, not with a briefcase crammed full, winking at her from the desk across the room.

Sighing, Beth rested her head against the cushions. The trips to Shawnee were becoming increasingly hard. They took their toll, especially when she saw Amanda.

She took a sip of the mocha, then set it down on the table beside her. Her eyes once again wandered to the fireplace, but this time they targeted the brass-framed picture on the mantel.

Amanda Elizabeth Winslow. It didn't seem possible that it had been a year since she had given birth to the lovely child who stared back at her, the tiny rosebud mouth open in laughter.

When Beth looked at this picture or the one just like it in her wallet, she felt as if an iron bar was lying across her chest. Though she drove herself, using work as a panacea for the ache that pressure caused, it never let up.

Zach and her baby were forever on her mind, the baby she would never share with him. Her only salvation during the past year had been knowing her sacrifice had made Zach and Rachel happy.

They worshiped Amanda. As for her part in Amanda's life, she had kept it very low-key, though she spent as much time with her as her work schedule allowed. And Amanda adored her, which made their partings harder to bear. Whenever she left, it broke her heart anew.

Now, feeling the threat of tears brought on by her thoughts, Beth grabbed the cup of mocha and stood. Without looking at the picture again, she hurried out of the room.

"I had a wonderful time."

Michael smiled and toyed with her slender fingers. "Thank you for going. If my firm gets this deal, we'll have you to thank. You made quite an impression on Mr. Deaton."

Beth returned his smile at the same time that she withdrew her hand. "You're giving me too much credit."

"I'd like another chance to repay you."

"You already have, a thousand times."

He smiled proudly. "Well, it's late, so I'll let you go."

"Good night, and thanks again for a lovely evening."

Beth stood at the door until he was in his car and driving off. Twelve o'clock. Tomorrow she would pay for staying out till the Cinderella hour, she thought as she slipped off her heels and trudged into her bedroom.

She had just taken off her earrings when the phone rang. With her heart in her throat, she lifted the receiver.

"Hello."

"Beth..."

"Zach!" she whispered, an unnatural fear turning the breath cold in her chest.

"Where the hell have you been?"

A naked flash of anger replaced the fear. Who did he think he was, talking to her like that?

"I've been out," she said stiffly.

"I've been trying to get hold of you for hours."

The warning bell signaled inside her brain again. "What's...what's wrong?" Beth's voice was a broken thread of sound. Amanda. Oh, God, if something had happened to Amanda...

"It's...Rachel. She's...sick."

Beth grabbed hold of the table. "Sick...but I don't understand. How sick?"

Zach's raw sigh filtered through the line. "She...she has cancer."

"Cancer!" Beth put a hand to her mouth.

"It's...not good, Beth. She's...she's asking for you. Will you come?"

Thirty-Four

A gentle north wind caressed Beth's cheeks as she stood beside Rachel's grave. Rachel had been laid to rest beside her son three days ago. Beth had felt compelled to stop by the cemetery before she left Shawnee. Even in death, she needed Rachel's strength.

"Oh, Rach, if only you'd told me how ill you were...."

By the time she'd been summoned to the hospital, it was too late. She should have been there all along, to help nurse her, to give her support, to cry for her and with her....

Beth's eyes were dry, but they stung as if she'd cried buckets of tears.

First Randall, now Rachel. Who was next? Her daddy? Gran? *Zach!* She felt the tears jar loose for the first time since Rachel had been pronounced dead. She willed them back. She could not allow herself the depression that she knew tears would bring. For Amanda's sake, she had to be strong.

As with Randall, the entire population of Shawnee had turned out for Rachel's funeral. The small funeral-home chapel had overflowed. Speakers had been connected outside so those standing on the sidewalk and steps could hear the service.

Through it all, Beth had sat numb, flanked by Trent and her grandmother. In the pew in front were Zach, his family and Rachel's mother.

Very few words had passed between Zach and her. He'd made it a point to avoid her, just as she had him. What could they say to each other? Nothing. Mere words could not eradicate the pain, the regret, that each harbored inside.

When the casket had rolled past them, not only had she wanted to scream for herself, but she'd wanted to fling herself into Zach's arms and comfort him, smooth the pain off his face.

She hadn't, of course. She had stood silently and nursed her own grief, wondering how she was going to keep her promise.

She was still wondering that now as she bent and laid a single rose on the grave.

"What are you doing here?"

Beth held herself rigid, feeling her stomach tighten with anger at the coldness in Zach's voice. Slowly she turned around, her cheeks reddened by a rush of blood. "I loved her, too, you know."

He didn't say anything. He just stood there and raked his eyes over her. She could feel them on her face, as if he were determined to peel off the skin, probe, pinpoint the flaws, the severed nerves.

Beth refused to back down, though she felt as if she were about to gag. Even in anger, he radiated the kind of raw physical presence that warned her to keep her distance.

But there was too much at stake to let anything interfere with her mission. In the flushed silence she took a step forward, hands outstretched. There were only a few feet between them now. For all the good it did her, it might as well have been an ocean. His piercing green eyes reminded her of shards of glass.

"Please, Zach, can't we at least carry on a decent conversation without—"

"No." The word was sharp edged, the tone whiplike.

"Why are you doing this?" Her voice sounded foreign.

"Rachel's death hasn't changed anything." Zach rubbed his knuckles. "We still don't have anything to talk about."

The sun bathed his features, highlighting each tiny line that marked his eyes and mouth like twisted crow's-feet.

"You're wrong. We do have something to talk about."

"If you're referring to Amanda, forget it."

Her eyes cut him to shreds. "No, I won't forget it."

"I know what Rachel wanted. I know she wanted you to be part of Amanda's life. But I . . . I told her I . . . we didn't need anyone else." His features were ravaged. "God only knows why she was so adamant."

Careful, Beth, be very careful. "Because she is . . . was my best friend. Because she knew how much I cared about Amanda. But even if I didn't, I'd still do everything in my power to keep my promise."

Zach's eyes narrowed menacingly. "You don't care about that baby. You're the most selfish person I know."

"That's not true!"

"Well, it doesn't matter." His tone was flat and bleak. "What does matter is that you forget about taking *my* daughter under your wing."

"I won't accept that!" she cried, horror-struck.

"Oh, yes, you will. You have no choice."

"But . . . why?" An ache ripped open inside her. "Is . . . is it because of . . . Randall?"

Zach looked as if he might break. "No, absolutely not!" His voice shook. "I blame God for that."

There was a frightening silence during which their eyes met and held. Crippled survivors, she thought. Barely ambulatory. And still hurting.

"Stay away from her, Beth. For all our sakes."

"And if I refuse?"

"You won't."

The wind had risen and was as unrelenting as the headache that pounded like a jackhammer inside Beth's head.

"You're wrong," she said so softly that, for a moment, she wasn't sure he'd heard her.

"Go back to where you came from, to the glitz and glamour of the big cities." There was an icy threat in his voice. "You aren't wanted here. You don't belong. Not anymore."

His words cut to the quick. Beth wanted to lash back, hurt him as much as he was hurting her. But the insides of her mouth felt full of cotton, strangling her.

"I made a promise to Rachel, Zach," she stressed again, tears scalding her eyes. "And I'm going to keep it."

He took a step forward. His gaze stabbed into her. "Wanna bet?"

"You don't frighten me."

A sneer added to the lines of hostility on his face. "I'm not worried. You're only in and out of Shawnee like a swinging door."

"Not for much longer," she said quietly.

"Just exactly what does that mean?"

She thought his face was hard enough to have been hacked out of stone. "Guess."

"Don't you play games with me!"

"I'm going to open another shop."

"So? What else is new?"

"You don't get it, do you?" High color flagged Beth's cheeks. "I'm moving back to Shawnee, Zach. So you see, there won't be any way you can stop me from seeing Amanda."

Part III

Thirty-Five

Summer, 1990

Her bags were packed, the boxes stacked neatly. There was nothing more to do, Beth told herself. The condo was as clean as the day she'd moved into it. As soon as the movers came and went, she would be free to leave for Shawnee, this time to stay.

"Anything else you need me to do?" Tracy asked, breezing into the living room.

Beth thought a moment. "Nothing that I can think of. But even if I could, I wouldn't ask. You've done far too much as it is."

"Ah, pooh." Tracy grinned. "You would've done the same for me." Her grin widened. "I will admit, though, you've got more than your share of junk."

Beth feigned anger. "I'll have you know nothing I own is junk."

"Ha, you're an even bigger pack rat than Mamma."

Beth chuckled. "You're right. But I'm afraid if I discard something, I might need it."

"What you need right now is to wipe that smudge off your face."

Beth raised a quick hand to her cheek. "Oh, my. Do I really have a dirty face?"

"Yep. So do I, probably."

They were both dressed in shorts, the skimpiest of T-shirts and sandals. Tracy's long hair was pulled back in a ponytail at her neck, while Beth's short curls were swept away from her face.

"Actually, you look fine," Beth said. "If you'll keep an eye out for the movers, I'll take a quick shower and change clothes. I'd hate to arrive at Gran's looking like I just crawled out of a trash can."

Tracy made a grunting sound. "Give me a break. You couldn't look like that even if you tried."

"Wrong. But I don't have time to argue. I'll be right back."

In record time Beth showered, then slipped on a pair of walking shorts and a cotton shirt. Tracy was standing at the window when Beth once again joined her.

"You can go now, Trace," she said, slightly out of breath from rushing. "And thanks again."

Tracy waved a hand. "You're welcome. Guess I'll see you next week."

"I can't believe we're about to open the store in Shawnee." Beth's eyes took on a far-off glaze. "I just hope it's not a mistake."

"The store or the move?"

"Both."

"Trust me, neither is a mistake." Tracy spoke with a lofty air of confidence. "Amanda needs you and—" she grinned "—the town needs The In-Look. They ain't seen nothing like it."

Beth laughed, but then her face turned grave. "That's what I keep telling myself, only—"

"No onlys and no buts, okay? It'll work out, you'll see."

Beth smiled weakly. "I have to believe you're right."

"Keep your chin up, kid."

When she was alone Beth wandered around the room, her thoughts refusing to settle. She still found it hard to believe she was going back home.

Once she made her mind up to make the move, she was eager to do so. Circumstances, however, hadn't cooperated. It had taken much longer than she'd thought to find a suitable location for the shop in Shawnee and complete renovations on it. Too, there had been personnel problems with several of the other shops.

But the main reason she'd waited was Zach. It had been nine months since Rachel's death and that violent encounter with him at the cemetery. She'd hoped he had mellowed.

She couldn't have been more wrong. She'd found that out the hard way the last time she visited Amanda without Zach's knowledge. During the shop's renovation period she commuted between Natchitoches and Shawnee, and she'd made it a point to see the child. Luck seemed to have been on her side, because she'd managed to miss Zach.

She would have missed him that day, too, except he had come home early from work to learn that his mother, who was baby-sitting Amanda, had given Beth permission to take Mandy to the park.

Beth hadn't asked to take Amanda anywhere. Out of the blue, Marian had offered. She hadn't questioned why, unable to puzzle through what had prompted Marian's unexpected generosity. But Beth hadn't looked a gift horse in the mouth; she had taken the child and spent an hour playing with her.

She could still hear Mandy's laughter the minute she'd set her down. The little girl had run toward the hobbyhorses, her short, chubby legs churning as fast as they could.

A sudden smile eased the tension around Beth's mouth. Although she had been only a few steps behind, it hadn't been close enough. Just before Amanda reached the ride, she lost her balance and fell. Immediately, a scream pierced the air.

"Oh, Mandy darling," Beth cried, scooping her up in her arms and holding her close, "you're all right. Shh, don't cry."

Mandy clung to her for a second. Then, drawing back but still sniffling, she pointed toward the wooden horses. "Horsey. Me down."

Beth laughed and hugged her tightly. "Only if you hold my hand, okay?"

"Okay," Mandy mimicked, struggling to get down.

The instant Amanda's feet touched the ground, she turned and headed for the merry-go-round, giggling out loud.

Beth followed on her heels. "Amanda Winslow, you're a naughty girl. You promised to hold my hand."

Mandy stopped a safe distance from the ride and pointed again. "Horsey."

"Would you like to have a rocking horsey for your birthday?" Beth asked.

In two months Amanda would be two years old. Beth already had a trunkful of presents. What the heck, she thought; there was always room for one more.

"Me ride horsey?"

"What do you say?"

"Pease, Bef."

No matter how often Beth looked at Amanda, she marveled anew that she and Zach had created a perfect child who resembled neither of them. Amanda had a face all her own. If she favored anyone, it was Rachel, uncanny as that was.

Mandy had a delicate heart-shaped face with huge black eyes, Gran's eyes, and a head full of black curls that shone like satin. Her rosebud mouth and rosy cheeks made you want to hug her the second you saw her. And her smile was like morning sunshine.

"You're a stinker, you know that?" Beth said, sweeping Amanda into her arms, then seating her atop one of the horses.

When she was with Amanda, Beth could forget that her daddy remained a vegetable in the nursing home, forget that Gran's heart was worsening every day, and forget that Zach hated her with every fiber of his being.

"Hold on, now," she cautioned, close to Amanda's tiny ear. Then she leaned over and punched the button. "Here we go."

Amanda squealed with delight as the horses bobbed up and down in time to the music.

Standing beside Amanda and holding on to her tightly, Beth looked up. Even if the weather was on the hot and humid side, she couldn't have asked for a lovelier day. The sky was as blue and perfect as a field of Texas bluebonnets.

"Daddy!"

Beth went rigid, while the blood slowly seeped from her face.

"Daddy, lookey! Me ridin' horsey."

Mandy's shrill voice did little to cover the sound of Beth's pounding heart as she lowered her head and watched Zach make his way toward them.

The sunlight that before had dappled the road now fell on him. For a minute, looking at him, Beth forgot about the past, forgot everything except how beautiful he was. She had thought it years ago, and she thought it even more now. Though she had known his body as well as she'd known her own, there were times like this when, in a burst of fresh awareness, she had to stop and catch her racing breath.

A snug-fitting T-shirt hugged his chest and shoulders, while a pair of cutoffs showed off his dark, hair-roughened legs. His hair, parted slightly on the left and much too long, lay trapped against his neck.

But it was Zach's face that claimed her full attention. Although it still bore the marks of long suffering and pain, that wasn't what made the blood in her veins turn to ice water. It was the livid anger she saw there.

"Daddy!" Mandy cried again, clamoring to get down.

Glad to have something to do with her hands, Beth lifted her off the horse. "There you go, pumpkin."

Without hesitation Amanda toddled toward Zach, her arms outstretched.

"How's my girl?" The anger seemed to melt from Zach's face as he bent down and scooped his daughter into his arms.

"Bef playing wif me."

"I see that."

Mandy gave him a gooey kiss on the cheek.

Zach laughed and kissed her back before easing her to the ground. "Daddy wants to talk to Beth a minute. You go over to the sandbox and play."

Wordlessly the child scampered to the piled-up sand, where she immediately latched on to a shovel and pail.

Delaying the verbal battle she knew was about to take place, Beth licked her lips and deliberately stared beyond Zach's shoulder. As if mesmerized, she watched the leaves on a maple tree ruffle in the breeze.

"Surely you didn't think you'd get away with this?" His voice was frigid, his eyes dark.

Refusing to let him intimidate her, Beth lifted her chin a notch. "I wasn't trying to get away with anything."

Zach snorted in disgust. "What do you take me for? I told you to leave Amanda alone, and I meant it."

Unexpectedly, Beth's eyes watered along the bottom rim and her lower lip trembled. "Do you really . . . hate me that much?" She swallowed. "I thought . . ."

"You thought what?" His voice was as cold and harsh as winter.

The smell of the hydrangeas and the wet earth was so strong it was almost like a drug. But it was not nearly as drugging as being close to Zach and unable to reach out and touch him, wipe the pain off his face.

Beth found she couldn't even answer him, and despised herself because she still wanted him. The fire inside her refused to die. But she would never have him, because he didn't feel the same about her. Her heart experienced that knowledge like an arrow straight through it, yet she couldn't make her feelings go away.

"I . . . I thought that time . . ."

"Well, you thought wrong."

With every harsh word he uttered, her heart became more pulverized. But she wouldn't let him know that. "I don't want to fight with you, Zach. Surely we can reach a compromise. Rachel . . ."

He groaned suddenly, as if something had broken inside him.

"You . . . miss her, don't you?" Beth's voice had fallen to a hoarse whisper.

For a moment he didn't respond. The silence tore at both of them.

"I didn't realize how much," he said, almost as if he were talking to himself. "Until . . . I woke up and she wasn't there anymore."

Beth felt his pain as if it were her own. Searching desperately for something to temper it, she said softly, "Thank God you have Mandy and the mill."

"But not in that order, I'm sorry to say."

For a second Beth was almost too stunned to answer. They were actually talking without shouting at each other. Fearing the manna from heaven wouldn't last, she quickly made the most of it.

"Speaking of the mill, how are things there?"

As if he read through her ploy, he smiled mirthlessly. "Fine."

"How's Trent doing?"

"Workwise all right, but something's bothering him."

She managed a smile. "He's getting cold feet, I imagine."

In the fall Trent and Vicki were finally going to make their relationship official. Beth was delighted, thinking that it was Vicki's influence that was slowly turning her brother into a decent citizen. Credit also went to Zach. When they had promoted him at the mill, Trent had blossomed. It had been months since he'd asked to borrow money or mentioned selling the shares in the mill.

"It's more than that."

She frowned. "You don't think he's gambling again, do you?"

"I don't know. If he is, I'll boot him out on his ear."

Before Beth could respond, Amanda cried, "Lookey, Bef, see what I gotted?"

Mandy was coming toward them, hand outstretched, a worm dangling between her fingers.

"Oh, no!" Beth cried through her laughter.

Zach rolled his eyes, then smiled. "That's my girl."

Amanda grinned.

Simultaneously they hurried toward her and knelt to her level. But instead of touching Amanda's hand, they touched each other's. The contact was electrical.

For an instant neither moved. Their eyes met and held for the merest breath of time.

Beth sucked in her breath.

He flexed his jaw.

"Zach . . . ?" Beth's voice was a feathery whisper.

As if the strangled sound of his name on her lips was too much, he flushed dully. Then a look of remembrance, followed by flashing scorn, jumped into his eyes.

"Shit," he muttered and lunged up.

Swallowing against the scalding pain inside her, Beth turned her attention to Mandy, who now had the worm in the palm of her hand.

"Oh, honey, no," she said, shaking Mandy's hand until the worm fell out. "A worm is not something you play with." Beth got to her feet and reached for Amanda's wrist. "Come on, let's go back to the sandbox. Why don't you make Daddy and me a sandman?"

Mandy clapped her hands. "Me make man."

Beth walked back to Zach, who was leaning against a huge sycamore tree, his back to her. She stopped at a safe distance.

He swung around, his chest rising and falling with his breathing.

The heavy, dead silence stretched.

"Tell me something, will you?" he asked.

"I'll . . . try."

The hesitation in her voice brought on another humorless smile. That soon disappeared, and his features once again took on a sinister look. "If you're so crazy to be with Mandy, why didn't you ever marry and have a child of your own?"

Cold pain filled Beth's chest, and for a second she reeled under its impact. She had no one else to blame. She had asked for this; she had opened herself again to be hurt.

"Go to hell," she whispered suddenly, furiously, striking back.

"Come on, now," he taunted. "Surely there's been someone who tempted you." Before Beth could defend herself against his hurtful attack, he laughed a bitter laugh. "Save your breath. I already know the answer. You didn't want to take time off from your precious job. Or was it because you didn't want to mar your perfect body?"

Beth flinched as if he'd sucker-punched her in the stomach. It was all she could do to remain upright. "That's despicable! *You're* despicable!"

"Truthful."

"You don't know anything about me. Why, I could've gotten married. In fact, I almost did."

"So why didn't you?" His words came out as a sneer.

Fearing that he would end up getting the truth from her, she blatantly lied. "I . . . I still might."

He stared at her for another long moment. "When you make love, do you still make that funny little noise in your throat?"

Beth gasped for breath, but the hot, humid air seemed to have sucked it all away. "You'll never know, will you?" she taunted.

His face twisted into an ugly scowl while silence beat between them like the steady tick of a clock.

Finally Beth whispered, "Zach, please, can't we call a truce?"

He continued to look at her, seeming to lose himself in the depths of her eyes. "Why did you have to come back?" he asked in a tortured voice. "And why do I care either way?"

Beth's heart swelled and, without breaking eye contact, she reached out.

He shook his head, stopping her cold. "Fuck it," he said, as though an insatiable rage had broken free inside him. "Stay away from me and from Amanda. Stay the hell away!"

Beth stood rooted to the spot and watched as Zach strode over to Amanda. Without looking back, he swept her up into his arms and strode toward his car.

Confused, Amanda turned around, her lower lip trembling. "Bef come, too, Daddy?"

"No, honey, not now. Not ever."

Those words were still very much on Beth's mind even as she shook the memories out of her head and walked to the door, having heard the moving van pull into the driveway.

Zach might have won the battle, but the war was far from over.

Thirty-Six

Beth filled the vase on Randall's headstone with fresh flowers, then moved to Rachel's, where she repeated the action.

The day was hot, breathless and cloudy. Her gaze strayed upward, across the sky. The clouds hinted at rain. The weather, like her mood, was dismal.

She had been in Shawnee over a month now. During that time she hadn't stopped. Her apartment was in order, even to the pictures on the wall. But making the rented home livable had taken more effort than she'd thought. In addition, she had spent time with her daddy and grandmother, which she had enjoyed very much.

Gran was delighted she was back in the fold, and even Trent seemed to have accepted her return with good grace. But then, her brother viewed the world through rose-colored glasses as his wedding day grew closer. He'd stopped by Gran's, and she had scrutinized him closely, looking for the signs of worry and discontent that Zach had spoken of in the park. She'd seen nothing to indicate either.

Her leisure time, starting tomorrow, would be at a premium. She shuddered to think of the work that still lay ahead on the new boutique. Releasing a pent-up sigh, she let her eyes dip back to Rachel's grave. It was hard to believe that her friend had been dead almost a year. Not a day went by that Beth didn't think about Rachel, about the good times they'd had, about how proud Rachel had been of Amanda, how much joy the child had brought her.

But Rachel was gone, and life had to go on. It was that thought that had driven Beth to the cemetery today. She'd finally had to face the cold reality that sorrow and loss do not necessarily ease with time. And that commitment to them did not benefit either the living or the dead.

Beth had also come to the realization that her life had to change. Things could not go on as they were. *She* could not go on as she was. After her confrontation with Zach in the park, she was suddenly no longer confused. Everything became crystal clear.

Beth paused in her thoughts and straightened a flower that was determined to droop.

"Oh, Rachel," she whispered, her eyes blurred with tears, "please forgive me. But you were right all along. I still love Zach. I always have, and I always will."

Not only did she love him, but she didn't want to be without him any longer. She wanted to be a part of his life. *I want to be his life.*

Beth knew Zach felt something for her other than anger and animosity, despite his actions and harsh words to the contrary. She had seen it in his face that day; she had felt it in his touch when their fingers had accidentally met.

In reviewing the years that had separated them, Beth was forced to ask herself a painful question. Had she made a mistake when she forced Zach out of her life? Until now she hadn't dared probe the dark recesses of her mind and heart for fear of what the answer would be.

Now she had to ask that question, if for no other reason than to reassure herself she had made the right decision, and it ripped her up on the inside to think she might have wasted all those years. Unfortunately, the answer and the peace she sought were not forthcoming. If she had it to do over again, would she handle things differently? She didn't know. She honestly didn't know.

At eighteen, fear for herself and love for Zach had been such powerful emotions that she hadn't known what to do other than play the hand life had dealt her. That no longer applied; she was in a position to deal her own hand. In doing so, she was prepared to commit herself to something other than work.

Beth went weak all over when she thought of trying to convince Zach that she'd never stopped loving him. The battle that lay ahead didn't bear contemplating, because the stakes were much higher now. Seventeen years ago there had been no child.

But to approach him would take nerves of steel. Despite the desire Beth had seen in his eyes, his angry words still burned their way through her mind like an out-of-control fire. Still, the risk was worth taking. And she planned to take it. Today.

While waiting for her appointment with Richard Walsh at the bank, Beth drove to Cottonwood.

She remained behind the wheel and let her eyes wander across the wide expanse of lawn and then to the house. She felt the same old tug in the vicinity of her heart. This time that tug had new meaning.

Because Cottonwood stood vacant, hope festered inside her, threatening to erupt.

Beth stifled the urge to get out of the car and see if she could gain entry to the house. There was no time. Anyway, with her luck she would get hauled to jail for trespassing.

Smiling ruefully, she nosed the car onto the street and headed toward her destination. She had high hopes that the day would end on a positive note, even though it hadn't begun that way.

Once Beth had made up her mind to talk to Zach, she'd gone to the mill, only to find that he was out of town on business. Then thoughts of visiting Amanda had surfaced and pushed aside her disappointment. That plan had run into a snag, as well. Marian had taken Amanda with her to visit a friend.

Determined not to waste the day, she had called the banker, spurred by the knowledge that Cottonwood had been vacant for a long while.

Minutes later, as she whipped into a parking slot in downtown Shawnee, a smile laced with self-confidence softened her lips.

The first of many changes in her life was about to take place, and it felt good. It felt damn good.

Richard Walsh sighed, leaned back in his leather chair and laced his fingers behind his neck.

"So, Ms. Melbourne," he drawled, "you're back in Shawnee to stay. Or is that just a rumor?"

"Why, Richard, you know I've moved back," Beth responded with false sweetness, "the grapevine being what it is."

For a long moment he remained silent, appearing flustered, as if the use of his first name had thrown him off balance.

"Well, I guess that's best, since you're opening a business, which, by the way, I congratulate you on." He unlaced his hands and sat up. "Any new endeavor is always good for the entire town."

Beth had planned to keep her dislike at bay. But whatever there was about this cold, taciturn man, it never failed to bring out the worst in her. Maybe it was because he reminded her of Taylor Winslow. In her opinion, they were two of a kind: they both waited until your back was turned, then plunged the knife into it.

She kept her hands folded calmly in front of her. "My sentiments exactly."

"So how's the family? Foster, in particular."

"No change, but thank you for asking."

Walsh shook his head. "Damned shame. Such a waste."
He smiled then, the gums surrounding his white-capped
teeth shining like a neon sign. Why hadn't she noticed that
gumline before? "But you didn't come here to discuss your
daddy's health, did you?"

Beth spoke politely but crisply. "That's right, I didn't."

"So what can I do for you? If it's money you need . . ."

"It's not money, Richard." Beth paused for emphasis.
"It's Cottonwood."

He stiffened visibly before his eyes flickered away.
"What about Cottonwood?"

"I want to talk to the owner about purchasing it."

He swung his eyes back around, but his features were
bland. "Cottonwood's not for sale."

"Are you just guessing, or do you know that for a fact?"

He blew air out his mouth, as though his nose was
stopped up. "I know that for a fact."

"Well, if you don't mind," Beth said, relentless in her
pursuit, "I'd like to talk to the owner myself."

"Now, why would you want to do that?" Richard's tone
was as bland as his features.

Two could play this cat-and-mouse game, Beth thought,
and forced a half smile. "Oh, I think that should be obvious."

"You know I'll do anything I can to be obliging—"

"But not when it pertains to Cottonwood, right?"

Richard smiled a plastic smile. "Exactly. And I'm sorry,
of course. But I can't do what you're asking."

Beth didn't bother to curb the anger boiling through her.
"Can't—or won't?"

He looked at her with a cultivated air of dismissal. "I
don't have to explain my actions to you."

"I wouldn't be too sure of that, if I were you."

His shoulders tensed, but still his tone held no rancor.
"Are you threatening me?"

"Maybe."

"Ah, come now, Ms. Melbourne," he drawled, "you're blowing this all out of proportion. Even if Cottonwood was for sale, which I must stress again it isn't, the asking price would be way beyond your means."

She cut him off, anger and resentment filling her veins like poison. "How do you know? Or have you made it *your* business to know *my* business?"

Richard flushed. "That accusation is unfounded." Beth could see that he was fighting to hang on to his patience. Only he didn't quite pull it off. When he spoke again, his voice was haughty and edged with contempt. "I have never—"

Again Beth cut him short, this time by standing, tired of the entire charade. "Please, spare me the platitudes regarding your integrity."

"Now, you listen here, young lady."

"Just tell the owner I want to talk to him." Beth's tone was brisk. "Or give me his name, and I'll call him."

Walsh's eyes filled with instant hostility. "Forget Cottonwood." He stood so that their eyes were level. "It will never belong to you again."

There was a heavy, brittle silence.

"We'll see, Mr. Walsh," Beth said flatly. "We'll see."

When she reached her car a few minutes later, she was shaking. But she was far from defeated. She was not about to give up. Where there was a will there was a way.

Cottonwood *would* be hers again.

Thirty-Seven

Zach's heart pounded so furiously that he was forced to concentrate on his breathing in order to slow it down to an acceptable level. Still, as his running shoes slapped the hard surface, the adrenaline pumped through him.

He knew it was futile to take his dark thoughts out on his body, punishing it so brutally. But he couldn't seem to stop. Somehow it dulled the agony that was his constant companion. It seemed as though that agony was wedged in a too-tight space, crowding him more each day.

First Randall, then Rachel. How much could he endure and keep his head above water? Zach had asked God that question, only God hadn't been listening. Misery saturated every level of his consciousness, so much so that the correlation between time and events blurred together, and Zach didn't care about anything. He wished he was dead.

Would he ever be able to stitch the loose threads of his life back together? Would he always carry this guilt inside him? If only he'd loved Rachel more...if only he'd paid more attention to her...if only she hadn't kept her illness from him for too long....

She had been brave all along. And still smiling. They hadn't had much time together toward the end, but what little they had had, Zach made it count. He remembered the last hour in the cloistering silence of the hospital room. Rachel had opened her eyes to find him sitting beside her.

That was when she had smiled, a weak but beautiful smile. "Zach..."

"I'm...here, honey."

Her face, rarely pale before her illness, was now drained of color to the bone.

"Zach...there's so much I want to say...so little time...to say it."

"Rach—" His voice broke.

"Shh, my darling." Her voice was now only a whisper. "It's going to be all right."

His breathing burst savagely from his throat. "No, nothing will ever be all right again."

"Yes...it will. You...you have Mandy. You...you must take care of...her. You...and...Beth."

"Oh, God, Rach!"

"Remember...you promised...Beth promised..."

Zach grasped her fingers in his cold strong ones.

"Sweet Zach," she whispered, her eyes glazed. "You look...so tired...."

He buried his face in the side of her neck. Her fingers lightly stroked his hair.

Thirty minutes later she was dead.

In the end, and just as Rachel had predicted, it had been Mandy who had saved his life. And the mill. Still, there were times, like now, when the pain nipped at him like a mad, hungry dog at a bone.

Recently Zach had tried to find relief in booze and women. He wanted to curse and screw, to stick his hand up some girl's skirt and press against someone's braless tits.

But that hadn't worked. If no one was around, if no one demanded anything of him, he need no longer pretend he was something he wasn't. He could act the way he felt, which was like a miserable SOB.

So women were out. Zach found he had no use for them. And that included Beth.

Beth.

His stomach suddenly cramped.

No. Don't think about her. She doesn't exist anymore. Forget her. But he couldn't. Therein lay the problem.

The farther he stretched his stride, the faster the wheels of his mind raced. Like an out-of-control tape, his mind repeated, Beth is back, Beth is back.

When the moving van had arrived with her furniture, Zach had been out of town negotiating a timber deal. That hadn't made any difference, though. Anything involving the Melbournes, even after all those years, remained a hot topic for the gossip mongers.

Beth's return and the reason for it were the type of juicy tidbit the townsfolk gnawed on with relish.

Though he hated like hell to admit it, he'd been gnawing on it, as well, except that it had stuck in his throat, almost strangling him.

Zach blinked against the harsh sunlight as if cognizant of it for the first time. Five o'clock in the afternoon was a piss-poor time to run, but he'd been too busy to run this morning.

He forced himself to slow down to a semitrot, feeling as if the sun had a direct line to his brain. Zach fought for breath, gulping huge pockets of air into his lungs.

Nothing he did, however, seemed to quiet his soul.

Why did she have to come back to Shawnee? He had asked himself that question a hundred times. More to the point, why did she have to come back *now,* when he was so vulnerable?

Zach had felt all chewed up on the inside. While he ached to honor Rachel's wishes, he also ached to protect himself, conscious of the void inside him. He had to be careful or he would fall in. Just by talking, Beth had the power to thaw his heart. How, after all this time, was such a thing possible?

He would just have to be tougher. She'd made a fool of him once, and that was enough. She wasn't going to get another chance.

By the time Zach headed down the road that led to the new brick home he'd had built shortly after Rachel died, his breathing was back to normal. His head no longer throbbed. It was as if someone had mercifully loosened the vise around it.

He paused and removed his sweatband. When he finished wringing it out, he stuffed it into his back pocket, then started walking at an even slower pace, once again in charge of his emotions.

That feeling lasted only until he rounded the corner and lumbered into the backyard. He stopped still as a dead man. She sat in the swing, holding a sleeping Amanda.

"Beth!"

He wasn't aware that he'd spoken aloud until she jerked her head up. Shock registered in every tense line of both their bodies.

Her face was as pale as his. Faint shadows were etched below her eyes. Wisps of hair rippled against the skin of her cheeks in the hot breeze.

There was a squashing sound in his ears. He was certain he was having a heart attack.

Unwittingly Zach's gaze moved over her. She wore a simple sleeveless cotton blouse in light orange, collarless, with a scooped neck. The flesh between her collarbones was creamy and hinted at what was below.

No bra.

Beth appeared calm and in control, yet something about her hinted at a sweetness that couldn't be overlooked.

He wanted her. Another pang of anger and guilt struck him like a blow to the solar plexus.

"Zach, I—" Beth got no further. Amanda stirred, and she peered down at the child in the crook of her arm.

The heat was smothering; clothes withered and clung to damp skin. Amanda's cheeks were scarlet, as if the color had been painted on with a brush. Her tiny upper lip and temples were beaded. Someone had bunched the silky mop of curls on top of her head and tied it with a pink ribbon.

Beth shifted the child in her arms. Zach was suddenly struck by a devastating sense of tenderness; something in Beth's face and the way Amanda's head rested against her breasts stirred his heart in the oddest way.

He refused to analyze his feelings; he only knew that he found something undeniably touching in the relationship between those two. *She should have been our child, Beth. Yours and mine.*

"I tried to get her to go inside," Beth was saying, "but she . . . she wanted to play a little while longer."

Zach wanted to tear his eyes away from them, but he felt like a child himself, one who had dipped his hand into the cookie jar and found it full. Once it was in there, he couldn't pull it out.

He knew he should break the tenuous connection that still linked them with the strength of raw silk. It was imperative that he not let this unexpected sight of her dismantle him to such an extent that he forgot his vows to himself.

"Why?" The simple word was twisted into a husky plea.

She didn't pretend to misunderstand him. "I knew you were back, and I wanted to see you."

His expression changed. "What the hell does that mean?" The voice was cast iron.

Amanda stirred again suddenly, demanding Beth's attention. She lowered her head, revealing the side of her bare neck. His features contorted with anger even as his insides roiled with arousal.

Before Zach could say anything, the back door of the house opened and his housekeeper walked onto the deck.

"Would you like me to take Amanda inside?" she asked, her gaze on Zach.

"Yes," Zach said more sharply than he'd intended. But he half blamed Ms. Yates for letting Beth in. He knew, though, that his reasoning was warped. He'd never told his housekeeper to bar Beth from the door. Even if he had, he doubted it would have done any good.

Flushing, the slightly overweight woman made her way down the deck steps and reached for the child.

"We had a good time, didn't we, Mandy girl?" Beth whispered against a soft cheek before placing her in the woman's arms.

When Ms. Yates and Amanda had vanished behind closed doors, Zach leaned against a pecan tree and jammed his hands into the pockets of his shorts.

"You're . . . furious with me, aren't you?" she asked.

Her eyes seemed to devour him, half wild, half afraid.

"What's with you, anyway?" His voice sounded thick. "Why can't you leave well enough alone?"

Beth stood and peered at him through round, sad eyes. "You know the answer to that."

He didn't hear a word she said; he was too busy thinking that no one that lovely ought to look that sad.

"When I made that promise to Rachel—"

"That's not why you came back to Shawnee."

"Yes, it is." Anxiety lowered her voice.

"No, it isn't. The real reason—*the only reason*—you came back is because of Cottonwood." Zach's expression was pasty. "You see, I know about your visit to Richard Walsh."

Beth lifted her eyes; they were swimming with unshed tears. "So what? I've never made it a secret that I wanted Cottonwood back."

"That house has always meant more to you than anything else." He was practically shouting now. "Hasn't it?"

"No! But it *is* important. After all, it's my roots."

"To hell with your roots!" His hands were whitened fists at his side. "Since when do they take precedence over a human being?"

"Oh, Zach, you're not being fair."

"Like I told you before, go back where you came from, Beth. Go back to the big city where you belong."

"But that's just it. I don't belong there." It was a broken cry. "I belong here—with *you*."

Silence.

"I...want to be part of your life again, Zach." Her voice had dropped to a reedy whisper.

Zach didn't move. He gave no indication that he'd heard her. But he had. Her words weighed like a block of lead on his chest. Only the unsteady beat of his heart reminded him of the passing seconds. He wondered if he was strong enough to survive this.

He must hold firm. His whole future, his daughter's future, depended on his doing just that.

"While my conscience dictates that I honor Rachel's dying request," he spat harshly, "it sure as hell doesn't dictate that I let you back into my life."

She took halting steps toward him, her gaze steady on him. She was so close now that he could make out the long sweep of each eyelash.

"Tell me you don't care. Tell me you don't feel anything for me, and I'll—I'll leave you alone."

Swearing, Zach looked away. He could no longer trust himself to look at her pale face, at her eyes, which were not bright but deep, black pools.

"Zach..."

No one spoke his name the way she did.

"Look at me...please."

Even as he turned, raw emotion balled like a fist in his throat.

"Give me...another chance."

"Don't . . . Beth . . . don't do this." It was getting harder for him to speak.

"I—I have to." Her eyes raked over him. "I have no choice."

"We all have choices," he said dully.

Her gaze didn't waver. "I love you."

Cold terror gripped his vitals. Yet it was all he could do to steel himself against the seductive words, the seductive sweetness in her voice. "It's . . . too late."

"Is . . . is that your final word?"

He didn't answer. He couldn't.

"I'm going now, Zach," she said quietly. "But I'm warning you, I'm not giving up."

Long after she'd gone, Zach continued to lean against the tree, using it to brace his trembling body.

When a heart was poisoned, it was about as much use as dead leaves blowing across the desert. Had his heart been poisoned too long? Was it time to forgive? To forget? He didn't know if he could do either. But he knew he was going to find out.

Thirty-Eight

He wasn't going to call. It was as simple and as complicated as that. And when you were waiting for something to
happen, three weeks seemed like a lifetime, much less three
months. Or at least it did to Beth.

Each day that passed when she didn't hear from Zach,
her insides shriveled a little more. Still, she kept on working long and hard hours. Just as she was now. Having been
at the shop the majority of the day, she had stopped put-
tering for a moment to survey her surroundings. She liked
what she saw.

The In-Look of Shawnee had potential to be one of her
best endeavors to date. The rich, forest green walls com-
plemented the plush raspberry-colored carpet.

In many respects it reminded her of the shop in Natchitoches, especially the layout. An abundance of freestand-
ing racks and accessory cases were interspersed carefully
between wicker planters loaded with live greenery. A small
sitting area dominated the middle, adding to the feeling of
fresh, cozy comfort.

The local women, both socialites and those who were
career minded, had shown enthusiasm for the trendy and
innovative new shop. The fact that Beth was a hometown
girl who had triumphed over tragedy and misfortune added
to the excitement and curiosity.

Circumstances had kept Beth from opening as soon as
she would have liked. Besides minor problems with the

contractors, she had spent two of the three months either
on the road or in the air. She had worked the fashion scenes
in both Paris and Milan and held managerial workshops for
her employees here.

She was also determined that her own design of light-
weight, papier-mâché jewelry would be ready for display on
opening day. That project alone had taken more time than
she had allotted. But her determination had paid off, and
now the workroom table was covered with a colorful array
of pins and earrings made by her own hands.

Sitting Indian-style on the carpet, clad in an oversize
sweatshirt and baggy jeans, Beth began thumbing through
the stack of job applications.

Tomorrow she had interviews lined up for salesclerks as
well as a part-time manager. While she wanted to work the
floor herself, that wasn't possible. She had too many re-
sponsibilities that only she could handle, although she'd
recently hired a full-time buyer to work closely with Tracy.

Tracy had left Shawnee yesterday and wasn't due to return until the official opening, slated in two weeks. While
much of the merchandise was in, there was more to come.
Beth wanted to have fully stocked racks and shelves before
making a splash.

She was pleased with what she had accomplished and was
eager to flaunt it. But the shop was not uppermost in her
mind. Zach took precedence over everything. After having
bared her soul to him, Beth had prayed he would respond,
but as the hours stretched into days, she began to fear that
she had allowed false hope to cloud her sound judgment.

Even so, she didn't give up. Before she left town she made
a point to record a message for her answering machine that
gave the numbers where she could be reached.

He never called. She would lie in her hotel bed alone and
dream of holding Zach in love, sliding her hands over his
rigid muscles, seeking the shadowed places between their
bodies.

But it was more than sex that Beth wanted. Their close proximity had whetted her appetite, had made her hungry for the little things—the sound of his devilish laughter, his sound advice, his warm friendship.

When no word was forthcoming, her hope diminished, though her doubts persisted. Had she been wrong? Had she misread his eyes? Maybe Zach was right. Maybe it was too late for them. Maybe there was too much pain and sorrow, too many years between them to ever bridge the gap.

It was a chilling thought, but perhaps Thomas Wolfe had known what he was talking about when he'd said you can't go home again.

Still, Beth wasn't sorry for her actions. No matter what the future held, she had no regrets. So why did she feel as if her whole life was some loose end unraveling, and she was holding only air? Was it because she herself had backed off? She had warned him that she wasn't giving up, only to do just that.

Reverend Broussard was having a birthday party at the shelter tomorrow. She wanted to take Amanda. More than that, she wanted to *see* Amanda.

At the risk of another cold rejection, should she call Zach? Holding that thought, Beth jumped up, locked the shop and drove to her apartment. The minute she walked inside she knew what she was going to do. Glancing at the clock, she noted it was six. If he wasn't out of town, Zach should be at home. She went to the phone and lifted the receiver. Taking a deep breath, she punched out the numbers.

She held her breath while it rang once, twice, three times. Answer, please, she willed frantically, feeling her heart in her throat.

After the fifth ring Beth decided that neither Zach nor Ms. Yates was going to respond. She was lowering the receiver when she heard Zach's terse, "Yes?"

"Zach?"

She heard his indrawn breath.

"Have...I caught you at a bad time?" She chose her words carefully because he could ignite—like a firecracker—into instant anger. Fearing her wobbly legs would fail her, she sat on the couch.

"Matter of fact, you have." His tone was clipped.

Beth waited for him to elaborate, and when he didn't she forced herself to continue in spite of the chill in his voice and the helpless feeling inside her. It was too late to turn back now.

"I'm helping Reverend Broussard with a party at the shelter tomorrow and I'd—I'd like to take Amanda."

"That's impossible."

It wasn't so much what he said as how he said it. He sounded at his wits' end. "What's wrong, Zach?" she asked.

"Mandy's sick."

"How sick?"

"Fever and upset stomach."

"You should have called me," Beth said irrationally, knowing she was the last person he would call.

"I haven't had time to call anybody. She just started throwing up a few minutes ago."

"Let me come over, Zach."

"I don't think that's a good idea."

She dug in her heels. "I do."

"She's sleeping right now."

"I don't care." Her tone was soft without being begging. "I want to see her...see you."

A minuscule silence ensued, but it was enough for Beth. "I'll be there in a few minutes."

"Beth!"

Ignoring the suppressed violence in his voice, she replaced the receiver, cutting off the remainder of his sentence. But it was a minute before she controlled her rapid heartbeat enough to dash into her bedroom, shower and slip into her clothes. Slinging her bag over her shoulder, she hurried toward the door. When she was halfway there, the doorbell chimed.

"Damn," she muttered, stopping in her tracks.

"Beth?" a voice called.

She frowned. "Vicki?"

"Please . . . open the door."

Even through the heavy door Beth picked up the hysteria in Vicki's voice. Trent? Something had happened to her brother! Without wasting another second, Beth yanked open the door.

"Oh, my God," she mouthed. "Oh, my God."

Trent stood on the porch, though not on his own merits. Vicki was holding him upright. Both eyes were almost swollen shut. His bottom lip was split and bleeding. He looked as if he'd been in a heavyweight fight and lost.

Swallowing her panic, Beth helped Vicki get Trent across the threshold and into the living room. They didn't let go of him until he was on the couch.

"Thanks," he whispered, closing his eyes.

Beth stared down into his battered face, trying to breathe around the crushing disappointment that was making her nauseated. She'd had such high hopes for Trent, especially after he had married Vicki last month. Opting for a quickie wedding, they had gone to Vegas. Since then he had been doing well, or so she'd thought.

Beth lifted her eyes to Vicki. "I'll call the doctor."

Trent reached out and grabbed her hand. "No, please. No doctor. I'll be all right. Nothing's broken. I'm just sore. They . . . they kicked me in the ribs a time or two."

Still facing Vicki, Beth demanded, "What happened? Who—who did this to him?"

Vicki's face crumpled, and she began sobbing. "They—they beat him up because . . ." She couldn't go on.

Beth quelled the urge to shake her. "Who are 'they'?" She heard her own voice reach the upper stages of hysteria, but she couldn't control it. "For God's sake, stop sniveling and tell me!"

Trent groaned, drawing Beth's attention back to him. His face was a study in misery.

"This is ridiculous, Trent. I'm calling the doctor," she insisted.

"No!" Trent tried to raise himself onto his elbows. "No doctor. I'll be fine. Just give me a few minutes."

"Please, Trent," Vicki begged, her weeping having subsided somewhat, "let her help you. Please, for my sake, if nothing else."

Trent turned his head into the cushion.

"Why?" Although she asked, Beth knew the answer.

Vicki sat down at the foot of the couch and placed a trembling hand on one of Trent's legs.

Trent licked his lips, then winced. "I'm in over my head to a certain loan shark. He's—he's been footing my bills at the track."

"Oh, Trent, how could you?" Beth whispered. "I...I thought you'd stopped all that, especially after you got the promotion."

"It hasn't interfered with my work." His tone was belligerent.

"Sure."

Trent peered up at Beth through only one eye. "I want to stop, but I...can't." He paused. "I...I thought this time they were going to kill me."

"Will you loan him the money, Beth?" Vicki asked in a small voice, the freckles on her pale face standing out like a bad case of the measles.

"How much?" Beth asked mechanically.

"Fifty thou," Trent said.

Beth gasped. "Fifty thousand dollars!"

Trent very gingerly eased into a sitting position, while a lone tear rolled down one cheek. Vicki began sobbing outright.

"I screwed up real good this time, didn't I?"

Beth couldn't speak; she could only nod.

"You've got to help him," Vicki pressed, sounding desperate.

Beth wrapped her arms around her chest, feeling cold through and through. "On one condition."

"Name it," Trent said.

"You get professional help. You check into a clinic that deals with this type of sickness."

If possible, Trent's face turned even paler. "All...right."

"When do they...want the money?"

"Tomorrow."

Beth went to the desk in the corner of the room and withdrew a checkbook. Moments later she ripped out a check and handed it to Trent. "No more. This is it!"

He looked down at the check and then back up. "Is this going...to...uh...ruin you?"

Beth ignored the lump growing in her throat and watched as Trent slipped what she had hoped would be the down payment on Cottonwood into his shirt pocket.

"No," she finally whispered. "What about Zach? Does he know?"

"He suspects, but when he finds out he's...going to kill me."

"I'd like to," Beth said softly, so softly that Trent looked at her as if he thought he hadn't heard her correctly.

"That's right, I'd like to kill you myself, but since it's against the law..."

Trent gulped, but he didn't say anything.

Beth spoke again. "Vicki, will you see that he gets in bed and stays there?"

"Oh, he'll stay there, all right, if I have to tie him."

Beth took in a slow breath. "Trent, don't go near Gran, you hear? If she sees you like this, it might trigger another heart attack."

Trent stood, though a bit unsteadily. The fact that he did so under his own power was a good sign. "I'll do anything you say." Then, with Vicki's help, he shuffled to the door.

"Trent?"

He turned around.

"You'd better think long and hard about what you promised, because I meant every word I said. Don't you think for one minute that I didn't. And don't you think I'll sell any of our mill stock to Zach or anyone else to help you. I won't. It's time you grew up."

Trent looked at her steadily for a long moment, his head tipped slightly back. "I know. And I owe you, sis."

With that he turned and, with Vicki at his side, walked out the door.

Beth felt a ridiculous shortness of breath. Still, she managed to ask, "May I come in?"

Zach stepped aside and motioned with his hand. Sweeping past him, Beth walked into the dimly lighted entry hall.

"I'd about decided you weren't coming." Zach's voice sounded strained.

She looked up at him. The connective force of their gaze was palpable. "Sorry. I . . . er . . . meant to come sooner."

"You've been crying, haven't you?"

Bypassing his question, Beth asked one of her own. "How's Mandy?"

He dragged a hand through his tousled hair. "Her fever's broken, and she's sleeping."

"Is it a virus?"

"No, it's her ears. They have a habit of giving her trouble."

They fell silent again. The cords stood out on Zach's neck. Beth stood transfixed, like someone who'd been drugged.

"Since you're here, you might as well stay for a few minutes."

His low voice jarred Beth into action. She followed him into a den that ran across the back of the house. It was a homey room, with a fireplace, brightly cushioned furniture and glass-topped tables. A lamp burned on a table next to the couch.

"You wanna sit down?" Zach asked, his eyes now shuttered.

Beth stood awkwardly in the middle of the room. "No, I'm all right."

Zach muttered an expletive and looked away.

He had on worn jeans, so worn they had a hole in one knee. His shirt was open to the waist, as if he'd put it on in a hurry. He looked tired and drawn and in need of a shave. A five-o'clock shadow covered his strong jaws.

Beth thought he'd never looked dearer or sexier. She longed to throw her arms around him and squeeze him. Instead she asked, "Are you alone?"

"Yes."

"Where's Ms. Yates?"

His expression changed. "What the hell is this, twenty questions?"

Beth's narrow shoulders bent under their burden of humiliation. Coming here had been a mistake. Nothing had changed. How could she ever have thought he still cared?

"I...I was just wondering, that's all," she whispered, sounding as if she had a tear in her voice.

Zach stared at her with hooded eyes, though when he spoke his tone was less harsh. "Ms. Yates is gone for the weekend."

Beth let out a slow, silent breath. "Does Amanda have trouble with her ears often?"

"Unfortunately, yes."

"That could...be serious."

"I know."

Silence.

"Something's wrong, isn't it?" he asked at last, his gaze holding hers. "You look awful."

"It's Trent, Zach."

His dark face showed no emotion at all. "Why am I not surprised? What's he done now?"

Beth told him everything. When she finished, Zach swore, then paced the floor. "Of all the stupid—"

"I think he's really scared this time," Beth cut in. "He has Vicki to consider now."

Zach stopped. "You gave him the money?"

She nodded.

He faced her with anger beaming from his eyes. "Why?"

"What else could I do?"

"Let them beat him within an inch of his life."

Beth wet her dry lips. "You don't mean that."

"No, but something needs to jerk a knot in his tail."

Unwittingly Beth rubbed her temple. "You're absolutely right."

"So does that mean you aren't going to let him get away with this?"

"He's going to enter a clinic."

Zach's lips twisted. "You sure about that?"

"Yes," she burst out. "He won't cross me on this. He knows better."

"We'll see."

"Look, do you mind if I see Mandy?" Beth asked, bridging another long silence.

Silently Zach gestured for her to precede him down a hall to the nursery. Beth went straight to the adorable pink-and-white bed where the child lay sleeping.

Zach followed her. As they stood side by side and peered down at her, Beth was aware of Zach with every beat of her heart.

"She's . . . about to lose a sock," Beth whispered, a tiny catch in her voice. With slightly unsteady fingers she began to slip it back on.

"I'll do it," Zach said curtly, nudging her hand aside.

Beth caught her breath and looked up at him, her eyes brilliant with unshed tears. "Do you hate me that much?"

Thirty-Nine

Beth's mortified tone, her hurt eyes, were more than Zach could bear. "I didn't mean—" He broke off and stepped backward, as if shoved by an invisible hand. His breathing was sporadic and his features grim. "Forget it. I don't know what I meant."

Beth uttered a faint choking sound, wanting to speak, only to find she couldn't. Her voice had deserted her.

"Don't look at me like that," Zach muttered, his tone biting.

In the stricken silence that followed, Beth closed her eyes, unable to bear the sight of the primitive anger her action had brought to life. After another choking attempt to speak, she whirled and fled the room. She didn't stop until she reached the dimly lighted den.

"Beth."

She knew he was behind her before he spoke, but she couldn't turn around. She stood rigid, barely able to hold herself together. Desire, pain and confusion formed a tight band around her chest. She struggled to breathe, but the pressure made that difficult. She struggled for control but could not find that, either.

It was all too much: Trent's dilemma, Amanda's illness, Zach's open condemnation. Her conscious mind simply refused to function.

"Beth," Zach said again, closer this time.

It wasn't the use of her name that drew her around to face him; it was the way it rolled off his tongue, both savage and tender at once.

"You . . . you lied to me," she whispered.

"No." His voice was sharp, wounding.

"You . . . told me you didn't blame me for Randall's . . . death."

"I don't."

"Yes . . . you do. That's why you . . . you can't stand for me to touch Amanda. You . . . you do blame me. You *do*." Tears coursed down her face.

Zach's hands closed until the knuckles were white and his fingernails bit into his palms. "No!"

"Oh, Zach, when Randall died, I wanted to die, too."

"Jesus . . . don't . . ." Pain throbbed in his voice.

Beth was weeping openly now, as she hadn't in months.

"Please don't," Zach pleaded in an agonized whisper, reaching out a hand, but still not touching her. "I can't stand it when you cry."

"I had only known him a short time," Beth sobbed, as if he hadn't spoken. "But I loved him, because—"

"You're breaking my heart."

"Because he was a part of you."

"Damn you!" Zach cried. "Do you have any idea what you're doing to me? What you've always done to me? It's killing me," he whispered achingly, "standing here with you like this, without touching you. I ache when I get near you, even if it's only in my mind."

"Oh, Zach, I'm so sorry for everything. I never meant to hurt you." Her enormous eyes fell, and when she spoke again it was in a raspy mumble. "Ever."

Outside, thunder exploded like an unexpected gunshot. They both winced as the first burst of rain slapped the windowpanes.

"You . . . believe me, don't you?"

"Beth," he breathed.

She shuddered.

He reached out and touched her. Her lips parted on an expectant breath.

His eyes widened, searching, holding hers.

"Do...you want me to go?" she whispered.

"God, no." His voice was thick.

"Zach..." Beth no longer seemed to be talking to him. She felt dizzy, as if she were about to faint.

Just as a violent flash of lightning ripped through the sky, his arms caught her. Then he simply held her.

A warm sensation spread through her, and for a moment it burned away the memories inside her, cleansing past pains and hurts.

His face was but a heartbeat from hers. She felt his strength and more, the pulse of him. Light-headed, unable to sustain her equilibrium, she leaned her malleable body into his. Instantly she felt his erection, so hard and tight she knew it must be painful.

Zach brought his lips down to hers and sipped from them as if tasting their sweetness for the first time. Then, brutally, he withdrew his mouth and hands.

"No! I can't. I *won't!*"

Beth's face twisted in torment. "You want me," she said in an agonized whisper. "I know you do."

"Beth!"

"Even if it's a lie, tell me you do."

"You're not playing fair. What gives you the right—"

"Loving you gives me that right," she pressed, her voice trembling with emotion.

His eyes flashed. "All right! I'm mad about you, and that's my friggin' curse! Is that what you wanted to hear?"

"Oh, Zach..."

His groan was lost against her lips as he pulled her against him once again. "Just this once. Just once—just this once!"

They kissed again, hotly, savagely as if they could never get enough of each other.

"I missed you so much!" she cried, clutching at him.

His body, hands and mouth were like poultices wresting the pain from her system. Her heart expanded, pulling him into her so fully that there was no room for anything else. For the moment she wanted only to feel, to forget everything else.

"My insides melt like wax when I touch you." Zach's voice came out a thick croak.

"Please...Zach..." Thunder clapped; rain drummed a cadence on the roof. "Make love to me. Now!"

He quickly discarded her clothes, then his. Never had Zach felt such urgency. The physical and emotional ramifications of his actions were both overridden by the need raging inside him.

When she'd begged him to love her, he'd swept her into his arms and carried her into the bedroom.

Now, as he peered down at her, he couldn't speak. It was as if he feared words would make him realize what he did not want to examine in the heat of the moment. Still, they rattled around in his mind until he wanted to scream.

Why did you leave me? he longed to ask. *Why did you hurt me so?*

Another bolt of lightning streaked past the window, offering him the light by which to see her.

She seemed so vulnerable, so fragile. To him her skin was as breakable as eggshells. Had it always been like that? God, it had been so long....

She held her arms up to him, beckoning.

With a muted cry he lay beside her on the bed. As their bodies came together, Zach gasped aloud. His hands roamed her body as if her flesh were on fire and he had been sent to put it out. He felt the nerves beneath his skin that had been dormant for years surge to life.

Her arms stole around his neck, her eyes looking into his. Her lips, soft as rose petals, were parted, and her sweet breath caressed his cheek.

He sighed into her mouth and tasted her, thinking he couldn't possibly get enough of her. Ever. His head pounded, and he felt the tension in his legs erupt into muscle spasms.

No matter how much he might despise her, despise himself, he had never stopped wanting her. He knew that now.

"Zach, oh, Zach," Beth whispered, "I thought I'd die before I felt your arms around me again."

His breath heaved as he clamped her to him, felt her warmth steal through him, melting his icy insides. At that moment his heart cried out, and he rose to his knees, then bent over and caressed the insides of her thighs. His face was close to the heat of her. Its warmth grazed his face as he touched his tongue there, at the same time inserting a finger.

"Ohh," Beth panted, thrashing her head on the pillow.

Her heart hammered against his arm as her secret flesh opened to him.

Just as Zach removed his mouth and slid another finger into her throbbing wetness, he whispered, "Let it go, darling, let it go."

"Yes!" she cried and dug her fingernails into his shoulders.

"You're beautiful when you come."

"Oh, Zach," she whispered, closing her hands around his burgeoning hardness and caressing it. "I want to—"

He stilled her hand, his eyes glazed. "Later. I can't wait to be inside you."

But instead of moving over her, he rolled off the bed, came to the foot and wordlessly grasped her gently by the ankles and eased her down to the edge.

Once there, he spread her legs, leaned over and eased the tip of his hardness inside her. His breathing stopped as he felt her warmth engulf him.

Together they watched in silence, breaths suspended, as he slid his hard shaft slowly in, then out, in, then out.

"Oh, Zach," she rasped, her eyes glazed, "I don't know how much more I can take."

He looked up.

Another burst of thunder shook the house.

His eyes blazed. "I love the way you're so tight...."

"Please...now," she begged, reaching for him, pulling him down. Her open mouth bit into his flesh.

"Oh, Beth...God..." Her mouth, her warmth, was almost more than he could bear. His lungs labored. Sweat drenched him.

With what little strength he had left, he bracketed her body with his hands and, without taking his eyes off her, sank deeper inside her, then eased out again.

"Don't!" she gasped, reacting as if a live wire had jolted her body. "I want all of you!"

"I've dreamed of doing this for so long—" his rhythm was slow and easy "—of watching your eyes, hearing you purr, feeling you come."

"I...can't...stand...it!" she cried, as if the heat he was generating had struck her like a blow across her breasts. Her strong fingers cupped him gently and squeezed.

It was too much for him. He groaned, then drove into her, hard, quivering with the images of her in the throes of climax.

"Oh, yes, oh, yes," Beth whimpered.

With every thrust, he felt the core of her surround him. He grew inside her, and at the same time he shifted, moving her on top.

Beth sensed the end was near and rode him rapidly, pressing her upper body into his. Their flesh slapped faster and faster. With total abandonment, he finally emptied his seed into her.

Locked to him, she felt the force of his explosion, and she exploded with him. Their cries of pleasure mingled with the long moaning cries of the wind and the rain.

Later, when she felt Zach ease out of her, she whimpered and reached for him, unwilling for him to leave her body.

"Oh, yes," he groaned. "Work your magic."

Soon, after careful nursing on her part, he surged back to life and brought them both to completion once more.

Forty

"If there's nothing else, I'm outta here."

Beth looked up from the papers on her desk and smiled at Tracy. "Drive carefully. And if you need me, don't hesitate to call."

Beth was at the shop in Natchitoches. She hadn't wanted to come, but there had been problems with the Houston store, and she'd had no choice. Tracy was being sent to try to muddle through the mess. The manager had given notice two days ago for no apparent reason and walked out.

"I can handle it. Don't worry."

Beth pushed her chair away from the desk and stood. "I don't doubt it for a minute." She paused with a smile. "Just in case I haven't told you lately, I don't know what I'd do without you."

Tracy grinned. "I planned it that way. It's called job security."

Beth laughed outright. "Well, if that's the case, you're definitely in for the long haul."

"That's good to know." Tracy's face sobered. "Are you going back to Shawnee today?"

"Yes. In fact, I'll be leaving after lunch."

Tracy hesitated, then asked, "How's your brother?"

"As well as can be expected, I guess." Beth's smile was rueful. "He hates counseling, but he's going every day, and that's what counts."

"I'm glad. I know you've been worrying yourself silly."

"True, only most of my energy has been spent on Gran. We tried to keep it from her, but we didn't succeed."

Tracy blew her a kiss. "You know I'm keeping everything crossed—except my legs, that is."

Beth shook her head and grinned. "You're awful."

Tracy's giggle stayed with Beth long after she sat back down and idly rolled her pen between her fingers. Her concentration had been broken, and she doubted she could get it back. But then, it had been broken a lot during the past two weeks.

Her thoughts had jockeyed between Trent, her grandmother and Zach. But, just as she'd told Tracy, Trent was making progress. One reason for that was Zach's promise. He had told Trent that if he would straighten up, he would seriously consider moving him to the new mill due to open in Texas.

The mill was doing well, as was her own business. Hopefully she would be able to recoup the cash she had doled out to her brother much sooner than she had expected.

Following up on her visit with Walsh was a moot point now, so she tried not to think about it. Still, someday, somehow, she intended to regain possession of her beloved home. It would just take longer than she'd thought, that was all. But she wouldn't let that get her down.

What *had* gotten her down was Zach's attitude. She hadn't thought it was possible for relations to worsen between them. But their passionate evening of lovemaking had done just that, even though Zach had been as hungry for her as she had been for him.

Thinking about it again now brought about the same panicked sensation inside her....

She had awakened in the wee hours of the morning. After peering at Zach's sleeping figure for a long minute, she had slipped out of bed, grabbed his shirt off the floor and put it on. Then she had gone into Mandy's room to check on her, finding the child still free of fever and resting peacefully.

When she returned to the bedroom, she stopped short. Zach, in cutoffs, was standing in front of the window staring into the inky blackness.

"Zach?"

He turned around. The door behind her was open, the night-light in the hall allowing her to see his face. The despair she saw there stole her breath.

"You're sorry, aren't you?" She felt as if a giant hand was squeezing her lungs until she couldn't breathe.

His shoulders sagged. "Right now I don't know what I'm feeling."

For a moment the room was silent.

"Your body wanted me," she whispered huskily, reaching out to him across the awkward silence, "even if your mind didn't."

His eyes were dark with misery. "Don't you think I know that?"

Staring at him, she suddenly felt sick with desperation. "What...what are we going to do?"

He blinked. "Do?"

"Yes...do."

Zach's mouth twisted into a nasty smile. "You think you've got me right where you want me, don't you?"

She had come this far, and she wasn't prepared to back down. She had prayed last night wasn't the end, but a new beginning. Yet he reminded her of a rainbow; you could blink your eyes and find it gone, faded to a memory.

Slowly, methodically, she turned away and reached for her clothes.

"Where are you going?"

"Home."

"Beth..." His voice sounded broken.

She faced him again and shook her head. "No...please. Don't say anything more." Distress left her breathless. "I couldn't bear it if we fought right now."

As soon as she'd managed to clothe herself decently, she had left. And he hadn't tried to stop her....

Since then she had seen him only once, at a meeting at the mill. He had been on edge around her, couldn't seem to meet her eyes. She hadn't reacted much differently. Because she didn't know where she stood with him, she'd felt vulnerable, as if her defenseless heart was an open invitation for him to step on all her feelings.

It was obvious that she'd expected too much too soon. But, damn it, he cared. She knew he did. His touch had told her that. But her hidden fears were coming to light. The old sins and hurts of the past stood like a brick wall between them. The thought that she would never be able to tear that wall down wasn't something she wanted to think about, especially not now.

It dawned on Beth that the tonic she needed for this attack of the blues was Amanda. Seeing her daughter would make her laugh.

And today Beth badly needed to laugh.

Sweat dripped from every pore on Zach's body, but he was oblivious to it as he continued to pump the iron high above his head. Instead of working weights, he would much rather be drinking himself into a deep stupor.

Since the latter wasn't possible, he'd settled for second best. Anyway, no matter how drunk he got, he couldn't erase his troubles from his mind. Front and center was the brouhaha at the mill. The hands were on strike and tempers were on edge. If that wasn't explosive enough, there was his bittersweet obsession with Beth.

Your body wanted me, even if your mind didn't.

The fortress around his heart, a fortress that he'd toiled for almost eighteen years to erect into an unbreachable shield against her, now lay in rubble at his feet, torn down, obliterated by none other than Beth herself.

She had accomplished that feat in only a matter of weeks. Layer by layer she had hacked away at the wall with her big, doelike eyes, her peaches-and-cream skin, her thick, silky hair, her luscious body, her unflappable tenacity in the fight to win him back again. With the expertise of a master carpenter, Beth had done what heretofore he had deemed impossible.

The blame sat squarely on his shoulders. But the moment he'd felt the heat of her naked body against his, stroked her plump lower lip, touched her uptilted breasts, tasted her rose-hued nipples, he'd been as defenseless as a newborn baby.

Every vital organ inside him had collapsed. She'd knocked down that steel door around his heart with featherlike ease.

Memories of those years filled with grief and hate and despair were vanishing from his mind, as well. As a last defensive resort, he was punishing his body. Only it wasn't working. He still hurt like hell.

"Want some company?"

Matt Thorne's unexpected drawl froze Zach midaction. "Anytime," he said, lowering the weights back to the rack and sitting down.

Matt's grin held no humor. "Good, 'cause I'm thinkin' I'm gonna have to strengthen my pecs."

"What's up?"

"The mood's turning awfully ugly, boss."

"Great," Zach said. "That's all we need."

"You know who's egging them on, don't you?"

"You bet I do, that scumbag Griffin."

Wade Griffin, the head of the union, had been and still was Zach's sworn enemy. For a reason Zach hadn't been able to uncover, Griffin hated him.

He voiced his thoughts. "Tell me, Matt, what the hell did I do to get that man's stinger after me?"

Matt grinned a lopsided grin and sat in the nearest chair. "It's simple. You wouldn't take his shit."

Zach snapped his fingers. "Why, I'll be damned," he drawled sarcastically. "Hadn't thought of that."

Matt chuckled. "Yeah, he's the type of creep who, once he's got you down and groveling, not only does he want to shit on you—"

"He wants to rub it in, too," Zach finished for him, mopping his face with a towel.

"You got it. So what'cha think?"

Zach made an exaggerated face. "I think it stinks, that's what."

They both laughed, a deep belly laugh.

When the laughter subsided, Zach asked, "Just what the hell more does he want, anyway?"

"You name it, he wants it." Matt threaded his hands behind his head and stretched his legs. "More money, more benefits.... But I think what really has him stirred is all the modernization. He sees that as a direct threat to manpower."

"That's bullshit, and he knows it. If we don't upgrade, pretty soon there won't be *any* jobs. He knows that, too."

"Hey, I'm not the one you have to convince."

"Sorry," Zach muttered darkly. "It's just that I've gone as far as I'm prepared to go. And Taylor—well, you know how he feels. He has less patience than I do."

"Well, I just wanted you to know that the rumblings are turning nasty. Word has it that some of the guys who have crossed the line have been harassed, even threatened."

Zach's face hardened. "You think Griffin's behind it all?"

"Yep."

"But no hard proof?"

"Nope."

"Well, it doesn't matter. If I have to, I'll stop that bastard myself."

"You may have to," Matt said seriously.

"Keep me posted."

"Will do."

The second Matt closed the door behind him, Zach reached for his weights again, but the relief he sought never came. Finally he showered, then walked out into the humid night air feeling more confused and alone than he had in years.

"Bef, read book."

"Oh, honey, I've already read you five."

"Pease."

Beth laughed, then lifted Amanda and swung her around. "You're quite a little con artist."

The girl squealed with laughter. When Beth stopped, she wiggled her feet. "Again, Bef."

"Bef has to go. It's getting late."

Amanda's lower lip began to tremble.

"Oh, honey, don't cry. I'll come back and see you soon. I promise."

Once Beth had made up her mind to visit Amanda, she had lost no time in coming here. She had found the child outside playing under the housekeeper's watchful eye. When Mandy had seen Beth, she had dropped her baby doll and run toward her.

That had been three hours ago. Now it was nearly six-thirty, time for Amanda to eat, then go to bed. And it was time for Beth to go home. She was exhausted, but pleasantly so. Amanda had certainly revived her spirits.

"Don't cry, please," Beth pleaded again while Amanda clung to her, tears wetting her shoulders.

Beyond Mandy's shoulders, Beth's eyes implored Ms. Yates for help.

The elderly woman smiled. "It'll take her a few minutes to settle down, but she'll be all right, especially when Mr. Winslow gets home." She paused and looked beyond Beth's shoulder. "And speaking of Mr. Winslow, he just drove up."

Beth sucked air deep into her lungs, as though she never meant to let it out.

Amanda's head popped up. She grinned. "Daddy. Me want to see daddy."

"Boy, are you fickle," Beth said, her voice off-key.

The child scaled down her body, then ran toward Zach. "Daddy, Daddy!" she cried.

Beth slowly turned around. She knew he would be furious at finding her here, but she wasn't about to apologize, no matter how riled he was.

"Hello, Beth," he said, concentrating on her rather than on Mandy, who was now in his arms and pulling on his earlobe.

The unexpected timbre of his voice loosened the grip around her throat. "Hello."

Zach didn't respond. Instead, he focused his attention on Ms. Yates. "How 'bout taking Mandy inside? I'll be along in a minute."

The child didn't squabble. She held out her arms to the housekeeper.

"Blow Daddy and Bef a kiss," Ms. Yates said.

Amanda giggled and did exactly that, placing her grimy little palm next to her mouth, then releasing it.

"Bye, pumpkin," Beth said, hating to feel her eyes fill with tears. "I'll see you later."

When Ms. Yates disappeared inside the house, Beth took her time before facing Zach again. She dreaded what she would see in his eyes.

"Look, I..." she began, still not looking directly at him.

"Have you eaten?"

Beth's mouth fell open; then, realizing how ridiculous she must look, she snapped it shut. Still, she couldn't quite get control of her scattered emotions.

"Well?"

"No... I mean..."

He watched her blustering with unreadable eyes, then asked, "You wanna ride to the mill with me, then grab a bite to eat?"

Forty-One

Beth stared out the window of Zach's silver Mercedes, still reeling from tiny tremors of shock at the unexpected change of events. What had prompted Zach to so casually ask her to dinner, as if his invitation wasn't out of the ordinary?

Well, no matter how he'd behaved, it *was* out of the ordinary. And the possibilities were endless, though she hadn't had a chance to sort them all out. Once she'd recovered enough to say yes, they had gotten into their respective cars. Zach had followed her to her apartment, where she'd left hers.

For the most part, the short ride to the mill had passed in silence. Now, as Zach nosed the Mercedes onto the road that led to the mill's entrance, the silence seemed to reach a screaming pitch. Each was aware of the other, each heated by the other's seductive warmth. And both were filled with anticipation, yet they were cautious about what might develop from this overture.

"Shit!"

Beth twisted her head sharply, saw Zach's tight profile, then followed his gaze. A group of men carrying signs were walking a picket line in front of Southland.

"Uh-oh," she said, wide-eyed. "Looks like trouble."

"Big-time trouble this time, as in Wade Griffin's involved."

"Who's he?"

"The man leading the pack, and someone you don't want to know."

"I gathered that from your initial reaction. But that still doesn't tell me who he is."

Zach didn't respond right away. Instead, he concentrated on nosing the vehicle cautiously through the gate; the picketers were slow to move out of the way.

Finally, when he pulled into his parking space, he faced Beth, but not before glancing quickly into the rearview mirror. "He's head of union negotiations."

"And not pleasant to deal with, I take it?"

Zach snorted. "If I didn't have to, I wouldn't let him through the gates, ever."

Beth saw movement out of the corner of one eye. "Even as we speak, here he comes."

"Figures," Zach muttered, slapping at the door handle. "The sooner I see what the bastard wants, the sooner we can get out of here." His gaze rested on Beth for a moment. "You stay put."

Beth laid a hand on his arm. "Zach..."

He looked down, then back up, an odd expression on his face.

"Be careful. Please." Her lips puckered in anxiety. "He...he looks—" She broke off with a shudder. "Mean."

Zach stared at her for another moment, then opened the door and got out.

"Well, well," Griffin sneered as he sauntered up to Zach, "if it isn't the high-and-mighty boss, who thinks his shit don't stink."

Griffin's megabreath nearly knocked Zach down. He didn't know which was stronger, the smell of liquor or the smell of garlic. Either way, the stench was repulsive. *He* was repulsive.

Short and beefy, with a refrigerator belly and a mustache that curved down around the corners of his lips, he offended on sight. But he was immaculately dressed in a pair of expensive slacks and a sports shirt. Still, nothing could overcome his social retardation, especially with a tattoo visible on his right biceps that said Fuck You, Too.

"Go home, Griffin." Zach took in a deep breath of fresh air. "You're drunk."

Griffin waggled a finger close to Zach's nose. "That's what you're countin' on, isn't it, me to turn tail and run? Well, lemme tell you, that ain't gonna happen. You rich Winslows and Melbournes have stuck it to these men long enough."

Zach tried to stymie the quick spurt of hot anger. "I'll tell you one more time. Go home."

"You'll tell me nothin', you hear? You're gonna listen to what I have to say."

The men walking the picket line had stopped and were not only staring but listening to every word they were saying.

The anger churning inside Zach had swelled to epic proportions and was eating its way up from the pit of his stomach. He could feel his face getting hot.

"Get outta my way, Griffin."

Griffin stuck out his chest. "Make me."

"I'm warning you, step aside." Zach's voice never wavered. "I haven't got time to mess with a turd like you."

Griffin laughed an ugly laugh. "You've been asking for this."

Zach barely saw it coming.

Griffin's hamlike left hand swung at him.

"Zach!" Beth cried out, standing beside the car.

Thrusting thoughts of Beth out of his mind, Zach sidestepped the punch, only to drive one of his own hard into the middle of Griffin's fleshy gut.

He grunted and bent double, but he remained on his feet. He grabbed Zach around the neck, drew back a fist and aimed for his face. The blow bounced off Zach's shoulder, then caught his right cheek, splitting it.

Zach jerked free of the other man's grip by shoving his balled fists under Griffin's armpits, then slammed his right forearm into the side of Griffin's head. Griffin tumbled back several paces, his breathing loud, his skin spraying sweat, before his knees connected with the pavement. He swore like an enraged bull, but he got up.

On guard now, he raised his hands, hunched his body and circled Zach like an animal stalking his prey. Zach moved to his right. Griffin moved with him, at the same time lowering his head and lunging his huge bulk into Zach. Zach jumped to the side again and stuck out his foot, tripping Griffin, who slid across the pavement. But with an agility uncommon in such a big man, he rebounded to his feet, whirled and came at Zach again. His nose was split, and blood was flying.

"I'm gonna kill you!" he spat.

Zach feinted with his right hand at Griffin's jaw, only to raise a knee into his crotch. Griffin hollered. While he was doubled over, Zach jabbed him in the face.

Griffin went down face first. This time he didn't get up.

Zach, breathing harshly, rolled him over with his boot. "Listen up, you bastard. You set foot on this property again, consider your ass mine!"

"Ouch!"

"Hold still."

Zach glared at her. "How the hell can I hold still when you're putting that lethal stuff on my face?"

Unruffled despite his disapproval, Beth continued to dab iodine on the cut.

They were at her apartment, sitting side by side on her bed. The minute they had gotten there, she had ordered Zach to take off his shirt and get comfortable while she gathered the necessary supplies to patch him up.

Although he had scowled at the idea of being ministered to, he had nevertheless done as he was told.

"There now," Beth murmured, spreading the last of the medicine on the wound, "that takes care of that."

She lowered her head then and began dabbing the ointment on the abrasion on his chest. Strands of her hair brushed across his shoulders. The air rushed from his lungs.

Her hands stilled, and she lifted her head. With their faces only a beat away from each other, their eyes locked.

"Beth . . ." he whispered thickly.

A light flared in her eyes, and she eased against him. Zach could feel her tremble like a trapped hummingbird as her lips opened over his. She moaned into his mouth, and their tongues embraced.

Wordlessly, and without taking their eyes off each other, they stood and removed their clothes. Zach held out his arms, and with a muted cry Beth dived into them.

"Oh, Zach," she whispered, her flesh fitting to his as if they were attached permanently.

He knew every luscious curve and dent in her body. He knew how to read the tremors that shook her now. He could easily have been blind, her flesh his guide, as he lowered their entwined bodies to the bed.

While his lips plundered hers, her hand snaked boldly down between their bodies and curled around his hardening length. Urgently she massaged, teased.

Zach's eyes closed, and he prayed for air just to breathe. "You're driving me crazy!"

A beautiful smile crossed her face. "I know, and I love every minute of it, too." She crouched over him and lowered her head, sending her hair over her flushed face. As though she was born for this, she replaced her hands with her lips.

He splayed his hands in those silky strands. "Beth, please, please."

No quarter was given. When he couldn't stand it anymore, he lifted her and turned her on her back.

"It's my turn," he whispered, bending all the way over and spreading her thighs. Her moans filled the small apartment. Then, rock hard, he positioned himself above her and felt her fingers surround him and direct him into her hot, pulsating center.

He thought he might lose his mind as she trapped his buttocks with her legs, embedding him deeper inside her. Sensations racked his body. He laid his mouth over hers, feeling the red-hot points of her nipples pressing with exquisite roughness into his chest. In that moment he tried to sink his soul into hers.

And he almost did.

Later Beth shifted from beneath him, then lay close, her cheek nestled against his arm.

"Mmm, am I in heaven?" Zach murmured.

She rubbed her head on his shoulder. "Feels like it, doesn't it?"

"Reckon it's better."

They were quiet for a moment.

"What are you thinking about?" she finally asked.

"You," Zach said, changing his position so he could look into her face.

"What about me?"

Her soft, raspy voice enveloped him. "Your breasts, how perfect they are."

"Oh."

He chuckled. "Why, Beth Melbourne, I do believe you're blushing. Fancy that."

"You're terrible."

"I know." His grin was wicked.

She punched him in the ribs.

"Ouch!"

"Oh, I'm sorry!" Beth cried. "I forgot you're slightly out of commission."

"Yeah, I bet you forgot."

She smiled demurely; then her face turned serious. "I'm worried about you, you know."

"Why?"

"I think that would be obvious, especially after tonight. What if things at the mill really get out of hand?"

"They can't get much more out of hand than they already are. But assuming they do, I'm going to push ahead with the offer I've put together. It's one I think the rank and file will go for."

"But not Griffin, huh?"

"It doesn't matter what he thinks. I meant what I said to him. Tomorrow I'm going to file charges. That'll bury him for sure."

Beth sighed. "I'm sorry Trent's not around to carry his share of the load."

"Me, too, but he needs to get his life back in his control."

"I know," she said softly. "I just hope this works. Otherwise . . ."

"Shh, don't think about that. Think on the positive side."

Beth nodded, and they fell silent again.

"Zach . . . I . . . want to tell you something," she began in a whisper.

Now that she had gotten a glimpse of the Zach of old, she felt rejuvenated and filled with hope that maybe a lasting relationship between them was no longer just a dream but a joyous possibility. Suddenly the urge to unburden herself, to tell him the truth about Amanda, couldn't be ignored. She wanted that secret out in the open.

"Not now," he said thickly. "I don't want to talk. I don't want to think about what tomorrow might bring. I just want to think about today, about *now*, about you being in my arms."

"But...Zach," Beth whispered brokenly, looking at him from the depths of her soul.

"Please...don't say anything...."

Her heart swelled with love. But mixed with that love were fear and remorse. And yes, guilt, too, because she felt that by not telling him about Amanda she was outright deceiving him. But would the truth carry too high a price tag? She couldn't deny the possibility that he would resent knowing that his greatest treasure, his daughter, had sprung from the woman who had caused him the greatest pain.

Her emotions waged such a war inside Beth that she almost cried out loud. But hadn't he told Rachel that he didn't want to know any of the details? Still, she should tell him, if for no other reason than her own peace of mind. With all her heart she longed to spill the words.

"Zach, I—" she said with more insistence.

He stopped her flow of words with his lips, and then there was nothing between them but a dialogue of tongues.

Before she could think again, she pressed her warm body against his, needing, wanting his warmth, his passion, his love, and needing to give hers in return.

Sweetly she whispered against his lips, "I love you."

Zach seized her then, kissing her with a feverish passion, as if he couldn't contain a sudden craving to devour her.

She responded with an eagerness that matched his. Within seconds they were making love again, frenzied, almost like enemies, grasping and urgent, crazy with wanting.

They heaved, sweated, thrashed about, sucked. They loved on the edge of savagery, yet when the time came for him to enter her, they pulled back and turned gentle and humble, as if an apology was in order before plunging headlong into the onslaught of desire.

After a while, when their climax could no longer be kept at bay, they descended as one into that endless, fiery furnace.

Later they lay exhausted, their breathing labored, their thoughts once again taking separate tracks.

Forty-Two

Happiness bubbled inside Beth like a rich warm wine, and she savored it. Nearly two months had passed since she'd tended Zach's wounds after his fight with Wade Griffin. During that time, which included both Thanksgiving and Christmas, she and Zach had been almost inseparable.

The holidays had been extra special because of Amanda. Christmas was for the young, Beth always said, and after seeing Amanda discover Santa Claus, she knew she was right.

Physically, she and Zach couldn't seem to get enough of each other, though after those first few frantic couplings they were ever mindful to take precautions. When they made love, which was often, it was with a hunger neither one could control or deny. But mentally and emotionally the same did not apply, at least where Zach was concerned.

He continued to hold himself aloof, refusing to discuss the change in their relationship. It was almost as if by not talking about it, he could ignore it. Because of his attitude, she hadn't told him about Amanda.

Still she longed for him to commit himself, to admit that he loved her as much as she loved him. However, she didn't push. But it was hard to suppress her anxieties, her hopes, her dreams. She was impatient. She wanted to know what the future held, and she wanted to hear Zach say what he told her with his hands and his mouth every time he touched her.

Today was one of those times. They were picnicking in the park on a lovely Sunday afternoon. Amanda had run and played until she was exhausted. They had managed to coax her into keeping her eyes open long enough to eat a small portion of the fried chicken, fruit and apple pie Ms. Yates had prepared for them.

Now Amanda was sound asleep on the blanket a few feet from them. They sat quietly, using a hundred-year-old oak as a backrest. Its bare limbs allowed the sun's rays to reach them.

Zach's arm was around Beth, and her head rested in the crook of his shoulder, but her eyes were on the child.

"Mandy's lovely, isn't she?"

For a moment Zach didn't answer, his gaze also on Amanda. "Yeah, she's a real piece of work." His gravelly voice was warm with pride.

Though it was January, the day was warm, like so many winter days in south Louisiana. Mandy's curls rippled in the gentle breeze, and her rosebud mouth had a fine sheen of moisture above it.

"I've decided her birth mother must have been a beauty."

A chill touched Beth, then her heart began to pump so rapidly, so noisily, that for a second she was certain he could hear it. She couldn't move, and she couldn't speak, her throat paralyzed with shock.

"Do you ever wonder what she looked like?" Zach pressed into the silence.

Beth gave her head a quick shake and forced words past her frozen lips. "I guess so. Do...you?"

"Naw, not really. It didn't matter then, and it doesn't matter now. I told Rachel from the get-go that I didn't want to know."

"Why? I mean...I find it hard to believe that you weren't the least bit curious." Even to Beth's own ears, the words sounded odd.

"At the time I didn't want another child. I was still mourning Randall. I guess shutting out the particulars of the adoption made it bearable."

"But you've never been sorry?"

"God, no. I know now that, without Mandy, I wouldn't have made it."

"I can...understand that," Beth said, licking her parched lips. *Tell him*, she insisted to herself. *Tell him the truth. Now! You have another chance. Don't squander it.*

But when she opened her mouth the words still wouldn't come. Fear held her mute. The thread that bound them together was still too fragile. She would wait. There would be another time, and she would tell him then.

Zach grazed her temple with his lips and whispered, "We have Rach to thank for our being together, you know. If she hadn't made you promise..."

There was a sudden sweet tightness in Beth's stomach. "I didn't think I'd ever hear you say that."

"I didn't think I ever would."

"It means a lot to me that you did. You...you know how I feel about Mandy."

"And she's crazy about her Bef, too."

Beth grinned at his use of Mandy's pet name for her. Then they fell silent and sober as memories intruded.

"You miss Randall, don't you?" Beth asked at length.

"Yes," he whispered, his voice sounding rusty. "At times I miss him so much I get physically sick."

"And...Rachel? Do you still miss her as much?"

"Sometimes."

"So do I."

"Beth..."

"Shh, it's all right. Remember, I loved her, too."

Another silence fell between them. Seconds later Beth realized he was smiling at her. Without thought, she did the same.

Time suddenly seemed of little importance as they basked in each other's presence, becoming reacquainted and finding a new and unexpected level to their relationship that the past had heretofore denied them.

"Oh, Beth," he said, "what am I going to do with you?"

She gazed up at him. "What do you want to do with me?"

"I don't know, that's just the problem," he said, nibbling on the side of her neck, then moving upward to her cheek.

She shivered. "You're making goose bumps all over me."

"Love bumps," he muttered, making his way to her mouth.

"What . . . what if someone sees you? Sees us?"

"Who cares?" He drew back slightly, tilted her chin and watched as the sunlight shone on her hair, burnishing it.

"Not me," she whispered, her open lips meshing with his slowly and so wetly. He groaned deep in his chest, the vibrations passing from him to her.

Her breasts tingled with expectancy as the kiss lengthened; his taste was like no other, as if it contained some secret potion unique to him.

His hand slipped down from her cheek and reached inside her blouse to surround a breast. The nipple, large and distended, was so hard she gasped when she felt his palm brush it.

She moaned as their tongues flickered and met again, as though feasting on a delicacy long denied.

When they parted at last, Zach's breathing was coming in spurts and his eyes were glazed.

"It's all I can do not to take you right here."

Suddenly Beth stiffened.

He groaned. "What's . . . the matter?"

"I think your daddy just drove by."

He blinked and pulled back. "What?"

"I said, I think your daddy just drove by."

"So?"

"Doesn't that bother you?"

"No. Why should it?"

"I'd call that spying."

"Spying?"

Beth heard the question mark, saw the troubled look that slipped over his face.

"Yes, spying." Her voice was thin.

"He's probably just out for a Sunday-afternoon drive." Zach's tone was light, his smile teasing.

Her lips puckered, deriding him.

"Okay, so maybe he's checking on his granddaughter." Again that light tone. "You know he's awfully possessive."

"Especially when Amanda's with me." Beth hadn't meant to say her thoughts aloud, but since she had, she refused to apologize.

Zach heaved a sigh. "As usual, you're exaggerating."

"Where your daddy's concerned, you mean?"

"Yes. I wish the two of you would take off the boxing gloves."

Beth turned her head. "You...you don't let him have Amanda when he's drinking, do you?"

"No, Beth, I don't," he said distinctly.

"Thank God."

"Hey, lighten up," he drawled, trailing a finger down her cheek. "I know something much more interesting to talk about."

Beth wrinkled her nose. "Such as?"

"Dinner tonight," he said softly, tightening his hold on her. "Actually, we have something to celebrate."

"Oh?"

"Yeah, ole Griffin got his comeuppance, just like I said he would. After I filed my report, his superiors in the union voted to demote him for his, er—" Zach grinned. "Shall we say his unseemly conduct?"

Beth answered his grin. "Revenge is sweet, isn't it?"

"Pretty tasty, especially in this case." He paused and kissed the tip of her nose. "So, are we on for tonight?"

Beth's eyes were colored with mingled love and lust. "Your place or mine?"

"Yours."

"I'll boil crawfish."

"Yeah?"

"Yeah."

"And then?" He was smiling like a satisfied cat.

"Oh, I thought we'd go shopping."

Zach's smile collapsed. "Shopping?"

She grinned saucily. "Had you going there for a minute, didn't I?"

"Why, you little tease. You'll pay for that."

"Promises, promises."

They both laughed then, only to find they couldn't stop. Laughter erupted into fits of giggles. Tears poured from their eyes. Their sides ached. But still they didn't stop.

It felt too damn good.

"Give me five minutes, Nancy, then let him in."

"All right," Beth's soft-spoken new secretary responded.

With a sigh Beth pushed her chair away from her desk and stood. So Taylor had come to see her. Well, well, she mused. She couldn't say she was surprised, because she wasn't. She'd been expecting him, maybe not here in Natchitoches, but she *had* been expecting him. And she knew the encounter would not be pleasant.

Sighing again, Beth smoothed a pleat in her skirt, then pulled her drawer out and removed a compact. After glancing quickly into the mirror, she decided she looked cool and composed.

She hadn't planned on this unexpected interruption. She had made a flying trip to Natchitoches this morning because there were problems that demanded her attention. But she was eager to get back to Shawnee, because she had another dinner date with Zach tonight.

Two days ago, as promised, she had fixed crawfish. He'd enjoyed them so much that he'd bribed her into boiling them again tonight. A smile relaxed her taut lips as she thought about the hours of lovemaking that were sure to follow.

Now, though, she had to deal with Taylor Winslow. Intuition as well as common sense told her that he was up to no good. Even if Zach hadn't thought it odd that Taylor had been spying on them, she knew better. He couldn't stand the idea of Zach and her being together, nor could he stand her being with Amanda. Well, that was just too bad.

He had played havoc with her life once already. He wasn't about to get another chance. She was no longer an innocent and frightened eighteen-year-old who had been scared spineless. She had learned to fight for what she wanted. She could hold her own now, with him or anyone else.

Clinging to that thought, Beth watched through narrow, cold eyes as Taylor crossed the threshold into her office, his stride that of a man with a mission. He didn't pause until he reached her desk.

"I won't waste time with pleasantries," he said, a nasty edge to his voice.

He looked awful, Beth thought, much worse than usual. The bags under his eyes were darker and extended down his cheeks, giving them a puffy, unnatural look. Added to that, he was sloppily dressed. On closer observation, Beth noticed that his clothes weren't even clean, and neither was his hair.

As the old saying went, he was stewing in his own juices.

A giddy feeling charged through her. The tables had finally turned. She had the upper hand, and it felt wonderful, deliciously wonderful. Hadn't she promised herself that one day he would get his comeuppance, that he would grovel at her feet? That day was here. But she would play the charade out to the bitter end and enjoy every moment of it.

"I don't know why you're here, Taylor." Her tone held just the right amount of innocence. "What could we possibly have to say to each other that would force you to drive all the way to Natchitoches?"

"Don't play the innocent with me, little lady. You know damn well why I'm here."

She almost slapped his face. Keep your cool, she cautioned herself silently. Don't let him rattle you. You're in command. Don't forget it. "Suppose you tell me," Beth said, her voice as smooth as silk.

Contempt bleached his lips. "You think you're smart, don't you? You think you've got me right where you want me? Well, I've got news for you." He leaned forward, an evil smile contorting his features. "Behind all that sophistication, you're still a scared little girl."

Suddenly Beth felt her courage desert her, and she was transported back in time, back to the day he'd raped her. Rage built inside her. She felt impotent against him.

"No!" she cried, placing her palms against her ears and rushing from behind the desk.

He followed her. "Yes, you are, and you're still scared of me," he said cruelly.

"You're wrong!" Her eyes were feral sparks. She was white now with rage. "I'm not scared of you. You take me on and you'll find out!"

For a moment there was silence in the room as they glared at each other, their chests heaving with their labored breathing.

"All right," Taylor spat. "What will it take to get you to leave Shawnee?"

Beth threw back her head and laughed, a cold, humorless laugh. "Money? I suppose we're talking dollars here, right?"

"Right."

"Why, you dotty old fool! Do you honestly think you can buy me off?" She got closer and leaned toward his face. "You ruined my life once by putting your vile, filthy hands on me, but never again."

Taylor cursed vehemently.

Beth ignored him and went on relentlessly, "Just so there won't be any misunderstanding between us, this is how it's going to be. I love Zach, and if he'll have me I intend to remain a part of his life, as well as Amanda's. And there's not one damn thing you can do about it."

Blood rushed all the way up Taylor's face, spreading into his scalp. "Oh, I wouldn't be too sure about that if I were you."

Beth went back to her desk. "I don't have to take this from you. You've got exactly five seconds to say what you came to say."

Instead of saying anything, Taylor reached into his pants pocket and pulled out a white envelope. Without taking his eyes off Beth, he slammed it down in the middle of her desk.

"Have a look-see, girlie."

Again it was all she could do not to slap his face. "What's that?"

"Look at it!"

She stared at him as if he were something less than human. Then she shook her head. "Oh, no, it doesn't work that way. Not anymore. We're playing by my rules, remember?"

Taylor smirked. "What's in front of you, little lady, is a deed."

For a split second Beth was caught off guard. "Deed?"

"Yeah, deed," he sneered, picking it up and shaking it in her face.

Beth's face was blank. "Deed to what?"

"Oh, I bet if you thought about it for a minute, you could guess."

The animal groan she heard came from deep inside her. "Cotton . . . wood?"

Taylor's harsh belly laugh rang loud. "Yeah, Cottonwood."

She finally lowered her head and stared at the white envelope. But it was a blur, as was everything else on her desk.

"And guess whose name it's in?" He chuckled. "Well, I'll tell you. It's in mine."

"Yours!" Beth whispered raggedly, then jerked her head up.

"Yeah, mine."

"It was you who . . . who bought Cottonwood from the bank?" Her tongue felt twice its normal size.

"Damn sure was," he said boastfully.

"But . . . but why?"

Taylor shrugged. "Why not? At the time it was a good investment."

"Oh, come on," Beth spat, having recovered enough to speak. "What do you take me for? You bought it to spite me and my family."

He smiled that evil smile again. "Why I bought it isn't important right now." He paused for emphasis. "What is important is that Cottonwood can be yours again. Now. This minute. Free and clear."

Beth couldn't believe her ears. Taylor was offering to give her the deed to Cottonwood. It was incredible. It was mind-boggling. When she no longer had the money to make a down payment on it, much less buy it outright, it was being offered to her on a silver platter.

Feeling suddenly as if gremlins had gotten loose insid[e] her, she crossed to the window. The glare seeping throug[h] the blinds hit her in the eyes, so that she almost staggere[d]. Her stomach was churning, and she was afraid she woul[d] vomit. Blindly she reached for the wall to steady herself. [It] didn't help. Her legs were as wobbly as jelly; nervous swea[t] dampened her neckline and under her arms.

Dear Lord, this was the moment she had longed for—Cottonwood returned to its rightful owners. But the pric[e] was too high.

"You promise to leave my son and granddaughter alon[e] and it's all yours," he stressed again.

Beth swung around, her face frozen into lines of fur[y]. "Why, you sorry piece of garbage!"

"Tut, tut, tut. Name-calling doesn't become you." Tay[-]lor scratched his bristled jaw. "But I'll let that slide, sin[ce] I know we're about to make a deal. Yeah," he repeated, "[if] you'll do like I say and get the hell out of Shawnee, tak[e] your business elsewhere, I'll sign this deed over to you.[]" When he finished speaking, he folded his arms across h[is] chest and grinned a smug grin.

Beth felt helpless again and utterly terrified. Inside sh[e] began to cry. But only for an instant. Idiot! she berate[d] herself. What's the matter with you? He can't hurt yo[u] anymore. You hold the trump card. Use it!

Adrenaline shot through Beth's veins, bringing her min[d] and heart back to life. She bolted around the desk and, i[g]noring the stench, got into his face, closer than before.

"Look, you slimy bastard, you can take that piece [of] paper and cram it! Sure, I want Cottonwood, but I wan[t] Zach more. Cottonwood is nothing compared to my fee[l]ings for him and Amanda. I won't be bribed or bought!"[]

Every ounce of color drained from Taylor's face, an[d] when he spoke, his voice shook. "We'll see about that. Yo[u] told me not to take you on. Well, I advise you not to tak[e] *me* on."

"Get out!"

When he got to the door he swung around, his face now purple with rage. "You'll be sorry for this."

"Not as sorry as you're going to be if you don't get out of my sight," Beth cried. "You make me sick!"

Forty-Three

Taylor Winslow cursed as he watched his hands shake. He couldn't even dial the phone. God, but his nerves were as tender as raw meat and just as exposed. He blamed Beth.

In addition to undermining his confidence, that ugly confrontation with her had forced his hand. Still, as he'd promised, he would have the last laugh. He refused to let her wheedle her way back into Zach's life. Too much was at stake to allow that. But he had to stop her now, before she had a chance to tell Zach the ugly secret that simmered between them.

That thought spurred him back into action. Ignoring the sweat saturating the collar of his shirt, Taylor lifted the receiver. This time he succeeded in punching out the number.

While it rang, sweat continued to pour off him. He swiped at it with a handkerchief and cursed again. That weasel Walsh better not have jerked him around. If he had, Taylor would take his money, every red cent of it, and put it in another bank.

Walsh had told him that he knew a detective who could find out anything, no matter how difficult.

"Well, I sure hope so," Taylor had spat. "Especially at the price he charges."

Richard Walsh had eyed him coldly. "You want him or not? Makes no difference to me."

"I want him."

Detective McPhearson had been hired a month ago, but to date he had come up with nothing. Zilch. Well, time had run out. Taylor needed the information he sought, and he needed it now.

A soft voice finally said, "Hello."

Taylor forced his mind back on track. "Is McPhearson there? Tell him it's Winslow."

"Just a minute." While he waited, he tapped his foot impatiently.

"I was just about to call you, Winslow," McPhearson said the minute he got on the line.

"You got what I need?"

"Sure do."

"Stay put. I'll be right there."

Amanda stuck out her lower lip and shook her head, her curls swishing against her cheeks. "Me playing."

"Me through playing for now," Zach said.

"No."

Zach laughed and tapped that protruding lower lip, then swung her out of the tub. "Up you go, sweetheart."

Mandy clung to him, then gave him a wet kiss on the lips.

"Want Daddy to read you a book before you take your nap?" Zach asked, wrapping her tiny body in a fluffy towel and sitting her on the commode lid.

"Daddy read book," Amanda echoed, grinning.

"You betcha. First *The Three Bears,* and *Little Red Riding Hood,* your two favorites. But now we have to get you dry and into some clothes."

"Mr. Winslow, is there anything I can do?" Ms. Yates stood in the door, twisting her hands.

Zach smiled. "Everything's under control."

"I'm so sorry she fell into that mud puddle."

"Oh, stop worrying, Ms. Yates. A little mud never hurt anyone." He paused and tickled Amanda in her side. "Isn't that right?"

Mandy squealed and kicked her feet. "Don't, Daddy!"

"Well...if you're sure." Ms. Yates didn't sound convinced.

"I'm sure," Zach responded, turning back to his daughter. "I'll put her to bed."

A while later, dressed in a pink jumpsuit, her curls brushed until they shone, Amanda lay in the crook of Zach's arm in the middle of her bed. But instead of listening to a story, she was sound asleep.

After simply looking at his daughter for a moment, Zach eased his arms from under, then leaned over and kissed her soft cheek. "Sweet dreams, darling. I love you."

He was glad he'd decided to indulge himself and take the afternoon off. Not only did he need to spend time with Amanda, but there were things he needed to do around the house that he'd been neglecting.

Later, as Zach made his way to the woodpile behind the house, he breathed deeply of the cool, clear air. It was a perfect day to chop wood or work with his horses, something he hadn't done in a long time.

It was also a perfect day to think. There was a lot on his mind, and he needed an outlet. Wasting no more time, he unbuttoned his shirt, tossed it aside and picked up the ax.

Even as he split the first log, he knew what he was going to do. When he went to Beth's for dinner tonight, he was going to tell her that he loved her, something he'd sworn he would never do again, something he'd sworn he would never *feel* again.

Had he ever stopped loving her, though? No, of course he hadn't. He could accept that now without feeling guilty.

For so long he hadn't been able to forgive himself for not loving Rachel the way he'd loved Beth. But Rachel hadn't seemed to notice, and they had been happy. And he had been faithful to her.

But now she was gone. He had finally come to terms with that. He needed a wife. Amanda needed a mother. More than either of those, he needed Beth for himself. Somehow, he knew Rachel had set this up. That was the reason she'd wanted Beth to be a part of Mandy's life, not so much for the child's sake, but for his.

He felt like a man who, after years of wandering in the desert, had stumbled upon a great treasure. His newfound happiness astounded him.

Zach stood still, feeling the life-giving air around him. He breathed deeply of it, hearing birds chirping behind him. He watched a pair of squirrels play tag, then disappear up the oak tree.

He reveled in the lightness in his spirit, like the crisp air after a stormy night. The slate was wiped clean. The lethal feeling that had dominated his life for so long had disappeared. He was a new man. Everything's all right, he thought, grinning to himself. Everything's all right.

He felt the sun on his face, but it was the thought of Beth that warmed his flesh. He turned his gaze toward town. Not far away, she waited for him.

His heart expanded at the thought.

"Zach."

At the sound of Taylor's voice, Zach turned around, his face and body drenched with sweat. He had been splitting wood for almost an hour.

"Hello, Daddy."

"Son."

Taylor was close enough for Zach to get a whiff of his high-octane breath, and his good humor fled. "At the bottle again, huh?"

Taylor's already heightened color deepened. "I'm not drunk, if that's what you mean," he said defensively.

"Drunk or not, you're still drinking too much." Zach paused and, still holding on to the ax, eased down on a stump next to the woodpile. "Look, Daddy," he said, trying to curb his disgust, "you need help. You're driving

Mother crazy, not to mention what you're doing to yourself.''

"I didn't come here to talk about my health."

"I'm sure you didn't."

"What's with you and Beth?" Taylor demanded suddenly, bluntly.

Zach's eyes narrowed. "That's none of your business, but since you asked, I'll tell you. I'm seeing her again."

"Is that all there is to it?"

"What do you think?"

"I think you're crazy about her."

"Could be you're right."

Taylor exhaled through his teeth, regarding Zach through eyes that were filled with hostility. "You know what else I think?"

"No, but I'm sure you're gonna tell me."

"You're right, I am. She's playing you for a fool."

"What?"

"You heard me."

"My relationship with Beth is not open for discussion."

"You'll change your mind when you hear this."

"So tell me," Zach said in a weary voice. "I'm tired of playing games."

"You're not gonna like it."

"Daddy!"

"Do you know who gave birth to Mandy?"

"No," Zach said emphatically. "It's never been important to me. But you know that."

"Well, then you're a bigger fool than I thought."

"Now, see here—"

"I did some checking, and I found out something very interesting, very interesting indeed."

Zach's lips thinned. "Just butt out while you're ahead, okay?"

"Yeah," Taylor went on, as if Zach hadn't spoken, a far-off glint in his eye. "It seems they made a deal or a pact or whatever you want to call it."

"What the hell are you talking about? Who made a deal?"

"Rachel and Beth." Taylor paused, then drew a cigarette out of his pocket and lit it, having long ago given up the pipe.

"Daddy!" Zach exploded again.

"Beth is Amanda's mother," Taylor said quietly.

Zach stood motionless and stared at him in fascinated horror. What was he talking about? What was he saying? Then, recovering, he screamed, "You're a liar! You're making this up! Say it, damn you!"

"I have the proof right here in my hand." Taylor held out the envelope. "Here, take a look. It's all right here in black and white."

"No!" Zach cried in anguish. "No! That can't be."

"I'll betcha everything I own it's Amanda she wants and not you."

A demented groan tore loose from Zach's throat, and his eyes blazed. "Don't say another word! Do you hear me? Don't say another word!"

Taylor backed up, as if afraid that Zach was going to strike him. "It's true, and you know it," he went on brazenly. "And you'd best face it before she—"

"Just shut the fuck up and leave me alone!"

Unable to remain standing under the weight of his pain, Zach's legs buckled, and his knees hit the ground.

It couldn't be true. It couldn't be. Rachel wouldn't have done that to him. *Beth* wouldn't have done that to him.

But in his heart of hearts he knew it was true; every stinking word of it was true. He wondered how he could have been such a fool, how he could have been so blind. The signs had all been there, if only he had realized it. His mind raced forward, then backward. Rachel's request. Beth's promise. Rachel's staunch defense of Beth. Beth's return to Shawnee. Her stubbornness in visiting Mandy despite his fury.

"Nooo!" he cried, dropping his head into his hands. "I can't stand it!"

With the same abruptness that his tongue-lashing had begun, it ended. Forcing himself upright, Zach felt like a ghost of his former self. Six foot plus, one hundred ninety pounds, and now nothing but a shrunken man.

Beth's betrayal had once again flattened his heart, twisted his soul out of shape.

In that moment, his love for her turned into burning hatred once again.

What a day this had been, Beth thought, her brain still spinning from her encounter with Taylor. But she felt good—wonderful, in fact. And she couldn't wait to see Zach.

Although she had gotten back to Shawnee only two hours ago, she was ready for him. She'd filled the tub with sweet-smelling bubble bath, then soaked until her fingers and toes were shriveled like prunes.

Instead of relaxing, her mind had buzzed with excitement. She'd been unable to curb it. She'd dreamed of getting even with Taylor, of hurting him as he'd hurt her. Hatred for him had been like a growth within her heart that she'd allowed to have a life of its own.

Now she found she no longer hated him. She no longer hated him because she no longer feared him. That thought flashed before her so clearly, so powerfully, that it made her head swim.

He couldn't hurt her again, especially because she was going to tell Zach the truth herself. Before the evening ended he would know she was Amanda's mother. The thought of telling him no longer frightened her. She loved him, and she knew he loved her. Therein lay her strength.

She had just slipped into a caftan and gotten herself a cup of tea when the doorbell rang. Frowning, she glanced at her watch. It was too early for Zach. He wasn't due for dinner until seven, and it was only five-thirty.

Shrugging, she made her way to the door and opened it.

Zach strode past her without a word, his body rigid, his face a molten mask. He didn't stop until he reached the window at the opposite end of the room.

"Hello to you, too," Beth said haltingly to his back. When he didn't respond, she whispered, "Zach...whatever is the matter?"

He swung around, his mouth drawn tight, his eyes trapped in a bloodshot net. "You bitch."

A stupefied look spread over her face. "What?"

"How could I have been so blind when it was right in front of my face all the time?"

"What—what are you talking about?" But she knew. Oh, God, she knew. Her pulse beat like a tiny drum in the hollow of her throat. *Zach, Zach,* her heart pounded against her rib cage. *I meant to tell you. I did, I did.*

"And to think I was going to ask you to marry me," he said dully, as if anesthetized.

"Oh, Zach..."

"Don't you dare 'oh, Zach' me!"

Beth's skin went white. "Please..."

"The funny part about it is, you could've gotten away with it."

"I...can explain."

"Explain?" He began to laugh, but the laughter quickly became maniacal.

Beth shook her head soundlessly, horrified at what was unfolding in front of her. "And...knowing makes a difference?"

"Oh, that's good. That's really good."

"You...you said you didn't want to know." The ground slipped harshly from beneath her feet.

"Didn't want to know?" His face was contorted with contempt and grief. "Do you honestly think I wouldn't want to know that *you* were the mother of my daughter?"

"If you *had* known, would you have given your consent?"

"No!" he shouted. "Not in this lifetime or any other."

Beth's pulse throbbed in her throat. "You...you know how desperate Rachel was for another child."

"So you're putting all the blame on her?"

"Yes...I mean no. I...went along with it."

"Why?" The word seemed ripped out of him.

"Because...because I saw it as a way to make amends...."

"Amends! Do you realize what you said?"

Beth spread her hands. "I never meant to hurt you. I always intended to tell—"

He laughed another cruel laugh. "Sure. Sure you did. Well, I'll have to hand it to you, not only did you stick a knife in my back, but you twisted the blade, too."

"Please...don't," she heard herself say but her voice seemed to come from another planet.

"Did you and Rachel laugh behind my back?"

"How can you even think a thing like that, much less say it? Creating a human being is no laughing matter."

"You're damn right it isn't!"

"I did it for Rachel...for you," she said brokenly.

"Oh, no." Zach shook his head. "You definitely didn't do it for me."

Tears erupted from beneath her quivering lids, stinging her eyes. "Taylor...told you, didn't he?"

"Yes." His voice sounded as heavy as her heart.

Beth laughed, a pitiful little laugh. "He...he said I'd be sorry," she whispered, more to herself than to him. Tears glazed her eyes and she bit her lip, thinking, you bastard

How could she ever have thought he couldn't hurt her again?

"Goddamn you, Beth! You used me. You made me fall in love with you all over again, and all you wanted was your daughter."

She covered her ears with her hands, his words pouring down on her like acid rain, making her hurt so much that she no longer wanted to live.

"That's not true! I love you. God help me, but it's the truth." Tears were running down her white face.

His hand dropped limply to his side. "It's Amanda you love. And the only way you could get her was through me."

Beth's big, sorrowful eyes looked up at him. "Are those your words—or Taylor's?"

"Leave my daddy out of this!"

"No! He's in this up to his drunken eyeballs!"

They were both shouting now.

"What does that mean?"

"It means that he's doing it all over again, just like he did eighteen years ago." Her heart was heavy with unutterable sadness. "He's tearing us apart."

He gave another ugly burst of laughter. "You can't take the heat, can you, Beth? But then, you never could. Always looking for a scapegoat."

"It's the truth!"

"Then tell me! Let me be the judge of what's the truth."

Pain stuck in Beth's throat like a stone. "No," she whispered bitterly. "If you want to know, then you'll have to ask him."

He stomped toward her, his face grotesquely twisted. "I'll do just that. But in the meantime I'd advise you to stay out of my way." He was shaking all over, and his voice was as cutting as razor blades. "Or I might not be responsible for my actions!"

Forty-Four

Although the sun still shone outside, Beth wasn't awa
of it. Inside her soul darkness dominated. She lay in abs
lute darkness. It pressed against her forehead and eyes. Sl
might as well have been blind. She had difficulty getting h
breath.

After Zach had left, she had crumpled into a ball on tl
couch, her heart roiling, the stench of fear hard on he
She'd been so sure her future was with Zach. She'd env
sioned them marrying at last, buying a house with the pr
verbial white picket fence around it, having more childre
But it was not to be. She had lost again. Again. But th
time she had lost everything: Zach, Amanda and Cotto
wood. She had made the ultimate sacrifice, only to have
backfire in her face.

She had remained curled on the couch, moving on
when deep sobs racked her body. Like now.

Which was why she didn't hear the door opening.

"Beth?"

Although she recognized her brother's voice, she couldt
answer. She didn't have the strength.

"Beth, where are you?" Trent called softly before ma
ing his way deeper into the room and switching on a lam

She tried to nod, but she couldn't manage that, eithe
Yet she was aware that her body was coming back to lif
Her limbs began trembling, and she began gasping, tryi
to pull much-needed air into her lungs. But when she tri

to lift her arms, they felt as if they no longer belonged to her. Again her energy failed her.

"Beth!" Her name was a sharp cry.

"Oh, Trent..."

Without warning, strong arms gently lifted her into a sitting position on the couch.

"My God, Beth, what happened?" Trent cried again, panic raising his voice an octave.

She leaned her head back against the cushions and blinked, the light shocking her eyes.

"Take it easy," Trent said softly. "Take it easy, sis."

She closed her eyes and breathed, fighting off a nauseating dizziness. Gradually her breathing began to return to normal.

"Better now?"

She nodded, not daring to try to speak yet.

"Are you sick? Do I need to call the doctor?"

"No." Hot tears burned her eyes. "I'm not sick. I'm... I'm just... upset."

"That's an understatement," he said. "What's going on?"

Having gained some semblance of control, Beth straightened and stared wide-eyed at Trent, as if realizing for the first time that he was beside her in the flesh.

"What are you doing here?" she asked, reaching for his hand and clinging to it.

"I was released from the clinic today with a clean bill of mental health." He seemed anxious to smile. "Your brother is now as fresh as the driven snow." He smiled big-time now. "What do you think about that?"

"Oh, Trent, that's wonderful."

He cleared his throat, his face sobering. "I came by to thank you for what you did. If... if it hadn't been for you—"

"That's all right," Beth whispered, grappling to get her mind off her misery and onto Trent's good fortune. "That's what sisters are for.'' Tears dripped down her cheeks onto their clasped hands.

Trent looked down then back up. ''What has you so torn up?'' he asked. ''Is it Zach?''

She nodded.

''Can you talk about it? I mean—can I help?'' He sounded awkward. ''After all, I owe you....'' He let his voice trail off.

Beth didn't know what caused her to pour her heart out to him. Maybe it was this new, gentle side of her brother that she had never seen before. Or maybe it was because she felt she would explode if she didn't tell someone.

When she stopped speaking, Trent stared at her in stunned amazement. ''You mean, you're...Amanda's mother?''

''Yes.'' Beth smiled through her tears. ''And if I had it to do all over again, I wouldn't hesitate a minute. I'll never regret creating Mandy. She's...she's very precious.''

''How did Taylor find out?''

Her smile disappeared, and bitterness reshaped her lips. ''That snake has his ways.''

''You're right. Nothing's sacred. If you have the money, that is.''

Beth gripped Trent's hand tighter. ''Because...because of something that happened a long time ago, he...he hates me. He'll do anything in his power to keep Zach and me apart.'' Her voice grew faint. ''Anything!''

For a moment Trent stared into space. Then he said roughly, ''Sis, I'm going to leave you for a while.''

Beth clutched his hand. ''Oh, please, don't go.''

''I have to.'' He sighed deeply, then gently removed his hand. ''I hope what I'm about to do will make up for what I should've done a long time ago.''

She wiped her eyes with the back of her free hand. ''You're not making sense. I...don't understand.''

"No, you don't. But you will." He withdrew his hand, stood, then leaned over and kissed her on the cheek. "Stop worrying, you hear? Everything's going to be all right. Trust me on that."

Zach climbed the steps at Wimberly two at a time, his breathing harsh and erratic.

If he had stopped and given in to the pain, the despair, that raged inside him, he couldn't have borne up under it. Instead of stopping to feel, to think about Amanda being Beth's child—and his—he had jumped into the car and, like a man possessed by demons, driven straight to Wimberly.

What had Beth meant when she'd said Taylor was responsible for their broken engagement? Something was definitely rotten in the state of Denmark, and he aimed to find out what it was, even if it was years after the fact.

Now, after flinging open the front door and charging across the threshold into the living room, he stopped in his tracks. The scene facing him could have come out of *Better Homes and Gardens,* he thought with cynical amusement.

Sitting in front of the fireplace, while a tiny fire sent smoke curling up the chimney, were his parents. Marian was clicking her knitting needles, and Taylor was holding the cat, rubbing its ears.

If Zach hadn't known better, he would have thought they were the perfect couple. But he did know better.

"Why, Zach, honey," his mother said, turning and facing him, a smile on her face. Instantly, a frown replaced the smile. "What on earth . . . ?"

"Mamma, I want to talk to Daddy. Alone."

As if she sensed trouble, Marian raised her hand to her throat. "Whatever for?"

"Mamma!"

"I'm not budging, Zachery."

"Do as he says, Marian," Taylor ordered before getting up and moving to stand in front of the fireplace.

Her eyes flicked from father to son. "No."

"All right," Zach said, his tone sharp. "Have it your own way." He refocused his gaze on Taylor. "Now, suppose you tell me what Beth meant when she said it was your fault she didn't marry me eighteen years ago?"

Taylor was taken aback. He opened his mouth as if to speak, but no words came out.

"Answer me, damn you!"

Taylor shuddered. "I don't have to tell you anything."

Zach sensed he had struck a nerve. He increased the pressure. "You'll tell me," he seethed, "even if I have to beat it out of you."

Marian lunged to her feet. "Zach!" she cried. "Do you know what you're saying?"

"She's nothing but a bitch," Taylor sneered. "She's just stirring up trouble because I told you the truth about Amanda."

"What about Amanda?" Marian demanded, her features now pale and drawn.

Taylor turned his attention to his wife. "Beth is Amanda's mother."

Marian gasped and grabbed her stomach. "Oh, my God." Then, recovering, she stammered, "How... I mean... how did you know?"

Taylor puffed out his chest. "I made it my business to know. When I had the proof, I told Zach."

"I wouldn't gloat, if I were you." Zach's voice was dangerously low. "Not just yet, anyway."

"Ah, son, surely you don't believe her. Like I said, she's just determined to stir up trouble in order to cover her own rear."

Gut instinct told Zach his daddy was lying, but getting him to admit it would be another matter altogether.

"Are you sure you're not the one who's lying?"

"I swear I'm telling you the truth." Taylor shook his head. "That bitch just keeps playing you for a fool. When are you going to see her true colors? I had nothing to do with your broken engagement. She's lying!"

"No, she's not."

At the sound of the quiet and unexpected voice, three pairs of eyes swung toward the door.

Trent was leaning against the doorjamb, his arms folded across his chest as if nothing out of the ordinary was happening.

"Trent, what are you doing here?" Zach asked, a muscle ticking in his jaw like a time bomb.

Trent had eyes only for Taylor. "If you don't tell him, I will." His stance had turned rigid.

"Just who do you think you are, you little creep?" Taylor ranted. "You can't just waltz into my house and make accusations you can't back up."

"Oh, I can back them up, all right," Trent said, maintaining his calm. "And you know it."

Color flooded Taylor's face; he looked ready to explode. "I don't know any such thing!"

Trent moved away from the door and closer to Taylor. When he was only a breath away, he jabbed a finger into the older man's chest, his features dark and menacing. "Look, you horny old son of a bitch, either you tell Zach the truth or I'm going to!"

"What the hell's going on?" But Zach's booming voice had no effect on the scene being played out in front of him.

Trent bounced a finger off Taylor's chest again and again, forcing him to back up. "I was there that night you came to see my daddy. You didn't know that, did you?"

Taylor's eyes grew wide with fear. "I—I don't know what you're talking about."

"I'm talking about the night you raped my sister!"

A shocked silence fell over the room. No one moved. No one said a word. They stood like zombies. Then, as if his part in the play was over, Trent stepped aside, giving Zach free access to his father.

"*No!*" Zach screamed, feeling the blood rush into his face like a blast from a hot furnace. His eyes felt as if they were springing out of their sockets. His lungs burned, forcing him to gasp for every breath. He thought he was having a heart attack.

"Zach!" Marian rushed to his side. "Are you all right?"

Glassy eyed, Zach pushed his mother away just as a wave of pure hate washed through him—hate for this man, this merciless liar, this back-stabbing bastard who had robbed him of everything he held near and dear.

With the cry of a wounded, crazed bull, Zach charged forward.

His face filled with terror, Taylor stumbled backward, but he wasn't quick enough.

Zach reached out, grabbed him by the collar and shook him until the old man's false teeth actually rattled.

"Zach, no!" Marian screamed.

Taylor grabbed his son's arms in an attempt to stave off the attack. Finally, in a halting, croaking voice, he begged, "Please . . . stop. . . ."

"I oughta kill you!" Zach choked, continuing to shake him. He could break every bone in his daddy's body. He wanted to. God, he wanted to.

"No, Zach!" Marian screeched again, racing toward father and son, grasping Zach's arms. "Stop it! Stop it right now!"

As quickly as he'd grabbed him, he let Taylor go. But Zach's face never changed; it remained cold and twisted with hate. And something else, something so dark and inhuman that you couldn't look at him without wanting to hide your eyes.

"Now I want to hear what you did to Beth from your own lips."

Taylor dropped his head to his chest and began sobbing.

Zach was unmoved. When he spoke again, his voice shook with rage. "Tell me!"

Little by little, Taylor sobbed out the sordid events of that day so long ago.

"Oh, God," Zach whispered. He didn't want to hear this. He thought he might pass out. Yet in the midst of his pain, at the core, he knew he had to hear it. He had to know what Beth had suffered at Taylor's hands. *Beth, Beth, Beth.*

"There's more," Trent said, walking up to where Zach still towered over his father. "He tried to bribe Beth with the deed to Cottonwood if she'd agree to leave you and Mandy alone."

Zach grabbed Taylor again, his eyes still ablaze.

"I'm sorry," Taylor sobbed again. "Please give me another chance...."

"You'll get nothing!" Zach's face took on a distorted, wild look, a mask of rage. "If it weren't for Mamma, I'd call the law and have your ass hauled to jail on assault charges."

Marian sobbed quietly from behind him.

Zach ignored her. "But I'll tell you what I *am* going to do. If you ever come near my house, my daughter or Beth again—" Zach was shouting now, making no effort to throttle back his blistering rage "—I'll beat you within an inch of your life! You'll wish you were dead!" He turned and strode away.

"Zach!" Marian cried, reaching out to him.

His footsteps didn't falter. When he reached the front door, his mother's sobs and his daddy's pleas for mercy rang in his ears.

Still, he didn't hesitate until he reached his car. Then he stood there, trying to wipe the tears from his eyes.

Forty-Five

Cold and shaking, the sweat dripping off his skin like the rain outside, Zach reveled in his self-induced punishment. In fact, he wished he could inflict more.

His pain and rage were both so deep-seated that they had a stranglehold on him. When he'd left Wimberly he hadn't gone home. He'd waited for Trent and gotten the rest of the story, then come to the mill, and now he was holed up in his weight room, beating up on himself.

Zach eyed a heavier weight, but instead of picking it up, he paced the floor, his fingers clenched, his mind on fire. Blind. Deaf. Dumb. And stupid. Those were the adjectives he applied to himself. How could something like that have happened? How could he not have known?

He stopped his pacing, feeling his heart swell into his throat as something broke within him. Groaning, he leaned forward until his forehead touched the woodwork. Like a baby, he wept, wept for Beth, for himself, for all the lost years.

His tears failed to wash away the sorrow. He had to face her, had to beg for her forgiveness. That was the only way he could gain any peace. But then reality blew over him like a cold winter wind and chilled his insides.

Would Beth see him? If so, would she forgive him? He didn't know.

And that was what terrified him the most.

* * *

The clock chimed midnight. Beth's fingers didn't miss a stroke as she continued to fold her underwear, arranging it neatly in the open suitcase sprawled across the bed.

It had been hours since Zach, then Trent, had stormed in and out of her apartment. She had finally forced herself to move from the couch. But the minute she had, the pain had set in. Pain so palpable that it took on an actual presence. It congealed in the center of her heart, forming a lump. It cut her nerve endings, leaving them raw and bleeding. It was without end. For without Zach and Amanda, life meant nothing. They *were* her life.

How could she leave Shawnee again? Beth asked herself, even as she stared down at the clothes strewn across the bed. Was running away the answer? No. But at the moment she saw it as her only option; her very sanity depended on it.

Still, she had obligations in Shawnee that she could never shirk, no matter how fast or far she ran. Gran needed her. Her daddy needed her. But she'd kept the road well traveled for years, and she could do so again.

Strangely, Beth couldn't cry. The tears no longer came; it was as if they had dried up along with her heart. She moved like a robot, refusing to think about Zach, about Amanda, about Taylor. The preservation of her sanity depended on that, too.

Thirty minutes later she had finished packing, had slipped into a robe and was on her way into the kitchen when she heard a tap on her front door.

Zach! Could it be Zach? Her heart soared, only to suddenly plummet back to earth. It's over, Beth, she told herself. The sooner she came to terms with that, the better. The numbness seeped back into her pores, slowing her movements to a snail-like pace.

Before opening the door she gazed through the peephole. She saw only a flash of lightning and heard a bolt of thunder. When had it begun to rain?

"Who is it?"

"Zach."

With a trembling soul, sweaty palms and shaking fingers, Beth unlatched the door and jerked it open.

Zach's face, barely recognizable, greeted her. She had never seen him look worse. His eyes, with the light gone from them, were sunken black holes in his head. His skin was almost translucent. Lines dented his face, the ravages of time on human flesh. He needed a shave. His shirttail hung out of his jeans. He wasn't wet, but he was shaking as if he were.

Beth knew she looked no better. Her own face was pale, her eyes streaked from crying, and her hair was a riot of tangles. A thought from long ago flared into her mind: the walking wounded. Barely ambulatory.

"May I come in?"

In a voice as thin as tissue paper she whispered, "Of course."

Neither said a word until they reached the dimly lighted living room. He stopped first and stared at her across a small space.

The clock on the wall ticked loudly.

Zach opened his mouth, but no words came out. A nerve in the side of his cheek worked tremulously.

"Why... why are you here, Zach?"

"To say I'm sorry." Tears broke from the corners of his eyes. "To ask... to *beg* you to forgive me."

Beth could not breathe. She tried to inhale, but it was as if she had been locked in an airless space.

"Why?" she finally got out. "Earlier... you hated me...."

Her words seemed to pierce him physically. He flinched. "I... I've been to Wimberly."

"And?"

"I...I know...oh, God...I know he...raped you." Zach's shoulders began to shake as if he were crying inside.

Beth's heart turned icy and her knees buckled. She doubled over as if to vomit.

He stepped toward her.

She slowly lifted her head.

His features wore an expression of agony that seemed beyond all understanding. "When...I found out what he'd done to you, I wanted to die. And I still do. Can you ever forgive me?" he added brokenly.

Seeing his tears, hearing his plea, the passion she had been desperately trying to keep at bay spilled out and she cried, "Oh, Zach, there's nothing to forgive."

"Yes...there is. And I'm sorry...so terribly sorry." Again his voice broke.

"Zach, please don't cry." She ached to touch him, to hold him, to comfort him. But she didn't move.

"Why didn't you tell me?"

"I...couldn't."

"Why?"

"For one thing, I didn't want to...couldn't ask you to choose between Taylor and me."

"Oh, Beth." He sounded as if something had snapped inside him.

"Don't you see? I thought I was doing the right thing. I loved you too much to put you through that, so I sent you away."

"My darling, my darling, how could you not know there was never any choice, that it was made long ago?"

"I ached to believe that, Zach, but I was so scared."

"Will you ever forgive me for being such a pigheaded, stupid fool?"

Beth licked the tears off her lips. "I love you. That automatically wipes the slate clean."

"And I love you," he said thickly. "I always have, and I always will. Even when I hated you, I loved you." He held out his arms. "Come here."

With a burst of exhaled breath, she cried out and plunged headlong into his open arms.

Love hovered on his lips, in the coiling, slippery mating of his tongue with hers. How long had she waited for this moment? All her life, she knew for certain. She felt giddy. She felt free. Most of all, she felt loved.

"Hold me."

"Always," he groaned, sweeping her into his arms and heading toward the bedroom.

Once they were naked and on the bed, Zach gathered her to him and held her tightly. It was as if their pulses were one, as if their skin had melted together, linking them forever. Zach felt his heart split, felt the bitterness rush away through the crack like a cleansing force, leaving him both weak and jubilant.

Zach wedged her head between his hands and peered into her face, a sight he could not get enough of. Her lips were moist and slightly parted. He groaned and covered her mouth with his. When their tongues twined, a simultaneous shudder rippled through them.

She clawed at his back, thrusting to meet him as he entered her.

"Zach, oh, Zach!" she moaned against the side of his neck.

He felt their tears mingle as he possessed her and she him. The connection was so painfully sweet that he thought for a moment he might black out.

She thrust her hips against him, moaning, and when their release came in a long shudder, they were transported into orbit, to another world and beyond.

With her head curled on his chest, he listened to her heartbeat.

Soon Beth lifted her head and kissed his damp flesh. "Oh . . . yes . . . Don't ever stop."

"I love you," she whispered. "I love you."

He could feel the places on his skin she had kissed. Her lips healed him.

"Beth," he said. "My Beth."

"I'm here, my darling."

And silently he wept, knowing that she was truly back.

Zach opened his eyes and heard the rain still pounding on the roof. He turned on his side and stared at Beth's sleeping face. She lay curled in a ball like a warm, satisfied kitten. She was breathing slowly and deeply, her eyelids fluttering from time to time.

Then, unexpectedly, her leg moved over his. Her mere touch intoxicated him.

"Hi."

"Hi yourself."

"Whatch'a doin'?" Her voice was tinged with sleep and contentment. She moved closer to him and placed her palm over the flesh above his heart.

He shut his eyes, listening to his own heartbeat, savoring her touch as she stroked him.

"Beth," he said after a moment, "thank you for Amanda."

Her hand ceased to move. "Oh, darling, what a beautiful thing to say."

"How did you ever give her up?"

She closed her eyes, and he was instantly apprehensive. "I'm sorry . . . I . . ."

"Mandy," she whispered, her arms all at once ribbons of steel around him. "When . . . oh, God! When I held her that first time . . ."

"You wanted to keep her."

She opened her eyes. They were nakedly honest. "Oh, yes," she whispered. "She was *our* baby. And I wanted her."

Zach pressed his cheek against hers. "Well, now you have her, love. And hopefully, one day, we'll have another baby. I want to see your tummy swell. I want to be there when you put my child to your breast to nurse. I want to see all the things I missed."

"I . . . love you."

He blinked. "I couldn't bear it if you ever left me again."

"I know," she murmured, kissing his shoulder.

"I'm so sorry about Cottonwood, too. I know how much you wanted it."

Her eyes widened. "You know about that?"

He nodded.

"I have no regrets, Zach. Losing Cottonwood is only a small price to pay for our being together."

"Maybe one day—"

"No, I don't want to think about that now. I just want to think about us being together and savor our happiness."

Zach reached for her hand and turned her palm to his mouth. "We deserve some happiness, don't we?"

She nodded, smiling.

"Will you marry me?"

She smiled through her tears. "Is today soon enough?"

He laughed at the same time that he grabbed her in a bear hug.

Later Beth peered up at him and asked, "Was it . . . Taylor who told you what . . . what he did to me?"

"Yes and no."

"What kind of answer is that?"

"Trent forced him to tell me."

"Trent?" Her voice was shock filled.

Zach sighed. "I know he plans to tell you himself, but under the circumstances—"

"You're not making sense," she interrupted. "Come to think of it, Trent didn't make sense, either, when he left here. It was almost as if he knew something...." Her voice drifted off.

Zach leaned his head in the palm of his hand and stared down at her. "That night... that awful night years ago, Trent walked in just as my—Taylor—was...getting off you and... and straightening his clothes."

She gasped in horror and stared at him wildly.

"I hated to tell you...."

"You... you mean...?"

"Yes. And for whatever reasons, Trent kept it to himself all these years. I'm sure there were times when it must have eaten a hole through his insides."

"And... and he never said anything? Never told anyone?"

"No."

Beth continued to stare at him in stunned disbelief.

"He's in a world of hurt over this, and I know he plans to make it up to you."

"He already has," Beth whispered, wiping the tears from her eyes. "The fact that he came forward and stood up to Taylor on my behalf is payment enough."

Zach raised her hand and kissed each fingertip, then said in a strangled voice, "You're something special."

"I'm glad you think so."

Zach ran a finger across her moist lower lip, his own not quite steady. "Did he..." Zach's voice collapsed. He couldn't go on. At length he took a deep breath and continued. "Did he hurt you... badly?"

"Yes... only the hurt was more mental than physical."

"All the time he was telling me what—" tears clumped his thick lashes together "—what he did to you, I wasn't sure I was going to live through it."

"Don't," she begged, placing her wet cheek against his and clinging to him. For a moment they wept together.

When he had regained his control, Zach pulled back. "I wanted to kill him, my own daddy. Does that shock you?"

"No. That's all part of not making you choose."

"But you haven't told me the real reason yet, have you?"

Beth turned away.

"Look at me," he groaned. "Please. I don't want any more secrets between us."

"I . . . I was afraid you'd think it was my fault."

"Oh, Beth, Beth . . ." His voice cracked.

"That you'd think I was dirty."

Another cry tore loose from deep inside him.

"And that . . . every time you made love to me you'd think about . . ."

He grabbed her and crushed her against him. "How could you have thought that, when I loved you more than life itself? I'm so sorry. . . ."

"Shh." Beth shifted away from him. "Don't ever say that again, you hear? We've already made enough apologies to last a lifetime."

"But simply loving you doesn't seem to be enough. I won't make up for—"

Beth placed her hands on either side of his face and gazed into his eyes. "That's not true," she said in a breathy whisper. "Love is always enough."

"I'll make it up to you, you'll see," he said fiercely.

She smiled. "Once I thought I'd never be whole again, that no amount of happiness could ever make the pain go away."

"And now?" he choked out.

"Now it has. So, you see, your love *is* enough. It's cured me. It's made me whole."

Zach's eyes brimmed with tears. "I . . . love you."

"And I love you."

"Forever this time?"

"Forever."

Epilogue

Summer, 1991

"Lookey, Mommy!"

Beth smiled at Amanda as she pedaled her tricycle around the covered pool area. "That's wonderful, darling," Beth said warmly. "Mommy's proud of you."

Amanda braked. "Daddy, come push me," she pleaded, her rosebud lips in a pout.

"Not now, darling."

"Pease."

"In a minute."

"Okay."

Beth smiled again as she listened to the verbal interplay between father and daughter, thinking what a perfect pair they were and what a perfect day this was. So perfect, in fact, that they had decided to have a late lunch, picnic-style, on the deck.

Now, after filling their stomachs with fried catfish and peach cobbler that Jessie had fixed and brought over, she and Zach shared the huge hammock that swung between two pecan trees not far from the deck.

"Mmm, you smell good," Zach said, sniffing her hair.

"Thanks," she murmured. "But it's a wonder I don't smell like food."

Zach chuckled. "You've got a point there. Lemme see now, how many pieces did you eat?"

"Five," Beth admitted shamefacedly.

"Five! Why, that's more than I ate."

Beth made a face. "I know. It's awful, isn't it? But they were so good."

"You're tellin' me."

She cut him a sharp glance.

He grinned. "Reckon we could hire Jessie to cook for us, too?"

"Are you saying I'm a lousy cook?"

"How would I know? You don't ever do it."

Her eyes twinkled. "Well, you oughta be glad."

"Believe me, I am."

They both giggled.

"Happy?" Zach whispered after a while.

Beth made a purring sound in her throat. "Happier than I ever dreamed possible."

And she was. She and Zach had been married for six months now, and they had been the happiest six months of her life. She knew the same was true for Zach, too. He had never looked better. The gaunt lines had disappeared from around his mouth and eyes, and the rakish grin that had always been his trademark, that always made her breathe a little faster than normal, was readily visible.

The stark thinness that had made her appear almost ethereal was no longer visible, either.

"Your curves are back intact," Zach had told her recently, grinning warmly.

Yes, married life definitely agreed with both of them. Amanda had accepted Beth as her mother and after the first month together even began calling her Mommy.

Still, life was not perfect. Her daddy's inactive body was slowly deteriorating. It broke her heart, but there was nothing she could do, though he continued to get the best care available. And despite Gran's strong spirit and sharp mind, she, too, was going downhill by the day.

Because of her family commitments, Beth had gradually given over most of the responsibility for the shops to Tracy. When the time was right, she would become active once again. After all, one day she hoped The In-Look would belong to her daughter.

During this time of warmth and love, she and Trent had also formed a new and lasting bond. On the other hand, Zach had had no contact with Taylor. It was as if his daddy had ceased to exist. When his mother visited them she never mentioned Taylor, and they never asked.

"Hey, pretty lady, remember me?"

With a start, she faced Zach. Her heart skipped a beat. His eyes were lazy and filled with desire.

"What are you thinking about?" he asked in his velvet drawl close to her ear, the tip of his tongue circling the soft skin inside.

Beth shivered. "You love giving me chill bumps, don't you?"

"Is that all I give you?"

She popped him playfully on the leg. "You know it isn't."

"Wanna tell me where else my kiss affects you?" he whispered huskily.

"You know where."

"Mmm," he murmured, sliding his hand down her stomach until he reached the warmth at the apex of her thighs. "I bet I made you wet."

While Beth still had enough of her faculties intact, she removed his hand. "Shame on you, Zachery Winslow," she whispered, though her eyes were glazed and her voice unsteady. "You're not setting a very good example for your daughter."

"Ah, she's not paying any attention to us."

Beth looked to the right of his shoulder, then chuckled. "Wanna bet?"

Groaning, Zach turned and followed her gaze. Amand
was making her way toward them as fast as her legs coul
pedal.

Zach lifted his eyes. "Kids."

"Aren't they wonderful?"

"Yeah, especially trying to make them."

She grinned. He grinned back, and for a sweet momen
the world seemed to stand still.

"Mommy! Daddy! I see a big man."

Zach sat up in the hammock. "What, honey?"

"A big man gotted out of his truck."

"He got out of his truck, darling," Beth corrected au
tomatically.

"That's what me said, Mommy."

This time it was Beth who rolled her eyes.

Zach laughed as he slid out of the hammock. "I'll go se
what she's talking about. Don't go away," he added on
husky note.

He had taken only a few steps when the stranger cam
into view, dressed in a Federal Express uniform. He smile
pleasantly. "Good afternoon. How are y'all?"

"Just right," Zach said.

"Who are you?" Amanda asked, standing at Zach
side.

Zach cast her a quick look. "Hey, that's not nic
Mandy."

The man squatted and was almost eye level with th
child. "I have a daughter about your age."

"Can her come play wiff me?"

Both men laughed, as did Beth, who was watching th
exchange from the hammock.

Zach tousled her curls. "Why don't you get your dol
and take her for a ride?"

With an excited squeal, Amanda scampered off.

"Now, what do you have for us?" Zach asked, a pu
zled frown on his face.

The man handed Zach an oversize envelope and his clip-board. "Sign here, please."

Zach scribbled his name. "Thanks."

The man tipped his cap. "Y'all have a nice day now, you hear?"

"Same to you," Zach responded absently, his gaze on the envelope in his hand.

"Bye, man!" Amanda called out.

Zach sauntered back to the hammock.

"What is it?" Beth asked.

Without speaking, Zach dropped the letter in her lap. "It's addressed to you."

"Me?"

"Yep."

"Who's it from?"

"Dunno," Zach said.

"What does that mean?"

"There's no return address."

"Well, here goes," Beth said, ripping it open. The words inside leaped out at her.

Beth,
Cottonwood is yours with no strings attached. This is the only way I know to say I'm sorry and to beg for your forgiveness.

Taylor

"Well?"

She lifted her face; it was chalk white.

Zach looked frightened. "What's wrong?"

"Read it."

"Well, I'll be damned," he said after a moment.

"Can you believe that?"

Zach blew out a deep breath. "No."

"Me either." Beth's voice shook.

"What are you going to do?"

"Guess."

"Don't need to," Zach said. "You're gonna keep it."

"Right."

He grinned. "Atta girl. So what happens next?"

"I...I don't know. I don't want to think about that right now. I just want to savor the moment."

He flicked a leaf off his jeans. "Do you think you could ever forgive him?"

Beth's eyes had a faraway look in them. "I know you should never say never, but..."

"I know."

"If you want to know how I feel right now, the answer is just that, *never.*"

He didn't say anything.

"What about you? Can you forgive him? Can you forget?"

Points of light flared in Zach's green eyes. "Not as long as I'm breathing."

Beth shrugged. "I rest my case."

He grinned suddenly. "That's just as well," he drawled, tapping her on the leg so that he could rejoin her in the hammock, "'cause at the moment I have something much more important on my mind."

"Like what?" Beth asked demurely.

"Like kissing my wife, for starters."

"Oh, Zach, I do love you." Tears misted Beth's eyes.

"And I love you," he muttered thickly.

"Sometimes I don't think I'll ever stop smiling."

His lips were warm with love. "Me either."

Under the generous shadows of a nearby pecan tree, a reckless blue jay answered them, then took flight south toward the distant shades of Cottonwood, their home.

Take 3 of "The Best of the Best™" Novels FREE
Plus get a FREE surprise gift!

Special Limited-time Offer

Mail to The Best of the Best™

3010 Walden Avenue
P.O. Box 1867
Buffalo, N.Y. 14269-1867

YES! Please send me 3 free novels and my free surprise gift. Then send me 3 of "The Best of the Best™" novels each month. I'll receive the best books by the world's hottest romance authors. Bill me at the low price of $3.99 each plus 25¢ delivery and applicable sales tax, if any.* That's the complete price and a savings of over 20% off the cover prices—quite a bargain! I understand that accepting the books and gift places me under no obligation ever to buy any books. I can always return a shipment and cancel at any time. Even if I never buy another book from Harlequin, the 3 free books and the surprise gift are mine to keep forever.

183 BPA A2P5

Name	(PLEASE PRINT)	
Address	Apt. No.	
City	State	Zip

This offer is limited to one order per household and not valid to current subscribers.
*Terms and prices are subject to change without notice. Sales tax applicable in N.Y.
All orders subject to approval.

UBOB-296

©1990 Harlequin Enterprises Limited

Serena Bouchard had conned him with her irresistible charm—again. The fact was that Michael Hamlin couldn't deny his ex-wife anything.

Serena's brother, Jeffrey, was in jail in Rio for murder. Michael agreed to go with her to Rio to help clear Jeffrey, then get as far away from Serena as possible. But as they got closer to uncovering the real killer, Michael and Serena were drawn into a dangerous game they intended to win. They just had to survive their

LAST NIGHT IN RIO

by

JANICE KAISER

Available this December at your favorite retail outlet.

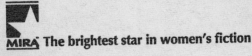

MIRA The brightest star in women's fiction

MJKNR